RUSSIAN AMERIKA

Stoney Compton

RUSSIAN AMERIKA

Stoney Compton

RUSSIAN AMERIKA

Copyright © 2007 by Stoney Compton.

A Baen Books Original

Baen Publishing Enterprises
P.O. Box 1403
Riverdale, NY 10471
www.baen.com

ISBN 10: 1-4165-2116-X
ISBN 13: 978-1-4165-2116-7

Cover art by Kurt Miller

First printing, April 2007

Distributed by Simon & Schuster
1230 Avenue of the Americas
New York, NY 10020

Library of Congress Cataloging-in-Publication Data: t/k

Compton, Stoney.
  Russian Amerika / Stoney Compton.
     p. cm.
  ISBN-10: 1-4165-2116-X
  ISBN-13: (invalid) 978-1-4165-2112-7
  1. Alaska—Fiction. I. Title.

  PS3603.O49R87 2007
  813'.6—dc22

2006100547

Printed in the United States of America

10 9 8 7 6 5 4 3 2 1

Dedication

To my Mother, Maxine Irene Stout Compton, 1926–1998
She would have been proud of my accomplishment.

To Sarah Maisie and Danford Gordon: my incredible children.

To Edna, the first to believe, and of course, Max: friends for life.

To Del Buhrman, oldest friend, constant supporter,
and fellow adventurer.

To Jess and Mary Herring, finer in-laws are not to be found.

To Eric Flint, whose friendship knows no bounds. Thank you.

And saving the best for last, to Colette Marie, my magical,
Wonderful dancer wife, with her all things are possible.

Acknowledgement

Over a quarter century ago I was hired by the Tanana Chiefs Health Authority to create a comic book designed to interest Athabascan youth in health careers. After the completion of the project I was put on staff as media specialist with this non-profit social services corporation. I was privileged to work with Tanana Chiefs Conference for two years. Those years and that job were an education into a culture I came to admire, respect, and to a large extent, envy.

This novel reflects my high regard for the Native Peoples of Alaska, and the Athabascan People in particular. As this is a work of fiction, I have taken a few cultural liberties, but have tried to stay true to the essence of the Dená People. Any and all mistakes are mine.

The names of my characters are similar to family names found in Alaska's Interior, however all are otherwise complete fabrications of my imagination.

Russian
Amerika

Russian Amerika
(Alaska)

Russia

Bridge
(Wales)

Russian
Amerika

Holy Cross   Nulato

Dene
Republic

Tanana

Toklat

Chena (Fairbanks)

Kodiak Island

Fort Yukon

St Nicholas Redoubt
(Anchorage)

St. Anthony Redount
(Delta)

Dot Lake

Tetlin Redoubt

Old Crow

Klukwan

New Archangel
(Sitka)

Akku (Juneau)

St. Dionysius (Wrangell)

T'angass (Ketchikan)

British
Canada

W

N

S

E

500 Miles

1

Clarence Strait, Russian Amerika, July 1987

Etolin Island lay to starboard and Prince of Wales Island stood fine on the horizon to port. All thirty meters of *Pravda* tossed like a cork in a pond. The graying seas broke into spraying foam at two meters and the wind shrilled warning.

Charter Captain Grigoriy Grigorievich couldn't drop anchor here, nor could he just abandon the wheel and go below to mediate what was sure to turn into rape, at the very least. Both passengers were below in the main cabin. He popped open the hidden compartment on the console and poked the tiny phone into his ear so quickly he hurt himself.

"No!" Valari said.

"You will do this with me for two reasons," Karpov said, sounding like a schoolteacher. "First, it will give us both comfort in this storm. Secondly, if you don't do it willingly, I will beat you and take you by force. This is inevitable; besides, you used to enjoy me."

"I was lying, you swine!" she shrieked. An oddly familiar *thonk* came over the phone, and Grisha realized that someone had just been hit with a bottle. A large mass fell on the deck.

He smiled and put the earphone away. Valari was beginning to appeal to him. She raged up the steps, clutching the vodka bottle by

1

its neck. Throwing it over the side, she grabbed the railing, braced herself on the heaving deck, and shouted at him.

"I wish to make a formal protest to be entered in the log!"

He gestured with his chin as he clutched the wheel with both hands. "It's right up there," he yelled over the building wind. "Make the entry yourself."

"But you're the captain."

"Do you want to take over?"

Hanging on to the railing with both hands she finally took in the sea around them. Huge swells of slate-colored water veined with submerged foam like fat in a rich man's steak roiled up around them, rising and dropping with unimaginable hydraulic force. Wind ripped loose foam off wave tops and hurled it at the boat where it smacked the hull and topsides like thrown sand.

Pravda rolled heavily from side to side and pitched up and down as she struggled from one wave to the next. Prince of Wales Island now lay behind a seamless wall of driving water and impenetrable cloud.

"By the saints, no," she said, nearly inaudible, swaying with the dance of the boat. She raised her voice. "Are we going to get out of this?" Water sluiced across the deck and gurgled into the scuppers as the boat labored through the shrieking elements.

"Of course!" He forced himself to smile and licked salt spray from his lips.

"You don't lie very well. Tell me the truth."

"We're not far from Fort Dionysus. If the storm doesn't get any worse we will make it easily."

"And if the storm gets worse?"

He shrugged. "Figure it out for yourself: we won't make it."

"Shit! This was such a stupid idea! Now we're all going to die. If I get out of this I'm going to get a new job."

"Why *are* you here?" Grisha shouted to be heard over the storm.

She gave him a level look and smiled. "Don't worry your pretty little head about it. The less you know the better off you'll be."

Grisha repressed the flare of anger.

Suddenly Karpov, blood streaming down the side of his head, erupted out of the companionway, slid across the soaking deck on his knees, and tackled Valari. She screamed and pounded his head with her fists.

"What are you doing, you ass?" she screamed at him. "Have you lost your mind?"

Still on his knees, the beefy man gripped her shirt with one hand, slapped her face with the other. Blood arced from her cut lip. The small sound from deep in her throat jerked open Grisha's gut anger.

Holding the wheel with one hand, he turned and snap-kicked Karpov as hard as he could in the side of the head. Still clutching Valari, Karpov flew backward and his head smashed into the fishing-gear compartment. The door to the locker swung open as he flopped on the deck, spasming as he tried to retain consciousness.

Valari squirmed out from under Karpov's twitching mass. "Thank you, Captain Grisha. I think he would have really hurt me this time." She staggered across the shifting deck and hugged him fiercely. He put one arm around her. "I owe you for that one," she said.

With a gasp she was wrenched out of his grasp and flung across the bridge deck by a seething Karpov. The large man didn't even look back at the woman. He stood glaring at Grisha, rain and blood running down his face as bruises and lumps purpled and thickened.

"I relieve you of command!" he said with a growl, and swung his massive fist at Grisha's face.

Grisha released the wheel, ducked under the swing and put all of his weight behind a two-fisted uppercut to Karpov's solar plexus. Air whoofed out of the larger man and he staggered back three steps. Grisha kicked him in the crotch as hard as he could. Karpov doubled over with a moan and fell heavily.

Grisha grabbed the spinning wheel and gave his attention to straightening the boat, which had immediately turned broadside to the wind. *Pravda* lurched sideways off a wave top and slid to the bottom of the trough with a crash. He felt thankful the boat hadn't rolled down the liquid incline.

Seawater crashed into the open bridge, soaking it and everyone on it. Gear spilled out of the fishing locker and slid around the deck. On the other side of the bridge, Valari pulled herself to her feet and clung to the railing, shivering.

Karpov shook his head and swung from the deck to bury his fist in Grisha's stomach, smashing him against the bulkhead and knocking him breathless. Grisha slid down on the deck, gasping. The boat again put beam to the wind and rolled heavily to starboard, hanging for an impossibly long time before rolling back to port.

More seawater inundated them. The bridge deck swirled with the increasing water the scuppers couldn't handle.

"Wheel!" Grisha gasped. "Get the wheel!"

Karpov threw himself on Grisha and hit him with three hammering blows. The vessel lurched in the moaning gale and crunched into a trough. Crockery shattered in the galley and Grisha twisted his body and threw Karpov off him.

He rolled over and pushed himself up, tried to hit Karpov but couldn't find a target the few times he could put any strength behind his fist. Valari grabbed the wheel and turned it back and forth uselessly.

"Into the wind!" he screamed. "Turn into the wi—"

Karpov's fist drove the oxygen from his lungs again. Grisha crashed back on the deck. The heavy man straddled him and began choking him with both hands.

Grisha stared at the hate-filled eyes in the bloody face. He dimly realized this was the first fight he'd been in since he got married. He felt his windpipe crackle and knew he was going to die very soon.

The lack of air became more pressing than the pain. He tried to struggle. But his arms lacked strength, pinned under the Russian's massive weight. Spots swam redly before his eyes.

Karpov lurched violently, his jaw dropped open and his eyes lost focus. The terrible crushing at Grisha's throat eased as the man collapsed on him. The medicinal scent of vodka mingled with his last shuddering breath.

Karpov suddenly rolled off Grisha and flopped on the deck, arms flung wide, and slid to the back of the boat in the quarter meter of water running across the deck. Valari pulled back the foot she had used to push Karpov's corpse and stood braced against the console. Blood and rain dripped off the steel spike on the halibut club in her hands.

"Get up and drive this goddamned thing!" she screamed, waving the club.

Even though Grisha felt like lying there and going to sleep, he rolled over and dragged himself up into the captain's chair bolted to the deck. *Pravda* rolled heavily to starboard again, and he grasped the wheel, turning to follow the roll, praying the tiller would grab enough water to keep from completely rolling over. Seawater seeped over the starboard gunwale as the boat pushed into multiple tons of brine.

Pravda edged slowly into the keening wind, the laboring diesel barely audible, and slowly, reluctantly, creaked back to port. His head and throat ached. Every breath felt like fire. The spots dancing in front of his eyes gradually evolved into rain drops.

"This isn't good weather for fishing," he said in a croak and shook his head. He pointed the bow into the wind and increased the throttle. *Pravda* surged against the storm and slowly made headway.

He estimated the waves to be ten meters from trough to top.

Valari huddled against the far bulkhead, braced and sobbing. "What are we going to do?"

They were both soaked to the skin. The ocean temperature rarely warmed more than eight or ten degrees above freezing. With the squall blowing in excess of fifty knots, they both were in the depths of hypothermia.

"We're going to live!" he said roughly, wincing at the pain in his throat. "We beat him, we can beat the storm!"

"I'm so cold!" she wailed.

"Go below, first locker on your right. Coats. Bring me one, too."

The few minutes she took seemed like hours to him. She reemerged bundled in a coat too large for her and handed him a foul-weather jacket. He shrugged into the dry coat and knew he was going to be all right.

"We m-must get rid of that," she said, nodding toward Karpov's bloody body. She was all business again, the tears gone but teeth still chattering. "B-but how?"

"Why do we have to get rid of him?"

"You f-fool! We've k-killed one of the Czar's co-cossacks! The Okhana will hang us both for that."

"Find something heavy," he said. "Tie it to him. Once we're out of the weather, we'll dump him over. Tell them he fell over the side when he was drunk. They'll believe us."

She gave him a look of respect and something else—he didn't know what. Despite the heavy weather she conducted a quick search, and dragged out Karpov's heavy tackle kit.

"Will this do?" Color had returned to her face and she no longer shivered. She only held the rail with one hand and didn't watch her feet. Grisha decided she was a natural sailor.

"Open it. He brought that onboard. I want to see what's in it."

Valari grabbed the halibut club and brought it down with on the kit with a crash. The broken padlock skittered across the deck. She unsnapped the clasps and threw the lid open. Oily metal glistened from the box.

"What the hell?" Grisha said.

Valari pulled out a gleaming pistol, twisted it about while she examined it and released the rail to pull the slide open to look into the chamber. She had handled weapons before. Grisha felt his stomach drop. Other pistols rested in the box.

"Kharitikoff, nine-millimeter," she announced. "Holds a clip of seven rounds, accurate up to twenty meters. An excellent weapon."

Over the last seven years Grisha had carried many illegal items on his boat, but never this. He had two rifles locked in their rack down in the main cabin, but pistols?

"Do you know what they do to you if they catch you with an unauthorized handgun?" Grisha asked, horror in his voice. "They take your dominant hand off at the wrist!"

She looked at him for a long moment, then returned the pistol to the box and shut it. "Where's the rope?"

Grisha pointed to another locker. "In there, but for now just hang on."

The boat dropped heavily into another trough as he worked his way toward land.

2

Four Days Earlier

It didn't take Grisha long to realize this was the charter trip from hell. He'd puzzled at it ever since the broker called to book boat and skipper for a five-day fishing trip to New Archangel, the capital of Russian Amerika, three hundred miles west. Most fishermen arrived at the dock the same time he did, eager to pursue the *chavych*, or Chinook salmon, or the monstrous halibut that could grow larger than a barn door.

Grisha had arrived just after sunrise. The summer sun hung two hand widths above tree-covered Mt. Robare when he finally spied the big man lumbering toward him down the dock. The client dressed like a fisherman, complete with trolling pole and tackle kit, but he walked like a cossack—arrogantly precise in a ruler-straight line and exuding the certainty he owned the world. At the edge of the dock he stopped and stared into Grisha's eyes, spoke Russian. "You are Charter Captain Grigoriy Grigorievich, yes?"

"Yes," Grisha replied in English. "Are you my charter to New Archangel?"

The man casually threw his tackle kit over the gunwale. When Grisha caught it, he nearly collapsed with the surprising weight of the locked metal box. The man climbed on deck and looked around.

"You have vodka on board?"

7

Grisha glanced at the chronometer in the console, it was half past eight of the morning. Stale sweat and bowel gas eddied around the large man, who dropped into the other seat bolted to the bridge deck.

Grisha watched the man look around at his nautical surroundings, obviously for the first time. So what was in the tackle box? This was obviously a smuggling run and would provide much more money at the end of the trip than previously agreed.

"Yes, and beer, even some California whiskey."

The man regarded Grisha with baleful, piggish eyes. "That is against the Czar's law, unless you have paid the duty, of course."

"Of course!" Grisha suppressed a grin while stowing the tackle box, which he estimated at ten kilos, with his own fishing gear.

Like this walrus ever worried about duty taxes!

Maintaining a professional mien, he slipped over the side onto the dock. "We're late. I'll get us underway." Quickly, he untied both lines and stepped back aboard.

Grisha edged the boat into gear and eased the throttle forward. "Do you have a name? *Other than Pig-eyes?*"

The boat gently left the slip and angled toward the channel. A warm breeze rippled the water and the sky stretched bereft of clouds as far as the eye could see. A charter skipper couldn't ask for better omens.

"I am Karpov. How long does it take to get to T'angass?"

"Depends on how much fishing we do on the way and how fast we go." Grisha snapped his head around and stared at Karpov. "Wait a minute, I thought we were going to New Archangel."

"There has been a change of plans. I wish to go to T'angass."

Karpov said. "We will fish on the way back. At maximum speed, how long will it take us to get to get there?"

"Today and two more days if we don't run into bad weather. If you're in a hurry, why don't you fly?"

"I enjoy the sea air. Where is the vodka?"

"In the galley." Grisha motored slowly past the harbor patrol, careful not to show any wake. So far he wasn't making all that much on this run, and a fine would put him in the hole, as well as add stamps to his license. Collect enough stamps and the license disappears; he loved the symmetry of Russian law.

Karpov disappeared into the cabin. Grisha decided he had a smuggler on his hands. Smuggling paid a lot better than charter fishing trips, so he would patiently wait for the proposal.

A ruble was a ruble, what the hell. His wife's face flashed through his mind and he slapped the wheel.

No time for that now. *It's either better when I return or it's over.* Small angry teeth bit inside his gut. They chewed at him a great deal these days. He felt pissed at himself.

"Sorry I slapped you," he murmured to the wheel, "I was aiming for someone else."

"Do you *Creoles* talk to yourselves all the time?" Karpov asked as he clumped up out of the galley. The bottle of vodka looked small in his wide, beefy hand.

"I talk to my boat when the notion strikes me," he said, edging his words with a glint of steel. Grisha forced himself calm. This wasn't the old days, even if Kazina didn't want him any more. But if this tub of suet kept up this "*Creole*" crap there would be trouble.

"You need some diversion on your boat for your passengers. Perhaps a *Creole* woman, heh?" Karpov laughed and drank from the bottle.

Grisha ground his teeth. It was going to be a long trip.

The boat burbled past the breakwater and into Akku Channel. He pushed the throttle forward, *Pravda*'s cutwater surged up onto the step, that portion of the boat where the vee of the hull flattens into a plane for moving at high speed, and raced cleanly toward the distant tip of Douglas Island.

Grisha thought it humorous that an island in Russian Amerika bore the name of an English religious leader. But custom in the old days of exploration decreed that all nations would honor the wish of whomever named it first. British Captain George Vancouver had accurately finished what his former skipper, Captain James Cook, had started, and charted the entire southeast Alaska coast in the 1790s before Imperial Russia completely dominated the region.

The constant rumble of stamp mills faded behind *Pravda*. They passed the whaling station on the island, scaring up part of the large flock of seagulls scavenging scraps. The station's stench caught them for an instant before the boat burst through the invisible miasma.

"Smells like the *Creole* part of town," Karpov said.

Abruptly Grisha pulled the throttle back to neutral and *Pravda*'s bow dipped with the sudden loss of power. The boat drifted.

"Why do you stop?"

"There will be an understanding before I go any farther. I am the captain and owner of this boat. You are my passenger.

"Despite the fact that my father was a poor Russian laborer and my mother was a Kolosh, you will show me the respect you would for any citizen, especially a boat captain. If you do not, I will return you to port so you can find a different charter to take you south."

"That would not be a smart thing for you to do. You would miss making a great deal of money. Also, your license might be forfeit."

"And your superior might ask many questions why I brought you back. Perhaps he has relatives who are *Creole*, or works with them. The Czar's ukase of 1968 said there would be no more prejudice because of one's birthright. That's nineteen years also, you should have heard about it by now. I don't want any more bigoted shit from you."

Karpov's squinting eyes receded even further into his face as he took another long drink.

"Drive your boat, I will say no more about your unfortunate station in life." As the beefy Russian lifted the bottle to his lips, Grisha pushed the throttle forward. *Pravda* reared like a cossack's horse and charged across the water. Karpov rocked back in his chair and vodka spilled down his neck and jacket front.

"You dung-eating Cre—, you ass!" Karpov shouted. "I would punish you for that, but for the fact I need to get to T'angass as soon as possible."

Grisha ignored him; a smile flickered at the edge of his mouth. More bullshit; if he wanted to get south as soon as possible he wouldn't have hired a small boat. His practiced eyes swept over the instrument panel and his mind ticked off the levels, amperage, RPM, and hull speed without actually thinking about them.

Kazina's face occupied his thoughts. Her dark hair framed the high cheeks and nearly jade eyes. Lilacs always attended her.

When they married just under six years ago he knew fortune had finally smiled on him. She epitomized the crowning accomplishment of his climb back from the lowest strata of the Czar's American possession.

The illiterate son of serfs, his father married a Kolosh woman of the *Kootz-neh-woo* people from Admiralty Island. As a *Creole*, a person of mixed race, Grisha found himself equally shunned by the children of low-caste Russians as well as by the children of the Auk and Taku *Kolosh*, including his own cousins.

At an early age he learned the three essentials of survival: a quick mind, lightning fists, and fast feet. After leaving the priest's school at fourteen, he crewed on a fishing boat. At seventeen he developed into a handsome combination of the ethnicities he represented.

Grisha's virginity went to a pretty barmaid during an equinox party. Women in every port of the Alexandr Archipelago watched for him. His other idea of a good time usually involved a drunken fight after which his opponent had to be carried away.

One night the fight was with his own skipper. Grisha won the fight but lost his berth. The next morning he joined the Troika Guard, the "Russian Foreign Legion."

Originally all the officers were Russian, but that had slowly changed over the years. However, all the enlisted were either minority races from the vast Russian Empire or foreigners. Never before had he been challenged on every level of his being, nor felt the degree of camaraderie, as he did in the Guard.

The Russian Army was a political beast complete with intrigue whose genesis went back centuries. The Troika Guard was tough, demanding, and received all the hard, dirty jobs. In essence, they were mercenary troops—which suited Grisha just fine.

He loved the Troika Guard. Starting as a sub-private he learned quickly and rapidly made his way upward to command sergeant in less than five years. His men loved him.

At the age of twenty-five he received a battlefield commission as well as the Imperial Order of Valor, the second highest decoration the Russian Empire awarded her soldiers and sailors. Four years later came French Algeria and dishonor.

His loathing of the Russian government began then and grew steadily over the years. Dealing with the day-to-day officiousness of Russian Amerika gnawed at him, but, like all other non-Russian residents, he endured.

The mustering-out money bought him his home and his boat but cost him his self-respect. He started over, going back to the things he had learned before he had killed his first man. He returned to the life he knew before the Troika Guard, fiercely holding onto the freedom of being his own boss. After a couple years fishing, smuggling, and building up a charter business, he met Kazina at a party.

She was a twenty-six-year-old bookkeeper with the Russian Amerika Company. Her extraordinary beauty lured him. Her intelligence hooked him. She made it plain she was on her way up and had no interest in a has-been.

He pointed out that he worked for himself and made a good living. They married when he was thirty-two, still the master of *Pravda*, a ten-meter fishing boat. He rigged the boat for sport fishing, which had turned into big business along the Inside Passage. Financial opportunities also occurred for skippers who knew how to lade cargo quietly and get out of port quickly.

At thirty-nine he could pass for a man ten years younger. Wiry and lean, with the exception of a slight paunch, he stood almost two meters and possessed open good looks that still attracted women who appreciated adventure.

Now, after six, almost seven, years of marriage, Kazina seemed distant. Grisha's past attempts to interact with her friends always came off stiff and wooden. None of them were *Creole*. He detected or expected their silent racism and ceased his efforts.

The marriage had been on the ebb for some time before tall, blond, Kommander Fedorov knocked on their door with an "Imperial Order for Lodging an Officer of the Czar." Grisha's small chart room became the sacrifice for the officer's comfort and fanned the embers of his anger at the government. But the sudden animation he perceived in Kazina proved the heaviest burden.

Until Fedorov arrived, Grisha entertained hope that he could find compromise with his beautiful wife. But she hadn't even said good-bye when he left for this charter. As a commander of troops he had learned the necessity of cutting one's losses. But this was much harder. The tiny teeth bit so hard in his stomach that he groaned aloud.

"Go ahead, talk to your boat," Karpov said with a slur in his voice. "I'm going to take a nap. Wake me when the evening meal is prepared."

As the burly man staggered down the steps into the cabin, Grisha steered sharply around imaginary flotsam, knowing the cossack would lose his balance in the narrow passageway. He heard Karpov crash into the companionway bulkhead.

"Damn your black ass!" Karpov's voice was muffled by distance and engine noise. Grisha smiled, trying to make it a victory.

Two days later, after pounding south at his top speed of twenty-four knots, Grisha still waited for enlightenment about the nature of his character. Maybe they were going to acquire contraband tomorrow in T'angass?

Much smaller than Akku, Fort Dionysus claimed to be the second oldest settlement in Southeast Alaska, after New Arkhangel. Grisha had fished out of the small town in his youth and still had friends there.

He pulled into the fuel dock, clicked the throttle back, and switched off the engine, letting the boat glide alongside the wooden dock. He grabbed the bowline, and nimbly jumped onto the bobbing dock to deftly loop two turns around a cleat.

As soon as he dropped the line he grasped the boat rail to keep the stern from yawing away from the slip. The station worker came out of his small shack as Grisha snubbed down the stern line.

"What ya runnin'?" The man said, and then blinked with surprise. "Grisha? That really you?"

"Alexi! By God, you're working a real job."

Alexi's face sported new lines and old scars. A limp now slowed him. He looked thinner than ever.

"Whose boat you workin' here?"

"Mine," Grisha said.

"So that's why you quit drinkin' with us, you were savin' your money."

"You got it, Alexi. How have you been?"

Alexi's grin dampened down to a polite grimace. "Getting by. You know, job here, job there, working as crew when the Chinook are running, or the czar krab fishery gets good. That don't happen much no more. Dimitri offered me a day job running his fuel dock, so I took it."

The suddenly diminished man ran an expert eye over *Pravda*. "Nice boat. Your home port is Akku these days?"

"Yeah. Even got a marriage that's going sour."

Alexi stepped back into the shack, professionally looked over his shoulder at Grisha. "Diesel or mix?"

"Diesel."

"So," Alexi said when fuel gurgled through the hose into the boat. "You got any kids?"

"No. All I have is my *Pravda*, here."

"Why'd you name it after something that doesn't exist?" Alexi asked with a flash of bitterness.

"She's the only truth I know," Grisha answered.

The boat rocked and Karpov came out on deck. "What is this place?"

Alexi grinned up at him. "Welcome to Fort Dionysus, home to *promyshlenniks* since 18—"

"I care nothing about fur hunter dens. Is food to be had here?"

"There's a lodge just up the street from the end of that dock," Alexi said, jabbing a thumb toward the shack.

Karpov gave Grisha a sour glance. "You will come and tell me when you are ready to leave, Captain Grigorievich." Then he stomped up the ramp to solid ground.

"Thought you was done with the military," Alexi stared at him under raised brows. "What you doing with a fucking cossack like that?"

"If I knew, I'm not sure I could tell you, old friend."

After Grisha paid for the fuel, he moved *Pravda* to transient moorage, then found his way up to the Canada House Lodge. Despite the late hour, the sun barely touched the mountains on Zarembo Island. Diners laughed, drank, and ate on the screened-in deck.

Grisha found a table, ordered, and had just swallowed his second mouthful of beer when Karpov loomed over him.

"When do we leave this place?"

"I'd like to get underway at oh-seven-hundred tomorrow, if you can be on board that early."

Karpov stalked into the lodge.

Why was the man pretending to be thicker than he really was? If they were smuggling something in the tackle box, when would Karpov broach the subject? Did the Russian plan to set Grisha up as a dupe, or think he could endanger boat and captain without a cut of the profits?

The next morning he glanced at the cloudless horizon, sucked hot tea through the sugar cube clenched in his teeth, and eyed the brass-cased chronometer on the console. The sharp, iodine-tinged smell of tidal flats filled his nostrils. At 0658, just as he allowed his tongue to seek out the final sweet granules, Karpov plodded down the steep ramp.

Fall and break your neck, Pig-eyes. I'll tell your keeper you didn't know what a low tide was.

Karpov did not fall.

Without a word Grisha untied the boat and pushed off. He wanted to make T'angass by early afternoon. One day of no clouds and bright sunshine was good. Three days of sunshine unnerved seamen in this part of Alaska—after a time it felt natural and if one took good weather for granted one would pay for it.

Grisha had attended ten funerals where the coffin was merely for show—the men, and one woman, lost to fierce storms on days that began this promising. The Alexandr Archipelago was legendary for its sudden bad weather.

Karpov again disappeared below and Grisha relished the solitude. Once he saw a humpback but didn't radio in the information. He enjoyed watching the huge, sleek mammals, and those whaling bastards never paid the spotter's fee anyway.

Twice he switched on the weather channel to ensure the high-pressure cell still held as expected. The air remained crisp and fresh, adding to his edginess.

For the rest of the six-hour run into T'angass the smooth wood of the steering wheel constituted his only connection with here-and-now reality. Despite himself, everything reminded him of Kazina's body on their wedding night. The texture of her skin had seeped into the steering wheel. The heavy, rounded console jutted toward him like her generous, gravity-defying breasts.

The sparkling light on the sea brought to mind her eyes when she laughed. He pulled his gaze away from the water, tried to concentrate on something else, break the train of memory. Two mountains on the mainland curved gently together, forcefully reminding him of Kazina's perfect ass.

He knew he would never enjoy her body again. With absolute conviction, he also knew if he didn't have this charter he'd be dead drunk by nightfall. Not even losing his commission had been this painful.

Revillagigedo Island loomed large on the bow when Karpov returned to the bridge deck. The big Russian made a show of examining his wristwatch.

"You've made excellent time, Captain," he said in heavy English. "Perhaps it is good I make you angry so you can concentrate on the job at hand."

Grisha's eyes ached from squinting at bright water. His kidneys throbbed from the pounding of a boat on step. The draining exhaustion of long, boring hours in open air weighed on him like a two-bottle hangover.

"Believe what you will, cossack."

Karpov frowned. "This is something you must not call me. If I do not call you *Creole*, you must not address me as cossack. Agreed?"

"You're the customer," Grisha said.

"*Da*. Very good. Pull into the fisherman's dock, we pick up our passenger there."

"Passenger? I thought you were getting off here." The vision of four beers lined up on a bar wavered.

"Last evening in Fort Dionysus I was apprised of a change in plans. We will pick up a passenger here and go to New Arkhangel immediately."

"That's out of the question! I've been pushing this boat for five straight days. The weather's been good for *over* five days and it's bound to turn. Besides, how do you know I don't have another charter?"

Whatever this was about, Grisha realized, it wasn't smuggling.

"Perhaps if your fee was increased?" Karpov asked, raising his right eyebrow skeptically. The corners of his mouth twitched, as if playing an elaborate prank.

Grisha stared at T'angass. A neon sign gleamed in the late afternoon shadows. He knew the owner of that bar, and she would be very happy to see her old lover.

It had been a long time since a good-looking woman had felt that way about him. He desperately craved reaffirmation from the gentler sex. The vision of beer dimmed further. He squinted back at Karpov.

"By how much?"

Karpov held out a wad of rubles that more than doubled the original fee. Grisha made the money disappear along with thoughts of carousing with Natalia Fialikof.

"I'll need to refuel and get some more supplies."

"Be sure to get plenty of vodka this time."

Fuel topped off, food and spirits stowed, Grisha had dropped onto one of the four passenger bunks and glanced around. Everything was shipshape. He peered at his watch.

He didn't want time to brood.

Where the hell is that damned cossack? I thought he was in a hurry.

He felt anxious they weren't smuggling. What else could this trip be for? Boat travel was no more secure than taking one of the new four-engine airliners, and a damned sight more tedious.

The boat rocked to port and a female voice said, "Give me a hand, would you, Nikki?" The English sounded accent-free.

Grisha's interest quickened. He had assumed the second passenger would be another cossack. Was this an elaborate assignation?

"Karpov. You will address me as Karpov while on this craft."

"Fine. Now give me a hand, would you?"

Grisha eased into the companionway and moved quietly up the steps to the bridge deck.

She wasn't much to look at, certainly not enticing enough to fetch all the way from T'angass. But then someone as ugly as Karpov might have to go to extraordinary lengths to get laid. Perhaps she was something else. A relative?

Short blond hair capped a face composed of planes and angles rather than the soft, rounded features expected on a woman. The full lips of her mouth made its excessive width enticing. Dark eyes flashed about, assessing the small bridge deck.

She wasn't nearly ugly enough to be Karpov's sister, but perhaps a cousin. Grisha stepped into view. Her agreeable proportions and medium stature heightened his interest.

"Ah, here is Charter Captain Grigorievich. We can leave at once," Karpov said.

The woman's eyes traveled over him slowly. *Nothing coy about this one*, he thought. He smiled.

"Welcome aboard *Pravda*. I'm Grisha. May I stow your gear?"

Her face softened a measure, adding attractiveness, and she handed him the canvas bag. It weighed nothing. An unknown, but delectable, scent touched his nose during the exchange.

"Captain Grisha," she said with the smallest of smiles. "I'm Valari Kominskiya." Her English sounded first-language. He wondered if her Russian was as proficient.

Grisha put the bag on the forward bunk and returned to the bridge.

"We can leave now." Karpov said again.

Fifteen minutes later, as *Pravda* motored north on T'angass Narrows, their conversation became cryptic.

"Did you have difficulty getting in or out?"

"No," Valari said. "My documents worked as smoothly as gold in St. Petersburg."

"Keep your subversive comments to yourself, or I'll take official notice," Karpov said with a growl. "What is the temper of Sam?"

What on earth were they talking about, more relatives? Grisha turned his head slightly to hear her answer over the engine noise. Karpov caught the movement.

"Wait," he ordered. "We'll go below to the cabin where there are fewer ears."

Grisha stared studiously through the windscreen while the two clumped down the steps into the cabin. He smiled to himself and slid aside a piece of the console molding. Some cargoes could speak, and additional knowledge had a way of turning into more rubles. After mounting the tiny phone in his right ear, he flipped the switch concealed in the opening.

". . . States are very nervous. One man told me they were 'waiting for the other shoe to drop,' whatever that means," Valari said.

"Which do they fear the most, New France or the Confederacy?"

"It's a toss-up," she said in fluent Russian. "They are allies. Tension is high between the governments. Texas is very friendly to British Canada. The great fear in Texas is of New Spain and the First People's Nation. Our historic ally, the Spanish, have been rattling sabers along the Rio Grande by placing additional troops at El Paso and Marronville. With New Spain as common enemy, California and Texas get along well. California is so friendly with British Canada that one may cross the Columbia River freely without showing a passport on either side."

"The religious country in the wasteland, is it anything we must worry about?"

"Deseret? The Mormons hate the other nations so fiercely they would sell themselves to the French Catholics before they would help any of them. They are neutral, you know."

"Neutral, in what way?"

"No matter who fights who, they will join neither side. Like Switzerland in Europe."

"So our U.S. friends are completely surrounded by antagonism," Karpov said.

"So it would seem. But what do we really care about North Amerikan countries?"

"We have internal problems you will be apprised of in New Arkhangel. If the southern countries were to act in tandem against us it would be very bad."

"I didn't see any unity or antagonism. But I saw a lot of spoiled people."

"You're becoming hardened," Karpov said.

"Not hardened, envious. Every one of our agents-in-place lives on a grand scale compared to what my family has in Russia. Our woman in Montreal owns two automobiles!"

Grisha blinked. Karpov was a spymaster? They chartered *Pravda* for a debriefing session? It did make sense, after a fashion.

"No!" Karpov's surprise carried clearly over the tiny earphone. "Perhaps we should pay them less?"

"At least she provides us with accurate information. She told me there is softening about us in the western republics."

"Didn't you just come through California?"

"Yes. But our man in San Francisco spends all of his money on cannabis cigarettes, which makes him useless for days at a time. All he wanted to do was make love and eat."

"Did you?"

"Did I what?"

"Make love with him."

"That is none of your *svinia* affair."

"It used to be."

Something thumped on the table, and Grisha realized Karpov had been drinking vodka throughout the debriefing.

"Not anymore, Nikki. You're just not my type."

"You'd sleep with our *Creole* captain, I saw it in your eyes."

"He is pretty to look at, but he holds no interest for me beyond the objectives of our voyage. I am weary of men and their strutting and crowing."

"You prefer women to sleep with, is what you mean?"

Valari stomped up the companionway. Grisha's heart lurched as he jerked the tiny phone from his ear and hastily stuffed the wires back into their hidden compartment. She stormed past before he could shut the false molding, but she had eyes only for her anger and the passing scenery.

"That bastard is such a *svinia*, a pig!" she said in a hissing voice. "Someday I will kill him."

"I believe he dropped out of finishing school," Grisha said in a theatrical Californian accent. He quietly pushed the small door shut. The molding blended with the rest of the console. He wondered what she meant by "the objectives of our voyage."

When Valari laughed she almost looked pretty. "You're married, aren't you?"

The question caught him off guard.

"At the moment."

"I've been out of the country for two years. What does 'at the moment' mean? Is it a marriage of convenience to obtain citizenship papers?"

"No. It means that at any moment she is going to leave me for another man."

"Oh."

Grisha made a show of checking his charts. He glanced at his watch and immediately powered up the radio.

". . . move across the Alexandr Archipelago by nightfall. Thirty-knot winds increasing to forty to fifty knots by morning. Seas two to three meters. For the outside waters, Dixon Entrance to Christian Sound, small-craft warning. Seas two to four meters. West winds forty knots increasing to fifty-five by morning—"

Grisha snapped off the radio and peered at the horizon. A dark line rapidly moved out of the west, staining the abnormal blue sky back to familiar tones.

"We're in for some rough weather," he said.

Her eyes widened. "Are we in any danger?"

He tried to laugh, but even to him it sounded more like a bark.

"One is always in danger in Russian Amerika, one way or another."

"Is this one of your pithy Native American sayings?"

"It's truth, like my boat."

"How can a boat be truth?" she asked with more than a hint of angry sarcasm.

"How can it be a lie?"

Karpov emerged from the cabin, vodka bottle in hand. "I'm hungry."

A gust of cold wind heeled the boat over to starboard. The temperature dropped ten degrees in as many seconds.

Karpov braced himself and stared out at the rapidly advancing weather. "Storm?" he said in a small voice.

Grisha started to smile at their discomfort but stopped himself. It would not do to laugh at the wind.

"*Da*," he said.

Karpov hastily drank from the bottle. He peered at Valari.

"You will go below with me, now."

She scowled back. "In the Amerikas they have the perfect expression for someone like you. Would you like to know it?"

Karpov quietly stared at her, eyes hidden in wrinkled folds of skin.

"Go fuck yourself, is what they say. I think you should do that now."

With surprising speed he lunged forward and slapped her open-handed. Her head smacked against the bulkhead with a solid thunk and she emitted a startled yell.

"Hey!" Grisha shouted. "What do you think you're doing?"

Karpov turned to face him. His English had gained polish. "This is none of your concern, Captain Grigorievich. You are being well paid. You will drive the boat and mind your own business."

Grisha clenched his teeth and said nothing. Karpov gathered Valari in one arm and hauled her down the companionway as if she were a sack of oats.

Then the storm caught them and Karpov started his last fight.

3

Tolstoi Bay, Prince of Wales Island

Pravda danced and jerked on the anchor line. The small cove on Prince of Wales Island sheltered them from the brunt of the storm. Grisha took a firm grasp under Karpov's shoulders.

"Ready?"

Valari nodded sharply.

"Hup!"

They swung the stiffing body off the deck and up onto the gunwale at the stern, balancing it carefully. The memory of butchering hogs flashed through his mind.

"Okay, I'll hold him, put the box on his chest."

She bent over and grabbed the box tied to the corpse with a short line, sat it in the middle of Karpov's chest.

"Push!" Grisha ordered.

The body splashed into the water and, spinning in a slow circle behind the heavy box of weapons, sank rapidly out of sight.

Numb lassitude spread over him, and he relaxed for the first time in three days. Suddenly Valari pressed against him, her hands moving over his face, chest, groin.

"I need you," she said. "Right now."

With a tired smile he pulled her into the cabin.

✧   ✧   ✧

The bright sky held no wind when he woke. For a long moment he lay in the bunk beside the woman and collected his thoughts. He tried to figure out how he could have changed the outcome.

This charter was set up by the government, even he knew that. Would the Okhana believe their concocted story about the loss of one of their agents?

"What's the matter, Captain Lover?"

Grisha turned his head and looked at her. The now-familiar mouth smiled, lips parted slightly as if anticipating a kiss. But Valari's eyes held a hardness unaffected through murder and sex.

He'd seen eyes like hers only a couple of times. They had belonged to desperate men whose only hope lay with the legal benediction of the Troika Guard. Both had finished badly, one shot for cowardice and the other killed in a barroom brawl.

He had let this situation get out of his control. With this woman he had helped murder a man and finally cheated on his wife. Too much, too fast. He knew nothing about her, yet she held his life in her hands. Amazing how an orgasm could clear the mind.

"What are we going to do now?" he asked.

"He got drunk and fell over the side during the storm." Her eyes searched his. "Isn't that what you said last night?"

"Yes, but . . ." Grisha licked his suddenly dry lips, "You must attest to what I say, no matter what. Agreed?"

"*Da.*" Valari's eyes narrowed and her mouth flattened. "But you must be very convincing and not waver."

"I can do that. But you worked for him, or with him, isn't there someone you could talk to, and make this be all right?"

Something deep in her eyes shifted and for a moment he thought he saw triumph before they became veiled. "Just who do you think I am?"

"I know you're an agent for the government. I know Karpov was someone you reported to. There's much that I don't know.

"Why did they hire a boat to bring you to New Arkhangel when flying would have been much more expedient? Why did Karpov hire me?" He felt angry. "Why, at my age, is everything in my life suddenly out of control?"

"I cannot tell you more than I already have. If you do not wish to face the Okhana we have two options. We can turn ourselves in and tell the truth, which would mean the gallows for both of us—"

"For stopping him from raping you? For saving us all from drowning because he imperiled this craft?"

"They rarely believe survivors who do not bring back a corpse."

"He fell over the side. We were in a storm, right?"

"Or we can go to California, ask for political asylum, and start our lives over."

"Political asylum? Who are we to ask for that?"

"I'm an espionage agent for Imperial Russia, you are my lover. They would give us asylum."

He allowed himself to think about it, to savor the idea like a bite of potato salad or a mouthful of good ale. His marriage was finished and he didn't want to be in the same small town where Kazina would be showing off her new Russian husband. He would forfeit the house but if the authorities refused to believe them he would also forfeit his life.

He had to depend on Valari. Of course, she already said she owed him, but he couldn't bring himself to trust her. A small part of his brain pointed out that this would be a new adventure, something he had sorely missed since leaving the Troika Guard.

He couldn't go on smuggling forever.

"We'll need money," he said.

"Do you have any?"

"Yes. I've put away half my earnings for three years now. At first it was for my children . . ." He turned his head and stared toward the overhead, focused on an image infinitely far away. "Then it was for my escape."

"How much?"

"Enough to live on for a year."

"It's on the boat?"

"No. It's in my workshop behind my house at Akku."

"Where your wife is," Valari said.

"And her lover," he agreed.

"Check the weather," she said, smiling.

"I don't understand it," he said, staring at the high cloud cover where blue peeked through in spots. "Yesterday the radio said it would be worse by this morning."

She laughed behind him. "How often are they correct?"

He grinned and snapped on the radio. The low-pressure system had inexplicably shifted far to the north and west where the storm now pounded from Kodiak Island to sprawling St. Nicholas, the huge military bastion of Russian Amerika on Cook's Inlet.

Good, I hope the Russian Amerika Company offices all wash out to sea.

They ran north as fast as he dared push the boat. Grisha settled into an apprehensive anticipation. Something about his feelings struck a chord in his memory.

Suddenly he was again a frightened five-year-old, watching his drunken father beat his mother. His mother grunted with the blows, trying to cover her face and chest. Grisha's fear for his mother finally overcame self-preservation and he attacked his father.

He pounded on his father with small fists. The next thing he knew, his mother was bathing his face with cold water. Pitr Grigorievich had knocked him out, realized the monstrousness of his actions, and fled into the night.

They had waited together, fearful and expectant, for the man to return and for it all to begin again. Which it did.

Grisha shook his head at the vividness of the memory. He knew he still harbored old anger for his father, but he thought the fear long vanquished. And how was this like that?

They spent the night at transient moorage in a small settlement on Mitkof Island. Fuel cost more there, but Grisha didn't want to run into anyone he knew. Not that Valari let him get that far from the double bunk in the bow and her insatiable needs.

By 0900 the next morning they were on the last leg of their trip. The fair weather held for the entire day and they made good time. Akku Channel lay quiet and empty in the late evening when they rounded the south end of Douglas Island.

The stamp mills sat silent, something that only happened on Christmas Day and the Czar's birthday. The last glow of light reflected on the water. Suddenly fireworks shouted across the sky as they neared town.

"What are they celebrating, a local holiday?" Valari asked.

Grisha thought hard. "No. There's no holiday in early July. I don't know what's going on."

He slowed as they passed under the bridge, but no patrol boats lurked in their usual spots. They idled up to the fuel dock, and he tied the boat while she stepped into the office.

"There's nobody here."

Laughter and music drifted down from the Harbor Hotel. Fireworks popped and whistled above them, the acrid stink of gunpowder drifted on the air. Grisha shrugged and filled the fuel tanks.

"This bothers me," Valari said. "I want to know what's happening."

He moved *Pravda* over to her normal berth as full darkness settled over an unusually boisterous Akku.

"You wait here. I'll get the money, and we'll go look at California."

"Be careful, Grigoriy," she whispered, then kissed him ardently.

He hurried away, wondering where they would be a year from now. From half a block away he could see that every light in his house blazed. People milled about, laughing and drinking.

A party. She's actually having a party.

He crept close enough to see Kazina radiant on the arm of Kommander Fedorov. She wore a dress new to him, and the kommander stood resplendent in full dress uniform. They made a handsome couple.

Surprisingly, the teeth didn't bite at him. He tensed in the old way, but they were gone.

It's over, and I don't care anymore, he thought. *A new adventure waits for me.*

The sense of freedom left him giddy. He hurried around the house to his well-built shop. Quietly he slipped in through the door and stopped, pulse drumming in his head.

He wasn't alone. Barely discernible noises exuded from the dark, sawdust-scented space. He peered at the workbench but could see nothing in the dim light other than a few tools out of place.

Three large electric saws dominated the center of the room. Sorted wood filled racks against the back wall, and his drafting table and books loomed on the left. The only thing against the right wall was his cot—

"Oh, Georg! Oh, my god!" exclaimed a young, feminine voice from the cot. Grisha grinned despite himself and moved quietly off to the left.

He had hidden the money in his file cabinet. Just a few more steps.

His foot hit a can of nails and knocked it over like a thunderclap in a hospital ward.

The woman gasped, and a male voice boomed out, "Who's there? Identify yourself. I'm armed!"

"Sorry, friend," Grisha said in a normal tone of voice. "I didn't realize there was anyone in here until after I had shut the door. Then I just tried to get my property without bothering you."

"I didn't hear anyone come in!" the man said.

The woman giggled. "I wonder why!"

Now Grisha could smell sex overlaying the sawdust. He thought of Valari and felt urgency.

"Well, just stay there, and I'll be out of your life in a moment."

"Wait," the man said. "Who are you? Our hostess said this was her husband's shop."

"I'm the husband," he said.

"But then you have just returned from New Archangel, yes?"

"Yes," Grisha echoed, surprised that Kazina had even remembered his destination, and more surprised she told anyone else. "Why do you ask?"

"What is the celebration like over there?"

"Celebration? What celebration?"

"Haven't you heard, man? The New Openness Treaty!"

"New what?"

"Openness!" the man and woman said together.

Finally his eyes adjusted, and he could see them in the dim light. They obviously believed themselves cloaked by darkness, as they made no effort to cover themselves.

Very nice breasts.

"I don't understand."

"New France, California, British Canada, and the First People's Nation have signed a treaty with us that drops political barriers and most trade and travel restrictions. The Cold War is over! We have true peace on this continent for the first time in over two hundred years."

Grisha felt numb. *Not now. Please, not yet!* "But what about New Spain, Texas? And Deseret?"

"Who cares? All are impossibly far away and none could conquer the rest of North America by themselves, or even in tandem. Peace! Isn't it wonderful?"

"Yes. Yes it is." He had the money bag in his hand, he edged toward the door. New Spain lay two thousand kilometers to the south. "I must have been in transit when this happened."

"Ah, your wife, sir," the woman said, "she and the kommander . . ."

"Never mind. I know. It's nice to see you two beginning a relationship that might go somewhere."

"Oh, we know where we will be going," the man said, laughing.

"Yes," the woman said with a giggle, "right back to our spouses!"

Grisha suddenly wanted to be anywhere but here.

He slipped out the door and into the dark night, jogging the four blocks to the boat harbor before slowing. The harbor lay quiet and dark.

He stopped, weighing possible actions. There might not be political asylum anymore. *Perhaps the thing to do is throw ourselves on the mercy of the crown. Karpov did start the whole thing, and wouldn't stop until he was killed.*

But Valari was right; they had disposed of the body. Honest citizens wouldn't do that. How would they explain that away? Tell them he fell over the side?

Valari would know, she understood the international political world. She owed him.

Grisha hurried down the dark dock to his boat. No sound or movement broke the stillness around *Pravda*. Concern enveloped him as he slipped aboard.

"Valari, are you here?" he whispered.

"Yes." Her voice sounded flat, official, disinterested.

Bright light stabbed out of the night and blinded him. Strong, rough hands seized his arms; he sensed many people around him.

"Are you Grigoriy Grigorievich?" an authoritative voice boomed.

"Yes, why?" He tried squinting to see past the glare.

"Is this the man, Lieutenant Kominskiya?"

"Yes," Valari said with a quaver in her voice. "He's the murderer."

Lieutenant? "Valari!" he screamed, cold fear tightening his guts. "What have you told them—"

The fist materialized out of the darkness and smashed into the side of his head. Dimly he felt them drag him off the boat. The smell of salt and tar flooded his nose.

"Time to hang a fuckin' *Creole!*" someone shouted.

Fireworks exploded in the air over Russian Amerika.

4

Akku

Consciousness brought pain on a level new to him. A small voice in the back of his mind noted that he must still be alive unless everything the priests taught him was a lie. He wondered if they were going to kill him.

Opening his eyes brought fresh anguish and it took three attempts before he could focus his squint at the gray expanse above him. Rock, or concrete, he decided. Slowly he turned his aching head and saw a wall of bars. So it hadn't been a nightmare, it was real.

Grisha felt so bereft and unanchored that he knew he had to be hollow. There was no more of himself to spend. His father, the Russian Army, his wife, his lover . . . all had used what they wanted and then discarded him.

The pain of the bruises, cuts, and scrapes covering his body abruptly lessened and he didn't need to wonder why. Could this profound detachment he felt actually be death? It didn't matter, he didn't care.

"Ah, our guest is back from the land of Winken and Nod!" an earsplittingly loud voice bellowed. "We must take him to breakfast."

Large, rough hands grabbed him by the arms and pulled him up onto his feet. If they hadn't continued to hold him, Grisha would have fallen on his face. Strength had fled his body and it took all his will to lift his head.

His squint functioned more smoothly this time and he beheld a small man dressed completely in black whose shaved head seemed to gleam. The bright grin under even brighter eyes gave the man an elfin cast.

"No, wait. Let's try him first and then decide whether to waste the cost of a meal on a condemned man. Bring him along."

The man turned and walked away. The strong hands dragged Grisha along in the man's wake and he idly wondered where they were taking him. He knew there would be more pain.

Through a doorway and suddenly the concrete floor yielded to wood and then carpet. Other people formed on the periphery but none moved to his aid. Abruptly he realized he was whimpering and he forced himself to stop.

To be frightened was to care. No reason to care, not anymore. He didn't even pity himself, he just moved further away.

Movement had stopped for some time and it took him long moments to focus on the words enough to comprehend.

". . . do you understand me?" a large man in black said in a calm voice.

Grisha tried to form the words but his scabbed lips, dry throat and aching jaw could only elicit, "Hnnn?"

"You are in the high court of His Majesty, Czar Nicholas IV, and accused of murdering one of his servants. How do you plead?"

Grisha again tried to speak; this time he did care. He hadn't killed anyone, he was guilty only of silence.

"Wad'r," he croaked.

"Give the prisoner some water," the big man said in his soothing voice.

The hands didn't slacken on his arms and a cup pressed against his lips and he gulped avidly as water poured down the front of him.

"How do you plead?" the calm man asked again.

"Not guilty," Grisha rasped. He couldn't tell if the man felt a flicker of disdain or mirth, but the corners of his mouth slightly twitched.

"Call the witness," the calm man said.

Grisha fell into the silence of waiting and his mind wandered far and fast. Noise turned into words.

". . . the man who cudgeled your superior officer, Kommander Nicholas Karpov of the Imperial Cavalry, to death on the Charter Vessel *Pravda* four days ago?"

"Yes, your honor, that is the man."

The sound of Valari's voice suddenly made him care, and hate suffused him, canceling all pain.

"She lies!" he rasped, willing his voice stronger. "She hit him in the back of the head with a halibut club while he was choking me on the deck."

The calm voice rolled over them again. "Lieutenant Kominskiya has a sterling record in the Imperial Cavalry. She was also prescient enough to predict your charge against her, even though she was also your victim."

"What?" Grisha croaked. "Victim? Of what?"

"Rape. Even the most casual examination of your berthing space condemns you."

"She—"

"The prisoner will maintain his silence while judgment is passed." His voice remained as calm as when he began the farce.

"Grigoriy Grigorievich, the High Court of His Majesty, Czar Nicholas IV, hereby condemns you to death for the murder of Kommander Nicholas Karpov, and the rape of Lieutenant Valari Kominskiya."

Grisha wilted and the hands struggled to keep him upright.

"However," the soothing voice revived the flickering flame of hope in Grisha's core, "His Imperial Majesty has decreed that in honor of the new Openness Treaty, for the period of one month, all capital sentences are commuted to thirty years at hard labor on the Russia-Canada Highway."

Grisha wilted again; it was still a death sentence. He glared at the impassive face of Valari Kominskiya as the guards pulled him from the courtroom and back into hell.

5

Akku

They beat him in his cell. Hours later they revived him by dumping cold water on his naked body and told him to dress; he had been deloused. The thin cotton prison uniform crawled with vermin but he pulled it on as quickly as he could.

Nothing of his former life remained, not even his boots. He pulled on shoes made of felt and the guards threw him into the back of a truck. Ten minutes later he was shackled to a long chain, the last in a coffle of twenty prisoners.

Different guards herded them up a ramp and into the cold, steel bowels of a transport ship. Grisha felt grateful for the straw on which they were allowed to sleep. After what must have been thirty hours, long past the fouling of the straw by all present, they were herded back into open air.

One glance of the Chilkat Range told Grisha they were on their way to Klukwan and the Czar's prison camp. They were all beaten upon arrival. Grisha thought he really might die, and the lassitude of surrender enveloped him once again.

When he woke the next morning, his hands were free of iron and one of the guards kicked his foot again.

"Get up, or you'll miss breakfast."

Grisha's stomach groaned loudly. He hadn't eaten since his last day on *Pravda*. His ribs looked like those of a corpse.

He staggered behind them, willing himself to take each step and not fall, knowing if he did he would never rise again. The aroma of hot, cooked food enveloped him and he dropped onto a bench where a steaming wooden bowl of gruel waited. Between burning his fingers, face, and lips, and the already raw condition of same, it took him almost ten minutes to empty the bowl.

He still felt ravenous.

He looked up at the guard.

"We'll feed you again in four hours. If you eat more now you'll just spew it all over the floor and have to clean it up."

For the first time since his trial he had the strength to look at the other prisoners. Men and women both were dressed in the same flimsy uniform. No attempt was made to segregate the sexes.

He pulled away from the women in gender hatred. First Kazina and then Valari had violated his trust. After supervising his anguished metamorphosis from cashiered officer to charter captain, his wife made him a cuckold.

Valari used him as a scapegoat for murder and exacerbated her infamy by claiming rape. Everything he attempted in his life had started with great promise, then ended in the most humiliating manner possible. And except for being cashiered, there had been a woman involved.

He noticed there were at least two men older than himself, and with the women there was no way of telling. Nobody talked except for one twitchy fellow who constantly murmured in conversation with something over his right shoulder.

The midday meal had flesh mixed in with potatoes and carrots. Grisha ate all they gave him. For a week they were fed and allowed to regain their strength. Toward the end of July Grisha and nineteen others were chained together in two coffles and herded into two army lorries.

The trucks growled north and east until they hit the Russia-Canada Highway and turned northwest.

The Russia–Canada enjoyed the term "highway" only by consent. Broken rock in fist-sized chunks formed the surface as well as the roadbed. In many places the top sank into the muskeg deep enough for narrow streams to traverse the roadway.

Leaving Klukwan and regular meals made all of them apprehensive.

"I don't think they are going to kill us," the oldest man said. "Else they wouldn't have wasted food on us."

"I agree," Grisha said, scratching at his beard. "I was sentenced to thirty years hard labor on the RustyCan, I think that's where they are taking us."

"Thirty years!" the old man exclaimed. "What was your crime?"

"They convicted me of killing a cossack. But I am innocent."

The other nine all laughed until they gasped.

"What's so fucking funny about that?"

The old man grinned at him. "Thank you, I haven't laughed since they sentenced me to ten years. We don't laugh at you, we laugh at ourselves. I doubt there are even two guilty persons in this truck."

"Why are you here?"

"My politics didn't hew closely enough to prescribed lines. I was the lucky one; they hanged three of my friends for treason."

"I thought they were commuting all capital offenses for a month. They did that to me."

"Which only points to your true innocence. What is your name, young man?"

"Grigoriy Grigorievich," he said with a laugh.

"Any you laugh why?"

"I haven't been called 'young man' for a very long time."

"I am Andreivich, and I have sixty years. You are younger than I am."

"By a third of your years, sir."

"You both talk too much," a burly, wild-haired man growled in a deep voice. "You should be trying to sleep."

"What is your name, woodsman?" Grisha asked.

"My mother called me Basil, after the saint. She may as well have named me Satan, now that I am in hell."

Grisha nodded in agreement.

"Thank your saint you are not a woman," a large woman with a gap between her front teeth said with disdain.

Grisha noticed the women had pulled as far away from the men as the chains would allow.

"We won't hurt you," Andreivich said. "Nor can we help you."

The woman pulled her haunted stare away from them, and looked out the back of the open truck at the cloud of dust billowing over the second truck. Equally great clouds of mosquitoes descended on them whenever the trucks stopped.

They arrived at Tetlin Redoubt and were pushed into a vast holding pen. The next morning they were fed and herded back into the trucks. Grisha found himself wondering where they would end their journey.

He was surprised that he cared.

A Zukhov K-28 tank followed the three trucks, one for army personnel and two for convicts, and Grisha wondered at the military decision behind its presence. Wherever they were going, a potential enemy lurked. Grisha smiled; it couldn't be all bad.

After traveling half the day the truck jolted to a stop and the engine died. Grisha stirred from his semiconscious nap.

"Get out here, you scum!" a deep voice shouted. "Quickly, or you'll miss dinner."

They all heaved to their feet and followed the woman at the head of the chain.

"She's mine, first," the deep voice roared.

"No matter what else comes out that truck?" a second harsh voice asked.

"Yes!"

The next three women were also claimed by unseen men.

Then Grisha jumped down to the ground and turned to help Andreivich. A stunning blow knocked him into the dust.

"You don't ever turn your back on me, slave, unless I tell you to!"

Holding his head so it wouldn't split, Grisha staggered to his feet and stared at the burly, bearded man in front of him.

The cossack sergeant grabbed him by the shoulder and thrust him away from the truck. "Keep moving, you dung-eater."

In moments Grisha took in his surroundings. They were in deep woods but the glint of moving water could be seen through the far trees. *Pravda* flashed through his mind but he wouldn't hold on to the memory.

Two rough cabins sat at the edge of a large clearing where most of the trees still lay after harvest. A coffle of nine emaciated prisoners sat in the dust at roadside. Grisha decided they were being taken back to Tetlin to be strengthened.

"How many were you in the beginning?" Grisha whispered to the closest one.

"Thirty," the man whispered back without moving his head. "The rest are dead."

"Move out!" the cossack sergeant bellowed.

The women shuffled toward the cabins.

Another cossack screamed, "Not that way! That's where we live."

They were halted at a wide trench floored with packed wood rounds. A ladder was the only way down or up. Two of the cossacks opened the heavy locks on each prisoner's shackles.

The men were ordered into the trench and the women were led away by the crowing cossacks. The soldiers who had traveled in the lead truck threw the men some food. They could hear the cries and moans of the women all night.

6

Outside Construction Camp 4, Mid August, 1987

Ten meters above the ground, Slayer-of-Men shifted slightly to take the pressure off his left foot. The tree limb remained motionless as the tall man smoothly transferred weight to his right foot so he could flex the numbness from his sleeping leg.

The cossacks below went about their wasteful ways, unaware of watchers. Not once had any of the bear-men looked up at the surrounding trees. They believed themselves complete masters on this part of the Tanana River. Soon they would know the truth. The Dená were reclaiming their ancestral home—despite the Czar.

Slayer-of-Men knew the location of all four cossacks, as well as that of the ten soldiers with the tank who followed their orders, and the twenty slaves who labored for them. One of the cossacks lay with a slave at the foot of the tree from which the Dená warrior watched. He glanced down with distaste at the couple.

The woman's head angled away from the cossack and the Athabascan Indian could easily see a dark bruise pushing her eye shut. If a man treated a free woman of the Dená like that, she would kill him or die trying. But then this woman was a slave.

The sound of hammers and saws echoed through the late summer foliage. A scattering of yellow and gold leaves heralded the imminent change of season; soon the birch trees wouldn't hide a squirrel, let alone a man.

His long, black hair was tied back from the blotchy face paint matching his camouflaged dungarees. The sleeves of his shirt bulged over well-muscled arms as he braced himself. Slowly, carefully, he continued to flex his leg.

With a grunt the cossack finished with the slave and pushed her toward the work site. The bear-man glanced around lazily, then lifted his gaze to the trees bordering the clearing. Slayer-of-Men thanked the spirits for his location at the man's back. The cossack strutted back toward the construction commotion and began shouting orders at those nearest him.

From his perch, Slayer-of-Men could see for miles over the wide, shallow Tanana River dotted with small islands scattered over the floodplain. The forest on the far bank presented a seemingly impenetrable wall to the uninitiated. Off to the northwest lay the Charley Hills and the great Yukon River.

The Dená warrior visually located every member of the Russian compound one more time before easing down the tree to those who waited for him. He felt certain this action would be like all the rest—completely successful and another victory for his People.

7

Construction Camp 4 on the Tanana River

Grigoriy Grigorievich ducked his head and pulled down hard on the crosscut saw. Sawdust and chips sprayed across him. He automatically shook his head before he pushed up and watched the man above him pull the long saw back to start the next cut. Four more cuts, he calculated, and the last log would be planked out.

"Pull!" Dimitri said above him, continuing the cadence. "Push. Pull. Push. Pull."

Halfway through the next downward cut, the last two pieces of the log fell apart into planks.

"Letting go!" Grisha said loudly and released the saw handle. He kneaded the hardening blisters on his hands while stumbling out of the saw pit. He shook himself off and brushed madly at his hair to dislodge as much of the chips and dust as possible.

Without raising his head he glanced around the clearing, locating all four cossacks. The soldiers would give a man time to catch his breath. But the cossacks interpreted a prisoner's lack of motion as a personal affront.

Grisha waved madly until the closest cossack nodded, then grabbed a handful of leaves and scuttled into the brush toward the malodorous slit trench. He dropped his ragged trousers and balanced narrow buttocks across the birch pole that served as a seat. Carefully he breathed through his mouth while his bowels released their

43

watery load. He allowed himself to dwell on the fact that he was still losing weight before forcing his thoughts elsewhere.

Unbidden, unstoppable, he thought of *Pravda* and the clean pleasure of running full out down some beautiful channel.

His sphincter clenched and he briskly used the leaves with his left hand. He pushed himself off the pole and bent to pull up his pants. A dizzying blow sent him reeling forward to fall full on his face, his clothing still down around his ankles.

Quickly he rolled onto his back and pulled his knees up over his exposed loins. Vich-something, the cossack sergeant, towered over him, legs wide, arms akimbo, and his gravel voice ground at Grisha.

"With good fortune you're blessed, pretty one," he said in Russian. "Out of twenty new mares, four of them are actually female. But soon you will know a stallion's strength, just like all the other animals on our little farm." He laughed without pretense at humor.

"Quickly return to work, you dung-eater! Or I will geld you now before your strength dissipates."

Grisha jerked the trousers up as he rolled over, lurching to his feet he ran toward the rapidly rising lodge. He knew he could kill one of them with his bare hands, but not four, especially when all were armed. He hoped to last long enough to kill at least one.

Basil, the wide-shouldered Georgian, grunted as he pried a log end up to secure the rope around it. Grisha skidded to a halt next to him, already on his knees, and pushed the noose over the squared-off tree trunk.

The straw boss, a thick Indian or *Creole* woman from somewhere to the west, barked a command and four women tightened the rope to take the log's weight off the pry bar. Grisha jumped up and helped hoist the log high enough to maneuver the end into the corner notch where it belonged.

At the other corner of the ten-meter wall, Basil, the wild-haired woodsman, hacked furiously to cut the place where the log's lower end would fit. Grisha scrambled up the wall and released the noose. Sallow-faced Andreivich, who had talked less and less as his strength drained, pushed the crude derrick around to position the rope above the back of Samis.

The burly army guard stepped forward and pointed his rifle in their general direction as Samis finished the cut before lowering himself to the ground. His short ax hung by a rope thong looped around his neck. He ignored the guard as he scrambled up onto the next corner. Taking a deep breath and careful aim he hacked out another joint.

As he went through the achingly familiar motions yet again, Grisha's thoughts drifted to the forest. This might be bad, but out there could be worse. Rumors told of work parties disappearing, cossacks, guards, and all, never to be heard of again.

They had been told cannibals lurked in the dense forest waiting for the unwary. No matter how grim their life under the cossacks, they continued to live.

However, he was sure they were in Dená country, or very close to it. Soldiers from here had served under him in the Troika Guard. If there were cannibals roaming the forest he would have heard about it long ago.

But slipping away without even a knife would mean starving to death, or perhaps ending up as dinner for a bear. He reflected that, in all his military travels, until now he had never been to the interior of Russian Amerika.

Irena poked him sharply with her elbow.

"You're cloud-gazing again, slave. Pay attention and help me pull the rope."

Grisha tugged obediently on the rope. Irena had arrived in the same coffle of prisoners with Grisha. He'd noticed her compact, pleasing body on the trip here, before sickness dominated his life. She was the first of the coffle to be raped by the cossacks. Even now her purpled right eye swelled as a result of further attention from one of their masters.

His willpower had dissipated in tandem with his physical strength and both approached their nadir. At the trial he had felt grateful toward the judge for saving him from the rope, even though was not sure he had received the most humane sentence. At least now the mosquitoes were nearly gone.

A breeze wafted through the trees and cleared the air momentarily. Instantly Grisha imagined himself on the deck of *Pravda*, the master of his domain, and free on the water. A frustrated tear leaked from the corner of his eye and he concentrated on hoisting the log onto the wall. Only three weeks completed out of thirty years.

Kazina's name stuck in his mind. But try as he might, he could no longer picture his wife's face. Last week he received official notice of the dissolution of his marriage. He used the paper at the slit trench and wondered if she still slept with the naval kommander.

Another tear broke free of his suppressed emotions and blended quietly into his sweat. In all of this upheaval and hell, he nursed but one teeth-gritting dream—to meet Valari Kominskiya one more time. He vowed she would not live through the encounter.

Hammers sounded from the small cabins grouped around the ever-growing lodge, bringing him back to grim reality. They all worked as hard as possible to finish before the subarctic winter snapped down on the land. All this for foreigners, he thought. Why would anyone pay money to vacation here?

"Put your back into it, you cockless mare!"

Grisha gripped the rope and did as he was told.

8

Outside Construction Camp 4

Slayer-of-Men kept one ear cocked at the distant pounding while he conferred with his team. All wore the same face paint and camouflaged clothing. None of the uniforms carried any indication of rank.

"Wohosni." His eyes flashed over the tall, thin man. "You take the cossack in the tent." His finger jabbed the twig model. "Paul, Claude," he glanced at the shorter men, one burly, one slight, "you deal with the three soldiers in the kitchen." A wood knot surrounded by smoothed dirt.

"Leader," said Malagni, a wide-faced, big-boned man whose muscular chest threatened to split the fabric of his large shirt. "I would like a cossack." His fingers caressed the skinning knife he held in his other hand.

"You take the one with the Kalashnikov. He has to die first, but not too early. And don't depend on your knife, use your bow."

"I understand," Malagni said through a wide smile.

"Heron." The man personified the bird. "You eliminate the soldier on the turret. Lynx, you take out the tank with the satchel charge. Remember, we want their slaves alive; that's the reason we're here."

"Maybe that's true for you, big brother," Malagni said. "But I'm here to kill cossacks."

"That's our second reason," the tall man said. "Alex, you move in on the left here"—he pointed at the twig standing upright—"and as soon as Malagni takes out his cossack, you destroy the radio with your satchel charge." Alex, easily the handsomest man present—despite the blotches of paint—nodded and displayed perfect teeth.

"Cora, you cover Alex; we have to get the radio. Wing, can you get two with your bow before they know what's happening?"

"Of course I can," the raven-haired woman said as she thrust out her finely chiseled chin. "You know that."

"Just checking. I want you to get the armed guard here"—his finger prodded dirt in the model layout—"and cover this one. If he makes a move to shoot, kill him."

She grinned, causing the scar on her wide cheek bone to bend back on itself. "Can't I just kill him?"

"No. We need trained people." Slayer-of-Men felt proud as he looked over the nine under his command. Each of them had commanded raids like this in the past.

They were the best warriors the Dená nation offered. He fervently believed that every day brought them closer to the time when the cossacks and their masters would be driven from Dená land. And people like these would lead new armies.

"You must all be in place by the time the shadows have moved from here"—his finger traveled less than a hand's width—"to here. I will signal and, after Malagni kills the Kalashnikov, the attack begins."

Murmurs of assent dissipated in the air and the team melted into the brush. Slayer-of-Men made his way back to the wide oval hacked out of the forest by the Russians. He waited and watched the huge cossack who sat on the small guard platform with an automatic rifle resting across his knees.

There would be more weapons like that in the camp. The cossacks ruled their world so completely that they felt only one of them at a time needed to be armed in this manner. Every one of their camps the Dená had attacked had been just like this one.

The only deference the Russians made to their previous losses elsewhere was the decrepit tank sitting on the riverbank. The tankers had lapsed into boredom and indifference over a week ago. The prisoners didn't need the machine to keep them working; the cossacks did that.

The cossacks wasted their own strength, Slayer-of-Men thought for the second time in less than an hour. He knelt and took his bow from its hiding place. Nocking a metal-headed arrow, he leaned back and calmly waited for his team to strike.

The shadows crawled inexorably along their appointed paths.

9

Construction Camp 4

Grisha could not ignore his thirst any longer. One of the many cossack rules forbade convicts more than one drink of water per hour. He felt sure dehydration due to diarrhea played no part in their calculations; a drink of water would improve his work. Perhaps if he just explained it to them.

The water station stood directly in front of the squat guard tower. A cossack corporal dominated the middle of the newly built square, a Kalashnikov resting across his muscular thighs. Fear threatened the tightness of Grisha's bowels as he spread his arms outward in the prescribed manner and shuffled forward.

As if it were animate, the barrel of the automatic weapon lazily centered on Grisha's chest. The corporal's blocky, bearded face remained bereft of expression. When Grisha was five meters from the drinking water, the big Russian spoke with a voice reminiscent of rusty iron hinges in use.

"What are you doing here, dung-eater? You guzzled more than your share of water much less than an hour ago."

Grisha stopped and braced as straight as he could. The weight of his hands multiplied every trembling second but he resolutely held them out.

"Yes, master, that is true." He felt overwhelming disgust for his self-debasement. "However I have the shitting sickness and my body does not retain the fluid—"

"Then shit in a cup." The cossack jerked the slide back on the weapon and released it to snap a round into the chamber. One pull on the trigger and Grisha would no longer need water, ever.

His knees trembled uncontrollably, the familiar burning told him he'd slightly fouled himself, and the stench of his body hung around his face like a rotten wreath. A raven called from deep in the trees. His tongue ran over cracked, parched lips, and he felt the last reserve of energy, and care, drain from his soul. Only anger remained.

The anger sparked a determination to end this animal-like existence. If nothing else, he would die like the soldier he once was. His arms dropped.

The corporal's mouth slowly twisted into a parody of a grin and he raised the weapon. "Go back to work now or you die."

Grisha felt incredible freedom. This moment would have presented itself sooner or later; why endure any longer in a world without hope? He squared his shoulders and lifted his head, a Troika Guard major and boat captain one last time, and finished throwing away his life.

"At least fight me bare-handed, you louse-infested sodomite." The insolence felt so good that he grinned.

The corporal snapped the weapon to his shoulder and squinted down the barrel. He shuddered and his expression shifted to surprise.

Grisha frowned at him, wondering at the hesitation. Could the huge fool actually be considering his challenge?

The Kalashnikov clattered to the ground.

Grisha jerked back in amazement.

The corporal slowly leaned forward, and picking up momentum, toppled off the platform into a heap on the ground. An arrow protruded from the base of his skull.

Grisha snatched up the automatic weapon and, dashing back to the water, stuck his whole parched head into the wide tin basin. After three huge sucks he threw himself to the ground behind the water tank and peered around, trying to make sense of the situation. Another raven called from the forest. Two women prisoners stood in the framed-in doorway of the lodge, staring silently at the dead cossack.

He checked the weapon. The chamber indeed held a round. He remembered the muzzle steadying on his chest and shivered.

Grisha twisted to see how the tankers would react. The soldier who always sat on the turret seemed to be patting the cannon; a feathered shaft jutted from his back also. Grisha realized the man was trying to escape.

The soldier gracefully slid around the barrel and fell to the ground. A figure popped up from behind the riverbank and deftly tossed a blocky object into the now-vacant hatch. Grisha blinked in disbelief as the figure vanished.

The camp was under attack.

Footsteps pounded behind him and he turned to see the burly army guard racing toward the fallen cossack. He pulled the Kalashnikov up to shoot the guard. The guard pointed his rifle from the hip, the muzzle bobbed back and forth.

Silence expanded like a bubble, then exploded with the tank. A piece of flaming debris scorched past Grisha's head and hit the guard, knocking him gurgling to the ground, his chest a mass of blood, ripped flesh, and mangled organs.

A Kalashnikov suddenly racketed off a burst. Another explosion blew the main cossack cabin into flinders. Chunks of wood rained down.

Out of the corner of his eye something moved rapidly toward Grisha. He recognized the straw boss, the *Creole* woman from west of here, what was her name?

The women all hated men. She could shoot him as well as Russians. He tightened his grip on the gun.

From the half-formed lodge a guard stepped backward on stiffened legs, staring down at his hands grasping the arrow buried in his chest. His thin scream died away and he fell over backward. The straw boss slammed into Grisha and hunched down beside him.

"If you ain't gonna use that thing, give it to me!"

"Who do you want to shoot?" he asked.

"Cossacks!" she hissed.

Chunks of wood exploded off the guard tower at their back as the sound of another Kalashnikov grabbed Grisha's attention. The sergeant, framed in the window of one of the finished cabins, sprayed the trees at the edge of the clearing, then again turned his weapon toward the two convicts huddled at the water station.

Grisha finally felt himself shift into combat mode. He squeezed off three rounds as the weapon bucked furiously in his hands. The window frame around the sergeant disintegrated and the man's face suddenly burst in a grisly spray.

"Pretty good shooting," the woman said.

"Thanks." He stared down at the rifle, then up at her. "Answer a question for me?"

She frowned and her eyes flicked around the area before coming to rest on his face.

"What?"

"What's your name? I've been trying to think of it for five minutes now!"

She laughed, showing gaps that remembered teeth. "Blue. My name is Blue."

Abrupt silence fell across the work site except for the crackle and pop of the furiously burning tank. The trees stood listless in the last surge of summer heat. Birds and insects, reeling from the cacophonous assault, remained silent lest they bring the racket anew.

His heart slammed against his rib cage and his hands shook unless he gripped the weapon tightly. He mentally eased back into slavery.

"I wish something would happen." He didn't realize he whispered the words.

Somebody tried to stifle sobs. The quiet became so loud that Grisha's ears began to ache. Blue moved beside him, her hand touched his.

"Don't be afraid." Her voice rose barely above a breath, but he heard her clearly. "These are my people."

His eyes flashed back to hers. Her face, alive with emotion, shone with sweat. He thought she looked beautiful just then.

"Soldiers of the Czar," a voice called in Russian. "Lay down your weapons and you will not be harmed. If you continue to resist you will die, slowly." A moment later the ultimatum was repeated in English.

"Who are they, your people?" Grisha asked.

"The Dená. The English call us Athabascans. We have lived here for hundreds of generations. This is our land." Even though she spoke softly, her words possessed backbone.

"My mother was a Kolosh," Grisha said. "She told me once that her ancestors traded with yours before the Russians came."

"And after, too," Blue agreed. "You have nothing to fear from us."

"I hope you're right. The last woman who told me that almost got me hung."

The tall Russian corporal everyone called "Professor," because of all the books he read, walked into the center of the square with his hands above his head. He didn't appear frightened, merely curious. Another guard shambled out of a cabin supporting a third soldier who dripped blood from an arm wound.

"Don't shoot! We surrender. My friend is hurt and in shock." They came to a halt near Professor and the wounded man slumped to the ground.

"I saw three of them die," Grisha said. "But there could have been more in the tank."

"Two," Blue said, "were in the tank."

"Then there are two more somewhere."

"The cabin that blew up?" she suggested.

The voice called out again, this time in a language Grisha didn't recognize.

From the other side of the clearing another voice answered in the same tongue.

"They're doing the same thing we are, making a tally," Blue said.

One at a time, voices reported from around the clearing. The birds began to sing again. The voices stopped.

Movement flickered in Grisha's peripheral vision. He jerked around to see a lithe youth, face painted black and green, dart into the edge of the square and take cover behind the corner of a cabin. The young man's movements, quick and deliberate, suggested much practice—or experience.

Blue called out a question in Athabascan.

The youth scrutinized her carefully.

"Blue?" he said in English.

"Lynx?"

A rhythmic pulse worked on Grisha's mind, persistent and bothersome. He watched the interchange between Blue and the person, Lynx. The pulse grew louder.

"Helicopter!" someone shouted. "Get into the tree line."

How did they know to send a helicopter?

"They radioed for help!" Grisha blurted.

Lynx glanced at him, then back to Blue.

"Usually the cossacks fight it out. One of the soldiers must have done it when the attack started."

"How far are we from Tetlin?" Grisha asked.

"Thirty kilometers at the most," Lynx said, "Why?"

"That's an incredibly fast response, unless this attack was anticipated."

The solid beat of rotors announced the impending arrival of the aircraft. Blue slapped Grisha on the arm and ran for the tree line. Grisha hesitated only a moment before following her. Professor thundered along behind them. Lynx had disappeared.

They ran into the forest for about twenty meters and threw themselves into a clump of alders. Grisha squirmed around so he could see the open square framed by trees. The unwounded soldier waved upward frantically.

The bright red helicopter hesitated in the blue Alaskan sky. Sparks suddenly danced across the bulbous fuselage as a Kalashnikov rattled.

The helicopter veered sideways and roared out over the river. Grisha watched, entranced, as it slowly turned back toward the camp, dropped to treetop level and bored in at high speed. The soldier still waved, grinning and hopping up and down.

Seeing only threat, the pilot fired his skid-mounted machine guns. The bullets threw up two walls of flying dirt, rock, and debris that raced across the square from left to right. The exploding tracks ripped across both soldiers, throwing them backward like sacks of bloody rags.

The Kalashnikov hammered again and a stream of greasy smoke threaded from the helicopter. The thread thickened into a tatter that rapidly ribboned into a banner. The craft turned awkwardly and labored out over the river again.

One island presented a long sandy expanse bereft of trees. The helicopter settled to within meters of the sand before it exploded. The blazing hulk ripped into pieces, some splashing down a quarter of a kilometer away.

Grisha turned to Blue with a wide grin. Two men flanked her. Both wore green and black paint applied in random patterns from the tops of their faces down to the neck of their dark shirts. The smaller one held a rifle that casually pointed at Professor, who sat quietly on the ground.

Grisha's heart lurched as ice filled his mind.

"I am Slayer-of-Men," the taller man said in English. "We are Dená. This is our land."

Grisha nodded, desperately trying to remember the names of his Athabascan Troika Guard troopers.

"We need your help and then you're free to go," the second man said. "Understand?"

"Yes."

"I'm Claude," he said. "What's your name?"

"Grisha." He licked his lips. "Grigoriy Grigorievich. I am a *Creole*. My father was Russian and my mother *Kolosh*. Until recently I lived in Akku, on Akku Channel."

His anxiety lifted. If they allowed him to keep talking, he would be all right. His determination to live swelled.

"Tell us later." Claude looked down at Professor. "How are you called?" he asked in Russian.

"Nikolai Rezanov. Please call me Nik," he said in perfect English.

Grisha raised a skeptical eyebrow; the man was named after the famous romantic Russian hero?

"Were any of those people your friend?" Slayer-of-Men asked.

"No. I expected something like this," Nik said, showing no fear. "Before leaving Tetlin Redoubt we were told to remain constantly on the alert. But the cossacks told us to stay out of their way, that they would tell us when we were needed."

"We kill cossacks," Claude said.

"Good."

"Was he cruel in his duties?" Slayer-of-Men asked Blue.

"Not that I ever saw. If anything, he was lazy, his nose in a book or scratching on paper all the time."

"He's afraid of the cossacks just like we were," Grisha said.

The Russian soldier glanced at him. "He's right. I am afraid of them. They're soulless animals."

Grisha glanced around. More painted Dená filtered through the trees, bringing the other convicts.

The one called Lynx jogged across the square and into the trees carrying a Kalashnikov. Blue stood and faced the youth.

"Are you Lynx Bostonman, son of Boston Jack and Bead Woman?"

Lynx dropped the heavy weapon and moved closer to her.

"Yes. And you're Blue. I thought my sister was dead."

They hugged. Grisha saw a tear run down Lynx's cheek. The others shifted away from the two and found tasks to occupy their attention. Some of the convicts murmured to each other.

Grisha touched Claude's arm.

"Are we . . . am I a prisoner?"

"He is," he pointed to Nik, "for now, time will tell. Like I said, you're free to do what you like. We're going to leave soon. There's another tank and more soldiers on the way here from Tetlin Redoubt. I'll be surprised if more aircraft aren't here within the hour."

Slayer-of-Men clapped his hands together.

"Now you will help us. All bodies go into the river, as well as damaged weapons. Let's get busy, we don't have much time."

All of the prisoners stripped the dead soldiers of their boots and field jackets; the long nights had been cold. Grisha found a pair of boots that fit and carefully wiped each clean of the pieces of flesh stuck to them. The previous owner had taken the brunt of an explosion in the upper body.

Once again Grisha found himself using weapons to weigh down Russian bodies for a watery grave. Both times involved saving his own life. He hoped this time the result would be very different.

Again Slayer-of-Men clapped his hands for attention.

"You people have to choose now. More cossacks are coming. We'll be gone long before they arrive. You can come with us or stay."

"If we go with you," Irena asked, "will we be slaves?"

"No. You can leave us at any time. But if you stay with us you'll work for your keep, but you won't be a slave."

"What about the cannibals in the forest?" Basil asked.

The tall Dená smiled and one of his team chuckled.

A thin Indian as tall as Rezanov clapped Grisha on the shoulder with a friendly hand.

"Who would eat this sorry litter of muskrats?"

"Heron is right," Slayer-of-Men said. "You wouldn't be worth cleaning, let alone cooking. There are no cannibals. We started that rumor to keep the cossacks and the army out of the bush in small numbers. If a lot of them come into the land, we know about it because of the racket they make."

"Where will you take us?" Basil asked.

"All over. This is a big land. We have many villages," Claude said. "You might even get a chance to join the Dená Army."

"But there are Russian Army posts in many of the villages," Nik said. "If we are seen things could get very bad."

"That's true," Slayer-of-Men said. "We must go now. How many wish to join us?"

Even Nik raised his hand.

"Why did we dump the bodies in the river?" Grisha asked.

Heron said, "They'll never be found. The Russians will think we ate them."

A smile creased Grisha's face.

"Everybody carry as many weapons as you can," Slayer-of-Men ordered. "Don't overdo it, we have many miles to go."

10

Construction Camp 4

Those without weapons carried bundles of clothing and other Russian supplies. In addition to a rifle, Grisha claimed a small, sharp knife with a curved blade. The camp lay completely stripped of useful material.

Barrels of petrol provided incendiary preparation for each structure. Finally Slayer-of-Men whistled. The Dená and their new recruits followed him into the forest.

Paul stayed in the camp to finish preparing the welcome for the Russian relief forces.

As he followed the man in front of him, Grisha ate steadily from his small bag of "squirrel food" given to him by the small, pretty woman called Cora. The squirrel food consisted of dried berries, small bits of dried fish, a variety of seeds, and clumps of congealed grease. It was the best meal he'd eaten since his arrest. He compared it to the iron rations given the Troika Guard in the old days and graded the squirrel food superior.

Paul caught up with them and they kept as fast a pace as the exhausted ex-prisoners could sustain. At one point the distant pulse of a helicopter put them on nervous alert, but the craft receded to the southeast. After nearly two hours on the trail they heard the distant crack of explosives.

"They pulled the trigger," Paul said. Everyone stopped to listen. Suddenly a quick, staccato rip of explosives coalesced into a gigantic roar, silencing the birds around them.

"My God," somebody said.

"Did you use all of your stuff?" Slayer-of-Men asked.

"Why not?" Paul shrugged "We're going home, aren't we?"

"What, exactly, did you do?" Nik asked.

"I placed petrol bombs in every building, used a Kalashnikov in the middle of the square as a trigger. When they picked it up, everything went off at once."

The column stood quietly, each one imagining the destruction.

"You've just pissed on their boots," Nik Rezanov said.

"Maybe scared them, too," Grisha said, smiling.

"I don't understand this pissed business," Andreivich said in a querulous tone.

"If you piss on somebody's boots, you have given them great insult," Nik said. "Unless they have no honor they will do their utmost to kill you."

"Actually, I'm worried," Paul said. "I didn't think they'd get anyone into the camp before tomorrow."

"Let's go," Slayer-of-Men said. "We have a long trip ahead of us."

Just before dark the column reached a cache of food and equipment. Each former prisoner collected a backpack, sleeping bag, rubberized ground cloth, small ax, and a sheath knife. Grisha felt fully equipped, but bordered on total exhaustion from carrying the heavy load of two Kalashnikovs since morning. In addition to observing his rescuers, he had spent the day dropping back into the mind-set of a major in the Troika Guard.

He dispassionately assessed the soldiers around him.

The largest and most fearsome of all the Indians, Malagni, built a small fire. The muscular man radiated energy. His long hair clouded around his head as he effortlessly performed one task after another, never resting, never asking for assistance.

Grisha decided the man had at least five years of paramilitary service behind him and no doubt improved the morale of the other soldiers by his mere presence. Malagni didn't trust any of the newcomers. He watched them carefully, but not openly.

He had yet to speak to any of the former prisoners.

With the help of Heron and Lynx, the two women, Cora and Wing, quickly made a stew using meat from a moose hindquarter they had previously covered with moss, wrapped in a shelter half, and tied high in a tree.

Any one of them would have done well in the Troika Guard.

Cora's quiet appearance hid a reservoir of strength that she applied to the task at hand. Her small stature and limitless energy produced an appeal not apparent if a man only looked at her surface. Far from unattractive, her inner glow enhanced the promise she carried like a badge.

Wing strutted, proud of her well-developed body, carrying herself with an authority backed up by a willingness to kill in an instant. The knife scar down her left cheek didn't mar her beauty—rather it heightened the observer's appreciation for her finely chiseled features. When she grinned, which was often, the scar writhed and bent double.

Grisha felt an instant attraction to her and quashed it quickly. He wasn't twenty anymore and his recent experience with women kept him at a remove. Still assessing recent events, he no longer trusted himself, let alone women.

The position of the others in the column didn't allow close scrutiny. Grisha spent most of the day perversely wondering what it would take to interest a woman like Wing. He ate constantly, glad his diarrhea had eased.

The moose stew registered somewhere between ambrosia and soporific. Grisha snored in his sleeping bag within minutes after eating his fill.

An insistent hand shook him out of sleep. When his eyes popped open, he thought for a long moment that he was still in the cossack camp. The sleeping bag brought him back to reality. The morning air felt good and smelled of fall.

Everyone else was up and moving about. He quickly pulled on his boots and packed his gear, bothered that he hadn't heard the general movement without being awakened. Cora came down the line handing out small bags.

"Here's your breakfast," she said as she passed.

More squirrel food. He grinned in the weak morning light when he realized he had confidence in these people and finally felt safe from those owned by the Russian government.

Lynx suddenly hurried into camp and murmured to Slayer-of-Men. The older man moved to the middle of the group and spoke in an urgent low voice.

"We're being followed. Lynx picked up a party of cossacks and *promyshlenniks* about a kilometer behind us."

Grisha felt alarm stab through him. *Promyshlenniks* seemed to be half man and half forest beast. Adventure tales about them had been in vogue in Mother Russia for decades.

Although skilled forest hunters and trappers, they would also kill their mother for a ruble. More often than not, they were the collectors of the Czar's share of half a man's yearly production.

"We have to split up now, they can't follow everybody," Slayer-of-Men said.

Samis, the woodsman, grinned at the Dená.

"Why not just shoot these people rather than leave them to those animals?"

"We won't leave you. We're just going to separate into smaller groups."

After a quick consultation, the Dená strike team broke into pairs and hurried over to the released captives. Wing and Claude came up to Grisha. "You and the soldier are going with us, now," Wing said.

Nik looked troubled. "Would it be possible for me to go with—"

"Either get in front of me or be rear guard," Wing snapped.

"By all means, lead."

Grisha had no idea which direction they took. He glanced back once at the camp, but the forest had already swallowed the others. He could hear Nik behind him, muttering under his breath.

He wondered how many were following them. Didn't matter, he decided, they would deal with the problem when they had to.

11

On the Tanana River Trail

Muscular Boris Crepov earned the name "Bear" from fellow *promyshlenniks*, who more closely resembled the ursine race than their own. Shaggy headed, his beard spanning from mid torso nearly to his black, distrustful eyes, he moved quickly through the forest despite his almost two-meter, wide-shouldered bulk. Following the Dená trail wouldn't have proved challenging to a St. Petersburg courtier.

The thought made him grin.

They don't know we're behind them. They think we were all killed in their hellish maskirovka. *They have no idea that we were patiently waiting for the word, or how quickly we moved out.*

The mixed force of cossacks, *promyshlenniks*, and Imperial Army rangers had been chosen for speed and woodcraft. At the last minute the general in charge of the mission had ordered the tank and regular infantry to accompany the ranger force. "Insurance," he said.

Insured to slow them down! Crepov thought contemptuously.

The cossacks had wanted to charge into the construction site. Bear Crepov knew better. He'd already been at two such sites in the past. There would be nobody there and the Indians always left a *maskirovka*—deception.

When he asked those he guided for a volunteer, six cossacks and two army rangers stepped forward, growling. He chose the biggest cossack and instructed him to look in every building, to carefully examine the whole area for fool traps. Through his binoculars he saw the man snatch up the Kalashnikov in the middle of the square and wave triumphantly before he and all the buildings around him were blown to fiery pieces.

That slowed both the cossacks and rangers down and they no longer questioned Bear as the obvious expert-in-place.

"Now you see what they are capable of," he told them in his rumbling voice. "The Dená Separatist Movement are not your normal fish-stinking Indians—not only can they kill, they like it as much as we do."

The tourist camp burned to the ground. Crepov didn't care about that. There were plenty more convicts at Tetlin Redoubt and villages full of lazy Indians to be inducted into service for the Czar if needed.

Only twilight stopped their pursuit. Crepov knew they were close but he didn't want to stumble over them in the dark.

Just before the sky bled to gray, his belly clock woke him at the final edge of blackness. He kicked his six men out of their blankets and gave them a few minutes to prepare their departure. Then he went over to where the six cossacks snored and farted. He prodded the foot of their sergeant, Tulubev.

"There is game to be hunted, my friend."

The cossack sergeant reared up from his blanket with a knife in his hand.

"Don't ever touch me without first asking permission. I heard you coming and recognized your lumbering tread, otherwise you would now be holding your guts in your hands."

"When you are done boasting, wake up your junior scouts here and see if you can find us." Crepov bared his teeth in a wolf's leer and turned back to his men.

Tulubev barked at his men and scrambled to secure his gear.

At least, Crepov reflected, he didn't have to deal with the forty army troopers and two tanks left behind at the burned construction site. Somebody had to clean up that mess, and he didn't want those children in uniform out here alerting the quarry. The rangers had reluctantly stayed at the camp to protect the relief troops in the unlikely event the DSM would return.

A breeze moved through trees now darkly silhouetted by the slowly lightening sky. He smelled someone out there who hadn't come down the trail with him, and they were close. Stepping next to his closest friend and best tracker, he bent over and whispered in his ear, "Company ahead on the trail. I'll go left."

Wolverine White wordlessly rolled into the brush and faded like mist. Crepov stepped into the trees and moved swiftly forward. The black spruce, birch, and willow grew far enough apart to allow a man to make good time if he knew how.

A flicker of movement, dark on dark, caught his eye. He froze, stared off to the side, slightly away from the location. Another ripple of shadow over shadow.

Crepov gazed intently now, easily smelling the man, wondering if he was alone. A slow deliberate step revealed the clear definition of an arm braced against a tree. The spy peered around the trunk, allowing only his head to show if someone in the Russian camp should glance up.

Bear unsheathed Claw, his razor-edged skinning knife, and crept forward, silent as death.

12

On the Tanana River Trail

Grisha plodded along mechanically, senses alert, closely followed by Nik Rezanov, who had ceased muttering to himself some time ago. Two meters ahead of Grisha, Wing moved steadily, effortlessly, almost gliding through the brush. He again wondered how many followed.

Grisha hated *promyshlenniks* almost as much as he hated cossacks. Ruthless opportunists who totally lacked discipline, they would wipe out a game population rather than use forethought and harvest animals with conservation in mind. Two islands near Akku no longer held the otherwise plentiful Sitka blacktail deer because of *promyshlennik* butchery.

As far as the hunters were concerned, the animals existed as a gift from God and Czar. Their proprietary manner in small communities often caused those of a different mind to move on to greener pastures. Grisha had never chartered his boat to any party containing *promyshlenniks*.

They also did the Czar's dirty work along with the cossacks. Half of every man's earnings belonged to the Czar. The *promyshlenniks* proved themselves foully adept at finding hidden potatoes, moose hides, and dried fish—not to mention money.

The year after his father's death, four *promyshlenniks* had come to his mother's door, demanding the Czar's share of her earnings.

She told them she was a widow with nothing to spare. They threw young Grisha out into the snow and spent the afternoon extracting what they wished from her while he beat his hands bloody trying to open the cabin door.

No more loathsome creature inhabited the subcontinent of Alaska. They prided themselves on being the worst. Grisha felt sick with loathing and apprehension, knowing that human weasels followed his party.

He pulled his attention back to the problem at hand. The sun came up over his right shoulder. They were moving west? But then did the sun really come up in the east this late in the year? Alaska's interior was as alien to him as the Republic of California.

Wing held up her hand, stopped, and cocked her head to the side.

"Listen," she said.

Grateful for the stop, Grisha tried to listen. All he could hear was his heart beating. Leaning against a tree, he opened his mouth wide to baffle the pounding pulse. Still he heard nothing.

Wing shook her head. "It's gone now. I thought I heard a scream."

"You did," Claude said from behind the panting Nik. "I think it was the last sound that person will ever make."

Grisha shuddered, glad he missed the whole thing.

"How many are following us?" Nik asked.

"Lynx said a dozen at least," Wing answered. "Alex was to get a better count and then catch up."

"Maybe they got Alex," Claude said in a low voice.

"That's the conclusion I reached about a minute ago," she snapped. Wing turned away from them. "Let's go."

Grisha stifled a curse and hurried after the fast moving woman. Nik followed and Grisha heard him ask Claude if Alex was related to Wing.

"Actually he was my cousin," Claude said in a low voice. "But he was her lover."

Nik cursed in Russian. "She must be in great pain," he said while trying to see her around Grisha. "And she just keeps going. What a woman."

Grisha glanced back at Nik. "Do you want to change places?" he asked in a joking tone.

"Yes!"

Before Grisha could respond, Nik darted around him and closed on Wing.

Grisha shrugged and wished his feet would stop hurting. As his still-wasted body ached into the rhythm of the pace, he forced his mind to range beyond the physical just as he had during his imprisonment. Movement became automatic. He concentrated on the country they traveled through.

Small tributaries fed into the Tanana, and every tributary rushed from the heart of a small valley. Some they crossed on fallen trees, others they waded through up to their chests.

Growing up on the Inside Passage of the Alexandr Archipelago, Grisha's idea of natural beauty differed somewhat from this. He loved the lush rain forest, the thirty-meter trees, the impressive fjords of Southeast Alaska, and the North Pacific Ocean.

The Tanana mocked him, hinting of the ocean to which it eventually traveled, which now sparkled forever out of his reach.

Valari Kominskiya entered his thoughts. Why had she thrown him to the Czar's wolves? They could have talked their way out of Karpov's death.

Had she set him up? No way of knowing. But there was no obvious reason for that. She must have just panicked. Her panic had cost him his old life, or what was left of it. He was surprised at how much he missed his boat.

At the top of a ridge the trail forked in a wide clearing. Wing signaled a halt and waved them up to her.

"Behold." She pointed. "The Great One."

A range of majestic snow-capped mountains lay unguessable kilometers in front of them. At the center of the range reigned a gleaming monarch reaching into the bright blue sky half again higher than any neighbor. Grisha and Nik stared dumbstruck.

"Claude," Wing said. "Watch the trail behind us."

"My God!" Nik said. "I've seen this from St. Nicholas Redoubt, but I had no idea it was this big!"

"That's bigger than Mt. St. Elias," Grisha said. "Even from here I can tell that. What did you call it?"

"Denali, the Great One." She stared proudly for a long moment. "That is the holy place of the Dená. You might say this the heart of why we fight the Czar and kill his cossacks—this is the only ikon in our church."

"But you don't kill his soldiers," Nik said. "Why?"

Her eyes flicked over both of them before settling on the soldier again.

"We've discovered that most soldiers of the Czar hate their life. They're merely slaves in uniform. We need soldiers too, but ours share with everyone else, they're not a lower class to be used like animals. They're respected."

"I find that difficult to believe," Nik said. "Will the people go into battle with them?"

"I am not a person?"

Grisha laughed as a look of consternation swept over Nik's face.

"You're twisting my words. Of course you're a person! But you're part of a paramilitary group, aren't you? You don't look like a schoolgirl to me."

"Once I was a teacher. My husband and I lived in Holy Cross where the Russian Army maintained a small garrison. One night three cossacks broke into our house, killed my husband, raped me"—her left hand touched the scar on her cheek—"and left me for dead."

It pained him to look at her just then, so Grisha stared at the mountain.

"Friends found me, hid me, nursed me back to health. I was introduced to others who were tired of being used by the Czar and living in constant fear. Through them I received training and began striking back. One of the most satisfying moments of my life was the morning I gelded those three bastards and left them tied in the forest to bleed to death."

"You've had a hard life," Nik muttered.

"Who hasn't? That's why we're here, to end the Czar's rule over our people and our homeland. We've been slaves to a man and a government none of us have ever seen, never will see. We've had enough, we're fighting back."

"You're talking about armed revolution," Nik said. "You'll never get away with it, you're too few and they're too many."

"I'm willing to fight," Grisha said. "And it's because they took my life from me, twice. Not quite as brutally as they took yours," he said, nodding at Wing, "but they took it just as completely.

"While serving the Czar I, and the men under my command, took the lives of countless men. We never questioned, never asked 'why?' because we didn't care. Now I've killed one cossack and I'm more than willing to kill more. And I know why."

Part of him stood shocked, aghast at his treason, but the rest of his being cheered as elation filled him.

"Well, by comparison I've had it pretty good," Nik said. "But there's certainly no love lost between me and the army."

"So you'll join us?" Wing asked.

"Conditionally."

"Good." She whistled, sounding just like a bird.

Claude came panting up. "There's someone behind us."

"How many?" Wing asked.

"Three, four, I'm not sure. They're good, they don't break the skyline and they skirt clearings."

"Who are they?" Nik asked.

"One cossack for sure, and two or three others. The rest must be *promyshlenniks.*"

"Damn!" Grisha said.

"They die just like anybody else," Wing snapped. "This is a perfect place to take them." She pointed. "Grisha, you take cover behind that fall of birch. Nik, over behind that large rock with the moss. Wait for my shot, then fire at whatever you see."

They all hurried to their posts. Claude and Wing disappeared to the left. Grisha quietly opened the chamber of the rifle he'd carried from the construction site. Shiny cartridge cases reflected redly in the light.

Algeria seemed a lifetime away. His service to the Czar was a subject carefully blocked from his day-to-day mind. The government had stripped him of two careers. He was ready to try a different tack.

"No," he hissed softly through clenched teeth. "They can't do that to me anymore."

He settled back and waited.

Off to his left he could see Nik. The soldier appeared calm and deadly. Grisha wondered about the man and abruptly realized he wasn't paying attention.

For long moments he stared first at one tree, watching for movement with his peripheral vision, before shifting his attention to another tree or rock. After ten minutes something flickered at the edge of the trees.

A hundred meters to the left, and right on the trail, a man stepped out in the open. He stopped at the brush line, clearly visible. Red collar flashes identified him as a cossack.

The cossack craned his head around, seeking a target. He shrugged and trudged up the slope to where the trail forked, as if hunting rabbits. He didn't waste a glance at Denali.

Grisha forced his eyes back to where they had been when he first saw the flicker of movement. Nothing. He stared at the spot, waiting. The cossack irritated him, bouncing up and down at the far edge of his eye.

He was always aware when someone stared at him; the skin on the side of his face, just in front of the ears, would tingle slightly. Suddenly the spot actually itched. A shadow moved at the other corner of his eye.

He swiveled his eyes over and slowly let his head follow. Another movement. Grisha finally made out the shape of a man. The woodsman was huge, with arms the diameter of stovepipe, wearing a great, dark beard that stretched halfway down his chest.

That's two. Beads of sweat rolled down his face. Where's the other one, two? He realized that the man on his far right was visible only to him. The others couldn't know about the *promyshlennik* because they couldn't see him.

Slowly he centered his sights on the man's chest, directly between the shoulders, in the middle of the beard. His target knelt and stared at the cossack, rifle butt resting on the ground beside him. Although Grisha's shoulders itched, he ignored the cossack. The man in the trees was a much more important target.

The *promyshlennik* suddenly gripped his rifle and rose to a crouch, peering at something.

Grisha glanced back, wishing Wing would fire the first shot. The only thing in sight was the cossack. He looked back at the woodsman.

He wasn't there.

His training instantly took over. Heart hammering, he abruptly knotted down into a crouch.

A blast from behind blew away a fist-sized chunk of the tree next to where his head had been. Grisha threw himself to the side as another blast tore into the space he'd just vacated. He rolled down the slight slope away from the attacker, but toward the cossack.

The ridge top erupted in gunfire. The cossack staggered backward under the force of hits and fell to the ground. Grisha leaped up and ran toward cover.

Expecting to be hit or killed at any moment, he grunted in surprise as he reached the relative protection of the forest. He hunched down, eyes flashing about, his breath shuddering in and out. He smelled sour, even to himself.

The air stood still, cooler now than earlier. The temperature would drop tonight, he decided.

He heard Claude call out, "Grisha! Where are you?"

Slowly his eyes moved over every object in his sight. Nothing moved.

Where did he go?

"Grisha? You okay?" Nik called from nearby.

"Stay down!" Grisha yelled. "There's another one over here."

Movement to his right. Claude edged into the trees like a large cat. Nik eased up behind him.

"Where?"

"I don't know. But he damn near got me, twice."

Wing suddenly slid up beside him. One of her hands steamed, covered in blood.

"We already got three," she said, her eyes searching out ahead of them. "Maybe he moved over and we caught him?"

"Big guy with a huge beard and biceps big as one of your thighs?"

"No. We didn't get anyone like that," she said in a low voice.

"There's one more and he's in there." Grisha nodded toward the thick forest at meadow edge. "He's very good. Well, good enough to make a fool of me," Grisha said and forced a chuckle.

"You're not green in the bush. You're just out of practice." She looked around and slowly rose to her feet. "C'mon." She nudged him and moved forward.

He glanced down at her hand. "You're hurt."

"Not my blood. C'mon."

Grisha put three meters between them so a near miss of one wouldn't hit someone else. They moved quietly ahead with Nik on one side and Claude off on the other. After a hundred meters all four stopped as if on command.

The forest stood in front of them, full of brush, wind fallen limbs, and rocks. Wing moved close to Grisha again and spoke quietly. "Are you sure he came this direction?"

"If he hadn't, one of you would have seen him," Grisha said.

"Well, since we haven't come across him by now, he's probably escaped," she said with a sigh. "We need to move on before it gets any later, we have a long way to go."

"I hope we got the bastard that killed Alex," Nik blurted.

Wing regarded him coolly. "You didn't even know Alex. Why are you so eager to avenge his death?"

"Because he was important to you." Nik angled away from them suddenly, pretending the brush forced his detour.

Grisha hurried back to the windfall where he had taken cover. With his sheath knife he dug the mushroomed slug out of the damaged wood. As they came together on the trail he held it out in his hand for them to look at. Nobody commented.

"Okay, Claude, you take point, I'll take flank," Wing said. "Nik, if you'll keep quiet, I want you back with me."

They set off toward Denali.

13

On the Delta River Trail

Bear Crepov slid Claw back into its sheath, put his rifle on safety, and eased out of the old wolf den. That had been too close. His heart still pounded nearly as much as it had when they came within a meter of where he lay.

He had been prepared to go down fighting. Two close calls in the space of ten minutes. Perhaps he was getting too old to be hunting traitors and DSM mercenaries. *These are well-trained people*, he decided.

He walked over to where the cossack lay frowning at the sky. Surprisingly, the rabble hadn't shot this fool as soon as they saw him. Three holes in the sergeant's chest testified to a quick death.

Crepov searched the corpse, found identity papers, six wadded rubles, and some coins. One coin was French-Canadian. He shoved everything into his pockets. After pulling the bandoleer off the cossack, he slipped it over his shoulder and went off to find his other dead.

Birds broke into song. Good, no more strangers around. Wolverine White grinned at the foliage with twin smiles. White's own knife still protruded from his throat.

Bear felt a shiver run through him. This wiry English turncoat had been his best friend. They'd done it all together.

He pulled the insulting knife out of the death wound, wiped it absently on his dirty cotton pants, and dropped it in his small pouch.

"I'll gut every one of 'em for you, Wolverine!" he said with a lump in his throat. "I promise."

He ambled back down the trail toward the construction site. For a moment he entertained the thought of seeking out the third casualty, but decided not to waste the time. Bukowski had just been a Pole anyway.

"Well, I got one ear for the Czar," he said to the trail. The Indian at dawn. Too bad he couldn't get the scum to talk. In a way the Indian had outsmarted him.

As soon as Bear had begun to skin him to loosen his tongue, the Indian had screamed defiantly in their face and thrown himself on the blade. "You have to admire a man like that," he muttered, lengthening his stride.

14

Toklat on the Toklat River, September 1987

In the six days it took them to reach the village of Toklat on the Toklat River, Grisha gained weight. Nik tried incessantly to talk with Wing, which made Grisha resentful.

On the second day she had finally stopped and all but shouted, "What don't you understand about 'shut up and be quiet'? We have no idea if we are being followed or not. We all have to maintain discipline, even you."

Nik didn't open his mouth for the rest of the journey. Grisha felt embarrassed for him, as well as vindicated. Nik had been getting dangerously loud.

The first snow of the season dusted lightly through the trees as they entered the village. A few barking dogs and two men, standing silent as sentinels, constituted their welcoming committee.

"Wing, Claude, we're glad to see you," the older man said. "Who are your friends?"

Quickly Wing introduced them to Chandalar Roy and Nathan Roubitaux. "Chan, here, is the grand old man of the movement," Wing said.

Chan's long, white hair hung down his back, tied in a ponytail; wrinkles of many decades crisscrossed his face. Sharp, intelligent eyes closely assessed the new arrivals. A spare and slightly stooped man, he stood half a head shorter than anyone else present.

Wing continued, "And Nathan is—"

"Let them learn for themselves," Nathan said.

Nathan's disturbing, piercing eyes glowed from his wide, pock-marked face. His dark, unruly hair stuck out in every direction. He stood half a head taller than Grisha, but probably weighed the same. The word *sinewy* came to mind as Grisha assessed him.

"Sure." Wing shrugged. "Any word from Slayer?"

"He is safe." Chandalar frowned. "Alex is—"

"I know. I heard him die."

"I mourn with you," Chan said.

She nodded. "These two are for you to train," she said briskly. "Claude and I must leave in the morning."

"To where?" Nik blurted. Grisha felt glad Nik asked the question; it spared him the impertinence.

"I'll be back in a month at most. You're still a prisoner suspected of Czarist leanings, so I can't tell you more than that."

"But what about—"

"That's all I can tell you." She stalked away in the failing afternoon light.

"She and Alex had been lovers for over a year," Chan said. "Come with me and we'll get you both settled."

Grisha snuck a glance at Nik. At first the man's face was stony, impossible to read, then it softened. He smiled and shrugged. They followed the gray-haired Chan.

Grisha felt Nathan staring at him. He brushed at a spot in front of his ear and turned to the tall, gaunt-featured man.

"What are you looking for, friend?"

Nathan gave him a frosty smile.

"You're very aware, Grigoriy. I meant no disrespect."

Chan opened the door of a cabin and motioned for them to enter. A cast-iron cook stove radiated heat, making Grisha aware he had been chilly for some time. Two oil lamps softly illuminated a pair of bunks built into the back wall, a small kitchen in one corner, and pegs and shelves in another. A sturdy wooden table and three chairs dominated the center of the room.

"I've stayed in much worse inns," Nik said absently as his gaze moved over the room.

"Four meters by four meters," Chan said. "Not exactly St. Petersburg but certainly adequate."

Grisha dropped onto one of the chairs and let his gear fall to the floor. "It's almost as beautiful as my boat. But right now some food would look even better. I am so tired."

Chan laughed. "No beating about the bush on your part. We have a meal waiting, come along."

Grisha threw his backpack on the bottom bunk and followed. Nik trailed him out the door.

"Thanks for giving me the top bunk."

Grisha glanced over his shoulder at him. "You'd have to fold double to fit into the bottom one. Besides, top bunks are always too warm at night."

"Well, I'm glad that our needs mesh," Nik said.

Chan led them to a large building.

"That's the biggest log structure I've ever seen," Grisha said.

"There are larger ones, but not close to Toklat," Nathan said beside him.

Large tables bisected the building. About twenty-five people stopped their noisy meal to look at them.

"This is Grigoriy Grigorievich, a Kolosh from Southeast, and Nikolai Rezanov, a former soldier of the Czar."

A few nods and a quick smile here and there made the best of it. Most of the men and a few of the women merely stared. Distrust emanated from the group and Grisha decided a meal wasn't worth sitting through this.

He turned toward the door and bumped into Nathan. The tall man smiled down at him, put his hand on Grisha's shoulder and carefully turned him around again.

"Come and break bread with me, killer of cossacks," he said loudly. Nathan's eyes found Nik. "You too. We have much to discuss."

The mood in the room perceptively altered. Someone put a large wooden bowl of soup in front of Grisha. He thanked the server.

"You're welcome," Cora said, smiling back.

"How did you get here before us?" Nik asked.

"I cheated. I went by river."

"We needed the exercise anyway," Nik said, giving her a full smile.

"It's good to see you again, comrade," Grisha said.

"I'm glad to see both of you," Cora said. "We need all the help we can get." She moved away across the room.

"Does she have someone like Wing did?" Nik asked.

"Cora's very independent," Nathan said, "most Athabascan men don't like that."

"Then most Athabascan men are fools, she's quite lovely."

"While we agree with the second part, we'll take the first part under advisement." Chan leaned across the table toward Grisha. "Why is your name familiar to me?"

"Did you ever serve in the czar's army, or the Troika Guard?"

"No. But my two nephews did, one was killed in some wasted action in Algeria—" Chan's eyes rounded as his voice abruptly stopped. "My God," he whispered. "You're that Grigorievich?"

"Da." Grisha pushed his empty bowl away. "Does that change anything between us?"

"You were in the Russian Army?" Nathan frowned, his eyes flicked back and forth between Chan and Grisha.

"You were a major and they cashiered you for disobeying orders," Chan said, staring at Grisha. "You had over ten years in uniform, yes?"

"You have an excellent memory, Chan."

"Moses, my surviving nephew, still talks about what you did."

Grisha smiled. "I wasn't aware my men knew what happened. I would like to talk with Moses some time."

"No time like the present." Chan left the table.

Nik gestured at Grisha with his spoon. "You people welcome him like a brother, yet he was in the army for ten years and I was only in for two—"

"That's right," Nathan interrupted. "And you are suspect."

Nik's eyes narrowed as he stared back at Nathan.

Why was Nik so tense? Grisha wondered. Hadn't he come with them in search of a better life? Didn't he hate the Russian Army? Was he so indoctrinated that he wouldn't be able to do this?

"Where are you from, Nikolai?" Chan asked as he sat down with a platter of meat. "Here, fellows, try some moose."

"I was raised in St. Nicholas Redoubt."

"What schools did you attend there?" Chan pressed.

"Primary, secondary, university, and military." He sounded nettled. "What else do you wish to know?"

"Why you are so defensive," Nathan said.

"I just deserted my life and family as well as the army. I tried to establish some rapport, but I really don't feel welcome here." He shut his mouth, jaw muscles worked under his skin.

"Look at the situation from our viewpoint. You're still an unknown to us, you could even be a spy."

Nik laughed. "Perhaps you're taking yourselves a bit too seriously?"

"Perhaps," Chan said. "But I'm afraid there are more questions I have to ask."

"The answers to which could help us a lot," Nathan said.

"What were you trained to do in the army?" Chan asked.

"To kill. To instantly obey any and every order given me by anyone with more stripes than I had on my arm, no matter how stupid the order or the person giving it."

"With your education I am surprised they did not offer you a commission."

"They did. I refused."

"Why?" Chan asked.

"A conscription lasts only three years. To obtain a commission one must commit to six. I had no desire to stay in the army for six years, even as an officer."

Chan smiled. "The military must have been hell for you."

"I'm here, aren't I?" Nik said. "They gave me every shit detail they could find and showed no sign of stopping. So I decided to desert. You people made it easy for me."

Chan and Nathan looked at each other. Nathan nodded.

Chan said, "With your military training we would like to have you in the Dená Army. Or you can help maintain the camp."

Nik glanced around at the three men. His eyes fastened on Nathan. "Is Cora in the army?"

Nathan nodded.

"She's a lieutenant," Chan said. "One of our best."

"I can believe that." Nik frowned. "I'll join your army."

"Enlistments are for the duration," Nathan said.

"Are you joining to fight or to be with Cora?" Chan asked.

"Does it matter?" Nik's voice carried an edge.

"Not really," Nathan said. He stared into Grisha's face. "And you, Major?"

First French Algeria, then all the wrongs visited on him since that last day on *Pravda* had filled him with a determined anger to hit back at the Czar and his corrupt machinery. These people not only had rescued him from certain death, they now offered him an avenue for revenge.

Before Grisha could respond, Chan said, "Oh, here's Moses now."

Grisha turned and immediately recognized Corporal Danilov. The ex-trooper stopped in his tracks, came to attention, and saluted. "Major, it's so good to see you."

"You're looking good, Moses." He held out his hand. "But call me Grisha, I haven't been a major for quite some time."

Moses shook his hand and smiled. "You're here in Toklat. Are you joining us?"

"Yes, yes I am."

"Then you'll probably be a major again, real soon."

15

On the Toklat River, October 1987

Grisha panted to a stop. Hiking in snowshoes proved as pleasant as whipsawing planks and reminded him of running through the desert in heavy boots. However, his speed and endurance showed improvement.

Nik stood on the crest of the small ridge ahead of him. The man's long legs made snowshoeing an easy exercise. Grisha tried to feel envious but couldn't; he'd always been comfortable with his compact size.

Nik was having a hard time of it. Not that he couldn't keep up with the physical training. In fact he'd started out in much better form than Grisha and was at least a decade younger.

Grisha knew the man's tight-lipped boorishness of the past few days was due to his frustration with Cora's continued evasiveness.

"I'm a deserted deserter!" he'd wailed in their cabin the night before. "First Wing told me how wonderful it was that I was going to be part of the movement and what an asset I would be with all the knowledge I had. Then she starts talking about Cora, her deep mind and her big heart.

"She even told me that Cora had commented on my preoccupation with books, that she liked intelligent men. Since then Cora has all but shunned me and Wing told me to shut up after one day on the trail."

"My God, you whine a lot. What, you need the help of one woman to win another?" Grisha laughed. "Maybe Cora is waiting to see if you can complete this little training course, maybe she wants to make sure you're all you're supposed to be."

Suddenly Nik fixed him with a hard stare. "What do you mean by that?"

Grisha frowned, shrugged. "What part of that didn't you understand? She probably just wants to see you become a fully accepted member of the DA before she loosens her heart to you."

"Hell, I don't know. I used to think I knew women and what they wanted, but over the past year I've been brutally disabused of that notion. Maybe you should follow my example and concentrate on what they're teaching us, forget about women."

"That'll be the day," Nik said with a grunt.

In the five weeks since their arrival in Toklat they and twelve other trainees met and conquered every challenge thrown at them by the DA. Most of them related to physical fitness and arctic survival skills. Grisha's body filled out and the convict pallor faded. He had regained his old Troika Guard physique.

"Think of this as a refresher course, Captain-Major Grigorievich," Chan had said, then laughed. "I'm sure it won't be long before you're in command."

Grisha had laughed with him.

But there was no way to lengthen legs. Finally, breathing heavily, he trudged up next to Nik, his training partner.

"There has to . . ." he gasped, ". . . be a better way to move around."

"They're quite functional," Nik said with exaggerated pomposity. "There's approximately a meter-point-five to two meters of snow beneath us. Think how far you'd sink if not for those fat webs hooked to your feet."

"True, they've kept me from sinking completely out of sight every time I fall over."

Nik sobered and gazed out over the flood plain. "Nice view from up here."

The frozen Toklat River wound between snowy, tree-covered banks. Grisha constantly compared the land and vegetation with Southeast Alaska. The variety of trees and shrubs were as varied as those of his childhood home, and almost completely different.

Tamarack, white and black spruce, birch, and a wider variety of willows had all been new to him. The best part was the lack of devil's club, the needle-spined broadleaf plants that grew in thickets in the Southeast. Grabbing the stalk of the plant would leave you with a handful of tear-inducing spines nearly impossible to extract.

Surrounded by mountains, the small valley before them appeared piebald where willow thickets and stands of birch stood naked waiting for new spring leaves. The tamarack and spruce appeared furry and deceptively warm from this distance. Already the temperature hovered at minus twenty degrees Celsius and only the exercise kept their faces from showing the cold.

"What's that?" Nik asked, breaking Grisha's reverie.

"Where?"

"On the river."

A row of dark spots well out on the ice snaked into view from behind the next ridge.

"Dog team," Grisha said, squinting mariner's eyes.

"Yeah, it is. I wonder."

"Don't you have your field glasses with you?"

Nik pulled off his backpack and unfastened the top cover, rooted frantically through the contents before triumphantly producing binoculars. He dropped the pack and focused on the distant team. The sled cleared the ridge, becoming visible on the seemingly glowing ice.

"The wide-shouldered Indian at the cossack camp, what was his name?" Nik asked.

"The brother of Slayer-of-Men, you mean?"

"*Da.*"

"Mugly? No. Malagni!"

"*Da*, Malagni. He's driving the sled. Looks like he has a passenger, full load anyway."

Grisha watched the sled move steadily down the river ice. Another dark object popped from behind the bluff.

"What's that? Sure isn't a dog team."

"Where?" Nik pulled the glasses away from his face.

"There, about two hundred meters behind Malagni."

The glasses went up to his face again. Grisha watched Nik chew his lower lip. The tall man suddenly grinned.

"Wing! It's Wing on skis!" He lowered the binoculars and grinned like an idiot. "She's back."

"Nikolai, my friend, don't get your hopes up. She might not stay, and if she does, she might not help you with Cora."

A shadow moved across Nik's face.

"You're right, damn it. I can't take anything for granted. I must stalk Cora like the woods creature she is." He bent over and put the glasses back in his pack, closed it, and lifted the straps over his arms. "But I'm sure Wing will help me."

Even though Grisha managed a ten-meter lead on Nik, the man passed him within minutes. By the time Grisha reached the bottom of the ridge only shoeprints remained to keep him company.

"God," he muttered to himself, "I hope she can match them up."

He maintained his pace and covered the last mile in under an hour. The unloaded sled lay on its side. The dogs, staked out and fed, slept curled on pallets of dried sedge with noses tucked under tails.

Grisha unstrapped his snowshoes and stepped away. He felt as if he could fly without the awkward bulk of them anchoring him. Leaning them against the wall, he pushed into the lodge.

"Here's Grisha, now," Chan said. Beside him, Nik, Malagni, and Wing faced the door. About half the village stood around the first two tables. All went silent.

A man Grisha didn't recognize turned to peer at him. The man's small stature, coarse, dark hair running down to the backs of his hands, and a clean-shaven, weather-beaten face that barely contained bright blue eyes gave him a fairy-tale aspect.

Grisha immediately thought of a gnome.

"So yer the cossack killer, huh?"

The clipped aggressiveness sounded like an alien variant of Tlingit. Grisha knew it to be a dialect from the eastern part of Canada or the United States. He once served with a sergeant who spoke with the same choppy-flat speech.

The room seemed to hang there, waiting for his response. Abruptly Grisha felt nettled for being singled out.

Probably more training for the ex-officer.

"I have killed one cossack. I was terrified at the time," Grisha said.

"Then yer nae fool. Good." He pronounced it "gud."

"Is there food?" Grisha asked the group, ignoring the little man.

"Haimish McCloud," the man said, holding a hand out to him. "Late of the great state of Vermont, U.S.A., proud ta be a Green Mountain boy."

"You fled the United States to live in Russian Amerika?" Grisha asked. The fellow didn't look like a boy to him, not with those raven's tracks around his eyes.

"I've come ta help create the Dená Republic, the Russians jist don't know they're beaten yet."

Everybody in the room laughed and the tension flowed out of Grisha. He shook the man's hand.

"I like the way you think," he said, smiling.

A tight, almost absent grin put even more creases in the man's face.

"That's good. I'm agonna be trainin' ya."

"You look a lot better than the last time I saw you," Malagni said with a sniff.

"I'm glad to see you, too," Grisha said, flattening his smile.

Wing led Nik over.

"You both have done well," she said, bending the scar on her cheek. "Tell me, Grisha, why is this one so distant?" She nodded at Nik.

"Do you want me to tell you right here?"

She peered into his eyes, frowned the scar into an arc again.

"No, I guess not." Her eyes moved all over his face like a blind man's fingers before she pulled her gaze away. "C'mon, Professor, take me for a walk." She pulled Nik toward the door.

Grisha exchanged glances with his friend as they left. Nik seemed more upset than ever. Grisha shrugged mental shoulders.

I'm glad I'm not in love.

"Here's food," Karin said, handing him stir-fried moose and late vegetables.

"Thank you." He watched her walk across the room. At eighteen she had attained complete physical maturity. The medical trainee, one of three being taught by Cora, easily claimed the title of prettiest woman in the village.

"I think if I were twenty years younger," Grisha muttered to himself as he watched her, ". . . you could make me do foolish things." He sat down and began to eat.

Chan sat down beside him. Haimish McCloud stood nearby, alone in the full room.

"Wing is correct. You both have done very well, all the trainees have," Chan said. "Now your training takes on a different aspect. Now you discover what it is you are really fighting for."

"I thought it was Denali," Grisha said around a mouthful of food, "and to keep all that one earned. That's what Wing told us."

"Denali is our ikon, if you will. But the heart of our cause is much more elusive."

"Chan, I'm just an old soldier and a new sailor. I'm here because I'm pissed off at the way things are in this country and I want to help change them. All that philosophy stuff is wasted on me."

"It's not philosophy, call it, ah, higher deductive reasoning."

"I know even less about that than philosophy."

"That's because you're not trained yet," he said, beaming.

16

Tetlin Redoubt

Bear Crepov stared at the photograph and wondered what the words at the bottom meant.

"Yeah, he was one of 'em. In fact I damn near killed him."

"Be thankful you did not," the cossack colonel said. "You'd probably have lost your balls."

"For killing a convict? That's what you people pay me to do!"

"This one is different. They want him alive." The colonel snatched the photograph out of Bear's hand.

"We didn't wait to notify St. Nicholas about the ambush before sending you out. However, they already knew about it and were adamant that we not 'unleash' any hunters." He absently rubbed a knuckle under his heavy mustache.

"There for a minute, I thought they were going to have my balls."

Bear didn't like the total bewilderment he felt. Somebody was busy pissing on his boots, but he couldn't figure out exactly who or how. Or what to do to stop them.

"Those bastards killed my best friend as well as another *promyshlennik* and a fuckin' cossack sergeant on top of that!"

"I'm sorry about your friend. Friends are much harder to come by than *promyshlenniks* or cossack sergeants. But for now you must not attempt revenge."

"I swore on Wolverine's body!" Anger surged through him. He'd have to visit Katti tonight. "How long do I have to wait?"

"I don't know. They're sending a cossack captain out from St. Nicholas to talk to you."

"I don't care if he is a captain. If they don't let me hunt those animals down, I'll tear off his head and piss in the hole!"

"Her head," the colonel said dryly.

"What?"

"The captain is a woman."

"Even better." Bear licked his lips. "I'll tear off her head and—"

"Get out of my office," the colonel said icily, "now."

"—fuck the hole!" he bellowed. He stomped from the office. As he went through the door, the noise of the combination army post and prison washed over him.

The wind blew from the latrine today, unusual for this time of year. He also smelled meat cooking and went in search of it.

17

Toklat, November 1987

"Don't rub all the bluing off, just pick up the piece and snap it in with authority," Haimish said.

Grisha stifled a curse behind his blindfold and tried to remember where the piece fit in the automatic rifle; it had been a long time since he had done this.

"It 'as its place, just like a person in any society. The weapon needs all of its parts to work. If just one piece is missing, the weapon doesn't function."

"And I suppose you're going to tell me that societies won't function if one person is missing?" Grisha felt waspish. The dimly familiar pieces under his fingers eluded him. The scent of gun oil brought back memories, and beckoned with a promise of strength and a precarious future.

"Human societies aren't nearly as perfect as the weapon in your hands. There are pieces beyond count that are interchangeable in our societies, and each piece slightly alters the direction, affects the warp and the weave of human enterprise."

"Y'know, Haimish," Nik said from across the small room, "you're the first person I've seen who could wear a man out from three directions at once. Do you ever stop talking long enough to give a body time to think?"

"Don't be cocky with me, Nikolai. You may be ahead of Grigoriy in field-stripping weapons, but yer jist as lackin' in political science."

"It all boils down to power," Nik said. "Those that don't have it, want it. Those that have it, want to keep it. What's not understood?"

"How to share it, that's what's elusive," Haimish said with authority. "In Russia the Czar rules with the advice of the Duma—which means he rules as he wishes. But he really isn't the power, he's only the figurehead."

Grisha pulled off the blindfold in exasperation and threw it on the table. He quickly reassembled the weapon and pulled the trigger. The hollow *clack* filled the small room.

"Who rules in Russia if not the Czar or the Duma?"

"The bureaucracy, the system itself, is the power in Russia. The Russian Amerika Company, the army, the navy, the foreign service, cultural affairs, even the cossacks, are all part of this huge mechanism continually fighting itself for dominance and it grinds up people like us to feed itself. Other countries have the same sort of mechanisms but wi' different names."

"What would be different about this 'Dená Republic' you keep nattering about?" Nik asked.

"Nattering, is it? The Dená Republic would borrow from every other republic in North America. But it would borrow only the best parts from each. Secret ballots, representational governments, an elected congress, absolute limits to elected terms, a separate, powerful judicial system, I could go on and on."

"We know!" Grisha and Nik said together.

"But who decides which parts to borrow, to keep?" Grisha asked.

"We all do," Haimish said with a wide grin, "by consensus."

"Everybody just works together with no strife," Nik asked.

"It's not quite that simple. There will be political parties, and factions within those also."

"Then why do we need to learn about weapons and bombs?"

"Because a lot of people don't agree with Haimish," Nik said dryly.

"Now you're catching on."

"But, Haimish," Grisha said. "Have you seen Tetlin Redoubt? Or St. Nicholas? Or even Akku Redoubt? How can a handful of escaped convicts, deserters, and Indians beat that?"

"I wish you'd stop calling me that," Nik said.

"To answer your first question, yes. I haven't personally seen the fortresses in Russian Amerika, but I have seen photographs of them. Very detailed photographs, I might add."

"So—"

"Wait, let me finish. We don't necessarily attack them frontally, nor do we attack them all. We pick a number of weak targets, go in, destroy them, and be gone before they know we're there."

"Just—"

"I'm still not finished. We pick targets that have high international visibility. Odious targets, like slave camps, or prisons. We make sure there are foreign journalists in every location."

"They don't let foreign journalists into the country." Grisha felt smug.

Nik shook his head. "You haven't witnessed the 'New Freedom' proclaimed by international treaty. In Alexandr Archipelago alone there are nearly a dozen foreign journalists. The Russian Amerika Company wishes to make riches off our southern neighbors in the form of tourism."

Haimish waved his arms around when agitated or excited. Now he appeared to be trying to fly. His face reflected an inner fire.

"They call this the 'last frontier,' wilderness unspoiled by man. That appeals to those in the North American Treaty Organization. They are crowded down there compared to the vastness of Alaska."

"We're going to attack prisons for tourists?" Grisha felt baffled.

"We are going to attack prisons because they are used to subjugate the people of the Dená Republic. If visitors are close and see the event, it will be widely talked about. If some of the prisoners escape, we have new recruits. Either way, the press will report it to their readers, and their governments. We will build international consensus to create a new republic."

"So you believe the Czar will give up the Dená Republic just so tourists will spend rubles in what's left of Russian Amerika?" Nik asked. His tone reeked with hostility.

"Nik, what's wrong?" Grisha asked. "It really doesn't sound all that far-fetched if you think about it."

"They'll send the cossacks and *promyshlenniks* into your villages to live. They'll rape your wives and daughters and make slaves of your brothers and sons. When they finally catch you they'll use torture for amusement before they release you to death. This is a madman's dream." He stalked out and slammed the door behind him.

Grisha gave Haimish a beseeching look. "What brought that on?"

"I don't know. But he's right. They will do that, you know, if they can. We have to pick our targets carefully and hit them all at the same time. The Russians can't be everywhere at once with a large army."

"Fragment them!" Grisha said. "Take bites and chew them up."

"Yes," said Haimish. "Now it's time to master the bow."

"Bows and arrows?"

"Exactly. They are deadly and quiet." Out of a rubberized bag Haimish pulled a common recurve bow. "This is our most efficient weapon. It's light, accurate at long distance in the hands of an expert, and absolutely silent."

"We never used these in the Troika Guard," Grisha said, running his hands over the smooth wood. "But we used pretty much everything else."

Haimish stared at him. "You were in the Troika Guard?"

"Ten years and a few months. Didn't Nathan tell you?"

"Nathan never tells me anything, him and his 'shaman of mystery' crap."

"Okay, let's go play with this and I'll tell you about my military career."

Haimish glanced at his wrist watch. "Too close to lunch. Let's go eat first."

The main hall swarmed with people. The rich aroma of salmon stew and baked bread filled the air. Nik and Cora sat at a small table in one corner, talking intently.

Wing's return seemed to trigger a realization in Cora. She and Nik now spent a great deal of time together, their mutual attraction obvious to all. Yet Nik appeared to be more tense than ever.

At first Grisha escaped their notice, and he wondered if he should impose on their conversation. Then Cora glanced up and saw him. She energetically waved him to their table.

Nik glanced up at him and then resumed talking. Grisha could tell by the way Nik hunched over that his friend was in a serious mood. Feeling reluctant, Grisha went to the table.

". . . the thing is either important or it's not," Nik said to Cora. "That's all I have to say."

Cora looked up. "Would you sit with us for a minute, Grisha?"

He sat down and smiled at her. "How are you?"

"I feel really good," she said. "I got good friends, and I'm attracted to a good man, despite the fact that he doesn't want to live with me."

"I do want to live with you," Nik said, "as man and wife."

"What do you think, Grisha?" she asked. "Should a man and woman have to marry to share their lives?"

He shielded his chest with his hands. "You're talking to someone whose wife left him for another man, and whose new companion got him thirty years hard labor for something she did. I think maybe you're talking to the wrong Ivan."

"I accept your reservations," she said. "Now answer the question."

Nik hid behind a flat stare and tightly crossed arms over his chest.

"Okay. After pointing out you two haven't known each other very long, I guess the first question would be, how long do these two plan to share their lives?"

"Exactly!" Nik said with a fierce grin.

"I don't see what that has to do with it," Cora said at the same time.

Grisha pursed his lips and nodded sagely.

"I think I see where the discussion has foundered."

"He says—" "She says—" they blurted together.

Grisha held up his hand.

"Nik, you go first."

"She says marriage is of no importance. If I love her I'll be happy to just live with her, no threads, no ties."

"You don't agree?"

"No! I want to marry her. I want to formalize what we feel for each other, I want to have a wife and someday have children. If we just lived together we'd be no better than the cossacks and their whores."

Cora's cheek turned red, and her smile went completely flat.

Grisha nodded to her. "Cora?"

"If a man and a woman love one another, why do they have to formalize it? We're both soldiers in a rapidly changing world, in a revolution. Who has time for sewing, cooking, babies, and warm goat's milk at night when there's a war to be fought?"

Her eyes shone and Grisha realized she was about to cry.

"This is our lives! Right now." A tear coursed down her cheek and dripped off her chin. "All of us could be dead tomorrow, or the day after, or. . . ." She turned to Nik. "There are no oaths or ceremonies that will stop death. I know. We must seize the time we have and live it to the fullest."

"Will you marry me?" Nik asked.

"Not until the Dená Republic is a fact. Then I will marry you. I'll marry you twice."

Grisha felt caught in their emotional energy. Once, as a young man, he crewed on a boat that lost power and ended up on the rocks. At this moment he felt very much the same way he had before the boat actually ground into the teeth of that North Pacific island—completely alive and scared, and knowing things were going to change drastically.

"Okay," Nik said. "When the Dená Republic becomes fact, we will be married."

"You witnessed this, Grisha," she said, glancing at him then back to Nik. "So when the time comes he can't get out of it."

"I'm done being a deserter," Nik said with a smile for her.

Suppressing his envy as best he could, Grisha pushed away and ambled toward the kitchen. Neither of them noticed.

"Snagging usually doesn't start until the ice goes out on the Yukon," Wing said, coming up beside him.

"Snagging? What's that?"

She laughed. "Mating season. You know, like the birds, go out and snag yourself a mate."

"I always thought snagging was an unfair way of catching a fish." Grisha liked looking at Wing and tonight she seemed more radiant than the last time he saw her.

"And your point is what?" They both started laughing at the same time.

"I haven't had a chance to ask since you got back. How was your trip?"

"Good," she said. Her eyes lost some of their sparkle. "There's just so much to do and so little time."

"So spread the work around, stop trying to do it all yourself."

"Don't worry, Grisha, there's plenty for you, too. We realize how fortunate we were when you decided to join us."

"Not as fortunate as I was when you saved my life. I'll do anything I can to further the movement. I'm collecting old debts, too."

"We know. Well, I have to meet with Chandalar before I can go to bed, so I'll say good night." She turned and went through the door.

"Good night," he mumbled, feeling bereft. He assessed his feelings and didn't like what he found. "Not good," he said, his voice barely audible. "You'll just get hurt again."

He pulled back into his mind where he sheltered his vulnerability. There was no time to waste being giddy and weak-kneed, he decided. Perhaps after the revolution.

Perhaps never again.

18

Tetlin Redoubt

Wolverine White, his skinning knife jutting from his gory throat, slapped Bear Crepov on the shoulder and demanded, "Where is their blood? You vowed to avenge me!" He slapped Bear a second time. "Where?" his voice gurgled with blood.

Again his shoulder jerked, more from the psychic blow than the physical one. The fourth blow made him dimly aware that it wasn't Wolverine speaking from the grave.

"Bear! There is someone for you," Katti said, slapping his beefy shoulder again.

" 'Nuf, you can stop punching around on me now," he mumbled. "Who wants ta see me?" He opened his eyes slowly, knew the vodka hangover needed only movement to explode behind his eyes and take his scalp off.

"A cossack," she said, and he finally heard the fear.

"A cossack wants to see me?" He sat up in the stained bed and dumbly endured the painful hammering in his head. "What for?"

"I don't know. But he knows you're here." Katti's chubby face usually maintained a shade of pink. Now the pink mixed with apprehensive gray and her wide-eyed gaze remained nailed to his face.

"Don't worry about it, Kat. He's just a damned messenger boy."

"For you, maybe. But for me he can be big trouble when you're not around."

Bear yawned and scratched his hairy belly before pulling on the soiled cotton trousers constituting his uniform. He carefully rose and shuffled to the cabin door and opened it. The cossack stood outside in the minus-thirty-degree weather.

"What do you want?" The cold air invaded the mat of hair on his chest and hardened his nipples. His bare toes tried to curl away from the cold but he wouldn't allow them to move.

"The colonel wants to see you, now."

"I'll be there as soon as I get dressed." Bear shut the door in the man's face.

Now what do they want?

He pulled on his clothes while Katti hovered, looking anxious in her ragged dressing gown. He'd taken her out of an arriving coffle two years before. She would allow him to do anything he wished to her to keep from facing the cossacks again.

She'd gotten fat, he decided. She really looked like a peasant now. Her eyes begged for answers, but he ignored her. Keep 'em off balance, that was the way. He pulled on his heavy socks and boots.

The cold bright daylight became knives that attacked his squinted eyes. He wanted a drink of vodka to numb the pain, but he'd emptied his last bottle the night before. Maybe the colonel would have some.

Despite his heavy coat, chill permeated him by the time the heavy barracks door shut behind him. He pushed into the colonel's office, leaving the door open, and dropped his bulk onto the wooden bench. The colonel looked up from the papers on his desk.

"What's the big hurry? I was in bed with my woman."

The colonel kept his face neutral and nodded toward the door. "The captain here wished to see you as soon as possible."

The door slowly swung shut to reveal a woman of medium size, a bit too much on the thin side to suit him, but not hard to look at. Her dark blond hair molded tightly around a face composed of angles and planes.

Her mouth was too wide for her face, he thought, and the dark eyes held more intelligence than he cared to deal with in a woman. He sat up straight.

"Well," he said, "now she's seen me."

"This man," she said holding out the photograph he'd seen in this office before. "You have seen him?"

"*Da*. I almost killed him in the bush."

"How fortunate for all of us that you did not," she said dryly. "Can you take me to the place where you last saw him?"

"Yes. Or I could show you on a map."

She pointed to a large wall map. "Do so."

He moved over and traced their trail with a dirty fingernail.

"This is where the construction site was attacked and destroyed. They went this way, along the Tanana River, there's a very old trail. They camped here the first night and our party stopped here."

"Didn't you check the construction site first?" she asked.

"I sent in one volunteer, a cossack, to look for fool traps."

"And?"

"He found one. He exploded with the rest of the camp. Everything burned."

Something moved in her eyes and she nearly smiled.

"So you sent in a fool to start with."

Bear stifled a retort about all cossacks being fools.

"*Da*, Captain. I did just that." He turned back to the map. "We caught an Indian the next morning, but couldn't get him to talk before he died."

"There are techniques," she began.

"He threw himself on my knife when I began skinning him."

"Oh. Please continue."

"That's when they discovered we were on their trail and they split up their party. We did the same. I followed the group with your friend in it."

"He's not my friend," she said in a flat voice.

"They set up an ambush here at the trail junction, right where I thought they would. We flanked them and moved in. Again I had a cossack volunteer who agreed to be first into the open."

Bear licked his lips and continued. "When nobody shot at him, he thought we'd been wrong. He walked up through the meadow toward the junction.

"But I had spotted the convict in the photograph. He also spotted me, so I pretended not to see him. When I wished to move, I stared at a tree behind him. As soon as he looked away in curiosity, I ran behind him and fired."

"How is it that you missed?"

"When he looked back and I wasn't there, he had the presence of mind to drop to the ground. My shot went over him. I fired a second time but he had already rolled clear, down the slope away from me."

"Hmm, perhaps his old training has resurfaced after all."

"He was scared pissless and reacting to the moment. Then much shooting happened and the cossack dropped. I slipped into an old wolf den and waited with my knife and rifle for them to discover me."

"You were outnumbered, weren't you?"

"I would not have died alone."

"They obviously didn't discover you."

"No. After they left I found my dead friend and then I returned here."

"How many were in their party?"

"Four."

"How many were in your party?"

"Four."

"How many of your party came back?"

"Only me. What are you trying to say?"

"I thought you *promyshlenniks* were the best woodsmen in Alaska."

"We are," he said with a growl.

"After the Indians, it would seem."

Bear glared at her but didn't respond. Her words hit too close to thoughts he himself had endured.

"You can show me this place?" she said.

"Of course. But there is no reason."

"Why not?"

"I heard them say they had far to go. They are probably in winter camp on the Yukon or lower Tanana."

"Actually," she said, "we know exactly where they are."

"Where?"

"Right here," her shellacked fingernail tapped the map once, "on the Toklat River at a village of the same name."

"If you knew this before you came, why do you ask me where I last saw the man?"

"I wanted to hear your story, firsthand accounts are always revealing. Besides, we need qualified people in on this, and between your experience in the bush and your raging animosity toward our quarry, you fit right in. You begin collecting field pay as of now."

"What do you plan to do about the traitor's camp?"

"Actually, it depends on the traitors." Her smile lacked warmth.

19

Toklat

"Often we send out two-man reconnaissance parties," Chan explained. "So for your final field test, you two are to go across the Toklat and follow the big game trail to the East Fork of the Toklat River. Go north up the East Fork until you come to a wide valley.

"Turn west there and follow the trail through the mountains until you hit the Toklat again. Then follow it home. This is about thirty-five to forty kilometers and will be an excellent exercise for you."

"How long do we have?" Nik asked.

"If we don't see you after two weeks have passed, we'll send out search parties."

"Looks simple enough to me," Grisha said.

"It always does, on a map," Haimish said.

"When do we leave?" Grisha asked.

"Within the hour."

"Can we use skis rather than snowshoes?" Nik asked.

"Whatever you wish," Chan said.

Cora sat off to one side of the small group, her eyes fastened on Nik.

"Good. If we had to use snowshoes, it would take Grisha a month to make the trip."

A few people chuckled. Grisha went into the main hall to get food for the journey. The tension generated by the meeting didn't dissipate. He wondered at it.

Wing stepped out of the kitchen and gave him a bulky bag made from soft moose hide. He stared at her face. Over the past few weeks they had fallen into conversation many times, on many subjects.

He found her intelligence impressive, but her courage awed him. At this point there existed a palpable tension between them that both chafed and titillated him. He felt good whenever he saw her.

"There's jerked moose, squaw candy, and trail mix." Her eyes moved over his face. "Be careful, okay? I'll miss you." She leaned forward and quickly kissed him on the mouth.

Before he could say anything, she hurried back into the kitchen.

It took most of an hour to get their gear arranged. Finally, burdened with backpacks and bows, they skied off across the frozen Kantishna into the November afternoon. Grisha hoped the tension would vanish once they cleared the village. It didn't.

After an hour passed, he pulled off the game trail they followed and waited for Nik to stop beside him.

"Are you worried because they made us take bows rather than rifles?" Grisha asked.

"No. I'm not worried at all." Nik's eyes constantly swept the land around them, his right cheek had developed a tic, and he chewed at his bottom lip.

"Okay, if you don't want to talk about it, that's all right with me."

"Good," Nik said, pushing off down the trail. Grisha stepped into the ski tracks and followed.

A man could come to love this sort of life. He thought back to his previous apprehension of the forest, of thinking himself unable to survive in it, and smiled.

It had all turned out like some fantastic hunting trip. His health had improved beyond previous experience. Not an ounce of fat could be found on his body, despite obvious weight gain.

He liked his new beard, but the things he missed most were his razor and beer. These people were worse than priests about alcohol. Wing told him once that vodka was liquid chains in a bottle.

"The *promyshlenniks* would get our men drunk before trading and then steal their furs and gold with more bottles." Her voice rang with intensity in his mind.

"Wait a minute," he said aloud to himself, faltering in his long, sliding stride. "She said 'gold'! Why the hell didn't I ask her more about that?"

He picked up his stride, remembering back to the afternoon. After snowshoeing all day he had been more interested in the immediate gratification of dinner than the acquisition of Athabascan Indian history. Gold?

Until this moment he hadn't given the Dená Republic decent odds of becoming reality. But if they had gold reserves they could eventually obtain anything else in the world. In Japan and the California Republic there existed things that to him were nearly unimaginable.

Radio that told stories and played music, not just weather reports and military communications. More than that, they could get electricity up here. He wondered if electrical power could be had outside the redoubts, or if it was only for Russians.

If you had gold, you could buy helicopters. He wondered if Haimish knew the Dená had gold. Probably; despite his philosophy there had to be a compelling reason for the small man's presence.

Ahead of him, Nik came to the base of a ridge and began to fishbone up the steep side. Why was Nik so nervous? Did he fear being away from towns or villages? He had said he was raised in the city of St. Nicholas on Cook's Inlet.

The farther they moved away from Toklat, the more agitated Nik became. Light began to ebb in the subarctic afternoon. They needed to make camp soon. Maybe tomorrow they'd try to make camp in the dark.

Grisha skied to the bottom of the ridge trail and shouted, "Nik! Hey, Nik!"

Working doggedly sixty meters higher, Nik hesitated and then stopped, looked back.

"You ruined my momentum. What do you want?"

"Are you in that big a hurry to get back to Cora?" Grisha manufactured a grin. "We can go a little slower. Besides, it's gonna be dark soon, we need to make camp."

"Already?" He glared at the sky as if to intimidate it. "Okay. We'll camp on the other side of the ridge."

"Agreed." Grisha started awkwardly up the hill. After flailing about on the skis for a few steps he stopped and took them off. The wind-packed snow easily supported his booted feet.

They were excellent boots. The Russian Army captain from whose corpse he had removed them had possessed excellent taste. The

Russian Army did not issue hand-made boots to anyone below the rank of colonel.

Life is strange.

Nik beat him to the top and glided off into the trees. Grisha plodded along until he found his companion's skis jammed down into the snow. The tall Russian was scrounging wood for a fire.

Grisha checked the sky. Royal blue sliding into purple, no clouds. Tonight the temperature could drop again, but probably no wind. He pulled the shelter half out of his pack and rigged it to reflect the fire's warmth onto his back.

After stowing his gear, he went looking for firewood. No matter how much they collected, it would not be enough to last the night. In this part of Alaska the temperature dropped to minus sixty Celsius in the winter and climbed to plus forty Celsius in the summer. The extreme temperatures dried wood to tinder. In Southeast Alaska wood never dried, it rotted.

The Dená Republic is an extreme place, he thought, *and so are the people*. Other than his military service, being treated as an equal had not been a part of his life in Russian Amerika. A few Russians paid lip service to the Czar's equality ukase, but only the priests took it seriously.

In the Dená Republic he not only commanded equal status, he was prized, needed; all due to reasons for which the Czar's government had thrown him away. He stuffed one more fragment of tree limb into the wad of branches clutched in his left arm.

But I still want my boat back. I want my life back—I know how to live it now.

He struggled back to the campsite, where a light plume of smoke already drifted above Nik's head. He dropped the load next to the strange, educated, taciturn man who had become his friend. Grabbing his hatchet, he cut fir boughs to put under their sleeping bags for insulation.

Nik rigged a holder and hung a pot of water up to boil. Tea would warm them up. As soon as he pissed, Grisha would turn in for the night. After putting down two layers of boughs he rolled out his sleeping bag, sat down carefully, and sighed.

"Starting out late today was a good thing," he said with a yawn. "Tomorrow it won't be as hard to get started as it would have been after a full day." He stared at the back of Nik, who prodded at an already blazing fire.

"What are you scared of?" Grisha asked in a vague tone designed to suggest indifference.

Nik stopped poking the fire. He didn't move. Grisha pulled out a piece of squaw candy and chewed the lightly smoked strand of salmon. He could live on this stuff.

Nik moved over to his pile of fir boughs and began to weave them into a mattress. He didn't speak or look at Grisha.

"I wasn't trying to be insulting," Grisha said. "You're getting me worried. You've gotten stranger and stranger since you took up with Cora."

Nik looked across at him, his eyes dancing through the curtain of heat.

"Don't you understand that this is a real war?" His voice rang hollow, as if bouncing off a rock wall. "People out there want to kill us, and we want to kill them."

"I don't particularly want to kill anybody," Grisha said.

"But you're expected to kill. Sabotage, prison breaks, raids on warehouses, and attacking cossacks all lead inevitably to killing or being killed." Nik's face became more distorted through the rising heat.

Grisha stared back in consternation.

"Well, of course people are going to get killed. But if we do it right most of them will be Russians."

"Exactly. And then they will retaliate and slaughter a village or two and everything will be over. Hundreds of Russians and Dená dead for what, a principle? An impossible idea?"

"I don't think it's impossible," Grisha said staunchly.

"That's because you're a *Creole.*"

Grisha's confusion instantly condensed into anger.

"And white Russians know more than everybody else!"

"No," Nik said, nearly moaning. "We're just more treacherous. They're all going to die, you know."

"Who, the Russians?"

"No, the Dená. Once their camp is identified with cadre training, they're doomed."

"The Russians don't even come into Dená country, especially in the winter."

"Grisha, the goddamned RustyCan runs right through the Dená country!"

"So what? That means the Russians own a three-hundred-meter-wide ribbon across a country that they couldn't hold if anyone tried to take it away from them."

"Not all their planes are helicopters. They have Yak fighters, too."

"Nik, the Indians own the forest."

"For the time being, yes." Nik crawled into his sleeping bag and turned his back to the fire.

Grisha fed the fire, deep in thought. The subarctic night settled. The temperature dropped, and the *aurora borealis* flickered teasingly before scrolling across the sky from horizon to horizon. The lights fascinated him.

The northern lights were not unknown in Akku. But the phenomena in southeast skies, when the clouds cleared, were usually subdued compared to this, even at their best. Above him they bent and circled in scrolls that had to be a thousand kilometers high. Bands of light winked on, broadening from a pinpoint to a swath of unimaginable width in the space of three breaths. Great sections of sky would suddenly present a mist of pink, green, or even yellow.

He wondered about Nik. What ate at the man so voraciously? What aspect of their current life could cripple him like that?

"You must be livin' a different life than me," Grisha mumbled through the flames at the sleeping form. "I really don't think it's so bad."

They're all going to die, you know.

That tone wasn't what Nik called rhetorical. He said it like he knew it for fact. Grisha frowned, tried to remember how the other guards had treated Nik.

They had left him alone. But to be fair, he was always reading and writing in little notebooks; maybe the other soldiers just thought Nik pretentious and avoided him, most of them couldn't read anyway. Grisha scratched his head and yawned.

He pushed himself up with a grunt and walked to the edge of the camp before urinating. The temperature had dropped for sure; his urine froze with a crackle in the air before hitting the snow with soft thuds. After piling more wood on the fire, leaving some for the morning, he crawled into his bag and closed the heavy zipper.

Moments later someone shook his shoulder, hard. He pried open one eye and peered at Nik's face.

"Let me sleep, okay?"

"It's time to get up. You've been asleep for hours." Nik stood and laid wood on the coals of the fire. Coals.

Grisha didn't feel like he'd slept at all, but he pulled himself out of the warm bag anyway. His full bladder added proof he had slept. As he relieved himself he noticed the overnight temperature had risen slightly.

"Nik?" he said, walking back to the fire, suddenly chilled.

"Yeah?" He was packing his bag.

"Why didn't the other guards talk to you?"

Nik froze for a long moment; then continued stowing his gear.

"Because I could read. Because I had gone to school for more than three or two years. Because my English is as good as my Russian even if I didn't come from southeast."

"That's what I thought," Grisha said with finality. "But I wanted to hear you say it."

"Why? Do you think me incapable of lying?"

"I think I could tell if you were lying, and I don't think you are."

Nik shook his head. "Are the Kolosh a perceptive people?"

"Sure, most peoples are or they wouldn't have lasted long enough to become a race. My mother's people can tell by a person's name who they are related to, where they fit in the house where they live, and even where they fit into the village."

"My God, that's even more stratified than Russian life!" Nik said.

"It's more complete, I think. It's also a clan culture, not something that would work in St. Petersburg and maybe not even St. Nicholas."

"Does anybody ever pretend to be something they are not in your mother's culture?"

"Why would they bother, to make a joke? Everyone would know they weren't telling the truth."

"But you're part Russian, too, Grisha. Did your father know where he fit in Russian society?"

"Yeah. At the bottom," Grisha said, his voice revealing the bleakness he suddenly felt. "I started from the bottom and worked my way to major's flashes in the Troika Guard. Then I was sacrificed for political reasons and had to start over, got back to where I owned a boat and was master of my life."

"What happened?" Nik asked, his face rapt.

"I'm not sure, and I've thought about it a lot. I took a charter job where the customer wasn't what he said he was, went places we weren't supposed to go, and did things we weren't supposed to do."

"Sounds like smuggling to me."

"No, at first I thought that's what was going on, too. But, we picked up a woman who knew the man and on the way back they talked about the other North American countries. You know, the U.S.A, the Confederacy, all them."

Nik nodded.

"Then Karpov, the guy, got drunk and tried to snag the woman, got real direct about it. So there was a fight and we killed him."

"We?"

"*Da*. While he was choking me, she hit him in the back of the head with a halibut club, the spiked kind."

"So why did you end up in Tetlin Redoubt? Did they only hang her for murder?"

"She told them I did it. They were going to hang me, but then they changed their minds and sentenced me to thirty years hard labor instead."

"You wouldn't have lasted another thirty days," Nik said with professional disdain.

"I thought I was going to die that day. If the Dená had waited another minute before attacking, I'd be dead. Life is strange."

"It's getting light. We need to go."

"Nik, I'm not going anywhere until you tell me why you've turned into a moody bear."

"I don't think you'd understand."

Grisha swallowed the anger that immediately flared through him. It left a bad taste in his mouth.

"Why not, because I don't have enough education?"

"You wouldn't like me anymore, take my word for it." Nik strapped on his skis and pushed off down the trail, heading for the cut that dropped into the next valley.

"Nik!" Grisha yelled. "I want a real answer, a real reason!"

The Russian stopped and looked back.

"I'm a traitor. I'm a traitor and I can't stand to live with myself."

Then he skied away and Grisha scrambled to follow.

20

Near the Toklat River

Bear wasn't sure about this helicopter stuff. He didn't understand what held the damned things up. But it sure covered the distance as they raced along twenty meters above the treetops in excess of sixty exhilarating kilometers an hour.

They had flown from Tetlin Redoubt to St. Anthony Redoubt the day before and spent the night there. They left early this morning, long before the winter sun rose, so they would be in the target area during the brief subarctic day.

He noticed the captain watching him with her superior little smile that said he was only shit and she knew it. He wished he could catch her without her bodyguard corporal and his machine pistol. Today the dog of a soldier even carried a Kalashnikov.

Between the three of them they could stand off a dozen Indians. He thought them heavily armed for this mission. The captain remained adamant about only the three of them going into Indian country alone.

With Wolverine White dead, there wasn't anybody he trusted to fight at his back anyway. Now he faced the world alone.

"Ten minutes to landing zone, Captain," the pilot said in his jovial voice. He would stay with the aircraft and keep the engine warm. If the other three weren't back in exactly twenty-four hours, he would return to base without them.

The captain and the corporal rechecked their weapons and gear. Bear stifled a comment and peered out the window. A *promyshlennik* never neglected his weapons; they were ready when he walked out the door of his cabin.

The two soldiers laid their automatic rifles down and tested straps and bindings. When they finished with themselves, they glanced at each other to double-check. Bear felt certain the look they exchanged wasn't regulation.

Cossacks were like that, he mused. The enlisted men were animals, the officers were clever at manipulation, and they all worked in tandem with the Czar's intelligence service. Bear had to keep telling himself that these people weren't really Okhana agents, merely hired mercenaries.

He didn't like them, but they paid good, steady wages and he didn't have to take their orders if he didn't want to. He could always quit. *Promyshlenniks* were known for their independent spirit.

"Are you ready, Crepov?" the captain asked.

"Am I ready for what?"

"Are you ready to take the field and find these men for us?"

"I wouldn't have entered this borscht-maker if I wasn't."

"Good." She turned to the corporal. "Crepov will lead, I will go behind him, and you will follow me."

"But, Captain, I think it's not good for you to be between him and me. What if he attempts—"

"Corporal, I *am* armed."

"*Da.*" The corporal evenly regarded Crepov, then stared out at the passing scenery.

You'll pay for that one, pet.

The engine changed pitch and they banked to the left. Crepov looked out his window and found himself staring straight down at a snow-covered meadow. A branch of the Toklat River, frozen and brittle, wound along about a kilometer away.

The craft dropped in a tight spiral and Crepov's heart tried to fly out his mouth. He swallowed in a vain effort to make it retreat. His gorge attempted to follow, but he successfully kept it down.

Just as Crepov thought the noisy machine would crash into the ground, it leveled off and gently landed. The engine died and the great blades swooshed to a stop. He slid the door open and stiffly dropped to the snow-covered ground.

After allowing his legs to know the earth for a moment, he turned and pulled his skis off the special rack on the landing skids. Mounted on the other side of the tubular skid strut was a 9mm machine gun that the pilot could fire after aiming his machine at the target.

Crepov decided there might be something to these things after all. He placed his skis, stepped into them and clamped the bindings over the toes of his boots. After stretching his legs for a minute, he struck off toward the game trail he had spotted from the air.

"Where are you going?" the captain snapped. "I didn't order you to move out."

Crepov stopped and twisted to regard her.

"I'm going to do my job. I will also do as I please. You may do the same." He moved out again, setting a track for them to follow.

Not until he reached the game trail did he look back. They were methodically closing his hundred meter lead. He carefully examined the trail.

Only small game and predator tracks; no ski had passed since the last snow. From the crust on the white mantle, he would estimate the last snowfall at over a week before.

The captain slid up to him, trying not to breathe hard. Crepov pointed to the trail.

"What?" she asked, looking at it then back at him.

"No human has been by here yet. Are you sure this is where our quarry will pass?"

"Yes, as sure as I can be."

"Then let's find a good ambush site." He skied down the trail toward the tree-covered ridges.

21

Near the East Fork of the Toklat River

Grisha and Nik sat and ate a cold lunch on a pile of needles under an unusually large spruce tree. After swallowing his last bite of moose jerky, Grisha said, "I want some fresh meat."

"We don't have any."

"I know that. I want to hunt for a while. This is a game trail."

"Not now. Maybe tomorrow."

"You don't have to hunt if you don't want to, General," Grisha said. "But I'm hungry for rabbit."

"But . . ."

Grisha abruptly stood and secured his poles to his pack before swinging it onto his shoulders. He put on his skis and finally picked up the recurve bow and his quiver.

"Grisha, please let me be in front."

"I'm a better hunter than you are," he said with a grin. "Better shot too. Besides, you've been in front all day long. It's my turn."

"Tomorrow you can be in front. Today I want to be first."

Grisha stared hard at his companion.

"I heard a saying once that they use down in the American countries. 'Go fuck yourself,' is what they say. And that's exactly what you can do." He skied away, pulling an arrow out of the quiver as he went.

The game trail wound through the woods and curved into a cut separating two ridges. He decided there could be game in the heavy brush at the cut. He nocked an arrow and skied as quietly as he could into the entrance.

Abruptly a snowshoe hare bolted out of the brush ahead and ran toward him for three lunging strides. Suddenly the animal saw Grisha and veered off to the man's right. For five seconds the hare presented an easily accessible target before disappearing in the timbered flank of the ridge.

Grisha didn't shoot. His heart thundered in his ears and he concentrated on maintaining his grip on the bowstring.

What scared the animal? Wrong time of the year for bear. Nik is behind me. Maybe a moose? St. Nicholas, please let it be a moose.

He crept forward a step, then hesitated. He glanced behind him. In the distance, Nik slid into his pack and took his first sliding stride toward Grisha.

He jerked his head around to face the cut again. The merest breath of a sound carried across the snow to his ears. The bow suddenly seemed like a child's toy as he recognized the protest of oiled metal against metal.

Another glance over his shoulder. Nik moved forward swiftly, craning his head to get a better look at Grisha.

Good. He knows something out of the ordinary is happening.

Slowly, quietly, Grisha eased the skis backward. No good—he had to keep looking back to judge his steps. He bent down and rapidly unfastened his bindings.

He pulled the skis up and jammed them butt down in the snow. Watching the cut as closely as possible, he carefully retreated back down the trail. Nik slid to a stop ten meters away and waited.

Grisha got to his friend's ski tips before he allowed himself to whisper.

"There's somebody in the cut."

"How do you know?" Nik stared past Grisha, watching the cut.

He told about the snowshoe hare, hesitated.

"Then I heard someone chamber a round."

"Your hearing must be extraordinary," Nik said softly, "or else you're imagining things."

Grisha felt his jaw muscles go taut and he squinted at the man.

"I know what I heard," he hissed. "There's somebody in there."

"Well, move then, let me see."

Nik swung a ski pole up and smacked it across Grisha's left arm. Instinctively, Grisha jerked away from the pole just before it made contact and fell flat in the slightly softer snow at trail's edge.

Nik skied for the cut. Grisha stifled a roar of anger and, gripping his bow and arrow in in one hand, flopped through the deep snow to the relative firmness of the trail. He scrambled to his feet as Nik passed Grisha's skis, standing like silent sentinels.

The Russian disappeared into the cut. Grisha ran to his skis, quickly dropped them on the trail and snapped down the spring-loaded clamp over the front lip of his boot soles. Then he was gliding along, smoothly, silently, swiftly, arrow nocked, adrenaline charged. He skied into the cut.

22

Near the Toklat River

As soon as Bear Crepov saw the cut in the ridgeline, he knew it perfect for an ambush site. He side stepped off the game trail and motioned for the captain to come up next to him. When she stopped beside him, the Kalashnikov lay cradled in her right arm, her finger on the trigger.

"What is it?" she said loudly.

Bear winced and nearly slapped her. "Quiet, you bitch! Do you want them to kill us?"

She blinked at him, whispered, "Are they close?"

"They have to be. Get your pet corporal into the brush line over there," he pointed, "and I'll take cover on the other side of the trail. You pull back into those spruce behind that large mound, I think it's a rock."

"Are you worried for my safety?"

He quickly searched her face for signs of mockery, but found none.

"I think you can take care of yourself," he said slowly. "But if there's shooting I want you out of the way. You're the only one who knows why we're doing this." He skied ahead another thirty meters, stopped, took his skis off, and hid his equipment in the brush.

The corporal quietly disappeared on the other side of the trail. Crepov glanced back down the trail but could see nothing of the woman. He carefully pulled the slide back on his weapon and chambered a round.

The quiet of winter settled on him. No birds this time of year, they had all gone south to the Confederacy and New Spain. He must be his own sentry.

A voice broke the stillness. Bear couldn't make out the words, but he knew it for human. He tensed when he heard skis on snow, moving fast.

23

Near the Toklat River

Valari Kominskiya saw the huge *promyshlennik* stiffen and raise his weapon slightly. She pulled back a little even though it was impossible for anyone on the trail to see her. She felt a thrill of fear when close to the woodsman and had yet to decide whether she liked it or not.

Vlad, her corporal, knew enough not to kill either of the strangers, and the woodsman had been carefully briefed and thoroughly cowed. Crepov's concern for her safety touched her oddly. She put it all out of her mind when a man skied swiftly through the cut.

He quickly traveled past the *promyshlennik*, who didn't have time to stop him, and their plan became obsolete. She had to stop him. She lunged out onto the trail, wondered which man she was about to face.

"Stop!" She held the Kalashnikov braced at her hip, ready to fire.

The man wedged his skis against the side of the trail and ground to a quick halt. Nikolai Rezanov glared at her with more feeling in his face than she remembered from their last meeting. What was wrong?

"So you did kill—" she began.

Grigoriy Grigorievich entered the cut. Crepov leaped out of the brush and knocked him off his feet.

"What?" Grisha blurted as he fell.

Rezanov twisted, gripping his ski poles for balance. Valari swung her foot and knocked away the pole holding most of his weight. He fell awkwardly in the snow.

Vlad emerged from the brush and stood behind Grisha. The corporal looked to her for orders. She jerked her head sideways.

"Get on your feet and move up next to your friend there," Vlad ordered.

Grisha got to his feet and picked up his skis.

Valari shook her head.

"Leave the skis," Vlad said sharply.

Obediently, Grisha dropped them and trudged forward. Crepov stayed off to the side, his Kalashnikov at the ready. Except for Grisha's heavy beard, it was just how she had imagined it would be; victory was at hand.

In his clothing Grisha looked like an Indian. He also looked larger than she remembered, probably due to the bulky furs. He still hadn't looked up at her.

"Hello, Captain Lover," she said coyly, a smirk on her lips.

Grisha stopped and his eyes fastened on her. In less than a second she saw astonishment, fear, hate, and death flash across his face.

"What are *you* doing *here?*" he spat. His features became expressionless.

"Why, I came by special helicopter to talk to you," she said.

"How did you know where to find me?" His stolidity began to annoy her.

"That doesn't matter," she said quickly. "What I have to say to you is very important, so listen carefully."

He nodded his head and she licked her lips.

"As agreed, we offer you your old life back."

"What do you mean? You aren't taking us back to Tetlin Redoubt?"

God, he could be so thick! "I mean you can have your boat back, or your commission in the Troika Guard."

His steely grin called her a liar. "I think maybe you're offering more than you own."

"We still have your boat."

"You planned to do this to me on purpose?" His face went expressionless again.

"Not at all. You were just in the wrong place at the wrong time. But once you struck Karpov, you became a criminal. You would have been given a year at hard labor." Her lip curled slightly.

"But Karpov, being the pig he was, had to drink too much. He reverted to a situation between us that had been over for years and tried to kill you when you interfered. You were more important than him at the moment, you could drive the boat, so I killed him."

"But why are you meeting me in the middle of Dená country?"

She smiled and licked her lips again.

"After your arrest, we examined your record. You're part Russian and part Kolosh. Historically your people traded with the Dená. You're also an ex-major with extensive military experience and demonstrated leadership qualities. You would be a prize for these traitors.

"By this time they have accepted you into their organization and soon you will be able to go anywhere, see anything. Correct?"

"So? What does the Czar care about a bunch of Indians in the middle of the forest?"

"They are trying to break away from Russian Amerika. They have attacked too many posts, killed too many people—"

"Cossacks," he said with a hungry smile, "they only kill the cossacks, and those who refuse to surrender."

Her jaw muscles tightened.

"The Czar and the Russian Amerika Company want them neutralized." Her voice matched the season. "We know there is a circle of leaders inciting the rest of the Indians to rebellion. We also know there has to be a revenue source to finance this travesty. We need their names and where they can be found."

She wondered why Grisha visibly relaxed.

"Then you're out of luck. I only know a couple of them. Got no idea where they get their paychecks. You'll have to find someone else to get the names for you."

"We know that you've been in Toklat since your 'rescue.' This is a long-term investment. But we need you in on the operation now, before any spring offensives are started."

"How did you know where I was? How did you find me now?"

"I'll tell you later—if you agree to our terms."

"Do you really think I would be fool enough to trust you or any part of the army again?"

She looked down at Rezanov.

"You were supposed to have won him over by this time, or killed him, Captain. Have you been derelict in your duties?"

"Captain?" Grisha said in astonishment.

Nik wouldn't look up. He sat on the trail and stared at Valari's snow-paks.

"I'm sorry I didn't warn you. You can't believe how convoluted this thing is, Grisha," he said calmly.

"Why haven't you enlisted him?" Valari hissed.

Nik looked up at her.

"Because once I saw the birthing of the Dená Republik, I realized how much I hate the blind, despotic greed of the Russian government and those who serve it."

"Birthing!" She kicked him in the face, knocking him back into the snow.

"There is no Dená Republik, you pompous ass!" she shouted. "The Czar will never allow mere savages to dictate to Imperial Russia. They must be stamped out, made an example of—just like the traitors of 1917 and 1935!"

She snapped her mouth shut and pulled back into herself. *This won't work*, she realized. *I must woo them, not break their arms.*

She reached down and helped Rezanov sit up again.

"Captain, you have lost your focus," she said gently. "These things happen. Now we must make the best of the situation."

Rezanov's eyes found hers. Blood leaked from his nose, and a dark bruise thickened across his right cheek.

"You only hear what you wish to hear, Captain," he said evenly. "I cannot do this to Grisha, to myself, or the Dená people."

Valari stifled the impulse to kick him again. She glanced at Vlad and Crepov. They stood watching her, close behind Grisha. Her gaze traveled back to Rezanov.

"You are speaking treason, my friend." She patted her Kalashnikov fondly. "You know what becomes of traitors."

"Just to save us all time, why don't you go ahead and execute me right now? That's why I made contact the last time, I want out of this charade."

"If you and your reluctant recruit here don't cooperate, that's exactly what we'll do."

A grunt of pain and sudden scuffling jerked her attention back to the others. Crepov was on his knees, bracing himself up with locked arms, trying to regain his feet. Blood ran freely from a slash across his cheek.

Grisha stood behind Vlad, holding a machine pistol to the corporal's head.

"No, don't," Valari said before she could stop herself.

"I thought I picked out the one you sleep with," Grisha said with a tight smile. "Now drop your weapon or I'll kill him."

She pointed her weapon at Rezanov's chest. "You drop your weapon," she said softly, "or I'll kill him."

"What do I care if you kill your own spy? Go ahead, then I want you down that trail as fast as you can go."

"You don't care if I kill him?" she said, doubt washed over her.

"If you don't care that I kill Corporal Lover, here." He jammed the muzzle of his weapon behind Vlad's ear. Vlad winced and tried to pull away.

Grisha tightened his grip on the corporal's collar. "I have nothing to lose. Now get out of here!"

Something sagged inside her. He was right. She, on the other hand, could lose everything if she didn't handle this correctly.

"Let us all go," she said quickly. "And we'll let you both leave."

The *promyshlennik* tried to stand but fell into the snow.

"Get away from me or I'll kill all of you," Grisha said.

"You can't get all of us before I get you." Her voice carried more of an urgency than she wanted to exhibit, but she had no time to think. "Do it my way and we all live."

Muscles moved beneath the dark beard. This man had changed a great deal more than expected in a few short months; he was no longer a defeated cuckold. She hadn't considered that possibility at all.

"Okay," he said. "Put down your weapon and carry your dog off."

"You must think I'm stupid, Grigoriy. If I put down my weapon you'll kill all three of us."

"All right then, you use the captain there for a shield and move back down the trail to where it turns. I'll back up with your corporal until I can find cover."

"Then?"

"Then the corporal helps your wolfhound move slowly down the trail—at the same time Rezanov moves toward me. Once they pass each other you won't be able to fire for fear of hitting the wrong people."

Her lips were very dry; she licked them again. Her mind darted over his words, searching for treachery, couldn't find any and knew she hadn't looked closely enough. But there was no more time.

"*Da*. It will be as you say." She looked down at Nik. "Get to your feet *very* slowly, with your back to me."

He turned away from her and rose slowly to his feet.

She grabbed his collar and prodded his spine with the Kalashnikov.

"Walk backward," she ordered. "If you try anything foolish I will spread your bowels all over your *Creole* brother."

He stepped back and hit the toe of her ski with his heel.

"Stop." She reached down and unlatched the bindings with her rifle muzzle. "Now step back over the skis."

Once he was across them, she stopped him again.

"Pick them up and hold them in front of you. If you try—"

"I'll do what you say, damn it!" he shouted. "Just shut up!" He bent over and grabbed the skis.

She glanced at Vlad as he shuffled backward down the trail away from her. This just hadn't worked out according to plan, she thought dully. Rezanov moved backward again.

The slow, awkward journey seemed to last for ulcerating hours. By the time they reached the bend in the trail, her back and legs ached. She peered past her hostage.

Perhaps Grisha outsmarted himself. The range of his weapon was considerably less than hers. But the assault rifle was not known for its accuracy at long distance either.

"Let Rezanov go!" Grisha shouted. His voice echoed down the valley.

Vlad and Crepov staggered slowly toward her. She prodded the traitor.

"Get away from me. There will come a time when I kill you, if your noble savages don't do it for me."

Rezanov hesitated for a moment and looked into her eyes. "There is a saying in the southern republiks that applies to you, Valari, go fuck yourself." He walked away down the path.

She nearly laughed. Sweat ran down her face despite the frigid cold. The men came together and each stepped off the trail slightly to allow the others to pass.

Vlad looked drawn and angry. Blood covered the left side of Crepov's face. How had Grisha done that? They shambled up to her,

Vlad released the *promyshlennik* and slumped beside the man when he fell.

Valari brought her weapon up quickly, but the trail stretched away cold, gray, and empty. They turned toward the distant helicopter.

A shot rang out and the sound echoed through the cut and past them, bounced off the frozen ridges.

They stopped. Crepov raised his head with an effort.

"He—the one that cut me—killed your cossack," he said thickly.

"So it would seem," Valari said distantly. Her eyes squinted in the dim midday brightness.

I wonder if Rezanov told him about the radio before he died?

24

Near the Toklat River

"There's one thing I still don't know," Grisha said, breaking the silence between them left by the gunshot.

They sat in the brush from where they had lost sight of Valari. No sense in trying to distance themselves from this place until the helicopter departed.

"What's that?" Nik said warily.

"How'd they know where we were?"

"I have a miniature Japanese radio that I reported in with periodically. Now you tell me something."

"What?" Grisha asked, staring into Nik's eyes.

"Why'd you just fire off one round? You didn't even aim it toward them."

"So they'd think I just shot an informer, before he could tell me about his radio."

"Huh?"

"Valari outsmarted me when I was still naive about her. No matter. But since she used me once, she thinks I'm stupid."

"*Da?*"

"It's my turn to outsmart her."

"Oh," Nik said with a frown. "Very well."

"Why didn't you tell me? Why didn't you explain?"

"And when do I do that, at the evening meal? 'Pass the salt, please. By the way, Grisha, I'm a spy and I must betray you and you're all going to die.' Something like that?"

"Why do you think we're all going to die?"

"Because they have helicopters, and fighter planes, if they need them. They have spies everywhere. They have two hundred tanks about two days from here. They have—"

"Look around, Nik! What do you see?" He waved his arm. "They can't get us in here with a tank. If we disperse, the planes can only blow up buildings, not kill people!"

"If your shelter is gone, you die."

"Not all the shelter is open to the sky. This problem has not been ignored. You knew that. But still you didn't tell me."

"I needed commitment."

"I gave you all that I had," Grisha said tightly.

"Not you. Cora. I mean, I knew you and I were friends, I knew you would understand once I explained it."

"Then why didn't you explain it?"

"Because if I told you, Cora would find out. I wasn't sure she would understand. In the beginning I was going to do what Capt— what Valari wanted."

Grisha felt as if he'd been slapped. Before he could find suitable words, a helicopter racketed toward them.

"Quick, pretend you're dead!" Grisha said. "Lay down on the trail."

Nik sprawled on the ground, facedown. "What if they put a few rounds into me to make sure I'm dead?" he muttered.

"They won't chance it, they're too big of a target and they don't know my location."

The helicopter roared over them. Grisha watched it pull up, wheel around in a tight turn and start back toward them. He pulled back farther into the thicket and aimed his Kalashnikov at the pilot.

The craft moved over them again, slower this time, but it didn't stop. A face peered whitely through the heavy plastic window. The rotor wash created a sudden snow flurry that quickly escalated into a miniature whiteout. The engine bellowed to higher decibels and the machine vanished over the ridge.

Grisha eased his weapon down to rest on his knees and sighed. "Okay, you aren't dead any more." He brushed snow off him.

Nik rolled over and stared at the ridge. "You don't think they'll be back?"

"No. Not if they want to stop that *promyshlennik* bastard from bleeding to death."

"What did you do to him?" Nik asked, getting to his feet.

Grisha stood. "Raked his face with this." He moved his wrist quickly and abruptly a small knife gleamed in his hand.

"How long have you had that?"

"It's been my talisman since the day we were rescued from the cossacks." Grisha stared at his friend. "Did you think I would tell on you?"

"I don't know, would you? Are you?"

"No, I'm not going to tell them anything: you are."

"They'll hate me," Nik said slowly. "Cora will hate me. I was a cossack."

"Just like she was a student nurse, in another life. You're a weapon for the Dená Republik now." Grisha began collecting his equipment. "You were actually a cossack captain?"

"*Da.*"

"You aren't old enough to be a captain!"

They skied into the late morning, following their trail back toward Toklat.

25

Toklat, December 1987

The pulsing beat of their engines reached far out in advance of the Russian gunships. In the village a hand-cranked siren shrilled into a wail for a full minute before the operator released the handle and fled into the forest.

The first helicopter buzzed in at treetop level, machine guns firing indiscriminately. More than forty Kalashnikovs filled the air with bullets.

Even from the ground they could see the effect of their fire; pieces of fuselage flew off, the engine sputtered as smoke leaked from it, one of the gunners collapsed, swaying in his safety harness. The gas tank abruptly ignited and the stricken machine exploded. The remaining door gunner screamed flaming to the ground.

Before the second gunship reached the village, the first already lay burning on the forest floor. The second machine strafed a different section of the forest and ran into another wall of lead.

The pilot must have been hit in the first few seconds. The second helicopter abruptly nosed over and crashed into the trees. The four surviving machines veered and circled back the way they had come.

They hovered a kilometer away, waiting.

A Yak fighter snarled over the village just ahead of its exploding ordinance. Three hundred square meters of forest blew into flying splinters and burning trees.

The fighter etched a circle and returned with cannons clawing out, searching for targets. Again the air filled with bullets. But the Dená were used to the slower helicopters and very few, if any, rounds found the aircraft.

The Yak didn't return. The helicopters swiveled and thwapped away to the southeast. The forest waited; only the crackle of small fires broke the stillness.

In excited jubilance, the Dená emerged from their bunkers and shelters.

"Where did you get all those Kalashnikovs?" Nik asked in awe. "The army had no hint you were so well armed."

"From allies who prefer not to advertise their aid," Chan said, his eyes gleaming. "One of these days soon you'll be serving in that branch of operations."

"Obtaining military aid?" he asked.

"Apparently you find it difficult to comprehend what an incredible asset you are to this cause." Chan pulled him away from the others and they slowly followed a path through a stand of birch. Their breath hung around them in the cold air as they talked.

"I, I do know a great deal about weapon procurements, but nothing about shopping for them."

"Why are you here, Nikolai?" Chan said abruptly. "How can you turn your back on a St. Petersburg education, an army commission, and a politically influential family?"

"I'm not turning my back on my education. I'm using it." He threw his arms out for emphasis. "I have never agreed with my father politically. That's why he got me a military scholarship—as punishment and challenge." Nik glanced out through the gleaming birch. The white trees held back the subarctic afternoon darkness.

"The academy was hell, but the mathematics, engineering, and electronics were worth the price of admission. For a short time I even worked with the command logic machine."

"The what?"

"The command logic machine. It's a calculating machine. It can solve great mathematical equations in a few tens of minutes."

"What do they use it for?"

"Mostly mathematics. But it's a wonder."

"I'm still wondering about your presence."

"At first I was scared to death. But I knew my mission wouldn't go on forever and so I decided to do the best I could and help you turn

Grisha into what you wanted and learn all your secrets at the same time." Nik hesitated, his burning eyes stared intently into Chan's face.

"Then I realized that you have the beginning of something here that could change the face of the continent." Enthusiasm bloomed in his voice. "And I wanted to be part of it."

"Why? You're not an Indian."

"Do I have to be an Indian to be part of the Dená Republik?"

"Of course not. But—"

"Then my race doesn't matter, only my attitude does."

"Go on."

"I know the definition of 'republik,' and I also know that Alaska will always be a Siberian colony as long as the Czar rules here."

Nik's words echoed back at him and he realized how loud he had become. He abruptly lowered his voice. "Sorry, I didn't mean to shout."

"You're saying you don't like the way things are out there? Why should you care, or want to be part of this? You're part of the aristocracy. Aren't you descended from the great Baron Rezanov?"

"Christ! What a cross to bear." Nik spat in the snow. "Yes, Count Rezanov was my eight-times-removed ancestor, as well as his lovely, and much younger, Spanish bride. The love story that secured a continent! Until history decreed something different."

"So why are you here, with us, when you have so much back in St. Petersburg?"

"Because it's wrong to keep a people down where they can't see the horizon," he said with a slight tremor in his voice. "And it's double-damned wrong when what's keeping them down are animals who are nothing more than pustules on the buttocks of decent humanity."

"My word," Chan said with a smile. "You're still a romantic."

"My only other choice was much worse. That's why I'm here now."

"Why did it take cossacks to get you to tell us the truth?"

"I was trying to obtain something here that was never available in St. Nicholas or New Arkhangel. But when I saw those slinking dogs in uniform, I realized that what I wanted had to be earned, not given."

Nik peered at Chan in the gloom. "My only chance to live the way I wish is to help you do the same thing."

"Welcome home." Chan patted the taller man's back. "Have I ever got a job for you. But first we've got to get this village packed up and out of here before daylight."

"What? We're going to evacuate everybody tonight?"

"That fighter will be back in the morning with a lot more just like it. Toklat has served its purpose. We knew this day would come."

"So where are we going tonight?"

"First to Minto. A council of war must be held in the next few days. Then we will go to many places. Some will go into Chena."

"Chena, on the road? There's a huge garrison there."

"We know," Chan said with a wide grin. "We know."

26

Minto, December 1987

Minto buzzed with excitement. Visitors from upriver and downriver crowded into the available guest space and spilled into the council chambers. The log building had been ordered built by the Imperial Army to serve as military quarters when needed.

Villagers had completed the project, which gave them a sense of ownership. Grisha found the fact amusing but doubted the army would. On reaching Minto he realized Toklat had been a military operation.

Minto swarmed with children, and the resident adults were not as enthusiastic about an impending Dená Republik as the people who had inhabited Toklat.

"You people are just going to bring the Russians down hard on us!" a middle-aged man bitterly informed Grisha. "They got an army, a navy, and an air force. How you gonna stop that with your fancy words?"

Grisha parroted Hamish's answer. "Politically and economically."

"Shit!" the man responded. "Them Russians hit this place 'cause of you—you're gonna be dead, one way or another!"

After that, Grisha asked quiet questions of Haimish, Chan, and Wing. The village was typical of the entire region, roughly thirty percent of the population were sympathetic to the cause, about forty percent seemed to tolerate it, ten percent didn't care one way or the other, and a vocal twenty percent adamantly opposed their goals.

"What's wrong with them?" Grisha had demanded of Chan. "Don't they want their own country?"

"They see themselves as realists who don't want to lose what freedom and property they already possess. Many of them consider themselves Russian even though they would play hell convincing the citizens of St. Petersburg of that."

"But if they had any vision, they could see the possibilities—"

"Did you?" Haimish snapped. "Face it, laddie, you were pushed into this by the Russian Amerika Company and the Okhana."

"So push them."

"Patience," Chan said with an enigmatic smile. "The day is coming when they will all choose. But they will see it as something they want to do. We won't have to push, the Czar will do it for us."

Grisha was beginning to appreciate how well the minds of Chan and Haimish meshed. Nathan arrived two days after the Toklat people reached Minto and spent long hours with Nik. The former Czarist soldier offered his memories to the Dená Republik, to mine for what usable ore they could discover.

While Wing operated a cunning little tape recorder from California, Nik recounted his life from adolescence to present, with Nathan concentrating on him. Nathan asked questions that sometimes seemed pertinent, sometimes pointless. Nik answered them all.

Grisha asked a few questions of his own about Nathan, and sometimes got evasions, sometimes pieces of answers. Chan allowed only that Nathan was a very perceptive man. Wing unwittingly revealed that Nathan had Russian, Dená, Yu'Pik, and Kolosh ancestors; she thought it common knowledge.

Grisha tried to slip into his charter-boat camaraderie in an attempt to hear if anyone ever entertained a negative thought about Nathan. If they did, they wouldn't talk about it. Few would even allude to the possibility of feeling negative about the man.

Slayer-of-Men told Grisha that he would never go wrong by following Nathan's orders. Finally he found one man, an old man who had weathered over sixty winters in Minto, who seemed open about the subject.

"Nathan Roubitaux? He was a strange kid. You could be pissed as hell at him, then he'd show up and all you could do was like the little shit. I gotta admit, he's done a lot for the People."

A faint apprehension slowly took shape in the back of Grisha's mind. In the meantime, Nik struck gold.

Gnady Ustinov wondered if he were wasting his time. For over a year he had been hearing stories about the Dená Separatist Movement fighting the wicked Russians in order to free the Athabascan People. At first he thought it was just a drunk's bull crap.

Then his good friend, Ambrose Ambrose had visited from Nabesna. They had only met a total of five times in the last twenty years but due to a heavy correspondence they were as close as brothers. Ambrose brought important news.

"My cousin in Tetlin Redoubt says there's going to be a war and many of our People will be killed." His eyes had grown large with earnestness and Gnady believed him.

"Who will kill them?"

"The Czar's army, and cossacks, and *promyshlenniks*."

"Why?"

"The DSM has been killing many Russians and the Czar told the Imperial Army to put a stop to it."

"I have heard the DSM is everywhere, how can the soldiers get them all?"

Ambrose grinned. "They can't, and that's a good thing."

"Why, my friend?"

"Because I am in the DSM, and I think you should be, too."

"And who would see to my store?" Gnady poked a thumb toward the structure he had built with his own hands before stocking it with a modest supply of goods he knew everybody needed or wanted. After five years he was making a good living, and he owned the land on which his store sat.

"What about Tatania?"

"My wife would rather talk than sell goods, I would be destitute within a week."

Ambrose laughed. Gnady smiled with him until Tatania smacked the back of his head.

"I can run our store just as good as you can, maybe better—people don't walk away from my bargains feeling cheated!"

The very next week brought news of this great council along with more rumors of war. So he came to find out what would happen if there was a war, and what would happen afterward. If the Dená drove the Russians out of Alaska, would the deed to his property still be valid?

Who would make what sort of decrees? The Czar had always been comfortably remote even if his cossacks and *promyshlennik* tax collectors had not. But the system had been in place for over a century and a half, it was a known thing.

Which Dená would rule the new government? Some half-Eskimo from Russian Mission or Holy Cross, way down at the mouth of the Yukon? This required his personal attention.

In the end, he and four others from their area brought two dog sleds down the frozen Yukon to Minto. He learned that news of the impending council of war had gone out to the frozen reaches of the Dená Republik by dog sled, skier, and in two ironic instances, via Russian mail plane. Over the following week delegates and freedom fighters began arriving.

Gnady talked with many people and learned of the recent success at Toklat. Many he spoke with didn't seem concerned about the Russian Army. There were many others who thought the DSM were a band of brigands and outlaws who in no way represented the average Dená.

Three weeks after the fight at Toklat, the War Council convened.

"I will act as chairman until this assembly elects one," Chandalar Roy announced. "And that will be our first order of business, so be thinking about who you'd like to nominate. Every man and woman in this room who has reached the age of fifteen, as well as those standing outside, have a vote."

Gnady listened closely, watching for word traps or ambiguity.

"We'll vote on everything," Chandalar said, "including who gets to make the hard decisions about where and how we'll fight the Czar. I suggest we use the rules in this little book to run our meeting, they make sense for this many people."

He covered the main points in *Robert's Rules of Order* and then grinned as shuffling feet and whispered conversations in the room began to drown him out.

"Okay! Nominations are open."

Chandalar was unanimously elected First Speaker. Gnady voted for him because there wasn't anyone else in the room he trusted that much, even though he'd never met the man before this night.

"Each representative will speak for one thousand people. In some cases that will be two or three villages, in others probably up to ten," Chan told them.

"So every delegate needs a voter herd?" somebody asked. They all found that funny.

"Within your area—" Chandalar pointed to a map with villages outlined "—nominate two candidates, people you trust, people you know will do a good job for you as well as themselves. Then the people from the same area will secretly vote for one of the candidates. Whoever wins will be your delegate to the War Council."

Gnady joined the throng at the map. His area included Circle and Eagle as well as his own village, Old Crow.

"There are signs with the names of the villages on them all around the room," Chandalar shouted over the din. "Go to the sign that has your village's name on it. If you can't read, ask somebody who can, we're all in this together."

Gnady knew eleven of the twelve people under the "Circle—Eagle—Old Crow" sign. A long-haired, mustached man with somewhere between forty and thirty years, wearing well-made moose-hide clothing leaned against the wall under the sign. His face proclaimed him to be angry.

They all stood around looking at each other as the people in the room sorted themselves out. Their number stayed at thirteen.

"I'm Waterman Stoddard," the man in moose hide declared. "I want to be your delegate."

"Why?" Gnady asked, surprising himself.

"I've been to university, I know how to talk to politicians no matter where they're from."

"But how do you feel?" Gnady asked. "Why do you want this, because you can talk? Who can't?"

"Feel about what?" Clara Oldsquaw asked.

"About this new government, about the old government!" Gnady threw his hands up. "If you think it's worth fighting the Czar, and for what? What do want to have happen when this is over? We know people by what they believe. So what does he believe?"

"Gnady's right," Clarence Oldsquaw said in his slow way.

Gnady completely ignored Clarence, as was his custom. "And where do you live and how long have you lived there?" He stared at Waterman Stoddard. "I sure ain't never seen you before now."

"I've lived outside Eagle for about five years. I'm from down in the Confederacy, originally."

"The what?" Clara asked.

"The Confederate States of America. They're just south of the United States and east of the Republic of Texas."

"Never heard of none of 'em," Clarence said, staring at the floor in a thoughtful manner.

"I know where they're at," Gnady said. "You come a long ways, Mr. Waterman Stoddard. Why?"

"No room down there for someone with an itch to be their own person and not bend into what's expected of you. I'd do a good job for y'all, and that's a promise."

"How do you make your bread? What is your work?"

"I hunt, trap, and fish. Never been hungry nor naked, want for naught."

"There is a problem, however," Gnady said quietly.

"Problem? What problem?"

"I, Gnady Ustinov, wish to be delegate." Stoddard opened his mouth but Gnady hurried on. "I am a property owner from Old Crow, where I was born. I have four years of Father Petroska's school so I can read, write, and cypher. I own the only store in town and everyone knows I do not cheat them."

Heads nodded within their small circle. Shouts echoed through the spacious room from larger, more divided groups. Gnady hoped these people liked him, which was something he had never before considered.

"So why do you have a Russian name?" Stoddard asked.

"My father was Russian, my mother is Dená. Many of our people have Russian blood, and English, and French, and Eskimo, and Tlingit . . . even Yankee and Rebel blood. I was born in fish camp in the middle of the dog salmon run."

"Why do you want to be delegate?" Stoddard asked, continuing to work his mouth after he finished speaking.

"Who knows what these downriver people will demand of us? We need a delegate who can see things as they are, not what might be."

"But if you don't have a glimpse of the future, aren't you stuck in the past?" Stoddard's eyes seemed lit from within. "This is all about the future. That's what y'all have to realize. We have a chance here to make something none of us have ever seen: a representative government that listens to our needs." The hunter chewed his invisible cud for a few heartbeats. "We need a delegate with vision, not just fear."

"That is easy for you to say," Gnady snapped, more stung than he wished to admit. "You have nothing to lose, no family to consider. Be a radical on your own account."

Catherine Alexander spoke for the first time. "Enough. We are to pick two people out loud and vote for one in silence. The rest of us have heard you both." She glanced at the others. "I nominate both you."

"So now what?" Clara asked.

"Somebody has to second the nominations," Waterman said.

Incomprehension stared at him from all eyes.

"Somebody has to agree out loud with her."

Gnady wondered if Waterman's obvious knowledge about how this meeting worked would take votes away from him. He nudged Clarence.

"Sure! I agree with her," the old man said and lapsed back into silence.

"Okay." Waterman looked around. Picked up a piece of paper off the table. "You write down who you want to be delegate on a piece of paper and then put the paper in here." He tapped a birch bark basket next to the stack of paper and box of heavy Russian pencils.

"What if I can't write?" Clara asked.

"Not a problem," Gnady said instantly, again surprising himself. "Mr. Stoddard and I will make little pictures for you. If you want to vote for me, you make an x beside my little picture, if you wish to vote for him, you put your mark next to his."

"What kind of little picture?" Soloman Dundas asked.

"Well, Mr. Stoddard hunts and fishes for a living, so I'll draw this little fish picture for him." Gnady looked into Stoddard's eyes. "That work for you?"

"Sure. What you gonna use for yours?"

"How about a pipe, the kind you smoke?" he quickly drew a simple outline. "Like that."

"I like this way," Soloman said. "It ain't confusing or nothing."

"I'll make thirteen ballots and we can get on with it." Gnady sketched them out quickly. There was a part of him that had yearned to create art, but he didn't know where to begin, so he ignored the tiny voice.

"There, one for each of us." He picked up a square of paper and walked over to a windowsill where he could brace the paper so only he could see it. Carefully, he put an X in front of the pipe.

Three other ballots already lay in the basket when he dropped his on top. He rubbed his hands together and, feeling self-conscious, moved over and leaned against the wall. He hadn't been this nervous when he asked Tatania to marry him. But, he thought wryly, she had been pregnant at the time and he would have been amazed if she'd turned him down.

He wiped sweat from his forehead as he looked around. Nobody here was pregnant.

"Who's gonna count them up?" *Clara speaks louder than she needs to*, Gnady thought, wondering if her hearing was deteriorating.

Catherine Alexander said, "Let's you and me do it, Clara."

Waterman Stoddard wiped his large forehead and leaned against the wall next to Gnady. "If I win, I want you to help me do what I need to do," he said so only Gnady could hear. "If you win I'll do everything I can to help you."

Gnady held out his hand. "Done."

They shook.

Catherine looked up from the two small piles of paper. "Mr. Stoddard, I'm sorry, but you didn't win."

Gnady's spirit soared upward from the abrupt dip it made when she first called Stoddard's name. One glance at his opponent told him Stoddard had just made the same trip in reverse. They both glared at her.

"But you only lost by one vote." She fanned the ballots out on the small table. "Everybody can see for themselves."

Gnady surveyed the room. Other winners and losers were being declared. Some of the winners looked more dejected than did the losers.

"Congratulations, Mr. Delegate," Waterman shook his hand. "I meant what I said. If I can help."

"Between us," Gnady said, "we know a great deal. I would that you help me watch them"—he nodded toward the noisy room—"to make sure our people are not meanly used."

"Sounds like a good idea to me." Waterman moved off through the crowd.

A bell rang and the room went silent.

"Would the delegates please come up here by me?" Chandalar called out.

Gnady felt many eyes on him and wondered if the other delegates felt as embarrassed as he did.

He found himself in the middle of the line. It felt as though a thousand people crowded the room, staring at them.

"This can stop anytime soon," a woman next to him muttered.

"From my right, over here, please introduce yourselves to the People." Chandalar made it sound like an order.

"I'm Blue Bostonman," the large woman said. "From Aniak." Gnady could see that she would be a difficult customer if she felt the goods were shoddy.

"Fredrik Seetamoona, from Elim."

"Ain't that an Eskimo name?" someone shouted from the crowd.

"My dad was Yu'pik, but my mom was Dená. How many of you are Dená and nothing else?"

Gnady liked Fredrik's sand.

"I'm Paul Eluska, from Kokrines, and my granny was Eskimo from up at Anaktuvuk Pass." He nodded at Fredrik. "Hell, me 'n' him are probably cousins."

The crowd laughed and the tension in the room, which Gnady hadn't realized existed, broke.

"Eleanor Wright from Nulato." She tossed her head and the long, black-shot-with-silver hair fanned briefly behind her stocky body. Her eyes defied one and all to cross her.

"My name is Claude Adams," the small, slightly built man said. As he looked around at the crowd, light flashed off his spectacles. He spoke in a soft voice and Gnady knew this one was smarter than himself. "I am from Holy Cross and am part Russian, Eskimo, Aleut, Yankee, and Dená. I don't how much of which, but it doesn't matter because I am here tonight."

Applause seemed to burst from the air.

The bell rang again.

"We have much to do," Chandalar said. "Next."

"I am Nicole Grey from Tanana. I will do the best I can."

Gnady had seen her before, but not in Tanana. He couldn't remember where it was, but he remembered she had the situation well in hand. It gnawed at him. Then he realized he stood next to her and all were waiting for him to speak.

"I am Gnady Ustinov from Old Crow. My grandfather was a *promyshlennik* who built an *odinochka* and settled down. The rest of my family is Dená and I was named for my grandfather. I own a trading post in Old Crow."

He stopped and allowed himself to breathe, waiting for someone to object to his presence. The crowd now stared at the man next to him. He smiled; everybody on the Yukon knew Andrew.

"I am Andrew Isaac of the Dot Lake Dená. My male ancestors probably slipped into a lot of strange beds, but I'm all Athabascan as far as I know."

The laughter and applause died quickly.

"Anna Samuel from Fort Yukon." She possessed extraordinary beauty and yet had to be in her middle-to-late years. She exuded self-possession.

"I am Alexandr Titus from Minto. We got Russian blood in the family, and pretty near every other kind, too. I got cousins in every village in Dená country. I'm proud to be here."

"Joanne Kaiser, I have a small lodge in St. Anthony. I always give full value and I've never let anyone go away hungry. My mother was from the Republic of California and my dad was a Russian-Dená soldier. But I'm here to help."

"Kurt Bachmann, from Klahotsa." The large man glowered at them all, made sure nobody else was speaking before he again opened his mouth. "I'm here to protect what is mine, what I have earned. I suspect what we just did is illegal, even treasonous, and I'm going to make sure everything follows the letter of the Czar's law."

"Mr. Bachmann"—Chan's voice sounded cold enough to shatter—"this is a revolution. We no longer wish to follow the Czar's laws and the purpose of this body is to successfully throw off the Russian yoke. Do you understand that?"

"So who's gonna run things, make the rules, enforce what laws?"

"We're working on it. But there is no way we can allow anyone loyal to the Czar to remain in this room. You either swear to serve the Dená People above all others, to fight their enemies, and defend their borders, or you leave now."

"I'm not a Dená, but I live here, I own a business, I serve as leader in my village. What you just asked me to swear allegiance to is everything I believe in, but why are we fighting the Czar?"

"You're in the fight, Mr. Bachmann, either on our side or the Czar's. Which is it?"

"I'm with you, of course, you've got me surrounded." He laughed and looked around at the others. Nobody laughed with him.

"Would the next delegate please introduce himself?"

"Joshua Golovin," the big man said, looking over at Bachmann. "Chena Redoubt, where the Russians treat you like moose shit. I need help to show them the error of their ways."

"I am Wing Demoski, from Beaver, I used to teach school with my husband until cossacks killed him and thought they killed me. Soon after, I joined the DSM and killed all three of the animals who took my old life. I have been killing the Czar's cossacks and *promyshlenniks* ever since. I believe in the Dená Republik!"

Everyone in the room applauded.

Gnady felt a thrill of pure pleasure when the last delegate spoke.

"I am Ambrose Ambrose from the village of Nabesna, on the Nabesna River. We're all related to everyone in Northway, just across the river."

"I thank everyone for their participation," Chandalar said in a loud voice, "and now ask all but the delegates to leave the building. We have much to do."

"We can't watch?" an old man asked in a querulous tone.

"I'm sorry." Chandalar's voice seemed made of stone. "But since we don't know everyone, we can't let anyone not on the council or their immediate advisors sit in and listen. We will make reports at the end of each day. Thank you all for understanding."

Gnady waved Waterman Stoddard over. "You're my advisor, okay?"

"Thanks. But let's call me chief of advisors, that way we can get more people in here."

Chandalar's voice boomed out, "Delegates, introduce your advisors if they exist."

Questions raised about the definition of "advisor" were quickly answered. During the quick debate more than one person yawned.

"We have a growing army," Chandalar said. "We need a general to run it. If there is anyone you know who can do a better job than Slayer-of-Men, I want to hear about it right now."

Slayer-of-Men was known the length and breadth of the Yukon and Kuskokwim Rivers. He had visited every village, every *odinochka*, every squalid "Indian town" clustered at the edge of the redoubts. Wherever he went, he insulted those who looked at the world differently, and recruited every malcontent he met.

His brother, Malagni, even more fearsome and far less diplomatic, always accompanied him. When they visited Old Crow, the thought had crossed Gnady's mind that these two didn't need anyone else, they *were* an army. Gnady couldn't offer an alternative.

It seemed no one could.

"Therefore we declare Slayer-of-Men the General of the Dená Army," Chandalar said in his best hard voice. "All in favor, say 'aye.'"

Gnady truly thought every person in the room said, "Aye."

"All opposed, say 'Nay.'"

"Nay," said Stoddard and Bachmann.

Chandalar glared at Stoddard. "Only delegates may vote!"

"Oh, sorry."

Nathan Roubitaux was elected Minister for War. Then the real work began.

"You there in the second row, do you have a question?" First Speaker Chandalar asked.

Gnady took a deep breath, glanced once at Bachmann, then said, "Yes, I have questions. If we win this war, what then? Who will take the place of the Czar for us? What kind of government are we going to have in a Dená Republic?"

Chandalar looked blank for far too long before answering.

"Those are very good questions, Gnady. Well, once the war is won we will convene a committee to write a constitution. Every village in the Dená Republic will select and send a delegate and those delegates will comprise that committee."

"What's to keep us, the council, I mean, from just taking over and running things from here on out?"

"Our word that we won't." Chan let his gaze move over everyone in the room. "Our People put us around this table for a reason. We're fighting a war against the Czar for our independence. When we have won that war, and we will, this council will disband and go home."

Nicole Grey stood up. "So who's going to make all the arrangements for this constitution meeting? Where's it going to be?"

"What we have now is called a provisional government," Chandalar said. "That government will run the Dená Republic until a new government is formed. I will remain as First Speaker until a new one is elected under the provisions of our new constitution."

Nathan stood and waited for the room to quiet. "What we have here is something between an experiment and destiny. There are no rules yet, we have to make them together."

The first War Council convened. Only the council members and key officials were allowed inside the room.

Grisha sat behind Wing—he had accepted her invitation to be her advisor. The fourteen men and women around the long table chatted for a half hour in an effort to get to know each other better.

Finally they debated what action to take first.

"We have to neutralize their air force or we're done before we start," Minto's Alexandr Titus said.

"They got a lot of planes over here, too," another added.

"For those of you who don't know," Nathan said, "we have generous allies who have already provided us military aid. Without their Kalashnikovs the fight at Toklat could have ended very differently. We have also received three antiaircraft batteries. What we need to do is ambush their air force."

"What do our 'generous allies' expect in return for their military aid?" Eleanor Wright, the Nulato delegate asked.

"There has been nothing asked in return to my knowledge," Nathan said; his voice level had risen and all registered his discomfort.

"Eleanor raises a good point," Andrew Isaac, the Dot Lake chief said. "Why would they risk the Czar's wrath for nothing?"

"Perhaps they have other differences with the Czar," Nathan said. His voice had leveled out and he sounded almost disinterested.

Claude Adams raised his hand. Nathan nodded.

"If we rely on assistance from the Lower Nine, we are merely changing masters. This has to be a predominantly Dená operation or we are doomed to another century of servitude."

"But if we throw off the yoke of the Czar," Ambrose Ambrose said, "what is to be expected in return? Can we back a military operation where the army we field takes over our lives and rules by force?"

"Your fantasies are entertaining, but have nothing to do with reality," Nathan said with heat. "For what purpose would you suggest that our army might subjugate us all?"

"For the most ancient of reasons, Mr. Speaker: power," Claude said, fervor in his voice. "Once power is won there are few men big enough or honorable enough to surrender the scepter. This is not a concept to be ignored."

"Nor is it a concept we should waste time with now," Joanne Kaiser, the lithe delegate from St. Anthony said. "We can decide later how we will rule ourselves, first we have to have something to rule!"

Fredrik Seetamoona rose to his feet and waited for a chance to speak.

"Every speaker here has brought up subjects that must be dealt with before we can become a nation. But the lovely lady is correct in her inference that we have nothing yet to rule. I live but a few *versts*, sorry, kilometers, from Bridge.

"I know how massive the garrison is in that place, I know we must mount an overwhelming assault in order to hold Bridge in order to deny more Russian armor from passing into the land of the Dená, the land of my mother. Therefore I implore you to first fight this war and then argue about politics. We have no time to waste." He sat down.

The room remained silent for nearly a full minute.

Nicole Grey, the Tanana delegate, spoke first. "First things first. What we going to use as bait for this attack on their air force?"

"How about their own radio?" Grisha suggested.

"Excellent idea," Nathan said from the head of the table.

"But where?" Alexandr Titus asked.

"I've asked our military people that very question," Nathan said. "Will you hear their answer?"

Every delegate nodded.

"Slayer-of-Men, would you share what the military has decided?"

The tall warrior stood. "I am honored. There is only one place that is midway between the aerodromes at Teslin Redoubt and Fort Yukon." He walked over to the wall map of Russian Amerika and tapped it. "Right here. Of course it helps that we have those three antiaircraft batteries dug in around the target area."

A few delegates laughed; most were thoughtful.

"That's our recommendation."

"Does the council agree?" Nathan asked.

It did.

Nathan rubbed his hands together. "Now we have to choose which Russian redoubts in the Dená Republik we will attack and in what order."

"Hit them one at a time?" Ambrose Ambrose asked sharply.

"Yes, but all over the Republik. Say first we hit Chena and then two days later we hit St. Anthony. If we can keep them off balance for a week or two, we might even achieve diplomatic recognition from other countries.

"There are silent allies in many North American governments who would advocate for us as soon as we make our cause more than small guerilla actions. But we will have to hold what we take to make us viable in their eyes. The most important thing is that nobody in this room says anything to anybody outside this room about what is said here. People like to talk and we can't let that happen."

Grisha spotted Haimish McCloud on the other side of the gallery. The small man wore a sardonic smile.

"Do we have enough people to hit all the redoubts at once?" Tanana's Nicole Grey asked.

"We'd have the element of surprise but hitting everywhere at once would spread our forces far too thin, especially since we have to consolidate our victories. Our army is not large." Nathan stared around the table.

"We have to use deception and fight with everything we have, otherwise we'll fail and the Czar will see all of us dead. We are fighting for our lives. If we lose this war, the Russians will kill every one of us. The lucky ones will die fast."

"Okay," Alexandr Titus said firmly, "how do we go about this?"

"First we identify the targets, and then we decide how to reduce them to rubble."

"Please explain to me that air force ambush," Gnady said.

Nathan moved to the large map on the wall. "If we put the transmitter here . . ." He tapped the paper where Slayer-of-Men had indicated. ". . . with our three antiaircraft guns ringing the target—" He drew a circle on the map. "—and put a few dozen Kalashnikovs here, here and here . . ."

"You think they're gonna send all their planes?" Joshua Golovin from Chena asked.

"What if this don't work?" Ambrose Ambrose asked.

Two more hours of debate changed nothing. After the assembly officially ended, most stayed in the room, talking about points on which they differed.

Grisha moved out into the night and stared up at the *aurora borealis*. Someone moved beside him and he glanced over to see Wing. She looked up at the northern lights.

"My granny used to say they could come down and cut your head off if you made too much noise when they were out."

"Did you believe her?" Grisha asked, glancing up uneasily.

"No. But I knew she believed it, so I didn't argue."

Grisha felt a rush of desire for her. The memory of her quick kiss weeks ago burned in his mind. He kept his gaze fixed on the glowing ions above, wondering what to do.

She moved closer to him.

"I think I should go back in," he said softly.

"Why?"

"Because if I don't, I'm going to grab you and kiss you." He looked at her then and her large brown eyes seemed to envelop him.

"That's exactly what I want you to do. But that's *all* you can do."

"Okay," he said, pulling her close.

Singly, in pairs, and small groups, the delegates left for their villages or joined the companies of volunteers raised by every village along the Yukon, Kuskokwim, Melosi, Black, Koyukuk, Porcupine, Stewart, and Tanana Rivers. Momentum for independence from the Czar built slowly but never faltered.

27

Tetlin Redoubt, January 1988

"Major Kominskiya, we're getting that carrier wave again."

Valari slapped down papers that eluded comprehension and smiled at the corporal in the doorway.

"Are you able to determine its location?" she said, elation in her voice.

"We radioed St. Nicholas and Chena Redoubt for a triangulation fix. We should have something within a half hour."

"Excellent!" She shot to her feet. "I'll be in the general's office. As soon as you have the location, inform me."

"Yes, Major." He saluted and vanished down the hallway.

She studied her appearance in the full-length mirror behind her office door. The uniform accentuated her slimness and the sharp creases mirrored the planes in her face. Deciding she looked competent and powerful, she marched smartly down the tiled corridor to her commanding officer's anteroom.

The tall, blond, rugged cossack sergeant fastened his blue eyes on her face when she entered the room. He stood and saluted.

"Good afternoon, Major Kominskiya." After she returned the salute he sat down. "How may I serve you?"

The code amused her. More than one quiet afternoon had been passed in each other's arms. She smiled and shook her head slightly. "I need to see General Posivich, now."

"Ah, I see." The sergeant stood again. "If you'll have a seat, I'll see what I can do." He stepped through the door behind his desk and closed it after him.

Valari Kominskiya sat and speculated on the signal's reappearance. After the costly attack on Toklat seven weeks ago, the carrier wave had stopped. She and others thought perhaps Lieutenant Rezanov had finally been killed in the attack even though no bodies were found when the Troika Guard investigated the site.

A squad had been dispatched to bring in his body when they thought him killed the first time near the Toklat. But they found nothing and she knew they had been victims of a charade. The memory of their last meeting still smarted; Grisha would pay for that one if it was the last thing he did.

Perhaps the redio had been tripped accidentally? she wondered. And was Rezanov still part of the DSM or merely going native and running a trap line or something equally droll? Or was it another deception?

"Major?"

She jerked in surprise and stared at the sergeant. "Yes?"

"The general will see you now. He has very little time."

She hurried through the door and knocked on the polished wood at the end of the small hallway.

"Come."

She entered, stood at attention and saluted. "Thank you for your time, General."

"Have a seat, Major." The commander of Tetlin Redoubt waved grandly and Valari settled into a padded chair. "What is it that has brought such color to your lovely face?"

"The radio has resumed transmitting a carrier wave. We are triangulating its exact position as I speak."

Posivich frowned in concentration for a moment. "Is this the same signal that brought our aircraft to Toklat?"

"Yes, sir. I suspect our turncoat lieutenant has accidentally switched it on."

His steady gaze unnerved her. Reading his eyes proved impossible.

"Perhaps the lieutenant and your sea captain have prepared another trap for our forces? No?"

She opened her mouth to disagree before realizing she had not thought it all out. "I, I don't know."

"It is something we should give careful consideration, Major Kominskiya. What action did you have in mind?"

"Ah, well, I was going to ask your opinion before promulgating any plans, General Posivich."

His grin glinted like steel. "You are very quick, Major, I like that in an officer. I will make no judgments. So, what was your first reaction when you received word of the signal's resumption?"

She smiled ruefully. "I wished to make an immediate attack with our wing of Yaks. Frankly, I feel that it is beyond the talents of the rebels to successfully carry off an operation that could withstand the strength of an entire squadron."

"The idea is far-fetched, I agree," the general said amiably. "But so was the notion that they could shoot down helicopter gunships with hunting rifles."

"True," she said in a low voice.

A discreet knock sounded at the door and the sergeant pushed through. "Excuse me, General, but the major wished this information as soon as we received it." He handed a sheet of paper to Valari.

"Thank you, Sergeant," they said in unison.

She stared at the paper.

"So where is the signal located?"

She looked up at him with a frown. "About sixty kilometers north of Chena Redoubt, at Chatanika Crossing, very close to the road."

"Perhaps they expect us to send in ground forces, since the signal is so close to the road," the general said.

"They wouldn't be expecting a flight of fighters to hit them and their puny trap," Valari said.

"I hope for the pilots' sake it is not an ambush." The general's voice had turned as steely as his grin. "But I have a hidden pawn; those savages won't know what hit them!"

28

Tetlin Imperial Aerodrome

Twelve Yaks roared into the air, following their flight leader and his wing man. Major Valari Kominskiya watched them buzz toward Chatanika Crossing until they blended into the sky. She hurried back into the radio room where General Posivich sat on a reversed chair, his chin resting on crossed arms.

"Have a seat, Major." He nodded toward a metal folding chair. She sat.

The speaker crackled and all eyes in the room focused on it. "This is Talon One, do you read me, Tetlin?"

"Yes, *podpolkovnik*. We read you clear and loud," said the corporal with the headset.

"Acknowledged. Talon Four, take your group and reconnoiter the target zone."

"Yes, sir. Talon Four, out."

Valari let her eyes slide over to the general. He sat with his face buried in his arms. A small sliver of anxiety worked its way into her composure.

"Talon One, this is Talon Four. We see only a cabin in a clearing. Over."

"Are there signs of habitation, Talon Four?"

"Yes, *podpolkovnik*. Smoke is coming out of the chimney."

"Tetlin, this is Talon One, did you copy our transmission?"

"Tetlin copies, Talon One," the corporal said. "Over."

"What are your orders?"

Valari glanced over at the general. He stared back at her. The corporal carefully looked to the lieutenant in charge of the radio room.

"Lieutenant?"

The lieutenant merely stared at the general.

"Your orders, General?" he said, standing at attention.

"Tell them to destroy the cabin," Posivich said. "I want to be through with this transmitting turncoat once and for all." He lowered his face back into his folded arms.

The corporal relayed the order.

"Talon Four, your people go first, Talon Eight goes next, then Georgi and me," the wing commander said. "Talon Six, you hold over the Tanana."

Terse acknowledgements crackled.

Valari felt her pulse quicken. Everyone else in the radio room seemed to be asleep. She felt like screaming.

"Direct hit, Talon Five. Good shooting." The voice sounded laconic, disinterested.

"Antiaircraft fire!" a voice blurted.

"Identify yours—"

"It's coming up from all sides!" a different, youthful voice shouted, breaking on the last word.

"Gain altitude! Get above it."

"They're bracketing us on all sides!"

"Andronivich just crashed, Talon One."

"This is Talon Three, I've spotted one of the gun positions. I'm going in after it."

"Where is it, Talon Three?"

Crackling dead air filled the room. Valari felt sweat running down her temples and wiped at it as unobtrusively as possible.

"Talon Three! Talon Three! Pull up, pull up—"

"Jesus, he crashed into the gun," a youthful voice said with evident awe.

"Tetlin, this is Talon One. We have lost two aircraft and the rest have sustained damage. We have destroyed one antiaircraft emplacement but are unable to locate others due to the amount of flak and smoke in the area."

"Tell them to return to base," General Posivich said wearily.

"Return to base," the corporal said into the microphone.

"Sergei's on fire," someone said in a tight voice. "He's going down."

"There's his chute, at least he made it out alive," another pilot said.

"This is Talon One, return to base. I repeat: return to base."

"Yes, *podpolkovnik*." The voice sounded relieved.

Valari felt nauseous and bewildered. Where had they obtained antiaircraft guns? Rezanov, with Grisha and his damned Indians, had suckered her and the Imperial Russian Air Force. The Dená were amassing quite the butcher's bill, and she could hardly wait for the day it came due.

"Major," the general said heavily, "your bright ideas have cost us a wealth of aircraft. Unless your 'special operation' bears successful fruit very soon, you're going to find yourself in the field like a common trooper."

"Send in the Troika Guard," she said quickly, hoping he would agree.

"Send them into a trap?" Posivich radiated hostility. "If the damned Indians can blow fighters out of the air they can no doubt handle a few ground troops."

"The Troika Guard is an elite fighting force." Valari's words stumbled over themselves in her rush to get them out. "They know how to infiltrate and decimate a hostile force. They did it three years ago in Afghanistan."

"Afghanistan doesn't have boreal forests in which to hide rebels."

"The other choice is to let them get away with destroying our aircraft," Valari said in a low voice.

"My first act of retribution is almost over the traitors," Posivich said, eyes gleaming.

"General?" Valari said.

"Switch to Combat IV," the general ordered.

The radioman complied.

". . . over the Yukon–Tanana junction." The voice sounded muffled, the speaker was talking in a small space. "Target dead ahead. We see smoke rising from where the fighters attacked."

"More fighters?" Valari asked.

"Bombers!" General Posivich said with a sinister chuckle.

"Bombs away!" the muffled voice said.

"The Indians aren't the only ones who can plan an ambush, major," he said, smiling widely.

✧   ✧   ✧

Glancing over at the burning pyre that had once been a Yak fighter and an antiaircraft gun, Lieutenant Sergei Muraviev stood calmly with his parachute bunched in his arms as the four men approached him with leveled rifles.

"Do you speak the English?" a sergeant asked.

"Somewhat better than you do," Sergei said with smile.

The sergeant scowled, made a prodding motion with his rifle. "Raise your hands!"

Sergei sighed and dropped the chute. The constant light breeze caught it and it started to billow.

"Gawd dammit!" the sergeant snapped at one of the privates with him. "Secure that damned parachute!"

"You should have let the lieutenant hold it, they're difficult to use as a weapon."

Sergei realized his captors were from two different armies.

The fourth man was totally at ease, while the men in matching uniforms seemed agitated.

"You do it your way, *Lieutenant*"—the sergeant actually lifted his lip in a slight sneer—"and I'll do it mine."

"I imagine the artillery does things differently than the infantry," the Dená said.

Sergei had never seen an Native with this degree of self confidence before. He stared at the sergeant's uniform.

"To what army do you belong?"

The sergeant stuck his chest out and smirked. "The Army of the United States of America, that's who."

Sergei looked at the Dená. "This means continent-wide war!"

The Dená nodded and started to speak.

A growing roar suddenly washed over the meadow. The Dená stared up with a gasp.

"Bombers! Get into the tree line and take cover!" Without waiting for anyone to agree, he sprinted for the closest clump of trees about sixty meters away.

Sergei started to follow him but the sergeant snapped, "Hold yer water there, Russki. We're going this way." He nodded back over his shoulder toward a gun emplacement already filling the sky with shells.

"Sarge, I think we should follow the lieutenant!" one of the privates said, his voice shaking.

The increasing artillery made conversation difficult.

"Do what I say!" the sergeant bellowed.

The shriek of falling bombs cut through the din.

Sergei ran as fast as he could but the explosions caught him, and he heard his deceased mother call out, "Over here, darling," and it was easy to go that way.

29

Outside Chena Redoubt, January 1988

"Well, do I look like a *promyshlennik*?" Grisha asked.

"Actually your hair needs to be more ragged," Wing said, squinting her eyes at him.

"He'd certainly pass in St. Nicholas," Nik said.

"Chena is only one berry compared to that bush," she said. "He looks too clean."

"Wait a minute," Grisha said. "I've seen *promyshlenniks* in much nicer clothes than these."

"Where, in Akku?"

"And Fort Dionysus," he said with a sniff.

"Chena is not part of that world," Wing said flatly. "The men that frequent Chena Redoubt are lower than the animals they hunt. They have no time for niceties. They would blow their noses on silk and spit on a hardwood floor."

"So make me look the part," Grisha said with an exaggerated sigh.

She rubbed grease in his hair and cut at it with scissors. Cora ambled up and watched silently. Nik moved to her side and they discreetly touched hips.

Chan walked over.

"I think he looks repulsive enough. Now we have to get his partner ready."

"Who's going with me?"

"Your *guide* will be Cora," Chan said, watching his face.

Grisha frowned and opened his mouth to speak.

"I will look and play the part of your woman," Cora said quickly and firmly. "You will be in charge as far as observers are concerned. The two of us will agree on our own actions."

"There could be fighting—"

Cora laughed. "Grisha, I helped rescue you. I've been a soldier for three years and you've been a lazy sailor for eight. If you want to know the truth, I'm a little worried about how you will stand up to this."

He throttled back his first impulse and thought about her words. Silence grew in the room. The rancid scent of old bear grease hung heavy in the air.

"That was stupid of me," Grisha said. He squinted up at Cora. "I'm sorry. To be frank, I'm worried about how I'll do. I know I'm a good field officer, but I've never done anything like this before. I'm glad you're going to be there."

"If you didn't have reservations," Chan said quietly, "I'd pull you off the mission. If they take you alive and discover your purpose, we'll have to change all our plans and lives will be lost for nothing. You must be completely alert at all times.

"There is another way into Chena Redoubt, but it is a door which would have to be breached. This plan will save more of our lives than would a direct initial assault.

"The Russians think they defeated us with their bombers. Our people did not die in vain. So set the hook and then get out quickly. Operation Defiant has started and time is precious."

Grisha nodded and glanced back to Cora. "You look far too fine to be with someone like this." He jabbed his chest with a thumb. "You'd better let them work on you."

"I've got an outfit, but my face needs work," Cora said, sitting down on the stool.

Grisha stepped back next to Wing and watched. He savored the kisses they had shared and looked forward to more. They both held a reluctance to move into anything more intimate. Each needed more time.

Tomorrow he and Cora had to walk into the twin beaks of the imperial eagle to set bait for an ambush. The comprehension of their audacity made Grisha feel like a mouse. He'd have to be a fast and smooth-talking mouse if he wanted to live. To succeed, Grisha must pass as a *Creole promyshlennik.*

Every Russian he encountered would look down on him. Their contempt might help him avoid suspicion, perhaps they would think him too cowed by their numbers and social standing to be dangerous.

Suddenly the small group around Cora stepped back to admire their work.

"What do you think?" Wing asked.

Cora's transformation to frightened, wild-eyed village woman went beyond convincing. For a moment he didn't even want to pretend that he was responsible for the pain and abuse evident in that furtive face. He suddenly smiled.

"You're good at this! Now if I can just remember to act as if I'm the bastard who makes you cringe like that, we might get through this."

"You can do it," Cora said firmly. "Now let's get our final briefing from Chan."

Chan said, "Good news, we've got the Troika Guard surrounded."

Grisha stopped and stared at the man. "You *are* giving them the chance to surrender and change their lives, aren't you? Most of them aren't even Russian citizens."

"Grisha," Chan spoke as if to a child, "of course we're giving them that chance. So far they haven't accepted. Just do your part and we'll do ours."

"Do you want me to talk to them?"

"Not to worry, we're telling them about you."

30

Chena Redoubt

The seven-meter walls of Chena Redoubt sprouted like malignant mushrooms from the buildings clustered close near their base. The RustyCan ran through the middle of town and past the front gate of the compound. As in every other town on the highway, the road boasted a convict-constructed stone surface.

Army lorries outnumbered civilian vehicles by a wide margin. Most people walked or rode the omnibus. The stench of diesel shrouded the town and trailed off into the surrounding forest.

Based on Tetlin Redoubt, Grisha's low expectations experienced a shock. The town of Chena stretched for five kilometers between the highway and the Tanana River, then widened to a kilometer on each side of the road near the middle of the strip. Neither Tetlin or any of the towns in Southeast Alaska came close to this size.

Conveniences such as electricity, sewer, and running water existed in even the poorest dwelling. Two nonparochial schools indicated the wealth of the local bourgeoisie. Education outside Russian Orthodox schools remained costly.

The priests had taught Grisha to read and write Russian. He had easily picked up street English, the *lingua franca* of the Pacific coast. Here, things seemed much more conservative and old-time Russian.

Every person moving about on the streets could pass for a character out of a Pushkin novel. New clothing styles had not gained a foothold here, nor anything else new.

This peculiar provincialism supposedly held an attraction for many people in the southern American countries. They called this the "Last Frontier."

Some people would buy anything, Grisha mused. Cora kept them moving at a steady gait past shops of all descriptions toward the forbidding hulk of the redoubt gate. Wing's assessment of the population held more skew than she realized.

Grisha blended with the lowest elements of humanity in Chena. His shabby appearance also created a barrier that many of the residents didn't care to breach. Few gave them a second glance.

Not that he minded their studied indifference. Quite the contrary. A half-track crunched past them and the soldiers manning its heavy machine gun shouted at Cora, offering her money for explicit sexual acts.

She scurried up next to Grisha, placing him between her and them. The soldiers laughed as they passed.

She gazed up at him and murmured, "Some of these soldiers won't get the same opportunity you did."

He nodded, trying his best to look dangerous and important.

They hurried up to the gate.

"I need to see the duty officer," Grisha said to one of the two guards.

The man rested his hand on the butt of his holstered pistol and looked them over contemptuously.

"What would a *Creole* want to tell an officer?" His rancid breath advertised ruined teeth.

"About Dená killing Russian soldiers and cossacks."

Instantly both men leveled their weapons at them.

"Don't move!" the more distant guard said with a bark. "Go get the lieutenant, Pitr."

The guard in front of the them turned and hurried through the gate.

"It's not *us* doing the killing!" Grisha said nervously.

"Quiet! Tell it to the officer."

Two armed men hurried out and took up position behind them. Cora stared at the ground, hands clenched together. Grisha did his best to appear as if he owned the world.

A youth of no more than twenty summers, wearing a rough gray uniform and glossy high black boots, strode through the gate gripping a machine pistol in his hand. He stopped directly in front of them and put the muzzle against the bridge of Grisha's nose.

"Who are you planning to kill?"

Grisha realized this was the lieutenant. "Nobody," he said carefully. "As I tried to tell these, ah, soldiers. I have knowledge about an ambush and I thought it might be worth something to you."

The lieutenant's lip curled. "Who would dare attack us here? Look around you. You can't even slide through the gate using your woman for grease."

Grisha stared at him with loathing. "I came to save lives, mine included. Maybe it's best that I don't bother you at this time." Grisha pulled back slightly. "After all, my woman and I are safe—it's the Troika Guard who are surrounded."

Grisha felt sick that his old unit was being used in this mess. But he agreed with Nathan and Chan that this would produce intense interest on the part of the Russians.

"Troika—" blurted one of the newer guards.

"Silence!" the lieutenant snapped. "Bring them." He hurried back through the gate.

With the wave of a gun barrel, the guards ushered them into the compound. Grisha tried to see everything he could without moving his head. Cora stared around wildly, rubbing her hands together in agitation.

The lieutenant sped across the courtyard, all but running. Grisha didn't try to keep up.

"Move your feet!" a guard snarled.

They trotted after the officer who disappeared into a two-story concrete building. Guards flanked the metal door. Bars latticed the windows.

Once past the alert sentries, they entered an immaculate hallway where their footsteps echoed off stone walls. The sour scent of urine fought the heavy chemical reek of government cleanser for domination of Grisha's nose. He also detected fear, and not just his own.

"In here," the lieutenant's voice echoed out at them. He stood in a small room furnished with four chairs and a heavily scarred wood table, all illuminated by a single bright light dangling from the dark, invisible ceiling. Despite the stone walls, the building's chill stayed in the hallway; the room felt quite warm.

The guards halted at the door. As Grisha and Cora stepped in front of the table the iron door slammed shut and latched behind them. Across the table sat a man in a soft gray uniform with the red tabs of a colonel on his collar.

Grisha tried not to stare, but he had never before seen a man so totally devoid of hair. The single light shone off his bald head as if reflected by a mirror. How the uniform remained spotless in such a filthy world was beyond him.

"Where did you hear the term 'Troika Guard'?" the man asked softly.

"At my *odinochka* between here and the Yukon," Grisha said.

"So you have a fortified outpost." The man's pale gray eyes glinted beneath wispy, light-colored lashes. "What manner Native are you?"

"I am a *Creole*," Grisha said, putting injury into his voice while straightening his posture. "My father was a Russian *promyshlennik*, as am I, and my mother was a Dená."

"That rabble!" the lieutenant said, slapping his leather holster.

"Shut up, Dimitri," the man said in his soft voice.

The lieutenant snapped to nervous attention.

"Where did you hear the term 'Troika Guard'?" the man repeated.

"May two good citizens sit in your presence?" Grisha tried to be unctuous.

"Yes. Now tell me."

They sat and Grisha leaned on the table to cover his shaking knees.

"A cousin of my woman came in the night and told me this thing. He had been shot. Before he died he said a lot of cossacks who called themselves Troika Guards had been surrounded by an army of Dená separatists, and were fighting for their lives. That when they finished wiping out the Russians, they would come after him and me."

"Why would they do that?"

"He was a *kaiur*, he worked for the cossacks. Some Dená who know him saw him escape. They know me, too. They say I ask too much for my goods. It isn't easy being a good subject to the Czar out there."

"Where is this supposed massacre taking place?"

"Near Yankovich Creek, where it meets the Nenana."

"Why haven't they radioed for help?"

"I should know?" Grisha shrugged. "If they have radio, why don't you call them?"

A thin wrinkle broke the shine on his scalp.

"We tried. Can you show me on a map where they are?"

"Yes, pretty close, I think."

The pale man pushed something on the table and a large map attached to a sheet of wood hummed from the darkness above them, bumping gently down the stone wall.

"Where?"

Grisha stood and peered hard at the lines and words. He tapped the surface.

"Somewhere in this area. My *odinochka* is right here. We could hear shooting to the west."

"You're lying of course," the man whispered and smiled.

Grisha's stomach knotted and his sphincter clenched.

"Why should I lie? Would I be here if this is a lie?"

"You are here because you are frightened. You don't care about Imperial soldiers. You want us to protect your smelly store."

"I would like that, to have my store be safe. But they are dying out there."

"Then we shall have to rescue them," the gray man said. "And you will guide us."

"I am not a warrior. I am a merchant, a trapper, a hunter."

"And now you're a guide. Your woman will be kept here just in case you had some alternate plan."

"But, she needs to be with me." Grisha didn't need to strain to put real pleading into his words. "She needs to be safe."

"Sasha?" Cora said sharply, fear emanating from her. Grisha wondered how much of it was acting.

"They say you must stay," he said in her language. Learning the Tanana dialect of Athabascan had been the most difficult part of his training. "I will come back for you."

Grisha turned to the bald man. "If she is harmed, I will kill you," he said flatly.

"That would be fair," the man said. "But it won't be necessary. She'll be quite safe."

The man lifted a steel helmet off the floor behind the table and strapped it carefully on his head. It bore the Imperial Army gold twin-headed eagle holding a sword in one talon and a wreath in the other, as well as the three stars of a colonel. "Dimitri, sound the alarm."

The lieutenant rushed out the door. Moments later an amplified bugle blared and even through the stone walls Grisha could hear running feet.

"Shall we go?" The colonel swept his hand toward the door.

31

800 Meters Over the Tanana River

The helicopter beat northward. That the Russians brought him with them gave him no surprise, but he hadn't anticipated flying. He nervously remembered the gunfire knocking down helicopters during the attack on Toklat.

"You're worried," the colonel said.

Grisha glanced at the man sitting next to him and nodded.

"I would rather be walking."

"We'll join the ground forces as soon as we ascertain there is indeed a battle under way. I don't want to send my motorized battalion into an ambush, do I?"

"No. Of course not," Grisha said, rubbing sweaty hands on his trouser legs.

"I thought all *promyshlenniks* relished a good fight, what's wrong with you?"

"How can I fight from this?" Grisha thumped the metal wall with his knuckles. "I do my fighting on my feet." He slid the razor-edged knife from his sleeve. "With this."

The colonel's eyes narrowed as he studied him.

"What did you say your name was?"

"Sasha. Sasha Dublinnik, free trader and expert hunter. What's yours?"

The colonel gave him a frosty grin and looked away to study the ground beneath them. Grisha did the same. Anxiety swirled through him.

He wasn't sure what they would encounter once they reached the battle site. A lot of people besides him had invested their lives in this complex operation. He would be the first to die if the Dená subterfuge did not work. Cora and many of the Chena assault force would also die.

"There's smoke ahead, Colonel," the pilot said over his shoulder.

"Circle the area first."

The gunship canted to the side as it turned. The left door gunner tightened his straps, slid open a Plexiglas hatch and, gripping his weapon, braced against the wall with one foot. Wind whipped in from the opening, displacing all warmth with withering cold. Their eyes followed the black column of smoke downward.

A Russian half-track burned furiously in the center of a snowy meadow. A figure in mottled white and dark camouflage ran out of the trees and waved at the helicopter, motioning it to land in the open space next to the burning vehicle. The gunship continued to circle.

Other figures in winter camouflage waved up at the craft, then went back to firing into the forest. Many men lay on the ground in various attitudes of death. Blood pimpled the snowy meadow.

"Drop the radio," the colonel said.

The right door gunner unhooked a parcel from the bulkhead. The pilot rapidly gained altitude in a tight spiral. The ground dropped away at such dizzying speed that Grisha nearly vomited.

"We're at a thousand meters," the pilot shouted.

"Send it down," the colonel said.

The gunner pulled an O-ring clear of the bulky pack and snapped it over a hook welded inside the aircraft. As he threw the pack from the helicopter a cord attached to the ring trailed out. Parachutes blossomed, dropping quickly toward the burning vehicle.

"Make sure our people get it!" the colonel shouted.

The gunship dropped, circling down around the course of the parachute cluster. Grisha forced himself to swallow his gorge before it could pass his lips. His throat burned, his ears ached and stung from the cold and constantly changing air pressure, he swallowed repeatedly to get his ears to pop.

"The package is down, Colonel," the gunner said. "Our men have it."

"Establish contact."

The pilot spoke into his microphone.

"We have contact."

The colonel pulled out a headset and held one earphone to his head. "This is Colonel Yuganin. Who am I speaking with?"

"Sergeant Malinski, Troika Guard," a tinny voice said. "We are surrounded."

"Let me speak to your captain."

"Captain Romanov is dead, colonel. All of the officers are dead except the major, and he's wounded. I am in command of fifteen effectives, sir."

A bullet punched through the side of the cabin, whirred over their heads, and dented the overhead before falling at their feet.

"Jesus!" the gunner said with a gasp, watching the spent bullet slide across the deck and fall out the door. "We're drawing fire."

Colonel Yuganin raised one eyebrow at the ashen soldier. "What did you expect, flowers?" He spoke into the headset, "Where are your enemies concentrated, Sergeant?"

"Between us and the road."

"Hold your position. We'll be back within the hour, Sergeant. And in force."

"Thank you, Colonel."

"Find our column, Major."

"Yes, Colonel," the pilot shouted.

The gunship swiveled and sped south.

32

Chena Redoubt

Cora knew at least one of them would come for her. She hoped no more than two would arrive together. When the bar on her cell door rasped to the side, she maintained her calm.

Like most of them, he towered over her, confident in his strength and size that he would prevail. Young and stupid. He stopped inside the door and sat his machine pistol on the small stool that comprised half the furniture in the concrete cell.

She quickly stood in front of the wood-frame cot. The door slammed behind him and someone outside lowered the bar. Cora took a deep breath and ran her right hand down the back edge of her skirt.

A quick grin flashed across the man's face and he relaxed slightly. She smiled too; he had predictably misconstrued her actions. The strip of silent-fastener hissed open under the pressure of her thumb and the skinning knife tipped out and fell into her palm.

The guard pulled his shirt over his head. Just as the cloth cleared his face, she kicked him as hard as she could in the crotch. He sucked in air with a small moan and bent double.

Cora slammed the knife down between the base of his skull and the knotted shoulders; the razor-sharp blade severed his spinal cord, killing him instantly. The body fell to the stone floor like a sack of potatoes.

"Please don't hurt me!" she said in Athabascan as she ripped his shirt apart. She pulled him over with a loud grunt. She cried out as if struck.

Quickly she searched the body, mimicking inarticulate sounds of pain every few seconds. Soon she had two clips for the weapon as well as a boot knife. She left two wadded rubles and a coin in the pockets.

She dropped her plunder into a small bag sewn to the back of the man's belt and fastened the belt around her. She picked up the machine pistol and made sure the safety was off, then rapped on the door with the muzzle.

"What a rabbit you are, Zabotin!" a voice boomed through the door. The bar scraped upward. Cora clutched the automatic weapon in her right hand, wedging the butt between elbow and ribs. In her left hand, the blade of the skinning knife jutted out, sharp edge up.

The door swung open. The man on the other side chuckled.

"Boom, boom, and you're done. I like that. It leaves more for m—"

She stepped forward, pushed the muzzle into his face and held the knife against his throat.

"Just one word and you'll be done too," she hissed in perfect Russian.

"Ah, God!" he breathed. His face went white and he swallowed, causing the skin on his throat to touch the knife blade. A whine of fear leaked from the corner of his mouth.

"If you do as you're told, you'll live." She glanced up and down the corridor. "Now turn around."

He turned obediently and stood, knees shaking, waiting for her next order.

"Where's your weapon?"

Keeping his hands high above his shoulders, he gingerly pointed down to his side. She glanced down to see the weapon hanging on a strap. She grinned quickly.

"Which hand do you write with?"

"I don't know how to write, or read."

"Okay," she said with a sigh. "Which hand do you wipe your butt with?"

He wiggled his right hand.

"With your other hand, reach down, unhook your weapon, and hand it back to me, very slowly."

"Yes." He moved with exaggerated caution while following the orders.

She expertly thumbed the release and caught the clip in her hand. "Very good. Now hold the weapon in front of you and open the firing chamber."

He put the machine pistol at present-arms and automatically snapped open the block. A round spun through the air and hit the floor.

"Who is in charge of this prison?"

"The colonel."

"Yes. I mean who is in charge of this place today, right now?"

"Ensign Kopectny, but he would be in his office."

"Dolt! Who do you report to if something goes wrong?"

When he hesitated, she jammed the muzzle into his right kidney. He jerked away with a small cry of pain.

"It's up to you," she said in a sharp whisper. "Die here, or do what you're told and have a new chance at life."

He held his weapon in the air and turned his head to speak. "Sergeant Brezhnev."

"Are the records of recent arrests where he is?"

"Yes."

"Can we get there without passing any other guards?"

"Yes."

"Do it."

They advanced down a long corridor and entered an office where Cora noticed a rack of automatic weapons with a locked chain running through the trigger guards. The sergeant behind the desk continued to scratch slow, labored words into a ledger for a moment without looking up.

"Speak and get out. What do you want?"

"The cell numbers of all prisoners arrested in the past four days," Cora said.

His head snapped up and his practiced frown changed to wide-eyed astonishment.

"Clasp your hands behind your neck," she ordered.

He did as he was told. "Who are you? What do you want?"

"Cell numbers for every Indian and *Creole* you've put in here in the past week."

"What for? You don't expect to get them out of the compound, do you?"

"Consider this; I am a very desperate woman, and if you do not do as I say, I will kill you."

He looked at the guard. "Where's Zabotin?"

"She killed him," the guard said tightly.

"And you surrendered."

"Or I would have killed him, also," Cora said. "Now I'll give you the same choice. I offer you a new life if you'll join us, amnesty if you cooperate, or death if you slow me up another minute." The knuckle on her trigger-finger whitened and resignation washed over his face.

"I need to turn the page on the ledger," he said, nodding at the book in front of him.

"Do it."

He quickly dropped his hand. Instead of landing on the desk, it fell behind the desk—out of sight. Cora shot him through the head with a single bullet.

The sergeant rocked back violently in the heavy chair and then fell forward onto the book.

"Get it before he bleeds all over it," she snapped at the guard. He snatched it from under the sergeant's ruined head.

"Hold it up so I can see it."

The names meant nothing to her. The cell numbers were evident and the dates beside them ranged over the past ten days.

"Can you read numbers?"

"Yes."

"I want you to take me to the last five cells listed. Right now."

They moved silently down the corridor past three doors before stopping at the fourth. The guard opened the door and she saw Wohosni lying on the rude cot, his face crusted with dried blood.

"Damn," she said fiercely and prodded the guard with the weapon. "Get in there."

"Cora?" Wohosni said in a weak voice.

"Yes. It's time. Can you move?"

"Water, I need water," he said with a gasp. "Then I think I can do it."

"Where's water?" she asked the Russian. He gestured toward the door with his thumb and she gestured with her gun.

She followed him to an alcove in the passageway. He filled a bucket and led her back to her friend. Wohosni had sat up. He grabbed the water and drank deeply.

When he finished, he cleaned his face and eyes.

"Who did that to you?" she asked.

"Two guards on night duty got bored and beat me up for the sport of it," he said tiredly. "Even though I thought this might happen when I was arrested, I'm real happy to see you." Wohosni stood. "Okay, I'm ready to go now."

They moved out into the corridor, Wohosni gripped the knife. They stopped at the next cell and the guard opened the door as quietly as he could. Anthony Cabinboy lay on the floor, staring sightlessly at the ceiling.

They looked at him for a moment and Cora pushed the muzzle of her weapon into the guard's side.

"Are they all dead?"

"N-no! Only this one. The sergeant killed him this morning."

"So that's why he tried—"

"Yes."

"What?" Wohosni asked.

"The sergeant didn't cooperate with me a few minutes ago, so I shot him."

"Ha." Wohosni's laugh lacked humor. "He didn't know you like the rest of us do."

"You never beat the prisoners?" she asked the guard lightly.

"Only if I must."

"In order to rape them, you mean?"

"Please. You said if I helped, you would let me live."

"Take us to the next cell."

A man with long hair tied back and sporting a moustache looked up from where he sat on the bunk. He wore beautifully made moose-hide clothing, and obviously hadn't been born in Russian Amerika.

"Who are you?" Cora asked. "Have we ever met before?"

"I'm Waterman Stoddard, from Eagle."

"I didn't realize we had elements that far east," Cora said. "What kind of an accent is that?"

Stoddard stood and smiled. "I was born in Virginia, Confederate States of America, but I've lived near Eagle for nearly seven years now."

"Why are you in here?"

"I did what that damn yankee McCloud told me to do, get arrested. So I picked a fight with two Russian ensigns and whipped both of 'em. That did it."

"So you're on our side?" Cora asked.

"Yes ma'am. I'm actually on Gnady Ustinov's staff and a captain in the Dená Army."

"Oh. Thank you for being here when we needed you, Captain Stoddard. We're going to get you a weapon as soon as we can." She looked at the guard. "There's supposed to be three more Indians in here, where are they?"

"I'll show you."

Heron unfolded his gangly body from the cot when the door swung open. Other than a bruise high on one cheek, he appeared to be fine. "It's about time. I was beginning to think it wasn't going to work. Where's the weapons?"

"After we get the last two," Cora said.

"Two?" His eyes moved over the group and back to her. "Don't you mean three?"

"Anthony is dead," she said softly.

His jaw clamped shut and his face muscles worked. "Who did it?" he said through clenched teeth.

"The sergeant. I killed him."

He nodded once and then looked at the guard.

"What about him?"

"I have offered him a new life if he cooperates with us. And I plan to keep my word."

"You're the strike team leader," Heron said flatly.

"Right." She frowned at the guard. "What's your name?"

"I-Ivan Yuvonovich, Private, Imperial Army, five, sev—"

"Spare me the numbers, Ivan. Just take us to the last two prisoners."

"Yes, Cora Leader." He moved out into the corridor, no longer hesitant. In moments he had the last two doors open. Claude and a small man named Ray emerged from the cells.

"Very good," Cora said. "Now let's see if I can remember my way back to the weapons." She easily led them to the office where the sergeant's corpse lay over the desk.

"Where's the key to that lock?" she asked Ivan.

"Ensign Kopectny has it. Do you wish me to lead you to Ensign Kopectny?"

"No." She picked up the heavy bayonet the sergeant had used as a paper weight, jammed it through the hasp of the lock, and jerked it down sharply. The lock fell apart.

"I'm glad it was a Russian lock," she muttered. "Get weapons, make sure you have ammunition."

Ivan stared at her and licked his lips.

"What do you wish now, Cora Leader?"

"Lead us to the radio room."

"We have to pass other guards to get to the radio room," he said in a hoarse whisper. "I do not wish to die. If they see me with my hands in the air, they'll kill me to get you."

"How many and where are they?"

"One, a turnkey like me, is three corridors away down there." He thumbed to his right. "Farther down the same corridor is the guard to the operations area. Sometimes he's out in the corridor and sometimes he's in the tunnel."

"What tunnel?"

"Operations is surrounded by two-meter-thick walls." He shrugged apologetically. "It's like being inside a rock."

"Operations is where the radio room is located?"

"Yes. There's another guard—" He swallowed heavily again. "—just inside the radio room."

"Three guards total."

"Yes, Cora Leader."

"Good." She glanced around at them. "Now here's what we're going to do."

With the redoubt on alert, the guard in Cell Block 2 looked up when the other guard turned the corner. He squinted, trying to make out exactly what the private was doing.

The younger guard thundered down the corridor at him, weapon in his left hand and pulling a struggling Native woman by—a gun barrel—with his right?

"Yuvonovich?" He saw the woman's left hand flash at her side. "What the hell are you do—"

With a quick, underhanded throw, Cora flashed the skinning knife into his throat, severing the jugular vein.

She told Yuvonovich to stop at the body. While she pulled the knife out, he glanced down.

"He wasn't such a bad fellow even if he was a corporal."

"Do you want to talk to the next one? Maybe save his life?"

He hesitated.

"Can't talk that fast?" she asked.

"I can talk that fast, but he listens slow."

"His loss." She motioned the others forward. "Move out."

As they hurried down the concrete corridor, a man stepped out of a doorway. He moved with the stately ponderousness of someone in charge of a secure world. By the time he looked up with studied indifference, Cora and Yuvonovich had closed to two meters.

"Sergeant!" Yuvonovich said urgently as he hurried toward the man.

"What?"

"Let loose of the barrel!" Cora snapped.

The sergeant grabbed at his weapon and she shot him once through the head. He slammed back and smeared down the wall. She shoved Yuvonovich to keep him from stopping.

"Get in there, now!"

He stiff-armed the metal door, ran down the short corridor to the radio room, and kicked the door open.

"Emergency! Emergency!" he shouted. Cora ran in behind him.

Two men wearing headsets sat in front of gray consoles. A third man, armed with one of the ubiquitous machine pistols, jerked to his feet, knocking over a cup of tea on the small table next to him. He brought the barrel up and pointed it at Yuvonovich.

"Get out of the way!" the guard screamed.

"Don't shoot! Don't shoot!"

The guard didn't hesitate. A burst of bullets threw Yuvonovich backward. The noise in the small room nearly deafened Cora.

She feinted to the side and put five rounds through the guard's chest, knocking him into one of the radio operators.

"What the hell is going on here? What are you doing?" the other radioman shouted. The other five Indians and Stoddard crowded into the room.

"Freeze right where you are," she said. "Put your hands on your head."

"Yes. Whatever you say. Please don't shoot."

The other radioman lay under the guard's bleeding body, his eyes wide.

"May I get up?"

With a quick thrust of her foot she shoved the body off the man.

"Yes. But very slowly. Don't forget I am a nervous woman with an automatic weapon."

"Yes!" The man got to his feet, sat his chair upright, and slowly sank onto the seat with his hands over his head.

Cora looked back at her people crowding around.

"Heron, you stay with me. The rest of you take up positions out in the corridor, I don't want to get trapped in here."

The radio crackled and a voice squawked from a headset on the floor.

"Put that on a speaker so we all can hear it," she told the man covered with secondhand blood.

"Yes." He turned to the console and pulled a switch.

"This is Imperial Eagle One. Do you copy me, Chena Redoubt? Over."

"Answer him." She jerked the weapon toward the bloodied man because he sat closest to her. "You close your eyes and put your head down on your hands," she told the other one.

"We copy, Imperial Eagle One, over."

"Imperial Eagle Leader failed to get a response from you, so we thought he might be blocked."

"We did hear a transmission, but it came in all broken up. Over."

"This is Imperial Eagle Leader, can you hear me now, Chena Redoubt?"

"Loud and clear, Colonel."

Cora smiled and nodded approvingly. The radioman gave her a tight smile.

"Contact Tetlin Aerodrome immediately. I want close combat support within the hour. Gunships and at least two Yak fighters. Read that back, over."

The radioman repeated the transmission back to him letter perfect. As he finished speaking, his eyes flashed up and then back to the console.

In that glance Cora saw her control questioned, threatened, perhaps challenged. She shook the weapon hard enough to make the strap slap against blued steel. The man's eyes turned submissive.

She pointed to the speaker and gave him a wide grin and a thumbs up. Heron pointed his gun at him.

"We'll send the message immediately, Colonel."

"I'm going to join the ground force. I'll be out of contact for a few minutes, over and clear."

"Acknowledged and out." The man regarded her with an expression of doubt. "There are other bases monitoring these signals."

"Don't count on it, *tovirich*. You'll tell him exactly what I say, nothing else, eh?"

"What happens when they come back, other than me getting shot for treason, I mean?"

"History is changing today. Do as you're told and you might live to tell your grandchildren about it." She handed him a scrap of paper. "Switch to this frequency."

The knob clicked as it turned. He waited for more instructions. Cora glanced over at the other radioman.

His head was still resting quietly on his hands. No—just one hand lay between head and console.

"You back there!" she snapped. "Get your other hand up where I can see it."

His head moved and his eyes gleamed like those of a cornered animal. His hand jerked up with a pistol in it.

He fired.

33

Outside the Walls of Chena Redoubt

Static issued from the radio speaker while the assault team waited, shifting from foot to foot and scratching imaginary itches. A light click sounded and the hum of a carrier wave took over.

"Somebody just switched to our frequency," James, the radioman, said. He didn't look up from the dials, knobs, and read-outs in front of him. The small shelter grew quiet as all six occupants stilled and unconsciously held their breath.

The radio hissed impotently.

"Maybe they've captured her and she told them the frequency," Paul whispered, "and they're trying to hear us."

"Quiet!" Nathan whispered back.

The speaker clicked and a strained voice carried easily to all of them.

"Cora is . . . she says to come now, quickly." Another click and silence filled the carrier wave.

All eyes centered on Nathan. He ignored them and began rubbing his temples. After thirty long seconds he put his hands in his lap and stared at James.

"I'm pretty sure that was Heron. Signal Assault Force Two. Tell them it's a go."

James keyed the mike twice and spoke clearly.

"Chena Two, this is Chena One. Go. I repeat. Go."

Throughout the town of Chena separate squads of the Dená Army went into action. The main gate of Chena Redoubt lost its guards within seconds of the radio message. Weapons appeared and men and women poured into the compound to spread across the parade ground.

As hoped, the majority of the personnel was at this moment going north at speed on a rescue mission. Only a skeleton force remained to garrison the redoubt. Nearly forty fighters streamed silently toward the offices, garages, barracks, and other support buildings when the sergeant of the guard stepped out of his office to make his rounds.

The noise of his weapon burst the bubble of silence. He killed one man and wounded two others before going down under immediate concentrated fire. Gunfire, screams, curses, and explosions filled the stone enclosure.

34

On the Russian-Canada Highway, Near the Tanana River

The half-track roared down the snowy road at an impressive forty kilometers per hour. Grisha, watching ahead carefully, bounced on the front seat between the driver and Colonel Yuganin. Behind them five trucks, carrying twenty troopers each, and a sixth truck loaded with reserve ammunition and weapons gamely kept pace. Three tanks followed at top speed, barely keeping up.

Engine noise threatened his hearing. Diesel fumes would have asphyxiated them had the cab sealed properly. Cold air streamed over their feet, producing borderline frostbite. Their bodies shook with the jarring violence of the ride.

The RustyCan wound between ridges in this part of Russian Amerika, and just ahead of them, the ridges came together. The half-track roared into a cut started centuries ago by the Tanana River and widened by Russian engineers forty years before during the World War. Off to the left lay the silent, frozen river and ahead on the right tilted the fifteen-meter rock known to the Dená as the Sentinel.

"I am going to burst if I don't piss!" Grisha shouted to the colonel.

"So burst."

They traveled another hundred meters before the officer shouted at the driver.

"Stop as soon as you can. The men will need to limber up before we get to the battle zone."

The driver obediently downshifted and flicked on his signal lamps. Moments later they stopped and the engine idled down to a mere growl. The colonel slid out and walked back to confer with his officers.

Grisha glanced over at the driver. The man urinated at the side of his half-track, stretched, and broke wind at the same time. At the far end of the column, tankers crawled out of their armored behemoths to join their comrades and relieve themselves in the snow.

Grisha wandered over to the river and looked down the ice-crusted bank.

A dozen weapons pointed at him before whispered word passed as to his identity. He grinned and stepped off the bank, slid down to join the string of pitifully few men and women who comprised this portion of the Dená Army. As soon as he stopped, others quickly moved up and took position.

Far down the twisting bank he could see figures hurrying toward the ambush site. Grisha thought there would be more people than the twenty he counted.

"Dublinnik!" the colonel's voice shouted. "Sasha Dublinnik! Where are you?"

A woman he had seen at Minto gave him a bolt-action rifle and a box of rounds. He quickly opened the chamber and peered down the barrel before loading. In a moment he was back to the edge of the bank.

He poked his head up slowly and carefully slid the weapon onto the icy ledge. He sensed movement next to him and Malagni whispered, "You get the first shot."

Grisha nodded and took careful aim at the colonel. There weren't enough of them at the edge of the bank to kill all the Russians. At least, he decided, they wouldn't have the colonel to contend with.

Colonel Yuganin twisted his head about, searching for Grisha, composure and control slipping.

"Sasha Dublinnik!" he shouted again. "Where are you?" His eyes ran along the snowy bank and suddenly locked on Grisha's face. His mouth dropped open in disbelief before he recovered and turned to scream at his men.

Grisha squeezed the trigger. The bullet hit Yuganin in the right side of the temple and blew the left half of his head into a pink splatter. The shot sparked a slaughter.

Murderous fire erupted from the riverbank as well as the ridge on the other side of the road—whipping the column in a crossfire. The sudden barrage startled Grisha into immobility for a long moment. Cossacks and soldiers went down like wheat under a lead scythe.

The Russians didn't get off a shot. Bodies littered the road, staining the snow red with blood. A whistle cut through the firing and the shooting abruptly stopped.

Two men sprinted out of the brush and darted up to the still-idling vehicles. The middle tank spun around on one tread and began to negotiate its way around the end machine. Another figure dashed out of the trees and scrambled up onto the clanking, lurching weapon. Grisha recognized Wing and an icy hand clutched at his heart.

She screamed something down into the tank. It stopped. She moved back and a pair of hands showed over the hatch rim. In moments the driver stepped out onto the turret, tears streaming down his youthful face.

Another whistle broke across the murmuring convoy and two waves of humanity converged on the tanker and his dead column. Grisha walked over to the colonel who lay facedown in the snow and rolled him over with his foot. Even in death what was left of Yuganin's face radiated arrogance.

Malagni walked up and slapped Grisha on the back. "Perfect. You couldn't have timed it any better."

"Any word from Cora? They locked her up."

"The attack on Chena is already underway, so she must have come through just fine."

Wing trotted up, a beatific smile curling her scar almost double.

"We did it! We really did it." She abruptly hugged both men at once. "Now we have to get back to Chena and prepare for the counterattack."

"When do we get to stop fighting?" Grisha asked.

"When the Russians surrender," Malagni said, striding away down the column.

"I don't think he could live without war," Wing murmured.

"When I saw you leap onto that tank my heart nearly stopped." He stared at her strong, proud profile, knowing that if he ever trusted his heart to a woman again it would be her.

"Yeah." She turned to face him. "I felt pretty good when I saw you get out of that truck. You're important to me, Grigoriy Grigorievich, don't forget that. But there's this thing called war that we gotta get through first."

"Where's Nik?"

She glanced at Malagni's retreating back. "He's with Nathan at Chena Redoubt."

"Oh."

"We haven't heard a word from them since they began the attack."

"How long ago was that?"

She finally looked up at him. "About an hour."

"What about the Russians of the Troika Guard I saw, are we going to finish them off?"

She smiled.

"The only Troika Guards alive at the battle zone had come over to our side. The battle you saw from the helicopter was a charade. But their commander wants to meet you as soon as possible."

"What's his name and rank?"

"I think he is a captain by the name of Smolst, do you know him?"

Grisha laughed and danced in a circle.

"I'll take that as a yes," Wing said with a smile. "Catch up with Malagni, you and he are going to take the lead."

Grisha gave her a level stare. "See you in Chena."

35

Chena

Nathan, Nik, and Haimish, surrounded by a squad of eight nervous, heavily armed soldiers, trotted down the deserted highway toward Chena Redoubt. Shops and homes stood quiet and still in the pale noon brightness. The civilian Russian and *Creole* population never knew what the cossacks might do next. When gunfire filled the air they went to ground.

Three men carrying equipment abruptly stepped from between two buildings. The Dená squad leader crouched and aimed at them. The squad followed her example.

"Wait!" one of the men shouted. "We're friends."

The squad leader glanced over at Nathan.

"What do you think?" she asked.

"Keep them covered, Eleanor," Nathan said in a low voice. Then he shouted. "What is that you have there, friend?"

The heavily clothed men walked toward them slowly with their hands in the air. One held a bulky object over his head. A thick, short barrel pointed from the front of the thing.

The second man carried a short tube with a knob on one end with wires running from the opposite end to a backpack carried by the third man. The man with the smallest load did all the talking.

"We're from RepCal Productions!" he said eagerly. "You've heard of RepCal, haven't you?" The three men closed to five meters.

"Stop or you're dead," Eleanor said in a flat voice, peering through the sights of her 9mm rifle.

They stopped.

"Look, we're just up here getting some footage for movie commercials," the man said quickly, pushing back his parka hood. "We just want to know what's going on around here. Is this a war or something?"

"Who are you?" Haimish asked.

"Benny Jackson. I'm a producer." He grinned quickly. "And this is Alf Rosario, my cameraman, and over here—" he patted the man carrying the knapsack on the shoulder "—is Jimmy Scanlon, our sound tech."

"That's a camera?" Nathan asked.

"Yeah, top-of-the-line 35mm camera."

"I saw one of those in St. Nicholas," Nik said. "They make movies with them."

"Yeah!" Jackson agreed. "Like the man says, we make movies."

"Why are you here?" Haimish asked.

"We've been traveling all through Russian America getting footage for commercials and maybe a documentary." Jackson paused and stared hard at Haimish. "You sure don't sound like the rest of these guys, where you from?"

"That doesn't matter. What does matter is that I'm here and helping birth a nation."

"Yeah? Who's gonna know about it if it isn't covered?"

"Covered—you mean observed?" Nathan asked.

"Filmed, baby, and shown to the public." Jackson patted the camera.

"You would do that for us?"

"Look, no offense, but you people are still in the stone age or something up here. Down south we got radio networks that span the continent and even go into New France, New Spain, and Brit Canada. We have a network of theater chains even more extensive, and the public is hungry for news and the unusual.

"The Russkies told us we could go anywhere we wanted in Russian America to shoot footage to entice people up here and spend money. But we didn't know nothin' about you people, or about any wars being fought."

"Actually it's just begun," Nathan said with a smile. "You can make money somehow from all this, can't you?"

Jackson grinned and spoke to Alf out of the corner of his mouth. "Start shooting, Alf. Jimmy, make sure you get sound levels on everything." He stuck the wire mesh knob in front of Nathan's face.

"This is a microphone, we can record your words with it."

"Answer my question," Nathan said.

"You must be a mind reader, mister. Yeah, we can make plenty off the rights to this stuff, even the Japanese will buy it."

"Perhaps we should talk before you begin."

Jackson's eyes narrowed and he reached down and snapped a switch on the machine in the backpack.

"So talk."

"We are not a rich people. It would be a good thing if you contributed a percentage of your profits to the Dená Separatist Movement. Sharing can open many doors."

Jackson smiled. "Ain't no moss growing on you, is there? Okay, how about fifteen percent?"

"Very generous, but twenty-five is the number I had in mind."

"Done."

"Make sure it tells the story we want people to hear."

"No sweat, baby. Roll it, Jimmy. You focused there, Alf? Okay." He held the microphone up again. "Just who are you people?"

"We are the Dená Army. For centuries our people have been exploited and oppressed by the Russians. As far as they are concerned, we are at the bottom of the social strata—"

"'Scuse me, but we got a war to fight," Haimish said waspishly.

"Let's go!" Jackson seemed delighted at the idea. "We can move and interview at the same time."

Nik and Haimish, surrounded by half of Eleanor's squad, ranged out ahead of the camera crew. The sun sank toward the early afternoon horizon and the temperature dropped with it. A few random gunshots echoed through the crisp air, shattering the crystalline stillness.

Two Dená holding Kalashnikovs emerged from the shadows at the main gate.

"We need the others, Hamish," Jimmy Burton said. "We've got the operations bunker and the prison. They have everything else, including the armory."

"How many 'ave we lost?"

"I don't know the exact number. Heron's over in the operations complex, I think he has numbers and names. Who are those guys?"

He pointed to the camera crew that busily recorded their conversation.

"They're movie people, telling the other North Amerikan countries about us."

"Who are you people?" Burton asked.

"We're harmless. Just pretend we're not here," Jackson said with a wink.

Burton shook his head and disappeared back into the shadows.

As they passed through the cell blocks, prisoners were being freed and herded into a large room where they could be briefed and offered positions in the DA. The camera crew slowed considerably in order to get shots of everything, including pools of blood and shattered buildings.

Nik hurried into the radio room, where a war of deception could still be won or lost. Six people crowded the room, removing bodies on litters. Half of the radio equipment lay in shards. Pockmarks from bullets cratered the walls and ceiling.

Two medics worked feverishly on someone whose face Nik couldn't see. He walked around them to get a better view. Cora lay on the litter, blinking up at the ceiling, her lower lip trembling.

"Cora! Oh my God, Cora!" Nik knelt down beside her and caught the eye of a medic. The medic shook his head slightly and went back to work stanching the flow of blood from her wounds. "Oh my darling, what have you done?" he said gently.

"I'm, so, sorry." She coughed up a large gobbet of red froth. Nik realized her lungs were destroyed and she was drowning in her own blood. ". . . I wanted, to be your, wife, but . . ."

The animation in her eyes froze into a glassy stare. The tears running down his cheeks surprised him for a moment before he began to sob.

Behind Nik, Benny Jackson tapped Alf Rosario on the shoulder.

"That's enough, Alf, it's a wrap."

They left Nik to his grief.

36

On the Russia–Canada Highway

Grisha pushed down harder on the accelerator. The increased speed caused the half-track to bounce even more, so he slowed again.

"We'll get there, Grisha, don't worry." Malagni peered out the side window. The man filled the cab, adding to Grisha's anxiety.

"Why don't they send us a message?"

"We agreed not to break radio silence until after all the attacks began. The other Russian bases might be monitoring every wavelength. The longer we can keep them out of this, the better."

"Six more kilometers," Grisha said through clenched teeth. "At this speed I could outrun the whole column on foot."

"We need every vehicle, every rifle, every bullet," Malagni said. "We need every break we can get."

Driving a half-track called for the same habits as piloting a boat. Grisha kept his eyes moving all the time, glancing from side to side, watching the rearview mirror, minding the ditches and keeping a keen eye as far ahead as possible. Diesel stench wafted through the firewall but he couldn't roll down the window without subjecting his ears to frostbite. He noticed they were near the end of a long straightaway and then glanced in the mirror.

As if waiting for his attention, the sound of a plane passed overhead. He glanced up in time to see a Yak fighter flash by in the fading light. The aircraft waggled its wings and flew in a wide circle around them.

"Colonel Yuganin," a voice rasped from the radio. "This is Talon Six. Chena Redoubt is under attack. Tetlin has lost radio contact with them. Over."

Malagni picked up the microphone. "We are advancing at top speed. Are there more aircraft to assist us?"

"No. Only three other aircraft exist in this sector. Four other redoubts are also under attack. The other three Yaks have gone north to hit Tanana Redoubt. We believe our garrison there has been nullified."

"And the other battles?" Malagni tried to put disbelief into his voice.

"In question," the pilot said. "Are you going to attack now?"

"Yes!" Malagni said. He dropped the microphone, pushed the roof hatch open and pulled on the mottled Russian parka next to him.

"Do you want me to stop?" Grisha asked.

"No, this won't take long." Malagni stood up behind the twin 9mm machine guns mounted above the cab roof.

Grisha heard the plane coming back over them. The machine gun fired four quick bursts. Trailing fire and smoke, the fighter angled down ahead of them, veered to the right, and dropped into the trees. The explosion lit the roadside forest for a blinding moment.

Malagni slammed the hatch shut and dropped onto the bench seat. "How's that for nullify? By all that's holy," he said wonderingly, "we might actually pull this off."

Complete darkness shrouded Chena when they roared down the street. The *aurora borealis* scrolled and winked overhead as the wood portions of the gates of the redoubt burned furiously.

Bullets *splanged* across the hood of the half-track. Grisha stomped on the brake, slewed the vehicle sideways, and roared off the street to crash through the wall of a house. The trucks behind them pulled to the sides of the road.

"By the Raven!" Malagni shouted.

"Are you hurt?" Grisha asked.

"Why are they shooting at us?"

"Perhaps they don't know who we are?"

"Good point, Grisha," Malagni said with a grin. "We *are* in a Russian half-track."

Both men broke into maniacal laughter.

Malagni crawled out of the cab and screamed into the night.

"This is the Dená Army! Who dares fire at us?"

"Friend," someone shouted. A figure materialized out of the gloom. Claude stopped a few meters from them and smiled. "I think you're just in time to make a difference."

"What do you want us to do?" Malagni asked, suddenly sane again.

Claude told them, then disappeared behind the walls. Malagni conferred with the other drivers, then jumped back in the cab with Grisha.

"Temperature's dropping fast out there," he said absently. "You ready to go kill some more Russians?"

"Do we have a choice?"

"No," Malagni said with a humorless laugh, "I guess we don't. Drive right up to the gate."

Grisha gunned the half-track backward and spun it around on one track until he was straight on the road again. He roared up to the gate and blew the air horn. Gunfire slackened inside the walls.

An iron shutter crashed open and a gun barrel poked out.

"Who is there?" a voice demanded in Russian.

"Colonel Yuganin and the remnants of the Troika Guard!" Grisha roared. "Open the gate, we're freezing out here!"

"At once, Colonel. There has been an attack. Rebels are inside the compound."

The gates opened swiftly and Grisha sped inside. The five trucks followed close behind him. When the tanks entered, they separated and scattered around the courtyard, stopping next to Russian strong points.

A sergeant with red flashes on his parka ran up to the half-track and pulled the door open.

"Colonel Yuganin. We must make an immediate assault. They have the operations complex."

Malagni put the muzzle of his machine pistol between the man's eyes.

"Cooperate and you'll live, Sergeant."

The man jerked to a stop and his breath puffed out in a cloud around his face.

"Where—where's the colonel?"

"Dead, along with the rest of his command," Malagni said flatly.

The tanks swiveled their turrets around until they menaced the armory from three directions.

"You can't win," the Indian said, "but you can live."

The sergeant lost all animation and his shoulders slumped.

"Very well, I'll signal my men to lay down their arms."

Before the men in the cab could say anything, the sergeant put a whistle to his lips and blew three short blasts.

A streak of fire shot out from the armory and exploded in the right front wheel well next to the sergeant, blowing him to pieces and fragmenting the cab door. The pressure and shrapnel blew Malagni against Grisha with such force that they both burst out through the driver's side of the cab into a heap on the frozen ground.

Weapons crashed and shrieked around them. Each of the tanks fired at the armory three times before hitting explosives inside. Suddenly the doors and windows blew outward with stunning concussion. Everything fell silent.

White sheets and towels appeared at the smashed windows of the barracks. Russian troopers crawled from their shelter with hands high in the biting air. Grisha sat up and held his hands over his ringing ears.

"Jesus!" he said with a croak. "What happened, Malagni?"

"Bad shit." Malagni sounded dazed. "Look what they did to my arm." Malagni's right arm hung shattered, connected only by a shred of bicep. Blood squirted in measured jets from the mangled flesh.

"Oh, God. We gotta tie that off!" Grisha pulled his belt off and looped it under Malagni's shoulder, pulled it as tight as he could and knotted it. The jets of blood dropped to a steady trickle "Medic! We need a medic over here!"

A woman ran over to them, glanced at the wound, and blew a sharp blast on a whistle. Two men appeared with a collapsible litter and the three of them rolled Malagni onto the canvas and hauled him away.

Hands pulled Grisha to his feet and led him into warmth and light. Equilibrium returned as he walked. He found himself in a large garage.

Paul emerged from a corner. "You're a mess, what happened?"

"I think they hit us with with one of those antitank weapons," Grisha told him. He tried to shake off the numbness he felt, and forced himself to focus on events around him, swallowing repeatedly to ease the ringing in his ears. The place stank of gunpowder and he felt chilled to the bone.

"What's happened here?"

"Most of them have come over to our side. We got about eighty new recruits. About twenty possess a usable skill other than cleaning or killing."

"Malagni's in a bad way," Grisha said. "Where's Nathan and Haimish?"

"Operations complex, through those doors over there. Chan's there, too, along with a camera crew from California."

"A what?" Wing asked, coming up behind them.

Paul explained about the visitors from the Republic of California.

"Casualties must have been light to have a bunch like that running around," she said.

"We lost some good people," Paul responded.

The door opened and Nik came out. One look at the Russian's streaming face told Grisha that he hadn't faced all the bad news yet.

"Oh, Nik, it's Cora, isn't it?"

Nik nodded dumbly, weeping uncontrollably. The sudden lump in Grisha's throat constricted his breathing.

"I am so sorry. Was it . . . quick?"

"She said she wanted to marry me, then," he swallowed, "then she died."

Grisha hugged his friend to him and Nik's head dropped to his shoulder and he sobbed.

37

Tetlin Redoubt

A quarter bottle of vodka filled the void behind Crepov's belt and fogged his brain when someone pounded on the door. Katti jumped like she'd been burned. Her jumpiness always pissed him off.

He lurched to his feet with a growl. This time he wouldn't take his anger out on the woman. With a violent jerk he pulled the heavy wooden door open creating a minus-thirty-degrees Celsius gust of wind.

Two Special Unit cossacks stared balefully in at him. He pulled up short, concentrated on the extreme cold, let it burn at the scar on his face to clear his head. They both towered over him.

"We must go immediately to headquarters and you must be with us," the biggest and ugliest one said.

"I get my coat." Crepov pulled his parka off its peg. He knew when to walk with the wind.

Katti shivered behind the door, ready to shut it as soon as possible. Most of the warmth in the single room had vanished along with his drunkenness. He hurried out, pushed between them, and strode rapidly toward the operations building.

The cold robbed him of anger. By the time he stormed past the sentry he had decided to first listen to the colonel before telling him to put this job sideways up his anus. He stiff-armed the office door open and jerked to a stop.

Valari wore the insignia of a major and the corporal had a third stripe. No good, he reflected, the man will always be a corporal.

The two flanked the colonel, who glowered from behind his desk.

"Good of you to come out on a night like this, Bear," he said with no hint of sarcasm. "We need your special skills."

Crepov saw the man's eyes flick over his scar before recapturing his gaze. He let himself glance at the other two. Nobody smiled in condescension tonight. He realized they didn't want him here any more than he wanted to be there. His interest flared.

"For what?"

"Something happened at Chena Redoubt. We need you to go take a look."

"Why don't you send one of your wonderful helicopters?"

"Do you refuse to go?" Valari asked softly, raising her eyebrows and tilting her head.

Her manner reminded Crepov of an attack dog anticipating trouble. In a rare flash of insight, he realized how well she fit that description. She was just more dangerous than other bitches.

"I need as much information as possible to make judgment," Bear said flatly.

"We cannot put an aircraft closer than a kilometer to Chena Redoubt," the colonel said tiredly. "They get shot down."

"What!" Bear's brain reeled with implications. "Chena Redoubt is not under the control of the Imperial Army?"

"Nor is Tanana Redoubt. Bridge Redoubt is under heavy attack and the *odinochkas* around Fort Yukon, Huslia, and Koyuk do not answer us at all. We believe the Dená Separatists are responsible. Either that or a well-organized mutiny."

"It must be mutiny, a very large mutiny," Bear muttered, more to himself than to anyone else in the room. "The Indians aren't organized enough to pull off something this big." He regarded the three of them thoughtfully.

"You can get me within two kilometers, can't you?" He added a smile for the pure spite of it.

"Of course we can." The colonel wouldn't rise to the bait. Crepov finally noticed the purple pouches under the man's eyes. "Can you leave immediately?"

"Yes. Within the hour."

"Would you like company?" Valari asked neutrally.

"You would be welcome," he said slowly. "But only if you left your pet corporal here."

"I'm a sergeant," the man said through clenched teeth.

Crepov gave him an amused look. "Your arm says that. But we know differently, don't we?" He turned and hurried back into the night.

Maybe he would find Grigoriy Grigorievich at Chena Redoubt. That would make it all worthwhile.

He grinned fiercely as the cold burned at his scar.

38

Chena Redoubt

Grisha huddled in the corner, nearly asleep, listening to the ever-lengthening interview.

"So this is a civil war?" Jackson asked Chan.

"No. We have never been part of Russian society, we have always been a subjugated people." The old man's eyes twinkled. "This is a revolution, we are finally striking back at a power which has oppressed us for centuries."

"Can you rig me a patch, Jimmy?" Jackson asked his technician.

"Ain't no way we're gonna get a radio signal out of here," Scanlon said.

"Only one way to find out, Jimmy, baby. And that's to try it."

"What is it that you wish to do?" Chan asked.

"Hook into our network down in California."

"Network," Haimish said. "You can communicate with California from here?"

"Let ya know in a few minutes," Jimmy said.

"Can you patch us through to the U.S.?" Haimish asked.

Jackson studied Haimish with an air of assessment.

"It might not be impossible," he said slowly. "But what's in it for us?"

"A place in history as a participant rather than a bystander."

"I need someone to help me," Jimmy said.

"The Russians have the technology to pick up any transmissions we make," Jackson said. "I sure as hell don't want to start any diplomatic hassles between them and the Republic of California just yet."

"I'll help you, Jimmy," Grisha said, pulling himself to his feet. "Every time I drop off to sleep I start having dreams."

"So you're just up here to make a few bucks and that's it?" Haimish said with barely concealed contempt. "Open up a new market and cash in?"

"And what the fuck are you doing here, Yank?" Jackson spat. "Founding an orphanage?"

"We need to put this on the roof, man," Jimmy said. "How do we get up there?"

Grisha picked up his parka and shrugged into it. "This way, I think."

"I'm a military advisor," Hamish said flatly.

"From the U.S.?" Jackson asked quickly.

"Does it matter?"

"If I'm putting my ass on the line, it does."

Grisha hesitated at the door, feeling the tension in the room.

"I'm a colonel in the United States Army." Haimish's voice carried urgency. "This situation has moved much faster than our intelligence people anticipated. If I don't get through to my superiors I'm afraid the Russians are going to flatten this place and smash the movement before it gets its wind."

"Get the antenna set up, Jimmy," Jackson said through a grin, "while I talk turkey with the colonel."

"C'mon, man," Jimmy said tiredly to Grisha. "I want to get some sleep tonight."

The cold stabbed through his parka and Grisha realized he was more weary than he thought. He held parts together while Jimmy clumsily fastened bolts without taking off his heavy mittens. At this temperature warm skin would be instantly frozen by metal.

"You guys are more than you're saying, aren't you?" Grisha said casually.

"Isn't everybody?" Jimmy said with a snort. "Hand me that wrench."

As he pondered the man's words, Grisha became aware of a pulsing in his ears.

"Helicopter!"

Jimmy lifted his head sharply and listened. "Yeah. About two klicks away, wouldn't you say?"

"But just one." Grisha frowned up at the brittle stars. "Why would they have just one helicopter up this time of night?"

"Reconnaissance," Jimmy muttered to himself. "That's the only reason I'd have a bird up in this deep freeze!"

"You're right. Are we done here?"

"Just about. Hold this cable up so I can hardwire this thing."

The sound of the helicopter receded.

"You got people out there?" Jimmy asked. "Patrols and all that?"

"I think that's where Slayer-of-Men went when he found out about his brother."

"I hope he's awake and on the job. Shit, this thing wants to fall over."

They grappled with aluminum rods and tie-downs as the *aurora borealis* rippled above them.

39

A Kilometer From Chena Redoubt

As the helicopter receded into the distance, Bear Crepov smiled at Major Kominskiya.

"I didn't think you'd really get off the machine. I thought you'd turn rabbit on me."

"This is not the first time you have misjudged me," she said, shrugging into her pack. "Shall we get to work?"

"We have much to do, you and me," Bear said carefully. "And not everything involves enemies."

She turned and looked at him. All he could see inside the ruffed hood of her parka were twin points of starlight reflecting off her eyes.

"I agree," she said, and pushed off to the northwest, toward Chena Redoubt.

Crepov tightened the hood down around his face and followed her. The cold burned in his scar and nipped at his nose.

Experimentally, he sniffed at the air. His nostrils tried to stick together. He immediately knew it was at least minus thirty-five degrees Celsius.

The survival habits of three decades unconsciously took over. He slowed his pace to avoid working up a sweat, yet skied actively enough to stay warm. He pushed out the fur ruff on his hood to its maximum in order to create a barrier of warm air between his face and the subarctic night.

He thought only of Valari Kominskiya's body and what he planned to do with it at his first opportunity. And there would be an opportunity.

The rest of his training kicked in and he studied the land around them. Chena Redoubt had been home to him more than once. He'd hunted caribou, moose, wolves, and men in this oblast. Bear knew this countryside as well as he did the streets of Tetlin Redoubt.

Valari skied ahead of him at the same speed he maintained. Good. There was nothing he hated more than worrying about someone else, whether he had to or not.

The fact clicked in his mind that she wasn't breaking trail, she followed one.

"Major!" he hissed. "Stop."

She slid to a halt and looked back over her shoulder.

"Yes?"

He pulled up beside her.

"This trail you are following must be known to the rebels if they have put out even one patrol."

"My God, you're right." She glanced around. "What do you think we should do?"

He grinned deep inside his parka hood. She was beginning to really interest him. Capable but submissive, he liked that in a woman.

"Follow me. I'll break trail and we'll come in behind the redoubt. There's a place where worthless items are thrown in winter and avoided in summer."

"Lead."

The *aurora borealis* flared into existence, danced and capered above them. Bear had to slow considerably as he broke trail. If one sweated heavily inside arctic coverings the chances of freezing to death attained unbeatable odds.

Between the dark, scattered cabins whose presence proclaimed the outskirts of Chena, the kilometer-long stone wall of the redoubt loomed before them. Nothing moved, no sound issued from the cabins around them. Starlight on the bright snow gave enough illumination to see they were alone outside the fortress.

"Perhaps everyone is dead?" she said.

"No. They are either tired or lazy. A lapse like this will not last if they know what they are doing."

"And?"

"I do not think they are lazy."

"They also seem to know what they are doing. Now what?"

Good question.

After a moment's thought, he stabbed his ski poles into the snow, unslung his weapon and carefully propped it against them, creating a pyramid. He shook the pack off his back and dug out the rope and anchor hook. He silently measured the height of the fortress wall with his eyes.

If anyone guarded the parapets above, he and the major would soon be dead or captured. He preferred death. Bear looked back at Valari.

"Step back, give me some room, and cover me."

He swung the hook in an ever-widening circle. Abruptly he released it and the metal claw sailed up and over the thick, slightly inclined wall. By the time they heard the soft thump as it landed, both their gun muzzles pointed upward.

Nothing.

Bear allowed himself to breathe again and slung his weapon over his shoulder. He bent down and tripped the bindings on his skis, straightened, and leaned toward Valari.

"I will find out what's up there and signal you when it's safe. Don't take any naps while I'm gone." He hauled himself upward, hand over hand, while his mukluk-encased feet silently walked up the frost-rimed stone.

When his head cleared the wall, he hesitated, searching the snow-filled roof for movement. The gleaming white and indigo shadows undulated away from him like a frozen wheat field. Paths where guards usually patrolled bisected the snowed-in roof.

Nothing moved. He pulled himself across the wide icy wall and jumped down into the trench worn in the snow. He crouched low, keeping his head below the surrounding walls. His breath puffed out and momentarily obscured his vision. He tried to breathe more slowly.

The path became a roofless tunnel through the deep snow and he hurried down straight sections, stopping to ease around corners. Very quickly it became obvious that the roof stood empty of anything other than the elements. However, something nagged at the back of his mind, a tiny, insistent warning that wouldn't allow him to stop until he'd covered the entire plain of connected stone roofs.

Those little nags had kept him alive in the past. Men who didn't listen to their gut usually died before their hair showed any gray. He crept around another corner—and froze.

Two figures shambled toward him, heads down. He couldn't see any weapons, but this was no time to take chances. He brought his weapon up and took careful aim.

The first parka-clad form stopped and pulled on a wall. A door opened, emitting a great cloud of warm air that instantly fogged around the figures. Once the cold ate the fog, the two were gone.

Bear continued to breathe slowly, keeping himself in the "look and listen" mode. It might be a changing of the guards. No, that wasn't it. The new guards always relieved the old ones on post.

What had the two been doing? He pushed the question to the back of his mind and finished his roof reconnaissance. Finally he became satisfied of his solitude.

He turned and hurried back to where Major Valari Kominskiya waited.

40

Chena Redoubt

"Getting anything?" Jackson asked with a tinge of anxiety in his voice.

"Shit, man, would you just give me some space?" Jimmy Scanlon snapped, rolling his eyes.

Grisha's eyes felt grainy, but he wanted to see if this little machine could capture words from two thousand miles away. Haimish and Jackson both wore smiles when Grisha and Jimmy returned. Nathan and Chan somberly whispered in a corner.

Jimmy turned a knob. Static gushed out of the speaker on the backpack. He twisted more knobs. The static lowered and then stopped. A low humming interrupted randomly by small beeps issued from the speakers. "That's their carrier wave," Jimmy said.

"All right!" Jackson crowed, and slapped Jimmy on the back. Alf Rosario picked up a microphone and spoke into it.

"This is Northern Lake, this is Northern Lake. We have a taped feed and a live feed for you. Do you copy? Over."

What an odd way to talk, Grisha thought.

"We copy, Northern Lake, transmit your feed."

Grisha felt his eyes bug out. It worked, it really worked.

"This is truly magic," Nathan said, staring down at the machine. "Are these your friends in California?"

219

"Yes," Jackson said with a grin. "Squirt the tape, Alf. They can check it out later. We probably don't have much time."

"Why not?" Grisha asked.

"The Russians will probably monitor the transmission and either jam us or try to take out the transmitter." Jackson pointed at the machine. "This is a transmitter."

Nik wandered in, rubbing his eyes. "What's going on?"

"Does the Russian military have monitoring devices that can detect radio signals?" Haimish asked.

"They have trouble picking up their own radio transmissions." Nik yawned and saw the small transmitter. "What's that?"

Nathan told him while Alf made the machine whine at high speed. It stopped with a click.

"Okay, Jackson, take the mike." Alf handed him the instrument.

"This is Northern Lake with a five-star performance," Jackson said. "Do you copy? Over."

"Wait one," a voice from the machine said. Clicks and short bursts of static quickly changed to a low hum. "Proceed," the voice ordered.

"The Dená Separatist Movement not only exists, but is receiving military aid from the United States of America. The DSM has captured a Russian armored column and used the materiel to capture a walled fort, Chena Redoubt, near the juncture of the Tanana and Chena Rivers. Most of the Russian-Amerikan fighter wing has been neutralized. Other redoubts have also been taken or are under attack as we speak. The elected government of the Dená Nation seeks diplomatic recognition as soon as possible." Jackson stopped and smiled around at everyone in the room.

"Can you get an ambassador out to address Congress?" the voice asked.

"Not by road," Jackson said. "We're surrounded by hostiles."

"Wait one." Grisha couldn't decide if the voice was male or female.

"Would you inquire about patching me through to my people?" Haimish asked.

"We have a representative of the United States here. Would it be possible to patch him through to the nearest U.S. Army unit?"

"Negative. But we can get someone from his delegation over here in about a half hour."

"That would be fine," Haimish said with evident relief.

"Please proceed on that, Five-Star."

"Acknowledged. Your transportation scenario is being dealt with, stay online, we'll be back as soon as possible."

Grisha glanced around the crowded room. People smiled at one another and hope became a palpable entity.

This might actually work.

41

"So it wasn't a mutiny," Bear muttered, peering down from the snow-laden roof of the headquarters building.

"They've captured the redoubt," Valari said. "How could they do that?"

"I told you they were a formidable enemy," Bear answered in a harsh whisper. "But you damn cossacks never believe anyone."

"Who was it said, 'The Indians aren't organized enough to pull off something this big'?" she countered in a hiss.

"We don't have time to argue." He turned away.

They could see the entire courtyard. A group of people dressed in foreign camouflage complete with flak jackets herded a coffle of Russian soldiers from a barracks toward the prison wing.

"That's not moose hide they're wearing," Valari hissed. "They're getting military aid from another country."

"They're all still inside the redoubt," he whispered.

"So?"

"Call in an air strike, level this place, and we stop their party cold."

"You are full of hidden talents, Bear. I like that in a man."

"There is much hidden about me that you have yet to appreciate. But this is not the time or place to show you."

"I am becoming very cold, could we leave now?"

"Do you have the radio?" he asked.

"Yes." She fumbled inside her parka and brought out the bulky box of knobs and batteries. "Use it quick, *tovarich*, before the batteries freeze."

"Not to worry." He snapped on the power switch and grinned appreciatively as the dials glowed to life. "I'm glad we preset the frequency before we left Tetlin Redoubt," he said absently.

"Do you want me to make the call?" she asked.

"I want you," he said heavily, "but I will make the call." He unhooked the microphone and held down the transmit button.

"This is Chena Probe to Imperial Tetlin, Chena Probe to Imperial Tetlin, do you copy?"

"Tetlin to probe," the voice from the radio sounded tinny, "we read you clearly, proceed."

"The Dená have the redoubt. Send an air strike now."

"Oh my God," the tinny voice said.

Valari gasped and Bear felt something hard press against the side of his head, his widened nostrils easily discerned the odor of gun oil. He pressed the transmit button three times in quick succession and hoped they were awake back in Tetlin.

"You will tell them," a calm masculine voice said softly, "that there was a mutiny here, and the traitors have been subdued."

The roof moved in the moonlight, suddenly populated with figures rising from the snow and shadows around them. A tall man closed on Bear and snatched the machine pistol from his hands.

He heard the safety click off on the automatic weapon pointed at his head. "*Da*," he whispered and nodded slightly. The muzzle eased back a third of a meter.

"There has been a mutiny." Even to him his voice sounded like an old man's croak. He swallowed quickly. "The traitors have been overwhelmed."

The radio sat silent long enough that Bear thought the batteries had frozen. Suddenly a new voice issued into the crystalline night.

"This is Colonel Rostov. Why do we not have radio contact with the redoubt?"

Valari's eyes widened.

"Tell them," the man said softly in Bear's ear, "Lieutenant Dimitri Andreanoff and his squad spoke to me. The radio room was destroyed by traitors."

Bear parroted the words into the microphone. "Do you copy?"

"Put the lieutenant on."

Bear turned and looked into the man's face in supplication. Neither light nor humanity rested in those eyes. He felt he was looking at a cossack.

"The lieutenant is leading his men," the tall Indian whispered, "but he left a corporal with us."

Bear lowered his gaze as he repeated the lie. For the first time in his life he felt helpless and used.

"Very well!" the colonel's voice snapped over the distance. "Put the damned corporal on."

The microphone jerked out of his hands.

"This is Corporal Danilev, Troika Guards," the Indian said in flawless Russian. Crepov recognized a St. Petersburg accent. "We've eliminated most of the traitors, but a small pocket still resists, sir."

"Don't kill them all," the voice on the radio snapped. "We want to know how this happened. Good work, Corporal. Give Major Kominskiya the microphone."

Another safety snicked off in the frigid subarctic night.

Valari reached out and snatched the instrument. Her eyes flashed about her. Bear felt his sphincter muscle twitch and he shivered. She grinned and snapped her mittened thumb down on the key with an exaggerated jerk.

"Colonel Rostov, this is Major Kominskiya. What would you like to know?"

"Do you agree with Corporal Danilev's assessment of the situation?"

"Yes, Colonel," she said smoothly, effortlessly. "Lieutenant Andreanoff has the upper hand from all I have seen." She glared at the tall, smiling Indian.

"Have the corporal report every hour, Major Kominskiya. Do you copy?"

"Yes," she said, her face falling slightly, "I copy."

"Tetlin Redoubt, clear."

"Chena Redoubt, clear." She dropped the microphone.

"Very good, Major Kominskiya," the tall man said. "Allow me to introduce myself, I am Slayer-of-Men." He smiled thinly in the moonlight. "And on occasion I also slay women."

Bear shivered again, his mind now as chilled as his body.

42

Chena Redoubt

"Yes, Mr. Ambassador," Haimish said, addressing the small speaker in front of him. "I have a message for Mr. Busch, he's on President Cuomo's staff."

"I know Keith. What do you want me to tell him?"

"Tell him that Operation Nicky is already at stage three, the stage three is very important, sir."

"And this will do what for your situation?"

"I'm hoping it means quick diplomatic recognition for the Dená Republik."

"Do you realize what you're asking? If the United States grants diplomatic recognition to the DSM at this point, every dissatisfied minority in the world would be out cutting throats in hours. I mean no disrespect to your hosts, but we have to back our diplomacy with our lives."

"Excuse me, Mr. Ambassador," Nathan said quickly, "but you have a double investment here, perhaps triple."

"Whom am I addressing, please?"

"Chandalar Roy, Codirector of the Dená Separatist Movement and President of the Dená Republic."

"Ah, pleased to meet you, Mr. President. I assume you have heard our entire conversation?"

"Sadly enough, yes, Mr. Ambassador. My illusions have fled."

"I'm glad you can assess the big picture from there."

"As I said, Mr. Ambassador, you have quite a large investment here in Alaska."

"Please elucidate, Mr. President."

"You have already blown most of your intelligence-gathering network by virtue of this uplink. Even if we do not carry the day very soon, the new treaty between the western republics and Russian Amerika will vaporize like piss at seventy below." Chan's voice hardened as he continued.

"We already enjoy political alignment with the United States of America. Events now demand that you are either with us or against us—neutrality is no help. As our situation is desperate, I need a reply in three days' time." He hesitated for a long moment before going on in a brisk voice. "We will treat the lack of a reply after that time as a negative response. You do understand, of course?"

"Yes, Mr. President, I understand. Now if you'll excuse me—" Static gushed from the speaker.

"Three days?" Haimish said wonderingly. "That bunch can't decide what to talk about in only three days. You've scuttled your boat, lad."

"Haimish, for Christ's sake stop that atrocious accent," Nathan said wearily, dropping onto a chair, "it's giving me a headache."

Grisha stared at the speaker, wishing it would tell something of California or the United States. The door opened and a group of people streamed into the room. Whatever retort Haimish was about to make died on his lips.

Grisha looked up to see Valari Kominskiya and the *promyshlennik* whose face he had scarred.

"What have we here?" Nathan asked.

"Scouts for the Czar," Slayer-of-Men said with a slow smile. "In the form of a cossack major and a *promyshlennik*."

"Where are you from?" Nathan asked the prisoners idly.

"Tet—" Bear began before Valari's bare hand slapped his cheek.

"Shut up, you fool! Information is ammunition for them."

"Major Kominskiya is correct," Nathan said. "Ah, Bear is it?"

Bear Crepov stared wonderingly at the man.

Grisha shook his head and slowly got to his feet.

"They were preparing to do us harm when we stopped them," Slayer-of-Men said. "Instead they made a very nice report about how

Lieutenant Andreanoff and his men were retaking the redoubt from mutinous traitors. We don't have much time, Nathan."

"Do we have three days?"

"Probably not."

Grisha pointed at Valari. "This woman is poisonous. She has absolutely no morals and will be your death if you trust her in the slightest." He blinked heavily, so tired he felt drunk.

Nik stepped out of the shadows at the back of the room.

"I'll second that. Major Valari Kominskiya is a member of the Okhana cossacks. She has attained two promotions in the past six months. Such speed through the ranks is unheard of."

Valari gave him a burning glance.

"I don't know about that," she snapped, "they made you a captain, didn't they?"

Grisha almost laughed. She had more scrotum than most men.

"She's one of the main architects behind the plan to infiltrate the movement," Nik continued. "She condemned Grisha to death."

Valari stared down at the floor. "Would you at least put me in a cell so I can get some sleep?" she said tiredly.

"She's hiding something," Nathan said with a rush.

"What's wrong?" Nik asked.

Valari and Bear began to unbutton their heavy parkas.

"There's something hidden. On her, I think."

Valari's hands stopped moving and she stared at Nathan. "Do you read minds?"

"Get her parka off," Nathan yelled.

Slayer-of-Men ran a knife down the front of the garment and jerked. Buttons hailed across the stone floor as he roughly pulled it off her. A small, flat-black box hung between her breasts on a cord around her neck.

"What is that?" Slayer-of-Men asked.

Nathan stood up, grabbed it and jerked, breaking the cord as well as off-balancing Valari.

"It's a location transmitter," Nathan said and threw the box against the stone wall as hard as he could. It broke into countless pieces.

Valari laughed. "If they paid attention, there's an air strike on the way," she said through a twisted smile.

Something snapped in Grisha and he raised his machine pistol to kill her once and for all.

The walls seemed to scream. Concussion beyond sound knocked everybody off their feet. The floor sharply heaved and every light bulb in the room exploded, plunging them into darkness. They heard explosions and the roar of attacking planes.

Screams and shouts filtered through sudden smoke. The room rocked with another blast. A light pierced the stygian blackness and a voice shouted above the din.

"This way! Come this way! It leads to the lower levels."

Grisha didn't try to stand. He maintained a tight grip on his weapon and scrambled toward the light on all fours. And ran into somebody.

"Sorry, didn't see—" With a stomach-wrenching jolt, he realized the person was dead. He rolled the body over and peered at the face. Haimish stared glassily upward toward the gory cleft in his head left by a piece of concrete. Despair washed over Grisha.

He dropped Haimish and continued moving toward the flickering light. People scrambled between him and the battery lantern, semaphoring messages of terror and flight. As he got to the door another explosion smashed them down.

The light disappeared. Grisha's mind swam hard against the currents of concussion. Something tugged at him.

"Grisha," Wing said with a note of anguish. "You must help me, I can't pull your weight by myself."

The urgency in her voice spurred him into dizzy action. He moved his feet blindly, and with her tugging at him, fell down an incline littered with hard edges. Dimly he realized he sprawled on stone steps.

"Wait," he said tiredly. "I need to clear my head a little."

"Very well," she said, releasing his arm. "But there is fire up there and the smoke will get to this level soon."

"I . . . know." He gently cupped his hands over his ears. Her voice sounded like a whisper, but logic told him that she must be talking very loudly—if not shouting. His head felt stuffed with cotton.

One ear leaked blood.

Shit. Maybe I'm dying.

Fear lifted him back to full consciousness. "I'm ready," he said loudly.

"You don't gotta scream at me," Wing snapped.

"Oh, I thought I was deafened."

"Come on." She turned and moved carefully down steps outlined by a glow of light from around a distant corner.

43

Inside the Ruins of Chena Redoubt

Bear's mind went from stunned grayness to the alert certainty he was alone in a burning room. He peered around. Numerous bodies reflected firelight.

Valari crossed his mind for less than an instant before he sought escape. He scuttled across the carnage of the shattered chamber. Fire licked at the logs supporting the damaged roof.

She hadn't told him about the transmitter. But then he hadn't asked, either. A huge explosion outside the building sent him burrowing under two corpses.

Smoke curled around his nose and he pushed his way over the bodies. The head on one flopped over and he beheld the face of Slayer-of-Men. Bear relieved the dead man of his automatic weapon.

Valari had been standing directly in front of this man. What had killed him?

Pieces of burning wood fell from the ceiling, landing next to Bear. He lost all curiosity about anything other than self-preservation. A door yawned open, emitting a slight glow of welcome and offering solid walls leading downward. He stumbled through and braced himself against the rough wall.

He'd been in this passageway before, years ago. The cossacks had tortured an Indian to death in an attempt to make him confess to pilfering supplies. A frightened Bear had witnessed both the pilferage and the torture.

The Indian died insisting he was innocent. Bear was pretty sure the Indian was the guilty party, but then he had been drunk at the time. He was drunk for the torture, too.

With a roar the burning roof collapsed behind him. No turning back now. Was there a back way out of the interrogation block?

There had to be, he decided, because bodies never came out the front of the building. Heat intensified on his back and he eased down the steps toward the bend in the passage.

Voices rose out of the dimness ahead of him and he stopped. For a long anguished moment he thought someone was coming back up the steps. But the voices receded and he moved downward again.

By the time he got to where the stairway made an abrupt right angle, the mild concussion eased to nothing. Dank air flowed past him, feeding oxygen to the burning debris above. He squatted and edged the top of his head around the corner.

A kerosene lantern hung in the passageway, splashing red light across the cold, icy stones. He saw no sign of a guard. That's because they believed everybody but them to be dead, he thought smugly.

Emboldened, he rose to his feet and moved purposefully around the corner and down the steps. Just as he remembered, the steps bisected a passageway where one had to turn right or left. His brow furrowed.

Which way had they turned that long ago day? He had been drunk on vodka and nearly blind with fear. The cossacks had insisted he watch the interrogation as an object lesson.

At the time he hadn't been all that sure they weren't going to kill him, too. Rarely did he let those memories surface. But the catharsis worked and he distinctly remembered turning left.

So, on that day he had turned left. What about now? Did the torture chamber have a door that led outside the redoubt?

Suddenly the steps beneath his feet lurched and he fell heavily on the stones. A muffled explosion sounded from above as the stone basement shuddered and jerked. A more immediate noise caught his attention and he looked back up the stairs to see burning rubble pouring down like molten lava.

He pushed himself to his feet and staggered quickly down the passageway to the left. Behind him a wall of smelly, smoking debris firmly blocked the passageway. One less choice to agonize over, he decided.

He tightened his grip on the weapon and moved carefully toward the torture chamber.

44

In the Bowels of Chena Redoubt

Even though his body ached and he wanted nothing more than to lie down and sleep, Grisha forced himself to follow Wing. Ahead of them, Nathan's large-bore revolver prodded a bruised and stumbling Valari.

The ice-sheathed stone walls glistened redly from two kerosene lanterns carried by the small band of survivors. Out of thirty-odd people who had been in the room above, nine now crept through the dim depths of the redoubt. Iron-barred cells, some containing frozen corpses, testified to the malignant nature of this level.

"Do you think they have recaptured the redoubt?" Grisha asked.

"I think they have leveled the redoubt," Wing said shortly, "thanks to that bitch's transmitter."

"They didn't care if they killed her," Grisha said wonderingly.

"You of all people should know how cheap life is in the Czar's Amerikan possession," Nathan said over his shoulder. "Weren't they going to use you as a Judas goat? Didn't they kill a cossack officer and blame you?"

"Why does anyone work for them, then?"

"Ask the major," Wing muttered.

Nik, in the lead and carrying one of the lanterns, suddenly stopped.

"There's no way out."

"Yes, there is, but it was always heavily guarded," Nathan said with authority. "I've been down here before . . ." He audibly swallowed, and there was a catch in his voice when he continued. ". . . when I watched them torture my twin brother to death."

"They killed your brother in here and you escaped?" Grisha asked.

"I . . . did. He died in this place, and . . . and I was with him when it happened."

"My God," Nik said quietly.

The group fell quiet, staring at Nathan, whose face shone with reddish tears. Grisha's ears reached out in the sudden silence, searching for something he hadn't been aware of until just now. They were being followed.

"Nik," he said quietly and crooked an index finger.

The tall Russian handed his lantern to a soot-streaked figure whom Grisha finally recognized as Karin. Her eyes blazed defiantly as she grasped the bail.

"Which way, Nathan?" she asked.

"Over, there—" he pointed. "I think." The band shuffled onward while Nik and Grisha hung back in the shadows.

Nik stepped next to Grisha, his eyes large and hollow-looking.

"What is it?" he whispered.

"Someone's behind us."

"One of ours, maybe?"

"They haven't identified themselves," Grisha said flatly.

Nik peered back into the gloomy distance, his jaw muscles tightening. "Good point," he murmured, easing off the safety on his weapon.

They pulled apart in mutual understanding, taking up station across the dark cavernous space from each other. Grisha leaned against the icy wall and willed his breathing to relax. Only an occasional murmur from the group, now thirty meters away, broke the silence.

Exhaustion tugged at him, seductively whispering how sweet it would be to let his eyes close for a few moments. Lassitude slowly washed over him and he felt as if he were floating above all the strife, carnage, and death he had witnessed in the past two—my God, only two—days.

Out in the darkness boot leather scuffed against stone. Grisha's senses prickled to full awareness and he pointed his machine pistol toward the spot from where the sound had emanated.

He strained to hear where the next step would fall, wondering what would happen then.

From across the space something bumped woodenly.

Gunfire filled the chamber.

45

Bear Crepov finally caught sight of the group ahead of him. Only nine. He smiled, feeling the scar on his face sting as it pulled tight. The clip in his weapon held fifteen rounds—this would be almost too easy!

He eased forward as silently as a hunting lynx. The light from their lanterns provided him ample illumination for his stalk. Before he fired a shot he wanted them all in plain sight.

His step lightened as adrenaline surged through his veins. Confidence suffused him and he recalled that just a short time ago these people had pushed him about as if he were a *Creole*. They would pay.

They would pay dearly.

His foot touched a loose stone on the floor, and even as he froze all motion, it rolled over with the smallest possible sound of protest. To Bear it seemed an avalanche. His mouth went dry and his eyes flicked about madly, searching for motion, seeking reaction to his self-betrayal.

Nothing. Mutters and louder bursts of sound came to him from the rabble ahead. They heard nothing. He smiled tightly in the darkness.

A good *promyshlennik* could outsmart an Indian any day of the week and twice on Sunday. His confidence returned and he moved forward with a touch more caution. Stone pillars blocked some of his view of the group.

He edged ahead, eyes jumping from floor to light to floor again. There they were. He allowed himself a cat smile that suddenly froze on his face.

Only seven forms stood around the two lanterns. His heart accelerated, thudding in his ears like the shoes of peasant dancers on a wooden floor. Clenching his machine pistol more tightly in his suddenly sweaty hands, he eased toward the wall on his left.

Maybe a pillar blocked two of them? Had they stepped into the darkness to relieve their bladders? His ears detected no careless splatter of urine.

His breathing sped up, puffing into small clouds of condensation that drifted off sideways. Where were they? He bit his tongue slightly to keep from screaming the question at the dark corners.

His elbow gently found the wall. He stopped and stared away from the light—trying to force his irises to maximum diameter. His senses expanded outward seeking information.

Murmurs from the group ahead of him effectively masked any other small sounds in the cavernous space. Also, the light they carried with them made the unlit portions densest black. Cold air moved across his face.

Had they escaped? He craned his head around and spotted his quarry. They filed through a door; they had found a way out.

He brought his foot up to hurry after them and his right mukluk scraped against the wall. Suddenly he sensed movement on the other side of the chamber. Something, someone, hit a piece of heavy wooden furniture, probably a bench, with a dull thud.

Crepov aimed at the sound and squeezed the trigger on his machine pistol. The brilliant muzzle blasts illuminated the area in chattering flashes. A figure reeled behind a heavy wooden post and Crepov followed with a stream of rounds.

Something moved in the corner of his eye and he dropped to his knees. A different weapon roared and Bear Crepov felt the hot breath of rounds as they snapped past his head and blew rock splinters out of the wall, lacerating his face and neck. He rolled away from the menace and regained his feet.

"Nik! Are you okay?" someone said urgently, panic in his voice.

Bear grinned and hurried toward the door. He had hit the turncoat Rezanov. Good.

"Don't think I'm okay, but I'm still alive," Rezanov said and coughed a short liquid bark.

Light gleamed in the dark and Crepov realized the group was returning with the lanterns. His ammunition was spent. He edged through the open door of a cell and flattened against the wall.

They streamed past with no thought other than getting to their wounded comrade. Bear saw Valari as he slipped out behind them. The door creaked as he pushed it open.

Heart-stopping cold swirled around him. St. Anthony Redoubt lay over a hundred kilometers to the southeast. The colonel mentioned an armored column but Bear hadn't paid attention, his thoughts centering on Chena at the time.

He pulled his parka hood up and thanked the woods spirits the Indian hadn't cut the buttons off *his* coat. He hurried into the dark forest to search for his skis.

46

Wing and Karin worked frantically on Nik, trying to staunch the flow of blood. They contained the arm wound, but the chest wound continued to seep. The bubbles around the edges weren't a good sign, either.

Wing stared at his face and found him staring back at her.

"Not gonna make it, am I?"

"Nik," she said softly, not wanting to admit even to herself that he was in a bad way.

" 'S okay, think I'll catch up with Cora." He coughed. She wiped his mouth with her hand and found dark blood mixed with the sputum.

"I thought I hit the bastard!" Grisha said, searching the area with the second lantern. "It was Crepov—I saw him drop."

"We have to get out of here," Nathan said. "Can he be carried?"

"How cold is it outside?" she asked.

"About forty below."

"Why can't we just stay in here?"

"Whoever shot Nik knows about the back door, Wing," Nathan said tiredly. "They'll be back with Russian troops sooner or later."

"Nathan," Grisha said from the darkness, "why don't we post guards and rest for a while. The Russians hit us with planes, not ground troops. Even if they do roll in soon, things have to be crazy up there. They won't search the ruins until they get reinforcements."

Thank you, Grisha, Wing thought.

"Okay," Nathan answered. "You take charge of the guard and I'll get everyone in here sorted out. By the way, Wing, when you have a minute, I think my arm is broken."

"Let me see." She sat back and looked up at him.

"No, you take care of Nik."

"Nothin' . . . she can do, for me." Nik said. "Let 'er . . . fix it."

Wing knew Nik was right, but she didn't say anything. "Let me see your arm."

Nathan awkwardly slid his coat off. She saw white bone, jagged and sharp, dripping blood, sticking out of his arm.

"My God, you've got a compound fracture. Grisha, give me a hand here."

Grisha moved out of the darkness and she saw tears streaking his face as he stared at Nik. She glanced down at the dying man. Nik's eyes were closed and his chest shuddered with labored breathing.

"Grisha," she said softly, "we have to go on or it was all for nothing."

"What do you want me to do?"

"Put your arms around Nathan's chest. When I say 'now' you pull him back a meter—just as hard as you can. Understand?"

"*Da.*" He wrapped his arms around Nathan's chest and watched her face with bright eyes.

"Nathan, this is going to hurt, a lot." She gripped his wrist with both hands. "Now!"

Grisha pulled the slightly taller man completely off his feet as he jerked his wrist in the other direction. The arm straightened with a liquid snap and Nathan silently sagged, a sudden deadweight.

"Lay him down. See if anyone has an emergency medical kit with them."

Grisha moved off into the gloom and she looked around for something to tie around Nathan's arm. The leather ties in Nik's mukluks caught her eye and she pulled them free without hesitation.

For a splint she tied a long fragment of wood to Nathan's arm. Grisha came back with a medical field kit.

"Give me the syringe," she said.

He started to hand it to her, then stopped.

"What's in this?"

"Morphine, I want him to sleep."

Grisha hesitated. "Nathan has to travel, soon. Why don't you give it to Nik?" His lower face shone with moisture.

Pulling her gaze from Grisha to look at Nik was one of the hardest things she had ever done in her life. His eyes were still closed and his chest heaved as his drowning lungs tried to process enough oxygen to keep his body functioning.

She remembered how happy he had been with Cora, how radiant the two of them looked when they were together. For both of them to die in such a short space of time broke her heart. She had unconsciously seen them as a test case for her and Grisha.

Abruptly she wondered if that had doomed the couple. For some reason, a spirit or god or something hated her. Violence had taken her husband, then Alex, and now these two beautiful people. She couldn't endanger Grisha in the same way; it wouldn't be fair to him.

Nik's eyes opened and stared at her. "Don't . . . waste time . . ." His chest gurgled with his words. ". . . waiting. Love him . . . now."

And then he died.

47

Tired of the frigid, icy dungeon, Valari felt it was time to make her move. Amazed at still being alive, she had instantly obeyed every terse order given to her by Jackson. She thought the Indians would kill her when they discovered she had brought death down on them.

Her anger at the command in Tetlin knew no bounds. They had been all too willing to sacrifice her and Crepov in order to kill the rebels. Someone would pay for that, just as this rabble would pay for their treason. She shifted her weight in a vain search for comfort.

Jackson stared fixedly at her and the barrel of the Kalashnikov he held didn't waver from her chest. She didn't know him, she reflected. Maybe she could lull him into a mistake and fall for one of the oldest stratagems a woman could use.

Only one other person remained awake, and he sat by the door that led to the frozen forest outside. She turned her attention back to Jackson and smiled tentatively at him.

"It's a shame we had to meet under such unfortunate circumstances, Benny Jackson, you're a very appealing man."

"In what way?" he asked quietly.

"You seem so virile." She hesitated and ran her tongue over her lower lip. "Perhaps we could explore that a little more?"

"What did you have in mind?" His voice remained quiet and controlled.

She slipped off her coat and unbuttoned her wool shirt, watching his eyes for the first sign of lust. As the shirt slid off her shoulders she unhooked the front of her French brassiere and let her breasts swing free. His eyes remained locked on hers.

"What's the deal? You screw me and I let you walk?"

"We can have sex first and talk about the rest later." She did her very best to sound aroused and sensual. The cold stone basement sucked the warmth from her. Goose bumps prickled her skin and her nipples hardened painfully. She shivered.

"Please, if you want me, let's begin. I'm getting cold."

"Stand up," he said with a catch in his voice.

She successfully refrained from smiling as she got to her feet.

"Take off the rest of your clothes."

The mukluks and thermal socks dropped to the floor and then she swiftly unfastened the belt and let the wool trousers fall from her hips. Stepping out of her undergarment, totally naked, she lifted her arms to him and stepped forward.

He stood up quickly and backed away.

"What . . .?" she began.

"Keep walking," he ordered.

"To where?" She slowed. "There's nothing over there except—"

"The door," he said with a wolfish grin. "I wondered how I was going to repay you for Alf's death."

"One of your friends?" she asked. Fear welled up in her. This chamber was balmy compared to outside. "I didn't kill him. It was the fortunes of war."

"Keep walking," he said harshly. "You killed him and a lot of other people with your secret transmitter. I want you to suffer more than the instant it would take for a bullet to kill you." His grin got wider. "And you suggested this yourself!"

"Please, no—I'll freeze!"

"That's the idea."

The guard looked up and the flash of hope she felt faded instantly. It was the other Californian, Scanlon.

He gave her a wry smile and stepped back, opening the door.

"Jackson and Alf had been an item for a long time, sister," he said. "You killed the love of his life."

"Get out!" Jackson snarled, and kicked her out into the brittle night.

She fell full length in the sharp, frozen crystals before scrambling up again. The door swung shut and and she looked around desperately. Above the ten meter stone wall, the sky reflected the burning redoubt.

So much warmth, so far away. The subarctic night pulled the heat from her and she knew if she didn't move she would die. Chena Redoubt was foreign to her, she didn't know the layout. The wall looked impossibly long in both directions.

The cabins held her attention long enough to see that they stood empty—all the chimneys stood bereft of smoke. A glow in the distance at one end seemed the most promising. She trotted woodenly through the snow and fought panic as the numbness crept up past her ankles, her entire body ached and many portions had already lost feeling. Focusing on thoughts of revenge in order to ignore imminent death, she ran whimpering into the night.

48

The slamming door woke Grisha. He rolled over and came to his feet clutching the machine pistol.

"What?"

Jackson moved over to him. "I just threw the Russian bitch out."

"What?" Grisha became fully awake. "Are you crazy? She's more dangerous than three men."

"Three naked men?" Jackson asked with a ghastly grin.

"Huh?"

"I threw her out naked. It's at least forty or fifty below out there; she'll freeze up and die in short order. Too short a time for what she deserves, but it'll damn well kill her."

"You're betting our lives on that." Grisha tried to contain his anger. "What if she doesn't die? They'll know we're here and how to find us."

"She won't last ten minutes. Nobody could," Scanlon said. "Could they?"

"We have to send out a patrol," Grisha said, glancing down at his weapon. "Karpov's out there somewhere. I'd hate to get surprised by those bastards."

"Can't argue with that," Jackson said. "But who would go?"

"I will," Grisha said.

"You're really worried that she'll live, aren't you?"

"Damn right."

"Then I guess I'd better go with."

Grisha looked over at Scanlon. "Do you have a watch?"

"Sure."

"If we're not back in an hour, get everybody out of here, head north for the Yukon, okay?"

"Sure, Grisha, whatever you say."

"Thanks." He pulled his hood up and nodded at Jackson. "Ready?"

Valari's tracks arrowed toward distant light. Jackson suggested they follow.

"Sure, but let's do it from about a hundred yards out, say at the edge of those birch, okay?"

"You Russians are sure a strange bunch," Jackson said.

"I'm not a Russian," Grisha said tightly, "I'm an Alaskan."

"What's the difference?"

"Valari is a Russian." Grisha trudged off through the snow.

They moved along at a steady pace, fast enough to stay warm but slow enough that they didn't sweat. As they neared the light, a fiercely burning structure almost completely consumed, they slowed.

"I sure didn't see her back there anywhere," Grisha whispered.

"How the fuck would you know? We weren't close enough to her trail to see shit."

"We'd have seen a body."

"Not if she fell flat, dammit," Jackson hissed.

"I'm not going to argue with you about this," Grisha whispered sharply. "I think she made it to help and I'm going to get our people out of there."

"Suit yourself. But I think me and Scanlon will just stay pu—"

An engine's metallic growl cut through the night. Both men instantly fell to the ground and huddled behind the dubious bulk of a copse of frozen birch. A beam of light sliced above their heads as a half-track turned from its original path and proceeded down the back of the redoubt.

"They're following her tracks," Grisha said, allowing his feeling of horror to shade his words.

"Wonder how many of them there are in that thing?"

"They'll hold twenty fully armed soldiers."

"Maybe they're our guys?" Jackson said with an air of supplication.

"The day your grandmother wears a crown!"

"Yeah, you're probably right."

Slowly the half-track moved along the wall, like a wolf stalking a wounded rabbit.

"They don't know what to expect," Grisha said suddenly. "She must not have been able to talk to them."

"I'm amazed she was even able to breathe," Jackson muttered.

"I told you she was more dangerous than three men."

"C'mon, let's give these bastards a run for their money." Jackson rose to his feet and checked his weapon. "I'd just as soon die on my feet as freeze to death out here."

"You're not used to cold, are you?"

"This isn't just cold, my friend, this is the dark underbelly of frozen hell. How can you people take this year after year?"

"To be truthful, this is my first winter in the Interior. We never have temperatures this low in Akku."

"Where I come from, we never have winter. This shit is for the birds."

"What birds?"

"Never mind, let's sneak up on those guys and ruin their day."

They trotted along, keeping pace with the machine grinding along a hundred meters away. Suddenly the half-track stopped and the lights winked out. Grisha and Jackson halted in their tracks, eyes wide and ears straining.

Dark figures dropped out of a hatch in the back of the darker machine and moved forward. Dull light glinted off a gun barrel. The half-track lurched and swung out away from the wall, toward the trees.

Grisha and Jackson dropped. The half-track spun around and stopped, engine idling. Two figures emerged through the roof, uncovered the heavy machine gun mounted over the cab and trained it on the wall of the redoubt.

The headlights flared like twin suns to illuminate a twenty meter circle on the stone wall. Exactly in the middle of the eye of radiance sat the door to the bowels of Chena Redoubt.

"We gotta warn them," Jackson whispered urgently.

"How? We make one move and those people will kill us."

The Californian spat in the snow. "Fuck!"

"Be patient," Grisha said. "We're not defeated. Think of us as a secret weapon. The last thing the Russians will expect is an attack from their rear."

"Would you be this blasé, if it was that Wing chick sitting on the other side of the door instead of Scanlon?"

"What are you trying to say?"

"All I'm saying is that I'm as attached to Jimmy Scanlon as you are to Wing, except that I don't particularly want to sleep with Scanlon."

Grisha pointed his machine pistol at the Californian's chest.

"Wait a fuckin' minute!" Jackson whispered harshly. "I know a man with a yen when I see one. I don't care if you don't want to admit it, but I think I made my point, no?"

"Yes," Grisha said, lowering the weapon. "So what do you want to do?"

"I want to take out that half-track, now."

"Once we shoot them, the others will turn on us and that will be it. Our people inside still won't have a chance."

"God, you can be dense. Must be from livin' in this stone-age culture up here." Jackson's smile reflected light. "If we capture the fuckin' 'track, we can wipe those other guys out and then we don't hafta walk away from here, we can ride."

The beauty of it overwhelmed Grisha. "Yeah." Part of his fogged brain wondered why he hadn't thought of it himself.

Both men moved determinedly toward the back of the half-track, where rapidly condensing engine exhaust clouded the frigid air. They could not have asked for better cover. They crawled through the back of the machine and paused, peering through the hatch at two men facing away from them in the gun tub.

"We know you are in there," an amplified voice blared English into the night. "If you surrender, you will live."

"Come on," Grisha said, and stepped into the canvas-covered box and waited with his weapon trained on the two soldiers. A moment later Jackson stood beside him.

"Shoot when they shoot," Jackson whispered in his ear, "we don't want to draw a lot of attention."

With a cold knot of fear and determination in the pit of his stomach, Grisha nodded agreement. They sidled forward.

One of the soldiers said something and the other one nodded. The machine gun fired a burst into the door of the redoubt. Without hesitation, almost in perfect unison, Grisha and Jackson shot the soldiers—ending the burst.

Their rounds blended into the cacophony of the heavier weapon. One soldier thudded into the wall of the vehicle and slid off the gun platform and down to the floor. The other bounced off the machine gun itself, knocking the muzzle into the air, before he too collapsed on the floor of the box.

"You have two minutes to surrender," the voice thundered again. "After that we will show as much mercy as you gave Major Kominskiya."

Grisha and Benny quietly crawled up onto the gun platform. They could see eighteen men ringed around the edge of the light, waiting to charge into the redoubt.

Jackson examined the machine gun.

"I know how to operate this," he whispered through a smile.

"The officer must be inside," Grisha said. "I'll guard the hatch from the cab and shoot anyone who tries to come back here."

"I really appreciate that, man." Grisha couldn't detect any levity in Jackson's voice.

Grisha heard a tiny voice and spied a headset on the floor. He picked it up and pressed one of the phones to his ear.

"-are you doing back there?" snapped a voice in Russian "I ordered you to blow the damned door to flinders!"

"Sorry, sir," Grisha answered in that language, "I was taking a piss."

"Who is this?"

"They want us to shoot," Grisha said.

"Bitchin." Jackson fired into the edge of the light. Five Russian soldiers died before the others realized something was amiss. Jackson swung the weapon in an arc, scything down the dumbstruck troopers.

The hatch on the cab burst open and Grisha sprayed the opening with a long burst. A scream curled up to an impossible octave and stopped. The door remained open. The machine gun ceased its thunder.

"Come out," Grisha called in Russian. "Or I'll throw in a grenade."

"*D-da!*" a strained voice said from the opening. The corporal wasn't wearing his parka, and the growing blossoms of blood soaked the chest of his field jacket. He tried to step toward them, but his legs buckled and he fell in a heap at their feet.

Grisha rolled him over with his foot. Sightless eyes regarded eternity. Grisha pulled a grenade from his parka.

Jackson frowned and held up his hand in admonition. Grisha twisted the grenade to show him the pin still intact, then he tossed it into the cab.

Silence.

"If there's anyone alive in there, they got more balls than I do," Jackson said fervently.

Grisha peeked inside, machine pistol at the ready. A cossack captain lay crumpled on the floor in front of the seat, dead. Grisha straightened up and smiled at Jackson.

"Let's get our people and get the hell out of here."

49

West of Chena on the Russia-Canada Highway

The half-track rumbled through the night as the glow in the sky dimmed behind them. The radio ordered Captain Romanov to report to base immediately. Five minutes later the order repeated.

"Shut that damn thing off," Jackson said drowsily.

"Go to sleep," Grisha replied as he steered the 'track carefully down the RustyCan. Between them on the bench seat Wing snored lightly, her head thrown back and her cheek resting on Jackson's shoulder.

"I want to know as much about their intentions as possible." From the heavier snores at his side, Grisha knew he was talking to himself again. He had done a lot of that through this endless night.

He glanced at the compass again to see if the road had yet swung due west. Their decision to make a dash for Tanana had been greatly weighted by a surprising statement from Jackson.

"You get us there, I can get us out of Russian Amerika, if need be."

Wing argued that their objective was not escape but independence. Jackson pointed out that anyone who wished could stay in Tanana. So they tied down the wounded in the back, secured the heavy machine gun, and smashed through five kilometers of birch and spruce forest before angling over and finding the road itself.

The two in the cab with Grisha supposedly served as guards in the event they came across Russian troops. After ten miles in the cab's warm confines Wing and Jackson fell asleep. Grisha felt thankful for his three-hour nap in the redoubt.

The subarctic night lay stiff and brittle on a land cloaked with snow meters deep. The northern lights capered unappreciated above them.

As he drove he thought about Nik and wondered if his family would ever know how bravely he died. Not that it made any difference. He also wondered if the lump in his throat would ever go away.

So many good people had died in such a short time that Grisha had trouble believing he would never see them again. Chandalar Roy had not come out of the redoubt. The loss of Slayer-of-Men would be felt throughout the Dená Nation. He wondered if Malagni still lived.

The half-track bounced as it went into the ditch and Grisha groggily steered it back into the middle of the road. He had almost gone to sleep himself. He pulled his foot off the accelerator and glanced at the other two. They snored on.

The track came to a stop and he put it in neutral, stepped out of the cab, and urinated on the ground. The hatch to the troop compartment popped open and Karin stuck her head out.

"Is there time for me to do that, too?"

"Of course. How's Nathan?"

"Still in the land of morphia." She jumped down to the road. "Look the other way, please."

He grinned and looked up the road as she made water. The grin evaporated as lights bobbed toward them.

"Company," he barked. "Unlimber the machine gun."

"Yes, sir," she said and clambered back into the half-track.

Grisha jumped in the cab, turned off the headlights, and pushed Wing's leg.

"Wake up you two, we have visitors."

"Visitors?" Jackson said, rubbing his eyes.

Wing sat up straight, eyes searching quietly ahead as if she had been wide awake the entire time.

"They have to be Russians," she said.

"Why?" Grisha asked. "Couldn't it be a relief column from Tanana?"

"It's only one half-track, not a column," Wing said. "But it could still be our people."

"What's the DSM frequency?" Jackson asked.

"One-oh-four kilocycles," Wing said.

Jackson turned the dial on the radio. Static popped and crackled on a discernible carrier wave. He picked up the microphone.

"Chena Two to approaching vehicle. Identify yourself or suffer the consequences."

Grisha put the half-track in gear and steered for the edge of the road. They all waited as the static grew in volume.

"Maybe it is Russians," Grisha muttered.

"Chena Two, who's in charge there?" The voice from the radio spoke English with a Yukon River accent.

"Identify yourself," Jackson snapped.

The lights slowed and came to a halt. Grisha estimated the other vehicle to be about three hundred meters from them. He twisted around and opened the hatch behind his head.

"Karin, you ready with the machine gun?"

"Yes, but I'm freezing my butt off. Let's shoot the bastards and get it over with."

"Not yet. I'll tell you when to shoot."

"Okay," she said resignedly.

"What does 'Tanana One' mean to you, Chena Two?" the voice asked hesitantly.

Wing grabbed the microphone out of Jackson's hand.

"It means Blue is in charge. Please put her on."

"Blue Bostonman?" Grisha said. "From the labor camp?"

She nodded her head and grinned, bending the scar nearly double.

"Wing!" a new voice issued from the speaker. "I would recognize your voice anywhere, even over a crappy Russian radio."

"Where are you going, Blue?"

"To join you. Before I say anything more, blink your headlamps for the number of brothers Malagni has."

"All right." Wing stared through the windshield at the distant lights. "Flash the headlights twice," she said in a tight voice.

Grisha complied.

"I see you, Wing!" Blue said. "Meet you halfway."

Wing hung up the microphone. "Do it."

Grisha let the clutch out and the half-track moved forward slowly, clanking along in low gear. "You're sure this is okay?" he asked out of the side of his mouth.

"Didn't that sound like Blue to you?" she asked.

"Yeah, but I couldn't see if anyone was holding a gun to her head or not."

"If somebody had been holding a gun to her head, she would have used the term 'squaw candy' when she spoke to me."

"Tell her we're hungry," Grisha said tersely. "Ask her if she has anything to eat."

"Jesus, but you're paranoid," Wing said with a growl. She picked up the microphone and repeated the question.

"Sure, we got food." Blue's voice all but chirped over the radio. "We got caribou, moose jerky, and even some squaw candy. I remember how much you like squaw candy, Wing."

"Oh, no," Wing said quietly. "She's a prisoner. How are we going to get her out of there alive?"

"We might not," Jackson said, now fully awake. "Depends on what the Russians have in mind."

"They don't know that we know they're there," Grisha said. "They expect us to be surprised."

"And defeated," Wing said with a ghastly smile. Abruptly she pulled the hood of her parka up, fastened the front, pushed open the hatch, and crawled into the back of the half-track. "Pull up and stop beside them, Grisha," she said over her shoulder. "Take out the driver. We'll handle the show from that point."

"Who's 'we'?"

"Warrior women." The hatch slammed behind her.

Grisha glanced over at Jackson. The Californian stared steadily at the approaching lights.

"Y'know," Jackson said absently, "if I'd met someone like that at the right point in my life, I might have developed a thing for women."

"I don't think I want to hear about it just now," Grisha said. He picked up the microphone. "Hey, Blue. This is Grisha. Remember me?"

"Grisha?" Her voice sounded tentative. "The little skinny guy who blew the head off that pig of a cossack sergeant?"

Grisha smiled. Blue knew her warning had been interpreted.

"Yeah," he said with a chuckle, "I've even killed a couple more since then."

Only fifty meters separated the two half-tracks. The other half-track suddenly stopped. Grisha braked and took his machine out of gear; the fight would be here.

"Jackson, get out on the running board. When I turn on my spotlight you shoot hell out of the driver."

"But, what about this Blue person, won't she get hit?"

"She knows what's going to happen." Grisha remembered the labor camp. "Besides, she's a survivor."

"Okay, you're the boss." Jackson swung out of the cab, leaned across the hood, and took aim at the approaching half-track.

Grisha rolled down the window and picked up the machine pistol in his left hand. Glacial air bit at his exposed skin. The other half-track lurched forward and closed on them in an obscenely short amount of time.

"Put on your interior lights," Blue said with an edge in her voice.

"I asked you first," Grisha said lightheartedly. He gripped the handle and swung the spotlight around to bear on the other cab. He thumbed on the light.

50

Wing turned from the hatch and saw Karin behind the machine gun mounted over the cab. Even though they moved at a snail's pace, the subarctic air knifing over the cab cut like cold steel. It won't be long, she thought.

"They're Russians!" she said clearly. "But they have some of our people."

"Who?" Karin demanded as she braced her foot against the wall and cocked the heavy weapon.

"Blue Bostonman, the sister of Lynx."

"Damn them," Karin said through clenched teeth.

"Who's able to fight down there?"

"Jimmy Scanlon, Heron, and that Eskimo guy, Simon."

"Get 'em out here," Wing said. "We need all the help we can get."

Karin disappeared and Wing studied the machine gun. Moments later, the men followed Karin back though the hatch. Everybody carried a weapon.

"Here's my idea," she said, talking fast.

Master Sergeant Lupasiac clutched his thirty years of service to the Czar in a grip of grim patriotic fervor. A bandage gleamed whitely, despite its crusted brownish-red edges, over the burly Georgian's dark face. His trademark vein of irascibility lay bare to the elements like an open pit mine.

"Keep them lulled," he growled. "We'll have this over in moments."

His prisoner seemed mesmerized either by the vehicle they crept toward or the knowledge she had only minutes left to live, condemned by her own friends. Just the same, he found it impossible to believe this addled cow could direct a battle as devastating as Tanana. The sergeant mentally dismissed her and growled over his shoulder to the corporal.

"As soon as I stop, kick the ramp down and surround their vehicle. I want them alive if possible, but don't take any chances."

"Yes, Wulff," the corporal said. "As you say."

Master Sergeant Wulff Lupasiac ignored the familiarity. Corporal Titov had earned the right to call him by his Christian name many years ago. His mind dwelt on the eight troopers in the back of the half-track.

Do we have enough men? Is there any way this cow of a woman can discover their numbers without alerting them?

He felt confident of total surprise. His men would surround the enemy vehicle in moments. Then he'd have something to show Tetlin Redoubt for the loss of his command, besides this ignorant savage beside him.

Unbidden, the overland fighting retreat from a destroyed and burning Tanana Redoubt kaleidoscoped through his memory. Pain, fear, hate, and hunger all fought to dominate his mind, but discipline hammered them down and allowed him to focus on revenge and duty. These vermin would pay dearly for their rebellion.

But why hadn't the Siberian fighter squadrons answered their call for help? The last he heard, all the Yak fighters in Alaska had been destroyed by the rebels. How could that be?

The point man apprehended this Blue person. At first she claimed the tea she brewed was intended for the Russian crew of the half-track in which she sat. His men searched for fifteen minutes but found no trace of a crew.

At no time had she offered any resistance to them, and even volunteered that she knew some of the rebels' code words. This information condemned her mere hours later.

"The leaders of each battle are called by the name of the battle," she said with a vacuous grin, following it up with a little giggle. "The battle leader at Tanana was called 'Tanana One,' and the leader at Chena was called 'Chena One,' you see?"

"How do you know this?" Wulff Lupasiac asked carefully.

"The sergeant who was boss in this half-track told his men about it. I overheard him."

Could this gap-toothed cow be as stupid as she seemed? So many questions, so many answers to puzzle out, and he was so tired. But the person on the radio, a woman he thought, had identified her as the leader of the Tanana revolt.

Nearly unimaginable.

"You shall die for this," he had told her. "But if you cooperate I promise you a quick, painless death."

Thus far she had cooperated completely. His blood boiled upon hearing one of the rebels boast of killing cossacks. He would personally torture that one until death ended his penance.

The only thing that bothered him now was that the rebel half-track had stopped moving. He peered into the dense night but could see no figures moving against the mottled forest background.

"Titov, stand by," he barked over his shoulder.

"Yes, Wulff. We're ready."

"Remember that you're cossacks."

He pulled up, nearly bumper to bumper with the other vehicle.

"Tell them to open their interior lights so we may see them," he said with a growl.

"Put on your interior lights," the woman said in a strange voice. Wulff glanced at her as she dropped the microphone and then rolled off the bench seat onto the floor of the cab. Alarm shot through him as all his instincts screamed.

"What are you—"

"I asked you first," a voice said over the radio.

"Titov!" he screamed. "Go!"

Bright light flooded the cab. Bullets, shock, and darkness crowded it out.

Wing held her breath as the half-track stopped. Light blossomed in the night. Bullets shattered the stillness. The loading ramp at the back of the half-track crunched down and dark figures poured across it.

"Fire!" she screamed.

Gun fire from three directions poured across the figures and into the opening. In moments nine bodies lay smashed and twitching, their blood leaking silently to freeze in the snow.

"Cease fire!" Wing shouted. She walked over to the bodies.

"Blue?"

Something scraped in the cab. Five gun muzzles moved toward the sound, hunting dogs tracking quarry.

"Wait!" a muffled voice cried. "It's me." The door abruptly flew open and a bloody body tumbled to the ground.

"Okay," The voice called out from the cab, louder and clearer now. "I'm coming out. Don't shoot."

Blue clambered down out of the half-track and peered around owlishly. Blood covered her head and parka.

"Blue, are you hurt?" Wing cried.

"It ain't my blood." She glanced down at the body.

Wing dropped her weapon, ran over, and embraced the older woman. "How wonderful to see you."

"Oh, that was such a close thing," Blue said, hugging her in return. "Thank goodness for code words."

"There's much I have to tell you," Wing said. "Very little of it is good."

"And I have much to tell you," Blue replied. "And most of it is good."

Jackson slapped Grisha on the back. "Good job, Captain. I'll take Jimmy and a couple others and drive the other half-track. Signal if you need me."

"I'm glad you're with us, Benny."

51

Russia–Canada Highway, Near the Yukon River

". . . and we know Yak fighters scrambled out of Siberia and Tetlin, but they never got to Tanana." Blue paused and stared at Grisha and Wing on the seat beside her. "Do either of you know why?"

Grisha concentrated on his driving, but managed one word, "Haimish."

"Yeah," Wing said absently. "His last act seems to have borne fruit."

"Hamish is dead?" Blue asked quietly. "What did he do to stop the fighters?"

"I think he arranged for help from the U.S.A., maybe got us a squadron of fighters. He worked for the Yanks, you know."

"No, I didn't know that, but I ain't surprised. You sure he's dead?"

"Yeah. And Chandalar, too."

"Ah, damn!" Blue's voice broke for the second time in twenty minutes. "Losin' all these people I love, who helped me be the person I am, makes me die a little bit with each one. I don't know how much more I can take."

The death of her brother, Lynx, didn't seem to jar her as much as hearing about Malagni and Slayer-of-Men. "You weren't sure about Malagni?"

"I know he lost his arm and a lot of blood." It seemed like a million years ago to Grisha. "But I won't believe he's dead until I see his grave."

"Yet Nathan the mind-bender still lives," Blue said shortly.

"He's hurt," Wing said testily. "He might even lose an arm."

Blue turned and stared at her friend. "But no bullet touched him, right?"

"His arm was broken by a piece of falling roof." Wing sounded defensive. "No, he has no bullet wounds."

Blue fastened her gaze on Grisha.

"What do you think, little brother? Is our Nathan a witch or just damn lucky?"

"Who knows? I believe he's especially intuitive. But if he can read minds he has an affliction I wouldn't wish on my worst enemy," Grisha mumbled. "There's no way to turn off what others are thinking. Think how awfully boring that could become."

Both women laughed, muting the tension.

Blue sobered quickly. "It might be boring, but I think he can control people around him."

"How can you believe that?" Wing asked incredulously. "He's been unconscious for hours and I don't feel any different than when he's awake."

"I can believe it 'cause he's the strangest damn thing to come downriver in my lifetime," Blue said. "Grisha, how about you?"

He yawned hugely. "I feel more awake when he's around."

"I'm serious, Grisha."

Grisha glanced past Wing at the larger woman. "If he's controlling me, I don't know about it." He paused. "But I almost wish he was, I'd have someone else to blame for my screwups."

Nobody laughed.

"What was the situation at Tanana when you left?" Wing asked.

"Mopping up. Most of the garrison were cossacks and knew they were dead even if they surrendered." Blue's tone grew bleak. "They didn't surrender, but we took the redoubt anyway."

"At what cost?"

"Fred Seetamoona and his assault team feinted to draw their fire, they all died. That's how we were able to take the place at all."

"Fred was on the council," Wing said slowly.

"We've lost five council members that I know of over the past few days," Blue said.

"How did you end up in this half-track with a bunch of desperate survivors?" Grisha asked.

"Pure, crazy chance. We captured three of these things and we only had two people who could drive them, so I volunteered to guard this one until somebody could come back for it." She grinned, showing the gap in her teeth. "The cossacks got there first and I just played dumb, which under the circumstances, wasn't too difficult."

"So what's next?" Grisha asked.

"What do you mean?" Wing said.

"We've got Tanana, Chena is in ruins and won't be of much use to them or us for a long time to come—"

"Not to mention Huslia, Koyuk, Fort Yukon, and Bridge," Wing said quickly.

"Where?" Grisha asked.

"Those are the other strongpoints on the highway now in our hands. We took Fort Yukon because we needed the airfield," Blue said. "Finish what you started to say."

"I already said it: what's next? Where do we go from here, attack south?"

"No," Blue said quickly. "We're fighting a revolution for independence, we have no legal reason to hold more than the land of the Dená."

"But Nathan and Chan mentioned attacks on St. Nicholas and Tetlin."

"Tetlin is inside the Dená Republik and is the strongest redoubt outside St. Nicholas. We hope to negotiate them out of there," Blue said with a trace of bitterness. "We planned an attack on the slave pens in each place, to gain more followers, but that didn't happen."

"Why not?"

"Too cold. The prisoners would have frozen to death before we could help them. As soon as the ice goes out on the Yukon, we'll hit Tetlin, if they haven't freed our people before then."

"Blue, you're pretty optimistic if you believe that," Wing said with a snort.

"Finish answering my question," Grisha said.

"We consolidate and negotiate," Blue said. "And, if we have to, we keep fighting."

"The Russians will definitely counterattack," Grisha said. "They won't give up this easily."

"We've hurt them badly here—" Blue began.

"Do you think this is the cream of the Czar's army?" Grisha said. "This is the frontier, a colony. This is where they send the people who are being punished or aren't worth the food they eat."

He licked his lips, hating himself for demeaning the sacrifice of others. "You were able to plant charges at the strongpoints before your initial attack, weren't you?"

"How'd you know what we did?" Blue asked.

"It's what I would have done. But the point is, the next Russian troops you see will be more aware, better trained, and possess few social skills. The real Russian Army will be a lot harder to beat than these trash-heap garrison troops."

Wing turned and stared at him. "We will fight until we die. I don't think the Russian Army cares that much about the Czar's holdings in Russian Amerika."

"The leaders do the thinking; all armies are paid to fight."

"If enough of them die, they will realize that to fight us is tantamount to death," Blue said with finality. "Their choices are to go home, join us, or die."

"Maybe you should tell them that," he said in a musing tone. "Perhaps they would come to their point of decision much faster."

"Propaganda's not a bad idea," Wing said. "Do we still have a printing press?"

"More than one," Blue said. "We'll print up small notices in Russian and English and distribute them in all the Russian-held redoubts."

"How will you deliver them?" Grisha asked.

"Getting in and out of their areas is easy. We're all worthless Indians or *Creoles* to them," Wing said, "we've just got to be very careful."

"They'll be looking at everybody twice from now on, especially Indians and *Creoles*."

"What's the matter, Grisha, don't you want the job?" Blue asked with a laugh.

"I think I'd be the wrong man for it," he said wryly. "Give me something else to do."

"I've been thinking about that," Blue said. "But I need to talk to War Minister Nathan about it first."

"If it helps the Dená Republik, I'll do it."

Blue glanced at Wing. "With Chan dead, how do we finance this war?"

"What do you mean?" Grisha asked. "What did Chan have to do with finances?"

"That's right, you didn't know," Wing said. "Chan was the money behind the DSM and the revolution. His grandfather discovered gold up in the hills north of Chena way back in the '30s, and had the presence of mind to keep quiet about it."

"Yeah," Blue said. "He kept the secret in his family. They operated that mine for years and years, hauled most of the gold down into British Canada to sell it."

Wing nodded. "They were rich, the whole family. Then one of Chan's uncles got drunk and told another Dená about it, and a cossack heard him."

"Oh, hell," Grisha said in a reverent tone.

"Yeah," Blue said. "Cossacks kidnapped the three brothers who had inherited. And their families were tortured to death in front of them. But no one told the location of the mine."

"Because," Wing said, hesitating for a beat, "the cossacks had missed getting Chandalar. He had been over in Nenana visiting a girl and her family. So the rest of the family died at the hands of the cossacks knowing Chan would revenge their deaths."

"Chan told the girl he couldn't marry, but would always love her, then went looking for other angry Athabascans," Blue said. "And he found a lot of 'em!"

"He recruited the first ten Dená Separatists," Wing said, "told them to find as many others as they could and he went down to the United States. He was arrested in a border town and turned over to the army. Within a week he was talking to someone on President Taft's staff."

"That's when Haimish came north the first time," Blue said. "I was just a little girl, but I remember him coming through our door and wonderin' what he was, cause he looked like one of those Eskimo billikens."

"But now they're both dead," Grisha said, sorry to pull them back to now.

"Yeah," Wing said in a husky voice. "But to answer your question, Blue, Chan willed the whole operation to the Dená people. We have bank accounts in British Canada, French Canada, and the United States with a lot of money in them."

52

Russia-Canada Highway, East of Tanana

A half hour later they came to a large tree lying across the road. Grisha started to drive into the ditch to go around it.

"No!" Blue shouted, her words nearly blurring in a staccato chatter. "This is our roadblock. The ditches are mined!"

Grisha, hands suddenly shaking in an adrenaline rush, jumped on the brake, bringing them to a sudden stop. Cries of pain and anger could be heard from the back of the half-track. The vehicle stopped with the front wheels off the road, resting in the ditch.

Grisha looked over at the two women, wondering if his face was as pale as theirs.

"Did you know this was coming up?"

"Yes," Blue said, panting, "I knew, I meant to mention it earlier. But we got to talking."

"Anything else you forget to mention?"

"Yeah, get out of the cab unarmed, with your hands in the air."

Grisha shook his head and grinned. "Remind me to talk to you about timing." He pushed the door open and stepped out on the running board with his still-shaking hands in the air.

"We're friends from Chena Redoubt," he shouted into the dark, snow-filled forest. The scent of wood smoke hung in the air, cold burned in his nostrils, the fresh air felt clean and good. "Blue is with us."

"Who are you?" a voice asked from the darkness.

"Grigoriy Grigorievich!"

"For what battle were you cashiered from the Troika Guard?" the voice demanded.

"Bou Saada, French Algeria." Grisha frowned and peered into the trees.

A figure strode out of the dark, stunted, frozen forest.

"It really is you, Major, isn't it?"

Grisha stared hard at the person but didn't recognize him until Heinrich Smolst grinned and grabbed him a bear hug. The two pounded each other on the back, laughing. Other figures materialized and surrounded the two vehicles.

"My God, Heinrich," Grisha gasped. "They told me you had come over to our side, but I thought you were among the dead at Chena Redoubt. It is so good to see you, my friend."

"The Russians made me a captain, and I still hated them for what they did to you. I've waited ten years for the exact right moment to tell the Czar to go fuck himself, and it arrived out there in the woods, when I was surrounded by your Dená."

The refugees climbed out of the half-tracks, adding their welcomes.

"Look me up tomorrow, Heinrich, please?"

"Of course, Major!"

"Not 'Major.' Grisha, just like when we were both private soldiers."

"Looks like we're in that category again anyway. I'll find you tomorrow, Grisha."

A cable and pulley easily swiveled the tree out of the road. The small convoy rolled across the frozen Yukon River to where Tanana slept under the scrolling northern lights.

The half-tracks pulled up onto the high riverbank and stopped in front of a large building bright with light. Shell holes in the walls and roof already boasted tarp bandages. Grisha realized he didn't have to drive anymore. The exhaustion he had been denying swept over him. He stumbled into the warm room and collapsed in a corner, fast asleep.

"Major Grigorievich, wake up."

The voice penetrated his dream of being on the water again. So vivid was the dream that when he blinked his eyes, he expected to see the interior of *Pravda*'s cabin. The crisp apparition staring down at him instantly brought him back. He moaned before his wits returned and he could stop himself.

"Heinrich, I'm not a major anymore," he said roughly. He stretched and, when the scent of cooking food finally registered, realized he was famished.

"About time you woke up," Smolst said. "You've been asleep for over a day."

To his amazement Grisha found himself undressed and in a bunk. He glanced around wildly. Three-high stands of built-in bunks filled the room. All the others were empty.

"How long have I been in here?"

"Since about oh-two-hundred yesterday."

"What time is it now?"

"Almost ten-hundred."

Grisha took stock, decided he felt pretty good. Voices wafted in along with food aromas. His stomach growled and he sat up, searching for his clothes.

The barracks contained a dining hall where nearly thirty people sat, talking, drinking tea, and eating. He blinked as he came out of the sleeping area into the brightly lit room. Heinrich prodded him from behind.

"Over there, near the wall."

Grisha blinked again and saw Wing, who saw him at the same time.

"Grisha. Over here."

He felt something he couldn't define when he looked at her. Relief that she was safe, the old deep-seated hunger he'd always felt but had denied, and finally something else he couldn't name—but it made his heart feel full.

She stood and embraced him. He couldn't remember anything that smelled quite as good as she did. He pulled back slightly and kissed her on her scar. She blushed and edged away.

"I want you to meet some people." She gestured at the five people sitting around the table: Blue, Claude, Nathan, and two other War Council members, an old man and a younger woman.

"I am honored to finally meet you," the old man said. Bright eyes flashed in the network of weathered wrinkles on his face. "I am Chief Andrew of the Dot Lake Dená." He held out his hand and Grisha shook it, completely at a loss.

A middle-aged woman with streaks of gray in her black hair smiled up at him.

"As am I," she said. "I'm Anna Samuel from Fort Yukon."

"Yes, I saw you both at the first War Council meeting, but I didn't meet you personally."

"Grisha is very confused," Nathan said gently, his intense eyes flashing from person to person. "Perhaps he should eat before we talk with him."

"Oh," Wing said, "of course. Pardon us, please." She led him over to the row of windows where the odor of cooked food became overwhelming.

Back at the table, as he wolfed down potatoes and moose steak, Wing spoke in a very low voice. The others listened quietly.

"We are in desperate straits. The Russians are massing troops on the Diomedes and at Tetlin. They're already moving north out of St. Nicholas."

Grisha's spoon paused midway to his mouth. "How many people do we have to put up against them?"

"That's a good question. A lot of Dená think we are mad to try this and are leaving the fortified villages, the redoubts, to go live with relatives in the bush. Other villages are fortifying against us, and announcing they are loyal to the Czar."

"How many do we know we have on our side?" Grisha asked through a mouthful of food, then paused to swallow. "That'll tell us what we can do."

"It seems we don't have to ask," Anna said to the others at the table.

"No," Nathan said with a smile on his pockmarked face. "He's already talking like a field commander."

Grisha nearly choked in the middle of a swallow. "Field commander! It's been years since I was a major, I'm not even a Dená."

"Don't forget we six are over half the War Council," Chief Andrew said in his careful voice, "Yesterday the Dená Republik officially declared independence. We're offering you a commission in the army, Colonel Grigorievich."

"Why me? There are so many others."

"You think efficiently during fluid situations," Wing said, holding up an index finger. "You have years of experience in the field and have proven yourself to be a commander of fighters." Another finger popped up. "You know the Russians—you've lived among them your entire life and served in their army. And we trust you to do your best." Four fingers splayed toward him.

"But I'm not a Dená, I'm only half Kolosh."

"There has been friction between some of our people," Nathan said, looking down at his hands. "Between 'upriver' Indians and 'downriver' Indians. People from Nulato don't completely trust people from Old Crow. There are factions in all areas."

"Why would they care, aren't we all in this together?"

"Some old, very old habits die hard. Everyone fights the same enemy, but when it comes to taking orders from someone whose people have always been suspect . . ." Nathan shook his head.

"There are soldiers in the ranks who know you, served with you in the Troika Guard, they speak highly of you. You've shown us all your mettle over the past few days."

"It doesn't feel right. I really think you could find someone else if—"

Chief Andrew raised his hand, palm out. "There's the other side of this aspect to consider. If we fail in our fight for independence, you would be the scapegoat in the eyes of many. You're not even of the People."

"But I plead with you to say yes," Nathan said. "There is much we think you can do."

Grisha considered Chief Andrew's warning along with Nathan's entreaty. He felt honored by the opportunity to lead these people he had come to respect and even love. This cause was important to him: much more immediate than anything he had ever done for the Czar.

But Chief Andrew was right: if his troops failed, Grisha would be blamed.

Which makes perfect sense to me.

He knew he would probably never see Akku or any other part of southeast Alaska again.

"Very well. Where do I serve?" Grisha tried to overcome the feeling of hollow unreality inside him.

"Colonel Grigorievich, you will be in charge of the Southern Defensive Force," Anna said crisply. "You are ordered to protect the highway between Chena and Tanana while retaking Chena for the Dená Republik."

"How many people are in my army?"

"A little over eight hundred, so far," Wing said. "Our scouts say the Russians haven't reinforced Chena yet. They're too busy building up Tetlin. They must think we're going to attack."

"What about the political angle?" Grisha asked. "Didn't the Californians offer some help, and Haimish's people?"

"The U.S. has a squadron of fighters on the ground in Galena but it's still uncertain if they are going to stay," Wing said. "The Californians are supposed to have an answer for us today."

"And," Nathan murmured, "here comes Mr. Jackson now."

Benny Jackson walked over to their table.

"Who's in charge here?"

"I'm the acting president," Nathan said, "if that's what you mean."

"Yeah, that's what I mean. Would you step over here, please?"

"Benny," Wing said firmly, "whatever concerns him as president also concerns us as the council."

"I got someone who wants to talk to the person in charge, okay?" He rolled his eyes at the ceiling and turned away. "C'mon, Mr. President."

Nathan followed him across the room, futilely running a hand through his unruly hair. Grisha got up and ambled after them. Jimmy Scanlon wore a headset with large cups over his ears behind a radio transmitter like the one back in Chena. A microphone on a stand stood in front of the other equipment.

"Where'd you get that?" Grisha asked.

"We left a cache here on our way to Chena," Jackson said, picking up a microphone. "Okay, Nathan, Mr. President, the person you're going to speak to is an undersecretary in the State Department."

"Of what must I convince him?"

"You must assure her that if the Republic of California grants your government diplomatic recognition you will grant us 'most favored nation' status in return."

"What does that mean?" Grisha asked.

"I thought Nathan was in charge here," Jackson snapped.

"So what does it mean?" Nathan asked, his raptor's gaze pinning Benny.

"It means the Dená Republik would grant the Republic of California first rights in trade agreements, political and military alliances, and extractive minerals exploration."

"So if the United States wanted to form an alliance with us, they'd have to wait in line behind you guys?" Grisha asked.

"Not necessarily, but you can't promise two countries the same things, you know."

"But we can have 'most favored nation' status with more than one country at a time?" Nathan pressed.

"Yes."

"Okay, we'll do it," Nathan said.

Jackson stepped up to the microphone and nodded to Jimmy Scanlon who twisted one dial. A speaker hummed into life.

"Benny Jackson, here. Are you there, Ms. Undersecretary, can you hear us?"

A pleasing contralto voice said, "I hear you fine, Mr. Jackson." She hesitated for a moment. "My heart goes out to you in your time of sorrow. Alf Rosario will be missed by us all."

Until now Grisha hadn't believed that Benny Jackson could ever be at a loss for words. The man straightened his posture, stared at the microphone, and licked his lips.

"Ah, thank you, Ms. Campbell. I genuinely appreciate that. I didn't know you were aware of his death." He nodded and stepped back, motioning Nathan to move closer.

"I am Sarah Campbell, Undersecretary of State for the Republic of California," she said crisply. "Whom am I addressing, please?"

"I am Nathan Roubitaux, President of the Dená Republik. I am honored to meet you, Madame Undersecretary."

"You'll forgive me if I skip the usual diplomatic puffery," she said. "Time is of the essence for you and I'll get directly to the point."

"I do appreciate that. Please continue."

"My government has authorized me to grant the Dená Republik full diplomatic recognition in return for most favored nation status and an exclusive extractive minerals treaty."

"Exclusive extractive minerals treaty?" Nathan echoed. "We're new to this sort of thing. Please explain."

"It's quite simple really. The Dená Republik would allow the Republic of California, but no other foreign nationals, access to your mineral or petroleum deposits."

"What if we didn't wish to allow anybody access to our deposits?"

"That is your prerogative. Our stipulation is that if and when you decide to seek expertise and, or, financial aid to utilize the minerals in your country, you come to us." She sounded cheery, with a smile in her voice. "Our cooperation would be very competitive, compared to the other nations of North America, I assure you."

"I will have to speak with the council about this. We already agreed on most favored nation status, but a minerals treaty has not been discussed at all."

Grisha wondered how someone as young-sounding as Ms. Campbell had risen to such high position in the California Republic.

"We have notified St. Petersburg that we are extending recognition to your government. I'm told we follow the First People's Nation and the United States in that regard, and in that order. The Russians continue to rattle their sabers.

"They contend this is an internal matter and we are violating their sovereignty. Our Defense High Command recommends that we station a squadron of Eureka fighters in your country as well as two mobile radar battalions and three antiaircraft companies."

"Where do you propose siting these elements?" Nathan asked in a soft voice.

"Strategically. On your borders with Russian Amerika. This is something your ambassador's military advisor and our High Command could discuss upon your party's arrival."

"We would be grateful if your air force could provide transportation for our ambassador and his staff. At the present time we have no transport aircraft capable of making the trip."

"It will be our pleasure, Mr. President. How many people will be in the ambassador's party?"

"Four. How soon could the transport arrive?"

"Tomorrow. Is Tanana aerodrome operational?"

"Yes. We'll send answers to your questions with Ambassador Adams and his party."

"Very well. We look forward to his arrival. Good day, Mr. President."

"Good day, Madame Undersecretary."

The speaker issued static and Scanlon switched off the machine. The room suddenly seemed smaller.

Nathan walked over to the table where the council members sat.

"We need to talk in private."

53

Tanana on the Yukon, February 1988

"Claude and his party will go south to negotiate military aid," Nathan said. "In the meantime we have to push the Czar's army out of as much of the Dená Republik as possible. If a truce is finally declared the battle lines will probably turn into borders."

"Any idea how many are moving toward us from St. Nicholas, or how many are already at St. Anthony?" Grisha asked.

Nathan hesitated, his eyes calculating. "Over two thousand troops are moving north from St. Nicholas, and they have armor. We estimate by the time they merge with the troops at St. Anthony they will be able to field over six thousand. We don't know how many they have at Tetlin or how many are being shipped from Russia."

Grisha felt light-headed. It sounded like he wouldn't be a colonel for long. "Claude better talk fast down there, I don't know how much time I can buy against those odds. Who do I have to help me with all this?"

"I'd like to be on your staff," Wing said.

"Captain Smolst and Heron have asked to serve with you, also," Nathan said.

Grisha glanced over at Wing. "As a subordinate?"

"We told you; you're in command." Her level gaze held more messages than he could decipher. "As a subordinate and where needed. I want to do what I can."

"Okay, you're now a lieutenant colonel and my chief of staff. Inform Captain Smolst that he is a major and responsible for the defense of Chena as head of Bear Team. Heron will lead our offensive elements, Wolf Team, also south from Chena and also as a major.

"We need to assemble our people, get them provisioned, and start for Chena as soon as possible. Do what you have to, but do it now."

"Yes, sir," she said quietly and quickly left the room.

"Who is the general I report to?" Grisha asked.

"Slayer-of-Men was our only general," Nathan said, "now it's just the council."

"I'm running my own war?"

"You have complete charge of the Southern Defensive Force. Paul Eluska is commanding the Northern Defensive Force."

Grisha pictured Paul as he first saw him in the rescue party on the Tanana River; compact, intelligent, and quiet but deadly alert. "Me and Paul are running the army," he said with a chuckle. "Things must be pretty bad."

"We have the utmost faith in both of you," Anna said, her handsome face earnest. "You're leading our sons and daughters."

The only Russians still at Chena Redoubt lay buried in the rubble. Those still breathing had pulled back to St. Anthony. When the Dená column moved into town, the people of Chena fled into the forest. No amount of shouting and assertions made the slightest difference; they would not return. The walls of the redoubt still stood where they met the highway.

Inside the gate was another matter. The huge administration and prison complex had become a mound of debris camouflaged by ice and snow. Wing and Grisha stared at it quietly, knowing the bodies of their friends and comrades still lay entombed inside.

"Colonel," Major Sherry said. "There's an equipment building that's mostly undamaged. Shall we put the command post in there?"

"Do we have all of our troops quartered, Heron?"

"Yes, Gri— uh, Colonel. They're all over town."

"Okay. Go ahead and make it the command post, and set the rest up as a hospital."

"Very good, sir." Heron turned and spoke to a corporal who instantly disappeared into the organized confusion.

"Wing, Heron, Heinrich, let's go look at the road." Grisha motioned and two of the four guards in their party hurried off to find transport.

Two trucks loaded with heavily armed troopers accompanied them down the highway. Once out of sight of Chena, all evidence of war faded from the boreal forest. The dark spruce and naked birch lay thick on either side of the road with a protective blanket of snow wrapped securely around the base of each trunk.

In their 160 kilometer retreat to St. Anthony, the Russian Army had left nothing behind. Grisha knew they would appear down the road within days, perhaps hours. For a few miles the road twisted and turned, following the contours of Chena Creek. After it crossed the creek, the road unwound and lay straight for nearly seventeen kilometers.

"This is where we'll hit them," Grisha said quietly. "I want scouts at least twenty kilometers down the road—we have to know when they're coming. I want everybody else out here to get the welcome ready. We've got a lot to do."

"Yes, Colonel. Right away." Heron turned to an orderly and snapped out commands. One of the trucks drove away toward Chena.

Grisha took a deep breath and held it a moment before making a cloud in the cold air. "This is as good a place to die as any."

Wing marveled at the energy Grisha exhibited. The man was everywhere, directing the cutting of firing lines, showing where to plant explosives and mines—no detail was too small, no concept too big for him. He threw himself at his work.

A good thing he is doing it this way, she thought. Grisha had been right: there had been rumblings from more than a few about a Kolosh-Russian being chosen to lead them. Wasn't there some worthy Athabascan in the army who could do the job just as well?

"No," Nathan had said when she first asked him that very question. "The man went from private to major in the Troika Guard. Judging from what I've heard about Bou Saada, he's probably the best tactician in the Dená Army. Furthermore, Grisha isn't related to anyone here. We're all Dená to him, he doesn't have prejudices about upriver Indians or downriver Indians. The only clans he cares about are still in Russian Amerika."

And he's doing fine, she thought. He had been there a hundred percent from the very beginning, but then he had nowhere else to go. Her thoughts about him started down an old familiar path and she focused her attention elsewhere to force a detour.

The Russia–Canada Highway had been built up on tons of crushed rock along this stretch of spruce bogs. In the summer the mosquitoes numbered in the billions and even animals avoided the area. But to the British and Russian engineers building a wartime emergency road, the flat, frozen ground looked wonderful and the entire section had been completed in the dead of winter.

An alien insect tone broke her reverie. She listened for a heartbeat and then screamed, "Aircraft! Take cover!"

The two-hundred-person work party scrambled into the woods. Weapons clacked and echoed through the forest as they cleared for action. The two trucks quickly backed into the largest spruce thicket available; hastily cut branches were tossed on top of them.

Grisha's voice sounded unnaturally loud. "If you think you can hit them, do it!"

The roar of fighters grew louder and suddenly a Yak fighter roared past, less than one hundred meters above the road, its huge propeller a metallic blur. Two more fighters roared past in formation at the same altitude. The forest erupted with gunfire. Sparks and bits of flying metal surrounded the planes, metallic mosquitoes biting at hawks.

The lead aircraft suddenly trailed smoke, pulled up sharply, and went into a wide turn. The right wingman abruptly nosed down and crashed into the forest. The plane exploded on impact.

Cheers broke out as the left wingman sheered off to the west, trailing smoke and fire. Moments after they lost sight of it a distant explosion boomed back at them. As even more cheers broke out, the first aircraft circled the area at high altitude. The wounded plane painted a dark smear of smoke across the sky.

"He's getting our position," someone shouted.

"Wolf Team, go to your positions. The rest of you people get all your equipment and fall back to Chena," Grisha shouted over the rising babble.

The fighter buzzed away to the east, trailing smoke. As soon as the air cleared, people ran onto the road and surrounded the trucks. Grisha was already there, directing events. "We can get twenty-five people in each truck. That leaves about a hundred and fifty of us to start walking. Radio back and get more trucks out here."

He detailed the rearguard, handpicked those who were to ride, and had the trucks racing away within the space of ten minutes. With both trucks gone, Wing edged out from behind a tree.

"What do want me to do, Grisha?"

He stared at her in perplexity. "Didn't I tell you to get on a truck?"

"No, Colonel. You did not."

"I meant to." He looked at everything but her. "Well, move out with the forward group there, take command. Send Heron back to me." He turned and walked away from her.

Wing wasn't sure what she felt, but she didn't want to be separated from him. "Grisha, wait a minute, I—"

He whirled and pointed his finger at her, a scowl twisting his face. "It's Colonel Grigorievich, Lieutenant Colonel Demoski, and I gave you an order—now obey it!"

He couldn't have stunned her any more if he'd slapped her. She jerked to a stop and came to attention. "Yes, sir, Colonel Grigorievich!" She scowled back at him, saluted like a Russian private, and started after the forward group at a run. When she passed Heron, she snapped, "Colonel Grigorievich wants to see you soonest, Major Sherry."

Grisha stared after her, feeling a biting relief. He'd made her chief of staff in hopes of keeping her away from the fighting. But in this war that was impossible on one hand and on the other she'd be angry if she found out.

Wing went everywhere with him. The more tasks he piled on her the more efficient she became; he couldn't slow her down enough to justify leaving her in camp. He couldn't tell her that he feared for her very life.

He felt he carried death for the people around him, especially those he loved. All one had to do was look at the list of friends he had lost in one way or another. And now they had put him in command of twelve hundred innocents, many of whom would die soon.

Heron jogged up. "Reporting as ordered, Colonel."

"I know Wolf Team has a big job. We've talked at length about this—you know what I want to have happen here."

"No problem, Grisha," Heron said with a smile. "It'll be an honor to hit them first."

"Don't just hit them, Heron. Maim them! Then get out, we need you." Grisha turned and trudged after his army. Two heavily armed, burly young men followed him, maintaining great vigilance.

54

Russia–Canada Highway East of Chena Redoubt

Heron called Wolf Team together. The five dozen men and women gathered around so the major wouldn't have to raise his voice.

"They're coming, and we're going to kill them." Grim smiles creased their faces. "People with radios, don't forget the code; tell us which squad, and one tap for sight contact, two taps you're pulling back, and three taps will tell us you're going to fire on the enemy. Be sure you state your sector so we know where they're at." He pressed once on the small radio in his hand and a tone issued from the other twelve. "Okay, you all know what you're supposed to do, so let's get at it."

The party split evenly, half going into the woods on the west side of the road, half to the east. Heron and two others moved into a bunker built with heavy logs. A large U.S. .50 caliber machine gun squatted on a tripod, the muzzle projected through a two-meter-long firing port.

"Sure would be nice to build a fire," Wally Sticks said wistfully.

"The Russians would agree with that," Heron said.

"Major," Riley Jones said, "maybe we should take turns getting some rest."

"Good thinking. Both of you try to get some sleep, I'll keep watch." Heron peered through the firing port for a moment before wandering back out into the fading afternoon. He found a tree to lean against and let his mind roam.

At first he had felt skeptical about the council's choice of Grisha as leader of the Southern Defensive Force. But after hearing about his military experience, he was unable to name another who fit the job better. And he sure as hell didn't want it.

Late winter dusk crowded in around the trees and Heron surveyed the perimeter. As he peered off to his left, movement caught in the right corner of his eye. He whipped his head back in time to see a large figure stop in its rushing advance and aim a weapon at him.

Heron threw himself to the ground as three slugs smashed into the tree behind him. He jerked his U.S.A.-issue machine gun up and put two long bursts into the attacker. The man spun with the impact of the bullets and dropped silently in the snow.

As an afterthought, Heron tapped his radio once and said, "Wolf One." How could the Russian have gotten past all the others? He moved quickly toward the command bunker. "Riley! Wally!" he shouted. "They've infiltrated!" He slipped coming around the end of the bunker and his feet went out from under him.

Bullets whizzed over his head at normal chest height. Heron instinctively sprayed a long burst at the muzzle flashes from the far end of the dim bunker before he stopped sliding. Two men jerked and fell in perfect unison.

The conviction they were his own people shot horror through him.

My God, why did they shoot at me?

He scrambled to his feet only to trip over something else. He peered down into the dead face of Wally Sticks. The feeling of horror grew exponentially as he realized the truth. All of his people were dead.

He hurried over to the closest figure and jerked open the heavy, white parka. The man wore a Russian field uniform. His collar flash featured a stylized leaping wolf. The Czar's elite, crack army ranger force was called the Wolf Pack.

The Russians had sent wolves after wolves. And the Russian wolves were better at their jobs. Heron stared wildly about.

The gunfire would bring others. Just to make sure he didn't harm his own people, he tapped the send key on his radio three times, said, "Wolf One, I'm gonna blow it." Then he reached down to the base of the log wall and grabbed the detonator hidden there.

Through the firing port he saw a scatter of figures rushing toward him. All wore white parkas.

He screamed, "Eat this, dog soldiers!" and violently twisted the rotary switch to the left.

Nearly two hundred meters of the RustyCan highway erupted in a sheet of fire. The bridge over the Chena blew into flaming splinters. The blast flattened trees and tossed the Russian rangers like rag dolls. The shock wave blew the bunker wall inward—burying Heron under bludgeoning logs.

He knew his chest was crushed and inkiness began to surround him. He wondered if he had died for nothing before the darkness rolled over him and he submitted.

The blast rattled Chena. Rubble shifted and the flash from the southeast silhouetted the gaping walls. Leaning against the back wall of the command post, Wing felt shock and surprise. She sat her cup of tea down. "Already?" she muttered to herself.

Grisha burst through the door and went to the radio being monitored by the War Council delegate from Nulato.

"Did you hear anything before the blast, Eleanor?" Grisha asked.

"Wolf One keyed his transmitter once, then about a half-minute later three more times—then it went off. That's all, Grisha."

Grisha stared hard at the walls. "Heron had the bunker. No report from the scouts. No other warning of imminent action, just the blast," he muttered.

Wing moved over and stood at his side. "Do you want to send a couple scouts out?"

"No. We've already lost too many people," Grisha said. "But I want everyone at their battle stations, now."

"Yes, Colonel," Wing said and turned to go.

"Wing," Grisha said.

She turned back to face him, conscious of others in the chilly stone room watching them. New lines etched his face and anxiety filled his eyes. "Colonel?"

"I want you to, please, be careful out there." For a long moment he was the old Grisha again and his dark eyes gleamed with affection.

"Of course," she said slowly, her eyes locked on his. "You be careful, too."

"Right, let's get our people ready." He was the colonel again: remote, hard, and driven.

Wing felt something move inside her and, with an almost audible click, she realized she was in love with Grisha. The thought frightened her—she didn't want to condemn him to death.

They haunted her, those men she had loved and lost. The Russians had killed every one of them. That was why the Russians had to be defeated before she could respond to Grisha the way she wished.

She recognized what she saw in his eyes when he looked at her, but she couldn't acknowledge it yet—it wasn't safe.

"Smolst," she snapped, "let's get 'em in their places."

55

Russia–Canada Highway, East of Chena Redoubt

Colonel Konstine Kronov sat stolidly next to his driver as they inched along the snow-covered Russia–Canada Highway. The last time he had been in Alaska was as a junior officer back in the '60s. His star had risen dramatically since then and he expected his troops to make short work of this rebellion.

Two days ago the Czar had personally given him command of all Imperial forces in Russian Amerika until this revolt ended. The rebels would hang, Kronov decided, as an object lesson for Mother Russia's other ethnic peoples. General rank waited at the end of this expedition, he felt sure.

He tried not to think about how few troops he had under his command, and how quickly he and his staff of four had thrown together this bare-bones response. What little intelligence he had about the rebels pointed to a small force, inexpertly commanded, and poorly trained. His response counted heavily on that intelligence. More troops were en route, but vast distances were involved.

"Captain Kashan to Colonel Kronov," the radio crackled.

Kronov picked up the microphone. "Report."

"Colonel, all of the Wolf Pack are dead. The road has been destroyed for nearly two hundred meters, including the bridge. There is no sign of the rebels."

"Thank you, Captain. We'll just have to drive on the taiga and ford the creek. Kronov clear."

He frowned. The Wolf Pack must have been ineptly led. How could a mob of savages and Creoles eliminate the best Imperial Army troops in Alaska? Those people were usually predictable.

The three tanks and two trucks in front of his command car detoured off the roadbed and crept between the shattered road surface and the dark stand of spruce and birch. The colonel stared at the wrecked road and wondered where the rebels had obtained the explosives. He'd forgotten how desolate Russian Amerika could be.

The command car bumped along behind the trucks. Behind the car rumbled a half dozen armored personnel carriers and a half dozen tanks. Reducing what was left of Chena Redoubt would be child's play with this much firepower.

It had been but a few weeks since the Imperial Air Corps had blasted the redoubt. High Command told him that most of the rebels there had been annihilated. This should be an easy campaign.

A heart-stopping blast shattered the truck directly in front of the car. A few screaming soldiers, bodies engulfed in flames, fell out of the back and thrashed on the ground.

Kronov grabbed his microphone and screamed, "Deploy, deploy, get out of line immediately!"

One tank turned and began grinding up over the rubble of the road. Suddenly an explosion went off under the lumbering giant, lifting it off the ground and blowing off one track—throwing the treads back into the trucks like shrapnel. Before the tank could fall completely to the ground ammunition stored inside exploded and the machine contorted like a living thing as it died.

"Mines!" Kronov screamed at his white-faced driver. "They've mined the roadside. Don't move this car another inch until our men have had a chance to clear the area."

The corporal pointed to the burning tank. "How did they mine something they already blew up?"

"What do you mean?" Kronov said in a shrill voice.

"Shouldn't the explosion of the roadbed have set off any mines this close?"

"Yes."

The tank behind them blew up. Ahead of them a streak of fire shot out of the forest and hit one of the two remaining advance tanks. Two men pulled themselves out of an escape hatch seconds before the inside of the tank exploded.

Gunfire cut the two soldiers down.

"It's an ambush," Kronov screamed into his microphone. "Take evasive action." He switched radio channels. "Tetlin Command, this is Kronov. We need air support immediately."

"What's your location, colonel?" the distant radio operator asked.

"Where the fighters were shot down. I was told this area had been cleansed." He broke off, suddenly conscious of the shrill panic in his voice.

"I'm sorry, colonel," the radio voice said, "but we have no operational aircraft close enough to support you at this time."

The last operational tank in front of him opened fire with its cannon and heavy machine gun. Two more streaks lanced out of the forest and hit the tank. The machine blew into bits, setting fire to the truck behind it.

Kronov expected soldiers to leap out of the truck and take defensive action but nothing of the sort happened.

He numbly dropped the microphone. "My God," he said to the corporal. "They all must be dead."

The corporal abruptly put the car in reverse and backed close to the burning tank behind them before jamming the gearshift forward and stomping on the accelerator. The car slewed around in a tight arc and bounced back past burning tanks and the bodies of soldiers. Kronov beheld a scene from hell.

Every tank was burning and all but two of the trucks were also in flames. The bodies of his soldiers lay scattered like toys after a child's game. The corporal grimly drove over a number of bodies in his haste.

None cried out.

For the first time in his life, Colonel Konstine Kronov felt true fear. He had never considered how helpless one might feel when afraid. Unbelievably, the command car roared up onto the undamaged portion of the highway.

Even here lay Russian bodies in attitudes of violent death.

Where was the enemy?

The car picked up speed as they passed the last bullet-riddled truck. The corporal jammed on the brakes and the car skidded sideways before stopping. A log barrier spanned the road, providing shelter for the heavily armed people behind it.

Kronov let his breath go and wondered how long he had been holding it. The sight of his enemies temporarily gave him something close to relief. At least now he knew they were fighting humans and not wraiths.

Someone shouted in perfect Russian, "Get out of the vehicle with your hands clasped to your head. Now!" The corporal kicked open his door, grabbed his head fiercely with both hands and stepped out of the car.

"Tell your officer that we will kill him if he does not get out of the vehicle."

The corporal bent down and peered in at Kronov. "Colonel—"

"I hear them, you idiot." He opened his door and stood full length before putting his hands on his head as insolently as possible. "I am Colonel Konstine Kronov of the Imperial Russian Army. Who are you and by what authority do you stop me from my duty?"

"You've got more balls than brains, Konstine," a man said in Russian. "But then, that's what the Czar likes in his cannon fodder."

"Who are you?"

"My name is Basil, and not all that long ago, I was a slave of the Czar's. Now I'm sergeant in the Dená Republik Army and under that authority I make you my prisoner."

"Why do you not kill me as you have my troops?"

Basil gave him a gap-toothed smile. "You'll see."

56

Chena Redoubt, March 1988

"What happened to Heron and the rest of Wolf Team?" Grisha asked.

"The Russians sent in their own wolves," Basil said in his deep voice. "By the time any of us knew of their presence, they had already killed a third of our people. Irena was the first to see them and pass the word to the rest of us."

"Why did you blow the road before anything was on it?"

"Heron did that. He must have thought we were all dead. The blast killed or maimed all the Russian Wolves."

"There were some left alive?"

"Some," Basil said with a slow grin. "But they didn't last long. As soon as we finished them off, we mined the roadsides and went back to our machine guns and antitank guns."

"You did well to bring in the colonel and the corporal. What's your rank, Basil?"

"Sergeant, why?"

"As of now you're a lieutenant and in charge of an infantry platoon."

"I'm not sure I want that, Grisha."

"It's Colonel Grisha and we need everyone working at the highest level they can achieve. When the rest of your team shows the initiative you did, I'll turn them into officers, too. We need them."

"Irena showed more initiative than I did, Colonel."

"That's why I've already made her a major and put her in command of Wolf Team."

"Oh. Okay, I'll take the platoon."

"You're getting some new people who haven't seen action. Teach them how to stay alive."

"Yes, sir." Basil grinned and left the room. The man sitting at the radio in the corner carefully kept his eyes on the gauges.

The door shut behind his old companion from slave days and Grisha sighed. Ever since the council pushed this command on him, he had expected his army to discover that he was only acting like a field officer, that too much time had passed since he last knew military life and battle. He felt what little he did know about cold-weather operations he had received from his conditioning with Nik, Malagni, and Haimish.

He felt the years as a charter captain had negated his long service to the Czar. Yet training completed over twenty-five years ago suddenly manifested when needed and helped him make desperate decisions.

The memory of his friends strengthened his determination to go on and finish this thing correctly. The Dená had saved him from certain death and he had vowed to help them any way he could. But he hadn't expected this.

A knock sounded on the door.

"Enter."

Wing stopped just inside the door. "Colonel, there's a contingent of forty recruits from upriver villages. It would be a good thing if you welcomed them personally."

"Forty," Grisha said. "We need so many more than that, but I had given up hope of getting more village people."

"Many of them thought the Russians would kill us all as soon as we attacked. The fact that we've held the highway from Bridge to Chena has made an impression. Now they know the Russians can be beaten."

"I wish I knew that," Grisha said as he moved around the desk toward her. "C'mon, let me at these people."

Wing led him over to a group eating from bowls. When they saw Wing they stopped eating and quietly watched her and Grisha.

"It's customary to show respect for the colonel by standing when he enters your area," Wing said in a low voice.

Everybody immediately began to rise.

"Thank you," Grisha said quickly. "I am honored. Please sit, you've all come a long way and I know you're tired."

They eased back down. One man remained standing. Grisha glanced over at him and had to force himself not to let his jaw hang open in astonishment. Slayer-of-Men stood there!

"How. You can't be standing there—I saw you die."

"You are Grisha, the boat captain?" the man asked.

Grisha felt relief. This wasn't Slayer-of-Men. The voice was different, higher than the steel bass of the dead warrior. "Yes, I'm Grisha. How are you related to my friend Slayer-of-Men?"

"I am Nikoli. Slayer-of-Men was my older brother, as is Malagni. They spoke highly of you and your dedication to the Dená Republik." Grisha was positive this is exactly how Slayer-of-Men sounded in his youth.

The words sank in. "Malagni is still alive?"

"Yes. He is healing. He said to tell you that he would be back soon."

"Thank you for the news. I thought both your brothers died that night."

"You're welcome." Nikoli nodded politely and sat down with the rest of the group.

For a moment Grisha felt as if he had regained a measure of his two dead friends in this person. Then he firmly suppressed the feeling. Nik wa— Nikoli was a whole new unknown and to give him that sort of measure to stand against wasn't fair. "Do you mind if I call you 'Nik'?"

The youth smiled. "That's okay. Everybody else does anyway."

They all smiled. Out of the corner of his eye he saw Wing sniff and look off to the side.

"I thank you all for coming to help. So far we have more than held our own against the Czar. The price has been high."

Grisha felt awkward at this kind of thing, he would rather sit around and drink beer with them and tell lies about fishing and hunting. But the cashiered major/charter captain had changed somewhere between slave and new soldier. Now he had to be a colonel.

"We'll teach you what we know about fighting the Russians. And because we must teach you quickly, we might wound your pride. You'll have to accept this as part of being in the army, so we apologize now and hope you remember then."

Nods eddied through the group.

"We need you on the lines now and so we'll put small groups of you in every part of the organization. Even though we are all constantly in danger, I will only take volunteers for the rifle companies—"

Forty hands shot into the air.

"—and I'll only take eight," Grisha said with a smile.

They laughed and all hands stayed in the air.

"I knew this wouldn't be easy," he muttered to Wing.

"You did fine, Colonel," she said. "I'll take it from here."

"Thank you, Colonel." He turned, left the dining hall and walked briskly toward his office, his emotions churning.

"Colonel Grigorievich!" a voice shouted harshly. "I demand my rights as an officer and a gentleman."

Grisha veered over to where Colonel Kronov stood chained to the wall. The Russian had enough chain to lie on the cot if he wished but he stood with the extra lengths puddled over his boots. A number of Dená stood at a distance watching him as if he were a rare beast.

"You're a prisoner of war," Grisha said. "We've shown you more humanity than we would have received at your hands."

"Only because you plan to use me for some sort of propaganda," Kronov spat. "This is not how an officer of the Imperial Russian Army should be treated."

"Okay," Grisha said tiredly. "I'll tell you what. As soon as we're done using you for propaganda, I promise we'll shoot you."

The growing crowd laughed. Pure hatred shone in Kronov's eyes. "You'd better shoot me. I'll kill you if you don't."

"They're sending a helicopter for you as soon as it's dark. You better rest while you can." Grisha turned back toward his office.

"You're a dead man, peasant. I'll make sure of that."

"Get in line." Grisha shut the door behind him.

57

Chena Redoubt

The helicopter circled once while the ground crew switched on lights at each corner of the square landing pad. The machine dropped quickly through the dark sky to hunch in the light like a live thing wary of circumstances. The rotors continued revolving as soldiers hustled Kronov out of his cell and lifted him into the aircraft.

Moments later they flew through an impossibly dark night. Kronov glanced down at his manacled hands and became aware that someone sat beside him. He looked up into gray eyes over an aquiline nose and perfectly trimmed moustache.

"Sorry I can't take those off for you, Colonel. But we've decided you're a very dangerous man." The man's voice held familiarity.

"This is outrageous," Kronov said. "I demand—"

"Allow me to introduce myself. Major James Douglas, United States Army Reserve. Actually I'm a journalist and just do this soldier-boy bit one weekend a month, until Mario decided he needed my talents."

"'Mario?'" Kronov said.

"President Cuomo. Think of him as an elected Czar."

"What do you intend to do with me?"

"Well, friend, I'm going to put you on the CBS radio network and ask how you came to be in the Dená Republik wrapped in chains when just a few days ago the Czar himself decorated you in St. Petersburg."

"This is Russian Amerika! There is no Dená Republik. I refuse to allow such a thing. I would rather die."

"That is the question, isn't it?" Douglas said. "Would you rather stay here in the Dená Republik—and it is a republic 'cause Mario told me so—or come down to the U.S. with me and cooperate enough to get furloughed back to the Czar?"

"This is possible?" Kronov said quickly in a low voice. "To be sent back to Russia, alive?"

"Of course." Douglas stroked his moustache. "We're not barbarians, y'know."

"If I went back to Russia alive, the Czar would have me shot."

"Your decision, of course. There are other alternatives available, and you can live quite handsomely in some of them."

Kronov thought furiously. He hadn't expected anything like this. Even if he escaped being used for propaganda, he couldn't go back to Russia. The Czar would have him executed for losing his elite command. The fact they shared a great-grandfather wouldn't make the slightest difference.

"Has the United States recognized this Dená Republik diplomatically?"

"This morning," Douglas said crisply. "There's been an incredible amount of military posturing on all borders, here and in Europe."

"Who else has joined you in this madness?" Kronov felt faint.

"Austria-Hungary, the Republic of California, and the First People's Nation so far. British Canada, New Spain, and our Confederate cousins seem to be siding with your Czar, but then they're like that."

"This means war."

"That, Colonel, remains to be seen."

"The Czar has no choice. If he doesn't put an immediate stop to this Dená nonsense other regions will attempt to break away from the Russian empire. All would be chaos."

Major Douglas gave him another wry smile. "Welcome to the twentieth century, colonel. Colonialism is dead."

"Tell that to Britain, Spain, and France!" Kronov spat.

"Besides," Douglas' demeanor became icy, "where would the Czar find allies if a war started tomorrow? He's already spent what little goodwill he inherited from his father."

"What is it you plan to do with me?" Kronov asked in a small voice.

"Propaganda, partner. Propaganda of the likes you've never seen before—we want you to tell the truth as you see it."

"About what?"

"Imperial Russia. Russian Amerika. How St. Petersburg views her North American holdings and what she plans for their future."

"I don't have all those answers. I'm a soldier, not a diplomat."

"That's what we're counting on."

58

Chena Redoubt

Major Heinrich Smolst worked his troops to their capacity. At his direction they dismantled the destroyed Chena Redoubt and sorted the material into orderly piles and rows. When they weren't working they drilled.

Soon Bear Team functioned as one. Smolst thought if he clenched his fist, every other fist in Bear Team would do likewise. Their military smartness warmed his Prussian-like soul.

After breaking their own record on the obstacle course for the fifth time, he threw them all a party. Finding enough beer had been his biggest challenge. But he persevered.

"This is a wonderful party, Major," First Lieutenant Sunnyboy exclaimed as he slapped his superior officer on the shoulder. "I've never seen anything quite like it."

Smolst grabbed the officer's wrist with a firm hand. "Lieutenants never slap the shoulder of anyone with higher rank, it works the other way around. Do you understand, Lieutenant?"

The lieutenant's eyes widened and he visibly wilted. "Oh, hell, I did it again, didn't I?"

Smolst released the wrist and smiled. "You're a good officer, Elijah. But you're a poor drunk."

"That's good, isn't it, Major?" Without waiting for an answer the lieutenant stumbled away.

"You're a good officer, sir."

Heinrich looked up into the lovely face of Karin Demientieff, one of their best medics. Just looking at her could heal a man, Heinrich thought.

"Thank you, Lieutenant. May I ask why you say that?"

"You know me too well to think I'm kissing your ass, sir. But I can see that you truly care about your people. Am I right in supposing you were once enlisted yourself?"

He narrowed his eyes and nearly lost his smile. "You already knew that, didn't you?"

Her expression snapped from knowing to surprise. "No!" she blurted. "You really were an enlisted man?"

"Started as a sub-private in the Troika Guard about ten years before you were born."

She swallowed. "I didn't mean to get personal, sir."

"Not to worry, Lieutenant. I'm not a Russian, I'm an Austrian."

"You served with Colonel Grigorievich, didn't you?"

"For nearly eleven years in the Troika Guard."

"I heard he was kicked out." Karin licked her lower lip nervously, but Heinrich thought she looked delectable. "Is that true?"

His mood abruptly shifted. The party swirled around them, everyone tipsy or downright drunk. He felt the alcohol lift from his mind and he clapped his hands twice.

"Bear Team!" he shouted.

The entire room went silent and, over a thirty-second period, they all straightened to attention.

"You have all done an excellent job so far. I think you've conquered the civilian in each of you and have formed into a fighting team unequaled in Alaska." He raised his glass. "I salute all of you." He threw the vodka into his throat and swallowed.

The room burst into applause. He grinned and held up his hands. They went silent and waited.

"Lieutenant Demientieff," he nodded toward her, "just asked me a question I know many of you are wondering yourself. Would you please restate the question for everyone else, Lieutenant?"

Color rose into her cheeks and she frowned at him. "I merely asked the major if it was true Colonel Grigorievich had been kicked out of the Troika Guard."

Many heads nodded. The rumor had circulated among the troops since the Second Battle of Chena.

"It's a good question, and the short answer is: yes."

Startled gasps and murmuring voices suddenly filled the room.

"The long answer, if you're interested, is this."

They abruptly went silent.

"In 1979, at the Battle of Bou Saada in French Algeria, then Major Grigorievich defied the orders of his commanding officer by commencing an orderly retreat rather than attack an impregnable position held by forces outnumbering his command three to one. The colonel, Major Grigorievich's commanding officer, held a pistol to the major's head and ordered him to attack the enemy."

Smolst shook his head and sipped his drink. "Imagine a large, thin loaf of rock, thirty meters high. Then add five more loaves of rock, each half again higher, one behind the other. Now add nearly a thousand heavily armed Algerians evenly dispersed through those loaves of rock.

"There is dust, and the sun is hot enough to boil your brains. I forgot to mention that the major and his men had been fighting up this miserable ridge for over seven days, were running out of water and ammunition, and had already taken thirty percent casualties. But as long as he led, they followed."

Every person in the room stared at him, completely mesmerized. Most had stopped drinking as they waited for his words. He smiled and continued.

"The colonel, a man who had spent his thirty years service behind desks from St. Nicholas to St. Petersburg and had wrangled a combat command to fill out his vanity-oriented career, ordered Major Grigorievich to take those ridges. He shouted the orders from a hundred meters distance, couldn't even face Grisha. The major crawled through heavy enemy fire to face the colonel and beg him to change his mind.

"The major was fortunate that his sergeant major followed. For when the major faced the colonel, the colonel pulled his side arm and pointed it at the major's head. 'Order your men to attack or I'll shoot you for mutiny on the spot,' he screamed."

Smolst glanced around. From their faces he could tell this was news to all of them, even Captain Danilov, who had been there. He also knew he was creating the seed of a legend here, but the Dená Army needed it. Besides, he was greatly enjoying himself.

"And?" Lieutenant Demientieff said.

"Major Grigorievich refused the order, said it was madness and he would not send his men to certain death. The colonel had lost control hours before and was now close to insane. When he started to pull the pistol trigger, the sergeant major shot him. Since they were all in the midst of battle, nobody knew where the shot originated, but they all saw it end in the colonel's head.

"Major Grigorievich was now in command and ordered his men to commence a fighting retreat. He saved their lives," Heinrich had to stop and swallow, "and the Imperial Army court-martialed him for disobeying orders. The bastards should have given him the Alexander Cross."

"You were there, Major?"

"Yes, Lieutenant, I was there. That was when I knew I would someday repay the Czar and his Imperial Army full price and when they least needed it. I have the Dená people to thank for the opportunity."

They burst into applause. He knew a Dená appreciated a good story as well as the next person.

"Let me buy you a drink!" he shouted. The party resumed and a line formed at the two kegs of beer.

"If I may, Major?" Lieutenant Demientieff asked.

"May what?"

"Ask what your rank was at the Battle of Bou Saada?"

"Of course you may." He winked at her. "I was a sergeant major."

59

Klahotsa, on the Yukon River

"The Dená Army has destroyed or captured two Russian tank groups, knocked down almost every Russian aircraft they've encountered, except for bombers, and more people are joining their side." Georg Hepner leaned on the counter separating the two men.

"Where's the Russian Army?" Kurt Bachmann demanded. "The real Russian Army?"

Hepner laughed. "I need something to drink, I've come a long way. Part of the army is massing on the Siberian side of Czar Nicholas Bridge, part is landing in St. Nicholas, and one wing of the Imperial Air Force and a tank battalion are staging out of Tetlin. The rest of the Russian military is beefing up their borders with other European and Asian countries."

Bachmann sat a bottle of vodka and two glasses on the counter of his store and again sat on his stool. "So everything the Russians have in Alaska is around the edges of Dená country, nothing here in the center?"

Hepner filled his glass and drank half. "I haven't been everywhere, so I can't swear there aren't Russian elements inside the country. But I'm good at asking the right questions and hearing what I need to know, and if the Russians have troops inside Alaska, they're well hidden."

"I didn't think the damned Indians could get this far," Bachmann said, sipping from his glass. "Did you find the Freekorps?"

"That's what you paid me to do, that's what I did."

"Where are they?"

"Just across the BC border. But that's only, what, a hundred and fifty men?"

Bachmann grinned. "A hundred and fiftly accomplished, well trained soldiers right here could make a very large difference." He smacked the bar top with his doubled fist.

Someone rattled the door.

"If the door's locked it means we're closed!" Bachmann bellowed. "Come back tomorrow."

"Must be nice to own your own town," Hepner said.

"There's a lot of responsibility," Bachmann said. "Keep the cossacks paid off. Keep goods on the shelves. Make sure the damned Indians don't go upriver to Tanana or down to Melosi to sell their game, furs, and crops."

"But still, you're like the king of Klahotsa. You got them all too scared to crap without your say-so." Hepner grinned and tossed back the rest of his drink. He reached for the bottle but Bachmann had already returned it to the shelf behind him.

"I want you to get a good night's rest. First thing in the morning you get back in your boat and go find Major Riordan and his Freekorps. Tell him I want to hire his boys for at least three months, and the sooner they can get here, the better."

"They're at least five days away, and they have vehicles, not boats."

"That's their problem. There is a road out there they can take, if they're tough enough to get through the Dená."

"I don't think the Russians will be too keen on them using it, either."

"Have them tell the Russian commanders that they're working for me, the Russians will let them through."

"This could take some time."

Bachmann smiled. "As long as they arrive in time."

60

Chena Redoubt

Three weeks inched by unattended by conflict. The sudden absence of the enemy proved more worrisome than coping with solitary fighters or squadrons of gunships. Grisha sent out more and more scouts, posted double sentries, constantly anticipating the sudden appearance of another Russian armored column or more camouflaged ground troops.

Where were the Russians? Grisha wondered, reading the pamphlets the Dená propaganda department printed by the bale.

The Dená Army constantly worked on rebuilding Chena Redoubt. More recruits drifted in to be turned into soldiers and the bitter truth of February softened into the false promises of March.

Bodies recovered from the broken redoubt were placed in an unheated building to wait for thawed ground later in the year. For three weeks, four men worked from dawn to dusk building coffins. Unless hers was one of the unidentifiable charred bodies, Valari Kominskiya did not number among the dead.

Grisha chafed and worried at the interminable waiting. "Anything from the diplomatic front?" he asked Wing for the third time that morning.

"Same as yesterday—the Czar's representative insists this is an internal matter for Russia to settle, and the NATO countries are saying it's a revolution. We should be thankful that the Yanks, the

First People's Nation, and the Californians have such an independence-minded history."

"There's more to it than their history," Grisha said, "I'll give you odds on that."

A truck roared up next to the building and labored in unmuffled cacophony for a long moment before shutting down. Doors slammed and Wing smiled over at Grisha. "I think we've got company."

The door to the outer office slammed and a loud indistinct voice could be heard through the wall. Knuckles rapped briskly on the office door and Sergeant Major Tobias appeared.

"There's a woman here to see you, colonel. She says to tell you she's blue." His eyebrows arched for a moment in disbelief and he whispered, "But she's no more blue than I am, sir. Should I call the guard?"

Grisha and Wing burst into laughter and the sergeant frowned. Describing himself as a "clerical mercenary," Sergeant Major Nelson Tobias had appeared at the front gate of Chena Redoubt a week before. With his expert assistance they put order to the command structure and the sergeant major became gatekeeper for both Wing and Grisha. The man was a military treasure but knew nothing about the Dená Republik or the Council.

"Her name is Blue Bostonman," Grisha said once he could speak again. "Do show her her in, and treat her as if she were a general."

With a muttered, "Very good, sir," he disappeared and moments later Blue hurried through the door.

"Where did you get him?"

"Where do we get any of them?" Wing said, crossing the room and hugging the older woman. "How are you?"

"Tired." She glanced at Grisha. "And the bearer of news."

"Good or bad?" Wing asked.

"Both. What do you want to hear first?"

"Bad news first," Grisha said, coming to his feet.

"You've been accused of war crimes by the Imperial Army. Armistice negotiations have broken down in San Francisco. The Russians refuse to continue until you are produced to answer their charges, or you're relieved of command and imprisoned by us."

"War crimes! What war crimes?"

"You're accused of throwing a Russian major, a woman yet, out into minus sixty degrees without clothing." Blue measured him with her eyes. "Claude maintains that you wouldn't do such a thing but we need you to go south, immediately."

"It happened," Grisha said softly and sat down in his chair. "But I didn't do it."

"Benny Jackson did it," Wing said flatly. "I was there."

"That's true," Grisha said. "I wanted to just kill her and get it over with. They want me to go south?"

Blue nodded. "The Californians are sending an aircraft for you."

"What does the council say about it?"

"The war seems to be in a hiatus while the negotiations proceed. We're eager for a resolution and a treaty. We feel very close to victory. There's a lot of pressure being generated in Europe and even Imperial Japanese warships have been sighted off Kodiak Island."

"It stinks," Wing said flatly. "There's more to this than meets the eye."

"I asked the council to let me be the messenger. We figure no more than three days down there should do it. Think of it as a vacation, Grisha."

"Am I being put on trial?"

"You're to answer questions put to you by a panel of representatives. Two representatives from each member nation of the North American Treaty Organization as well as Imperial Russia and the Dená Republik. They have no true authority over you, this is all politics and propaganda. Smoke and mirrors."

"Some vacation," Wing muttered.

"You need to come back to Tanana with me. They're going to pick you up in the morning. We'll have to drive all night."

Grisha felt his resolve waver. All of his instincts screamed in alarm but he could see no alternative. "I will obey the council's wishes."

"Grisha!" Wing moved between him and Blue. "Didn't you hear me? This stinks, dammit. There's something going on that they haven't told us."

"Who is they?" Blue said, sudden ice in her voice.

Wing swung around to face her. "This smells like a sacrifice to me. There are at least five witnesses still alive who could tell them that Grisha wasn't the one who threw that bitch out into the cold. Has anyone asked the Californians about it? Has anyone asked Captain Jackson about it?"

"He's a colonel now," Blue snapped. "This is a delicate political situation. We have to give every indication of complying with the wishes of the NATO countries in order to maintain their backing, the ones we have, that is. We're dead without them, don't you see that?"

"All I see is that Grisha didn't do what he's accused of, that he's doing a hell of a job and he's needed right here until this whole thing is finished once and for all."

"I have orders"—Blue tapped her pocket—"for Grisha to return to Tanana with me immediately. If you wish to question the council's intelligence I suggest you accompany us back to Tanana. But one way or another, Grisha is going with me."

"What do you mean, 'one way or another'?" Grisha asked.

"This wasn't my idea," Blue said. "But they sent a squad with me as security and escort."

"A squad!" Wing shrilled. "Do you realize this garrison would die for him if asked?"

"Yes." Blue seemed on the verge of tears. "So please don't push it."

"Am I under arrest?" Grisha asked quietly.

"No. We'd never go that far. But we need you to go south and talk to these people, Grisha. Will you please do that?"

"Didn't I tell you once that I'd do anything for the Dená Republik? Let me collect my things."

"You said something about good news?" Wing said.

"Malagni!" Blue shouted.

The big man pushed through the door. The absence of his right arm in no way diminished him. He grinned fiercely.

"Two of my most favorite people in the world. Things must be tough to make you a colonel. But I have to tell you, your little ambush out there on the RustyCan really impressed me. That fancy-ass colonel your guys captured is a cousin of the Czar, and he's blabbing his ass off."

Grisha and Wing embraced him, patted his back. Wing reached up and kissed his cheek. "We were so worried about you."

Grisha stepped back, looked up into the man's face. "Are you returning to duty?"

Malagni glanced at Blue. "You didn't tell them?"

"Not all of it."

He turned back to the others. "They made me a lieutenant colonel. I'm taking over Southern Command until you come back, Grisha. That okay with you?"

Conflicting emotions warred in Grisha's mind. He tried to smile, wasn't sure if he made it. "They couldn't have chosen anyone better.

Lieutenant Colonel Demoski is the best executive officer you could ask for."

"I know. I want you to know that I'm doing this for you—when you get back there's no question as to who's the skipper."

61

Russia–Canada Highway

The ride west to Tanana proved wearisome and tedious. Blue retreated into herself and spoke only when addressed. Grisha quickly tired of initiating one-sided conversation and lapsed into moody silence.

A new fortification bristled with armament on the near bank of the Yukon River.

"If the gate is breached, the bridge blows up," Blue said. "All the people on this side are volunteers."

"Is there anyone in this army who isn't a volunteer?" Grisha asked. The truck rumbled across the bridge and he stared at the rotten ice on the Yukon. "When will the ice go out?"

"Any day now," Blue said, clearly pleased to dwell on a safe subject. "We have a lottery going for the day and hour it goes. The engineers built a little box that's hooked to a clock on the shore. When the cable pulls on the clock it stops running—the ice has officially gone out and we know the winning time."

Grisha laughed. "Sounds like morale is high on the Yukon."

"It is. And let me tell you, Colonel Grigoriy Grigorievich is a hero to the Athabascan People. It pains me to be part of this dog-shit political posturing. But it's all for the Republik, right?"

"Right." Grisha felt embarrassed at her effusiveness. Blue remained in the scout car when Grisha got out.

"Good luck, Grisha," she called.

A matte-black twin-engined bomber with three gold stars triangulated on its tail waited on the runway built on the ridge behind the village, props ticking at idle. Two fighters roared in wide circles above. An entrenched antiaircraft battery manned by Republic of California troops bristled near the taxi strip.

Grisha entered the aircraft and a handsome, smiling woman took his bag and led him to a plush seat next to a bubble window.

"My name is Anita, Colonel Grigorievich. Please sit here and fasten your seat belt. As soon as we are in the air I'll get you something to eat and drink." She disappeared from the small cabin and Grisha wondered what the rest of the aircraft held.

The plane turned sharply and a muted roar filled the cabin. He stared out the window as they raced past the small fires outlining the field, and wondered if they were going as fast as he thought.

Then they tilted back and roared upward.

Once airborne, Grisha had his first beer in eight months. His last had been in T'angass the day he and Karpov picked up Valari Kominskiya for the trip north to New Arkhangel. Despite the memories the beer was excellent.

Anita walked toward him carrying a steaming tray. Suddenly the plane nosed downward without warning. She and the tray slammed into the overhead and hung there as the plane arced in a dive.

"Are we going to crash?" Grisha yelled.

Abruptly the plane pulled up and went into a steep climb. Anita crashed to the floor and steaming food rained across the cabin. The flash of an explosion above them pulled his attention briefly to the window.

"We're being attacked," he said to himself.

A fighter flashed upward and a rocket ignited under its wing as both streaked out of sight.

Grisha unbelted himself and hurried to Anita who sprawled moaning on the floor, grasping at seat legs. He picked the woman up, put her in a seat, sat beside her, and strapped them both in. He intently examined her for injuries.

A voice came from above their seats. "This is the pilot speaking. My apologies for that unannounced dive. We were under rocket attack from a bogey and I had to take evasive action. The two attacking aircraft have been destroyed. Would the stewardess please report to the flight deck? Once again, my apologies."

Grisha unstrapped and moved through the cabin to the flight deck. He rapped on the door and then pushed it open. A man wearing a headset sitting at a console of switches and gauges looked up and his eyes widened in alarm. Beyond him were the pilot and copilot.

"Hey, who're you? Where's Anita?"

"I'm Gri—, Colonel Grigorievich. The stewardess was injured and I've got her strapped down in a seat."

"I'll take care of it, Captain," the man said to the pilot. He pulled off the headset and unstrapped. "I'm Navigation Officer Donahue. After you, sir." He pushed Grisha ahead of him.

Anita's ashen and drawn face testified to her pain and shock. Donahue examined the woman. "Broken arm." He opened an overhead compartment, produced a first-aid kit and gave Anita an injection. He straightened her arm, wrapped splints around it, and positioned it in a sling before looking up at Grisha again.

"Who fired on us?" Grisha asked.

"Don't know, Colonel Grigorievich. But we nailed both of them."

"Were we attacked over British airspace?"

"No, sir. Alaskan."

Grisha nodded at the nearly comatose Anita. "I'll watch her if you like."

"Thank you, we appreciate that." Donahue beckoned toward the flight deck. "If her condition changes, just let us know."

Grisha strapped himself in. The aircraft hummed swiftly through the night and he wondered if he would return in time to see the ice go out on the Yukon.

62

Columbia, Ohio, Capital of the U.S.A.

Colonel Konstine Kronov, seemingly oblivious of the motion-picture camera, grinned widely at Major Douglas. Both men, now slightly drunk, had dropped formalities some days before.

"But, Konni, why doesn't the Czar modernize Alaska?"

"It's my theory he has a secret agenda, James," Kronov said carefully, struggling tipsily with English. "An economically viable Alaska would pose the same threat that the Indians are currently pressing. By themselves, however, they do not have the political and military clout to make the transition to a true republic."

"You don't think they can win this fight?"

"Not alone." Kronov leered and tossed back more vodka. "And if you or any of the other NATO members assist them, you are risking a full-fledged war on this continent, and perhaps Europe as well."

"Why would the Czar fight a war over Alaska?"

"Would not your president fight a war over Pennsylvania? Wouldn't the French fight over Quebec?"

"Ask the British," Douglas said.

"Pah! The British," Kronov said with a rude laugh. "Let them posture all they wish, who else would want it? But France still owns Quebec."

Major Douglas opened his mouth then pursed his lips without speaking. He regarded Kronov with stony eyes for a long moment before continuing. "The Czar hasn't developed Alaska. He's kept it in the nineteenth century for ninety years longer than any other part of North America. Why would he fight for it at this late date?"

"Do you really believe that a mere colonel, who happens to be a distant cousin, has the ear of Czar Nicholas? What his majesty wishes and doesn't wish is of paramount consequence to me, but there's damn all I can do about it, *nyet*?" Kronov tossed back another inch of vodka.

"Why do you think the Czar will fight for Alaska?" Douglas persisted.

"Because he thinks he can sell it," Kronov said airily. "Just as his great-grandfather attempted to do in the 1860s."

"To keep it from being absorbed by Canada," Douglas said triumphantly.

"British Canada," Kronov corrected.

"Then"—Douglas's face became animated and his eyes wetly caught the light—"do you believe he could be bought off?"

"Good question, Major. But who would do the buying, and more importantly, who's willing to be bought?"

Douglas blinked owlishly before recovering. "Nobody would be bought. But a nation might be aided financially by its neighbors."

Kronov laughed so hard his eyes watered.

"What's so damned funny?"

"You, you Yankees. You still think you're the only ones in the world who have a brain or know how to use it." Kronov's countenance went steely. "One of the most unsavory parts of being a Russian is knowing that our forefathers of the 1850s allowed themselves to be allied to you inept losers in your short civil war."

"You can relax now." Douglas shot to his feet, his lips a firm line. "I think we're through for today."

Two rangers eased into the room and stood on either side of Kronov.

The Russian stood and gave Douglas an exaggerated bow. "My thanks for the excellent vodka. Next time we should have bourbon, to which I'm sure you are more accustomed."

Douglas nodded, turned sharply on the balls of his feet, and marched over to the door.

"Good luck on your Indian purchase," Kronov called gaily as the door slammed.

63

On the Yukon River, Between Old Crow and Tetlin

"Who goes there?" The voice held menace.

"Friend! I am Georg Hepner, from Klahotsa, sent by Kurt Bachmann. I need to talk to Major Riordan."

"Keep your hands where I can see them and come forward."

Hepner put his hands on his head and moved forward in his customary loose, rangy amble. "I was here two weeks ago," he said in a friendly way.

"Yet you returned?" the mercenary said, motioning him to move down the trail. "If I could get out of this miserable mosquito factory there's no bloody way I would come back. I thought Scotland was a waste of dirt until I beheld this great sponge."

"Some of us like it here."

"Aye, you'll find the daft nae matter where ye travel. Stand tall, this is as far as I go." The mercenary was a raw-skinned man with a head of burnt orange hair and muscles that rippled under his shirt. He seemed sure of himself.

"Corporal of the Guard! Visitor at Post Three!"

Two men stepped out of the brush as if they had been waiting for their cue. "Who is this, now? Corporal Harris, Timothy me boy?"

"I'm not your bloody boy, O'Hara. This man says he was here last week, yet he came back for another visit. I'd say he was daft, wouldn't you?"

323

O'Hara looked Hepner up and down. O'Hara stood a foot shorter than the sentry, yet looked far more dangerous.

"Who are you and what's your business?"

"Name's Hepner. Work with Kurt Bachmann up at Klahotsa. Kurt's got an offer for your boss."

"If it's more than five California dollars, we'll take it," O'Hara said with a laugh. Harris and the large black man behind O'Hara laughed with him.

"What?" Hepner said.

"What do you expect?" Harris said. "He already told me he likes it here."

"I got 'im, Timothy, you go back to your post."

Harris nodded and disappeared in the brush.

"You visited us about two weeks ago, am I wrong?"

"Yes, I mean no!" Hepner didn't like people playing with his mind. "Yes, I was here two weeks ago. You're probably wrong in some very fundamental ways but I haven't the time to really help, or care."

O'Hara grinned. "Yer not as dumb as you look, that's good. You follow me and Private N'go will take up the rear."

The black man smiled, revealing brilliant white teeth filed to points. Hepner shuddered despite himself. He followed O'Hara through the mercenary camp, which consisted of dozens of tents, and stopped at a tent three times the size of any other in sight.

A small man emerged. French *captaine* boards rode his shoulders and he stopped at the sight of O'Hara. "I have explained already there is no whiskey to be had, Corporal O'Hara."

"I hadn't forgotten, Captain Flérs. It seems this gentleman has an offer for the major, and I hope to sweet baby Jesus that he takes it, 'cause there's no tellin' what a another missed payday might bring, sir." With an exaggerated salute, the corporal turned and marched away. N'go followed him, chuckling and glancing back over his shoulder.

"I know you, yes?" Captain Flérs said.

"I was here two weeks ago. I need to see the major, my boss wants to hire you fellows."

"Excited I am to hear this. Please enter in."

"Well, if it isn't our old friend, Georg!" Major Riordan stood and offered his hand.

He measured a few inches shorter than Hepner, but Georg thought none the less of him for that; Napoleon had been a lot shorter than either of them.

"What brings you out here beyond the pale?" He grinned and moved his lean body about as if he were on euphorics. "Missed my brilliant conversation and insights, did you?"

"Not as much as you would imagine. I bring you an offer from Kurt Bachmann. He wants to hire you and your men."

"For how long?" Riordan stood very still and stared at Hepner with the aspect of a very hungry lion.

"He said three months."

"Did he send money with you, to seal the bargain?"

"Do you want his offer in rubles or dollars?"

"Dollars, preferably California or Texas dollars."

"He offers three hundred forty-five California dollars per day, for three months."

"Shit on my grave, why don't you? That's less than five dollars an hour for each of us!"

"Take it or leave it."

"What does he want us to do?"

"Fight Indians, the Dená, I think. But he wants you and your men at Klahotsa."

"That's bloody days away!"

"You start getting paid today if you agree."

"I need an advance to show the men we're not getting rogered yet again."

"Then you you agree?"

"Yes, I bloody well agree!"

"Then sign this," Hepner pulled a folded page from his pocket and handed it to the major, "and I'll give you a thousand California on the spot."

"If you have that much on you, why would I not just kill you and take the money?"

"Because you would forfeit so much more for very little effort."

"How do we get to Klahotsa?"

"There's a road they call the RustyCan—"

"Don't be impertinent! You know there are Russians everywhere, you can't just glide through them like it's some bloody dance with an 'excuse me' here and an 'excuse me' there."

"You're an ally. You're fighting the Dená just as they are. Bachmann said you'd figure out something. Are you going to sign or do I need to look for professional soldiers elsewhere?"

Riordan glared at him, then down at the contract.

"Where do I sign?"

64

San Francisco, Republic of California

"Please state your name and rank for the members of this tribunal," the white-haired man in the gray uniform said.

"Colonel Grigoriy Grigorievich, Southern Army Commander of the Dená Republik."

"I object." A cossack major general stood and stared at Grisha. "This man is in rebellion against his legitimate government and claims fealty to a political entity which does not in fact exist."

"So noted, suh," the old man said frostily. "But we will hear him just the same."

"I made my objection for the record, at the wishes of my government, nothing more," the cossack said.

"Colonel Grigorievich," the old man said, "I am General Carter of the Confederate States Army. The other delegates elected me president of this tribunal—" his eyes flicked over the two Russians at the other end of the table, "—but I wish to assure you the vote was not unanimous."

Grisha surreptitiously surveyed the men behind the long table. Another man in gray sat beside General Carter. Next to them were two men in tan British uniforms flanked by another pair wearing the now familiar khaki of the Republic of California.

He decided the men in black were from Deseret and the two in pale blue from Texas. Kepis lay on the table in front of both New

France officers and their deep blue, red-faced uniforms easily captured the prize for most ostentatious. However, he had noticed that New Spain's officers wore highly polished, knee-length jackboots which gave them the most sinister air.

The United States had sent a gimlet-eyed admiral and a cadaverous general as their representatives. Even to Grisha's untutored eye, they seemed very chummy with the Russians next to them.

A tall, broad-faced man wearing a three-piece-suit and two long braids wrapped in ermine sat staring fixedly at him. Next to the tall man sat a stocky, dark-eyed man with a proud face and a prominent hooked nose. He was dressed in starched camouflaged dungarees adorned with a silver bison's head on each shoulder. The First People's Nation delegation, Grisha decided.

No representative from the Dená Republik was present.

Twenty judges. He suddenly realized the Confederate general hadn't finished addressing him.

". . . by our governments to ascertain if you are a war criminal or have led others in your organization to perpetuate atrocities on your enemies." General Carter paused for a long moment, his eyes never leaving Grisha's face.

"These are very serious charges, Colonel, and I must tell you frankly that more hinges on your answers than just your reputation among North American nations."

Grisha nodded. "I appreciate your advice, General Carter, and I thank you for it. I am here of my own volition, even though I have troops in the field under my command who expect a counter-attack at any moment." He gave the Russians a hard look before returning his gaze to the general.

"Neither I, nor any of the people fighting for the liberation of the Dená Republik, have committed any atrocities or other actions that could be determined criminal under conditions of war. I would like to make this appearance as brief as possible in order to return to my command."

"Your concern is well taken, sir," General Carter said softly. "However, the charge against you is of a grievous nature and must be dealt with before our governments will return to the conference table to help chart the future of your nation's political aspirations."

"Under the rules of the tribunal," Grisha said quickly, "am I allowed to call in witnesses of my own?"

"Certainly, suh. This is not a kangaroo court."

"Then I request that Colonel Benny Jackson be summoned to speak to this gathering."

"Under what flag does Colonel Jackson serve?"

"The Republic of California."

General Carter nodded to a Confederate captain standing by the door and the man hurried away. "Do you have any other requests, colonel?"

"I'd like to know why there are no representatives from the Dená Republik at this hear—uh, tribunal."

"They were invited to attend but they declined. Ambassador Adams said that you were quite able to handle anything we could throw at you."

Grisha felt a shadow flit across his mind, leaving Wing's *sacrifice* and Chief Andrew's *scapegoat* resonating in his memory.

"I'm sure the ambassador is correct, General," Grisha said, surprised that his suddenly dry throat could produce words. "Please continue."

"You are charged with exposing a naked prisoner of war to subzero cold," General Carter said succinctly. "Is this true?"

"No. I was asleep when Major Kominskiya was expelled from our shelter."

"Who, then, forced her into the night?" the Russian major general asked in acid tones.

"I did."

All eyes in the room shifted to the crisply uniformed man standing at the door.

"Benny!" Grisha blurted before he could stop himself.

"Would you please identify yourself to this tribunal, colonel?" General Carter said.

"Colonel Bernard Jackson, Special Forces, Army of the Republic of California."

"Please take the seat next to Colonel Grigorievich."

As Benny sat down he flashed a smile and muttered, "You're a colonel? Must be scraping the bottom of the barrel up north."

Grisha smiled and nodded toward the silver bear head on Benny's shoulder. "As if they weren't down here."

"Would you be good enough to explain what happened that night, Colonel Jackson?" General Carter said.

"I lost the person I loved most, and Major Kominskiya killed him," Benny said in a ringing voice.

Some of the officers muttered to each other and, with the exception of the Californians, the First People's Nation representatives, and the Frenchmen, all glowered at him. Both generals from Deseret sat back stiffly in their chairs.

"I realize that most of you find homosexuality offensive and therefore are probably incapable of understanding my feelings that night. But I'll relate it for you anyway." Benny told of the battle for Chena Redoubt in the bitter cold. He spoke of the people he knew for such a short time. Slayer-of-Men had impressed him and in Haimish he recognized a kindred spirit and fellow operative.

The capture of Valari and the *promyshlennik* caught the interest of the Russians and the U.S. military. As Benny related the discovery of the hidden transmitter, the Russian general interrupted him.

"How did you know she had a radio, Colonel?"

Benny hesitated for half a heartbeat before replying, "I think one of the Dená heard it."

"You're a liar, colonel," the Russian said softly.

A sharp intake of breath came from the California contingent and one of the Canadian generals mumbled, "I say!"

"The radio Major Kominskiya wore that night"—the Russian's eyes shone with eagerness masked from his speech—"did not have a receiver or a speaker. Nothing could be heard. I repeat, how did you know of the radio?"

Benny frowned and glanced at Grisha before replying. "That's a military secret, general. I'm sure you can appreciate that."

"It's a secret, all right," the general said in a controlled voice. "A hidden mutation used on behalf of these rebels. Do you deny that one of the Dená"—he spat the word—"read her mind in order to discover the hidden transmitter?"

"We deny nothing," Grisha said. "We merely wait for your proof."

The First People's Nation representatives conferred without taking their eyes off Benny.

"Please continue, Colonel Jackson," General Carter said, shooting a quick frown at the Russians.

"Colonel Grigorievich tried to shoot her on the spot. But at that moment Russian aircraft, homing in on her radio, bombed the redoubt, killing eighty percent of the people in the building. Alf

Rosario, my constant companion of twelve years, was part of that eighty percent."

Benny abruptly fell silent and stared down at the floor for a long moment. Grisha could see his jaw muscles working. The U.S. admiral broke the silence.

"Colonel Jackson, I would like to repeat General Romanov's question. How did you know Major Kominskiya had a transmitter?"

Before Benny could say anything, General Carter slapped the table with the flat of his hand.

"That's enough! We're here to determine if a war crime was committed—not to delve into intelligence matters despite how arcane they might appear."

The admiral scowled, pursed his fleshy lips, and nodded, leaning back in his chair.

"We found a stairway," Benny continued. He succinctly related the events in the frigid dungeon of Chena Redoubt, told of Nik's death as dispassionately as of Crepov's escape. Grisha listened carefully as Benny told about Valari's foolish attempt to seduce him.

"So I let her undress and then I threw her outside."

"Why didn't you just shoot her?" General Carter asked quietly.

"I didn't want her death to be quick." Benny's voice was a snarl. "I wanted her to suffer."

"I wish to call a witness," General Romanov said.

"Whom do you wish us to call?" General Carter asked, a puzzled expression on his face.

"Major Valari Ivanevna Kominskiya." The Russian's voice grated on Grisha's nerves.

"So ordered." General Carter nodded to his captain and the man vanished once more.

Benny leaned over and muttered to Grisha, "That bitch can't be alive."

"I told you she's tough," Grisha whispered back.

The door opened and the Confederate lieutenant pushed a wheelchair into the room. A beefy female Russian Army nurse followed him. A figure wrapped in dark shawls sat in the chair.

At first Grisha thought they had brought in a child, because he could see the person's legs ended a half meter above the foot plate. Then he realized that Valari had suffered as Benny wished.

The nurse walked around to Valari's side and pulled off the heavy shawl. The tribunal recoiled. In a prayerlike voice a Canadian general muttered, "Christ wept!"

Both legs ended at mid shin. Both of her arms, crossed on her lap, stopped at the wrist. Teeth and pink gums shone through an oddly serrated mouth and Grisha realized her lips were gone. But what remained of her nose, unnaturally bobbed with exaggerated nostrils running up between her closed eyes, proved the most horrific feature.

"Jesus Christ," Benny breathed softly. Then in a louder voice he said, "You kept her alive for this farce. And you have the guts to accuse Grisha of war crimes?"

Valari's eyes opened. Her gaze darted over the tribunal before she found Grisha and Benny. The hard intelligence still resided but something else tempered her stare—longing.

"Grsh," she said wetly with what remained of her tongue. She said something else, completely foreign.

"What did she say?" Grisha asked the nurse.

The nurse stared into his eyes. "Grisha, *pozhaluysta ubey menya. Pozhaluysta!*"

"What?" Benny asked.

Grisha spoke loud enough for all to hear. "She said: 'Grisha, please kill me. Please!'"

"Nurse," General Carter said. "Kindly remove your patient to the waiting room."

The blocky nurse wrapped the shawl around Valari.

"Peas!" Valari shouted, her face a nightmarish mask.

The nurse pushed the chair through the door held open by the white-faced captain.

"Peas!" echoed back through the door before it closed on the desperate voice.

"Colonel Jackson," General Carter said in a hushed voice. "Be careful what you wish for in the future, sir, you might once again get it."

The general raised his voice, "Colonel Grigorievich, thank you for your presence. It is obvious to this court that you are innocent of the charges brought against you and you are free to return to your command. This tribunal is concluded."

Not until the last of the gold-braided judges had trooped out of the room did Grisha realize Benny was sobbing quietly.

65

San Francisco, Republic of California

"This has all been bullshit," Claude said, pacing around the room. "Nathan and the War Council instructed us to boycott the tribunal to avoid the appearance of Russia ordering us around. We knew you didn't do it, and so did the Russians. So why did we have to go through this charade?"

"To buy time, to assess our strength, to dump every soldier they have into Alaska," Grisha said tiredly. "How is your part going?" He drank off the remainder of his tea and set the cup down. The ambassador's residence outshone anything in his prior experience. The building commanded a hill overlooking San Francisco Bay. With the sun sinking slowly on a liquid horizon, the view equaled the splendor of Denali, but in a much different way.

"It's as if we were a catalyst, causing every festering grievance in North America to pop like a pustule." Claude shook his head. "The Russians are dragging their heels at every turn. I agree, they're obviously stalling, probably pouring troops into Alaska by the plane-load like you said.

"The Californians and the First People's Nation are pressing hard for resolution, but they make very strange bedfellows. The Texans are firmly backing the Confederate States, who are backing the British—" Claude took a deep breath. "—who are allying with the

French and the Spanish. And the Spanish are rattling sabers on the Texas border!"

Grisha scratched his head. "This is really mixed up."

Claude grinned and continued, "The United States seems smug but supportive of us and solicitous of the Republic of California. The French and the Spanish are here purely out of avarice. The British Canadians are, oddly enough, firmly in the Russian camp and display animosity toward the United States, probably remembering their colony breaking away from them and now commiserating with another crown."

"What about the men in black?" Grisha asked.

"The religious fanatics from Deseret are like Stellar's jays back home—they'll take what shiny trinkets they can get and then fly back to their nest. They are of no consequence to us. I think all the posturing will be over soon, and to our benefit."

"The U.S. contingent seemed very friendly toward the Russians," Grisha said. "Are you sure the U.S. is siding with us?"

"The U.S. has its own internal problems. The current administration is liberal and, as you know, the military rarely leans in that direction."

"I want to get back to my command, as soon as possible."

Claude smiled. "Spoken like a true soldier." He flopped in his chair. "I wish I could go home."

"You can arrange to have me flown north?"

"I'll try." Claude picked up a telephone. "This is Ambassador Adams. I wish to arrange transport for Colonel Grigorievich back to the Dená Republik as soon as possible. Yes, thank you." He replaced the phone.

"Day after tomorrow." Claude seemed pleased.

"Why so long? It didn't take them that long to pull me out of Alaska. Are they using all their aircraft for something else?"

"Grisha, we are their guests. Two days is nothing in the greater scheme of things."

"Diplomatically perhaps, but a battle can be lost in a hell of a lot less time than that," Grisha snapped.

The door flew open and Andreivich rushed in. "Quick, turn on the radio," the old scholar said, panting.

Claude picked up a button-covered device and clicked it. The large speaker built into the wall immediately broadcast a voice, no static, no distortion; Grisha thought it sounded like the person speaking was in the room with them. The man seemed intoxicated.

". . . and I know that's why your government is willing to help the Athabascans." The man spoke with a Russian accent.

"There's more than minerals involved, Konni," a Yankee voice said. "There is a people yearning to be free."

"What crap, James!" The Russian swallowed something and the smack of a glass being set on a table with undue force came though clearly.

"We're both adults here. Don't give me grandmother tales. You couldn't even deal with your own aboriginals; they ended up with enough land to double the size of your country. You're after the gold, and the oil, and the silver, and the coal, and the lead, and the fish, and the whales—all of it—just like all the other NATO nations. And the Czar won't give it up without a fight."

An entirely different voice broke in. "To repeat, this tape was obtained this morning. We have just learned that the Russian government pulled out of NATO negotiations on Russian America this afternoon and continues mobilizing on the disputed Dená border."

The announcer's stentorious voice continued, "British Canada declared it will back the Russian government and has placed its military on red alert. Great Britain dispatched air and naval elements to North America within an hour of the Canadian announcement. Military forces in the United States have gone to red alert as a precaution."

"My God," Claude whispered. "This is going to escalate into a continentwide war."

"This just in." The man's voice became even more somber. "The Confederate States has withdrawn its ambassadors from the U.S. and California, and has announced it will treat any foreign military craft violating its air space as hostile. The U.S. announced the departure of the 77th Airborne Division to aid the beleaguered Dená Republic."

"But what are the Russians doing?" Grisha screamed at the speaker. He turned to Claude. "You've got to get me back right now!"

"I don't know if I can, but I'll try." Claude picked up the phone, held it to his ear for a long moment, and then set it down. "It's dead," he said listlessly, "and I'll bet the doors are locked from the outside."

Andreivich walked over and tugged on the knob, shrugged. Grisha felt despair wash over him. Claude glanced at both of them and then turned back to the radio.

"We've been in worse prisons," Andreivich said with a shrug, "and we have no cossacks to deal with."

Despite himself, Grisha gave the old man a smile. "When we were at the prison camp, I thought you were stiff and sullen. Yet you can find something in this situation to feel good about. I wish I could."

"We still live," Andreivich said crisply.

Grisha nodded and turned to Claude, who sat transfixed by the radio. "Claude, you've been talking to all these people. Why did we go with the Californians if the United States is that interested in us? Haimish even gave his life in an attempt to help."

The ambassador didn't take his eyes off the speaker. "Haimish was trying to tie us to the U.S. and the Californians beat him to the punch. They brought instant communications and a lot of weapons. Haimish only brought a few weapons and a lot of philosophy. We already had philosophy."

"But now the Yankees are sending paratroopers," Grisha said softly, "and what are the Californians doing?"

"I wish I knew, Grisha. I wish I knew."

66

The Presidio, San Francisco, Republic of California

"I don't care if we're with them or against them!" Colonel Bernard Jackson said to the officers around the mahogany table. "But we pulled Colonel Grigorievich out of his command and we have to get him back, now!"

"May I remind the colonel," a frosty-faced admiral said, "that he is the junior officer in the room and here only at our invitation and sufferance."

Benny forced himself to remain quiet. Telling this old windbag where to put it would only exacerbate the situation.

"Be careful, Admiral Clyde," a three-star R.O.C. Air Force general said, ". . . or he might throw you outside in the dead of winter."

Benny felt his face grow warm as the all the men and one woman present laughed. He realized there was nothing further to be gained here and stiffened to attention.

"Colonel Jackson requests permission to leave, sir."

General of the Army Davidson waved him toward a chair. "Take a seat, Benny, we're just getting started. In my opinion it took a lot of balls to do what you did, then admit it in front of a tribunal, and still walk away with your head and rank intact."

"Thank you, General. But Colonel Grigorievich was correct, I should have just shot the bitch rather than sink to her level. Not to mention that Grisha also wouldn't be our de facto prisoner when he is urgently needed at home."

"He's not a prisoner," Admiral Ramona Clyde snapped. "He is a guest of the Republic of California. We're going to give him military aid, for crissake."

Benny perked up. This was new.

"Indeed, Admiral, when?"

"That's why you're here, Colonel Jackson," General Davidson said. "You know the situation up there, what should we send?"

"Fighter wings, airborne troops, artillery, and armor, all with lots of ammunition, that should do it, General."

"You are aware that New Spain is moving troops and warships up from the south and British Canada is doing the same from the north, yes?" Admiral Clyde's voice could quick-freeze a tree, Benny thought. "Not to mention that when we dispatch military personnel to Russian America we will be at war with them, too."

"Russia has a small but modern navy with which to threaten our shores. So what would you have us do, what should we keep here at home for defense?"

"The fleet and the fleet air wings, Admiral. You could deploy the marines against the enemy land forces. I have heard many times from their very lips that one marine is worth five soldiers." He shrugged and kept his smile hidden. "I should think that would do it nicely."

Color rose in the admiral's cheeks. Marine General Louis Cole broke his silence with a near growl. "Is that a challenge, Colonel? Or are you making a joke?"

"Only repeating what I've heard, General."

"Okay, enough of this screwing around," General Burgett, the head of the Joint Chiefs of Staff said. "We're sending the Third Airborne and the 117th Fighter Squadron. Do you want to head up a Special Forces unit and go with?"

"Thank you, General." Benny's heart seemed about to burst through his dress jacket. "I'd love to do just that!"

"Then get your ass out of here and have at, you've got eighteen hours."

67

East of St. Anthony Redoubt,
on the Russia–Canada Highway

Major Riordan of the International Freekorps spotted movement ahead and slapped the driver's arm. The scout car stopped and Riordan peered through his binoculars.

"It's our motorcycle scout coming like there's something chewing his ass. Alert the column."

The driver reached out and hand-cranked a siren for five seconds. Behind the scout car, the men in the two armored personnel carriers and the five trucks didn't change in their aspect, but most of them woke up.

The camouflaged motorcycle purred up to the car and the rider stopped and saluted.

"Major, there's a Russian unit bivouacked about a mile up the road."

"How big a unit?"

"Three medium tanks, three APCs, five trucks, and a scout car."

"Could you tell if they were special forces or regular army?"

"Looked like regular army to me, but I don't know for sure."

"What the hell are they doing out here in the middle of nowhere?"

"I didn't ask, Major," the man said with a laugh. "And they didn't say."

"They see you?"

"No. I smelled the smoke from their fires and hid the bike before reconnoitering on foot. They must not be expecting trouble, their sentries were playing cards."

"Good work, Sergeant Percy. Let your radio antenna free and put a white flag on it. But first take a break, I need to talk to the men."

"Yes, sir!" Sergeant. Percy saluted and rode back down the small column.

"Duty Sergeant!" Riordan bellowed.

A large man swung down out of the first truck. His face bore scars and a nose broken many times over. "Yes, Major Riordan?" he said and saluted the smaller man.

"I want two pickets forward about two hundred yards. They are not to fire at anything until ordered."

"Yes, sir."

Captain Flérs dropped out of the lead APC. He saluted in the French manner and narrowed his eyes. "What have we, Major Riordan? Perhaps an engagement?"

"Pass the word for assembly, René. We're going to play nice and be friendly, until we see the lay of the land. At least until I whistle."

"We are going to engage the Russian Army?"

"Now, René, don't go all Gallic on me. We're not going to do anything stupid, okay?"

"*Oui, mon Majeur!*" He turned and shouted for assembly.

68

Chena Redoubt, April 1988

Wing picked at her food and wondered what had happened to Grisha. For a week the Southern Army had heard nothing of its commander. Malagni stiffened the patrols, drilled the troops mercilessly, and stepped up training for the new recruits.

If asked, she wouldn't have been able to explain the feeling in her gut, or the nervous twitch that ruled her left eyebrow. She felt a wrongness that magnified in proportion to the length of his absence.

In addition, two days ago Malagni went to Tanana to confer with the War Council and left her in charge. She shook her head and eased down on her cot. Maybe a nap would help.

Quick steps paused at her door long enough for someone to rap once before pushing it open. Sergeant Major Tobias poked his head in, eyes on the floor.

"Colonel Demoski, things are heating up."

"Come in, Sergeant Major," she said, sitting up. "What's the situation?"

He closed the door and stood with his back to it.

"What are the Russians doing?" she asked in a hushed voice.

"There's heavy fighting at Bridge and our scouts report a mechanized force moving toward us from St. Anthony."

"How large a force?" Here was the genesis of her anxiety, why her thus-far infallible intuition nagged at her. She pulled on her boots and grabbed her jacket—April could be capricious.

"Big, at least twenty tanks and twice that many troop carriers, last I heard."

"Sound the alarm. I want everybody into their bunkers. I'm amazed we haven't been hit by aircraft already."

"They're afraid of our antiaircraft batteries," Tobias said with a quick grin. "I'll sound the alarm. By the way, we've intercepted radio transmissions from the south. The Canadians are building up their troops on the California border and we think they have launched a major offensive through the First People's Nation into Minnesota in the United States."

"They must be madmen. Anything about California?"

"Yes, ma'am. They have broken off diplomatic relations with Russia and said if the Czar's forces attack the Dená, they'll declare war."

"Let's hope they aren't just posturing." She followed Tobias into the situation room. "I want an officers' meeting in five minutes. Radio Colonel Malagni of our actions."

"Yes, ma'am."

From the roof a klaxon broke the arboreal silence.

She paused at the radio room. Two women and a man sat at consoles with earphones clamped on their heads. All three scribbled madly on pads of paper. As they tore off the information-covered sheets a corporal collected them and hurried into the next room where a knot of people huddled around a map table.

Wing followed the corporal, a second cousin from downriver, and asked the room at large, "So what're they doing out there?"

A large man Wing didn't recognize straightened to attention.

"We were just going to send for you, colonel. I'm Captain Lauesen, U.S. Army Intelligence. I've been seconded to your command and am honored to be here. I also brought two enlisted men who should arrive momentarily."

"Welcome, Captain, we need all the help we can get. What do we know?"

"All hell's breaking loose here in Alaska, as well as the rest of North America."

"Give me our situation first, please."

"Yes, ma'am." He cleared his throat and his face remained free of emotion. "Thirty Russian tanks are advancing from St. Nicholas at roughly forty-five kilometers per hour. Behind them are troop carriers, forty-five at the very least. Reports are still coming in from our scouts."

"How far out are they?"

"There are some lead elements, three scout cars and a few motorcycles, ten klicks ahead of the rest who are approximately three hundred and fifty kilometers away. It will take them at least thirty hours to get get here.

"Much closer to home we have a three part battle group moving up from Tetlin Redoubt, some of their armor was already in St. Anthony, twenty tanks and forty trucks, which will hit us first, probably in less than two hours."

"They must not be too worried about mines and ambushes," Wing said.

"They have an advance force of rangers who are moving very fast. Our people have picked off about ten of them and we've lost five effectives."

"Two to one, not good enough," she said.

"To beat the numbers they're sending against us, we need to make it eight to one," he said with a nod.

"What else?" A sudden numbness crept over her and she had to concentrate to make sense of his words.

"Our 77th Airborne parachuted into St. Michael and, in concert with your Northern Defense Force, are engaging the enemy at Bridge. Mobile antiaircraft batteries are en route as we speak. There's so much happening down south that the only way to follow it is chronologically."

He glanced down at the paper in his hand and pointed a long stick at the maps. "British Canadian armor has struck across the corner of the First People's Nation, here"—he tapped the map—"and into the U.S., here. The town of Bemidji, Minnesota"—another tap—"is under siege. A second front at Detroit Lakes has bogged down and the town is under heavy artillery attack."

"Where are you from in the United States, Major?"

"Iowa, ma'am, out west in 'Confederacy Corner.'" His grin held no humor. "We're east of the First People's Nation and north of the Confederate States. We haven't had trouble with the F.P.N. since we gave 'em back Kansas and signed the big treaty back in 1877. If anything they would be allies, but so far they're just sittin' quiet."

More of her officers hurried into the room and stopped to listen.

"Will the United States lose to Canada?"

"Not likely. Our borders have been beefed up for decades, waiting for this."

"What else is happening down there?"

"Well, the Confederates are trying for a second win at Harrisburg, but our boys are holding without too much trouble since we aren't using muskets this time."

"It seems that fighting a two-front war is the fashion these days," Wing said.

A few in the room laughed—brittle, edgy barks lacking humor and evading release.

"Can anything down there change our situation one way or another?"

"On our way here," Captain Lauesen said, "Republic of California Air Defense told us to expect heavy friendly traffic from their direction. They didn't elaborate."

The door crashed open.

"What the hell is going on?" Malagni swept into the room, radiating energy. He glanced at Captain Lauesen, pinned Wing with his eyes. "Report, Colonel."

Great, he's in crazy mode.

"This is Captain Lauesen of the U.S. Army."

"Colonel," Lauesen said with a nod.

"He and the rest of us were assessing the situation, Colonel," Wing said. "It seems all of North America is suddenly at war with itself."

"What's our situation?" he asked with a nod to the captain.

"The Russians are fielding enough men that we're outnumbered eight to one," Wing said. "To be truthful, I don't know if we can hold them."

"Of course we can hold them!" Malagni's teeth bared under glinting eyes and Wing wondered if he smiled or snarled. He pressed on.

"Tanana Command is being beefed up by antiaircraft batteries from the U.S. and their new radar units show a large flight coming in from the R.O.C. All we gotta do is slow the damned Russians. Not that I would mind slaughtering every mother's son of 'em!"

"Any word on Grisha?" Wing asked.

"No." Malagni moved over to the map table and grabbed a pointer. The moose-hide shirt that covered his chest had only one sleeve. The right side flowed seamlessly over his stump. "Show me where they're at."

Captain Lauesen smoothly redelivered the report he had just given Wing. She edged back and watched as markers changed position on the table, strategies discussed and dismissed.

"Your people are fighting a two-front war?" Malagni asked.

"Three," Lauesen said with a grin. "We've launched an amphibious assault on the big naval yards at Norfolk and Little Creek, Virginia. Our marines are ashore and moving inland, as well as up into Chesapeake Bay."

"With that much going on I'm surprised the 77th came up to help us out."

"President Cuomo never backs away from his promises."

A U.S. Army sergeant moved briskly into the room and handed a sheet of paper to Captain Lauesen, who quickly read it.

"Well?" Malagni gestured at the paper.

"The Spanish are swarming across the Rio Grande into the Texas Republic from a number of positions. Everything south of San Antonio is under the Spanish flag right now." He took a deep breath.

"The Canadians are sending two armored columns against the Republic of California, with perhaps a third cutting through the First People's Nation."

"They've actually cut through the F.P.N. twice," Malagni whispered; Wing was sure he grinned. "The British are even dumber than I thought," he boomed. "They've really stirred up a hornet's nest now. Didn't they ever hear about Custer?"

He stared at the map table. "This is what we're going to do."

69

Capitol Building, San Francisco, Republic of California

"Ambassador Adams, Colonel Grigorievich, gentlemen, please be seated," Republic of California Secretary of State Frank Barnes swept his arm out toward chairs in front of his desk. The secretary sank into his own leather upholstery.

"Please accept the president's apologies for not keeping you in the picture over the past few days. The situation in Alaska has polarized our congress and nation. After forty hours of debate the Senate and House both gave President Reagan authorization to declare war on Imperial Russia."

"So we are now allies?" Claude asked.

"Very much so," Secretary Barnes said. He grinned. "I think the president gave the people one of his best speeches ever. 'There's an eagle in the woods, it has two heads and both wear a crown. It likes to eat baby republics.' He received a standing ovation on that one."

Grisha laughed. "Good imagery. Does this mean I can get back to my command soon?"

Secretary Barnes glanced at his watch. "Your flight leaves in a little over an hour. You'll be flying with a squadron of troop transports carrying the Third Parachute Infantry Regiment and a Special Forces contingent to Fort Yukon. Ambassador Adams and you other gentlemen will be flown out tomorrow, assuming we all agree on our current treaty."

"We certainly want to finish our mission before going home," Claude said.

Grisha stood up. "Where do I go to catch this flight, sir?"

Secretary Barnes pushed a button on his desk then rose to his feet and shook Grisha's hand. "Lieutenant Anderlik will take to your transport. I wish you Godspeed and victory, Colonel."

"Thank you, Mr. Secretary." He nodded to the Dená delegation and followed the lieutenant out of the room.

"Right this way, sir," the lieutenant said. They entered an elevator and dropped farther than Grisha remembered ascending. The door opened into a large bay filled with ranked equipment and military personnel moving in all directions.

"Please follow me, sir." Lieutenant Anderlik moved briskly through the confusion and Grisha had to pay attention to his guide rather than gawk at the activity around him. After traversing a second bay they emerged into the hot California afternoon.

A topless military vehicle with an enlisted driver sat idling while two officers leaned against it, smoking and chatting. When Grisha appeared both men stiffened to attention and saluted. The major remained silent while the colonel spoke.

"Good afternoon, Colonel Grigorievich. I'm Colonel Buhrman, commander of the Third PIR. You'll be riding with us. This is my exec, Major Coffey."

"I'm pleased to meet both of you, and grateful for the ride, not to mention deeply appreciative of your aid."

"Aw hell, we've always wanted to see Alaska," Colonel Buhrman said.

"We hear the fishing is fantastic," Major Coffey added.

"Once we kick the Czar out, I'll be happy to take you fishing," Grisha said. "I know a lot of good spots."

They rode three blocks to an airfield where a row of transports were filling up with men. Grisha noticed that every trooper carried far more than did his soldiers back home. To a man they looked formidable and menacing.

"How many are going north?" he asked.

"Nine hundred and sixty on this flight and we have the Fourth PIR in ready reserve if we need them."

"The last I heard there were over twenty-four hundred Russians heading toward our lines from two different directions."

"They aren't there yet, Colonel," Major Coffey said. "We also have—"

Three waves of five fighters buzzed over the field in tight formation. The paratroopers lined up outside their transports cheered and waved.

"—them," Coffey finished. "Those are P-61 Eureka long range fighters of the 117th Attack Squadron who will provide cover for us and then seek out targets of opportunity once in the combat zone."

Grisha couldn't stop grinning. "This is great!"

They pulled to up the lead transport.

Colonel Buhrman looked over at Grisha. "Going—"

A scout car roared up and screeched to a stop. Colonel Benny Jackson stepped to the tarmac. He nodded at the other two R.O.C. officers. "Del, Joe, glad to see good people are going north with me."

"You're going north?" Grisha said.

"Yeah, they're letting me take a Special Forces strike force to get your ass out of the jam we helped put you in."

"Benny," Colonel Buhrman said with a grin, "you're going with us, not the other way around."

"Sure, Del, whatever you say."

Colonel Buhrman looked at Grisha and motioned to the transports. "Going my way, Colonel?"

70

St. Anthony Redoubt

"Colonel Romanov, the last of General Myslosovich's supply train has left the area."

"Thank you, Sergeant Severin. Let us enjoy the silence for a while before we bring Captain Kobelev's motorized scout unit back to the garrison."

Romanov stepped to the window and opened the blinds. He loved this place more than he had loved any other thing in his life. Most of his men thought of their posting to St. Anthony Redoubt as punishment, but not him.

The Delta River joined the Tanana River less than a kilometer from his office. The redoubt enjoyed a view that few appreciated. Stepan Romanov felt drawn to this country.

Despite his aristocratic name, Roaanov's grandmother was a Yakut from Siberia and he held deep sympathies for the Dená. He tried to keep his attitudes to himself, but others had noticed.

A visiting colonel once asked for an Indian woman for the night.

Stepan had frowned. "I'm not a whoremonger, colonel, you'll have to solicit for yourself."

"You do not know women who—"

"No. You'll have to ask one of the privates."

Thankfully, the colonel let the matter drop. Romanov would not allow his men to molest the local women or mistreat any of the civilian population. He preached brotherhood to his troops and had a corporal lashed within inches of his life for beating an old Athabascan man.

Now this stupid war has made a hash of everything, he thought. Not that he blamed the Dená. In fact he felt they were right: the Czar and his ancestors had caused limitless suffering in Alaska and the time for change had long since passed.

Colonel Romanov glanced up guiltily at his sergeant to see if the man had interpreted his silence correctly. The sergeant was staring out of the other window at the same view.

Romanov grinned, then eased back into his military role.

"Very well, Sergeant Severin, notify Captain Kobelev to bring his people in, we have room for them now."

71

Russia–Canada Highway, East of Chena

General Taras Myslosovich pulled idly on his white mustache until the scout finished his report. His jowls shook as he turned to Bear Crepov sitting next to him in the command car. "They only shoot from concealment, like the brigands back home?"

"Yes, they are animals without courage. They cannot stand up to the might of the Imperial Army, so they attack like coyotes in the night." Bear kept his eyes in constant movement as the column clanked up the RustyCan. The Dená could be anywhere.

His loathing for the Indians barely eclipsed his hatred of the Russians. Fate had dealt him a deadly hand. The Russians didn't trust him and the Indians had put the price of five hundred California dollars on his head.

The Dená bounty was the only thing that kept the Russians from shooting him outright for leaving Valari behind at Chena Redoubt. They thought he should have died to save her, the two-faced bastards, after they had bombed the place flat! He spat out the window of the command car.

"Perhaps war is not to your taste, woodsman," the fat old general said, barely concealing a sneer.

"The way you wage war is not to my liking," Crepov said. "The Indians have already proven they can destroy your fancy machines,

353

whether they fly or crawl. We should be advancing quietly through the forest to surprise them in their beds."

"Reconnaissance shows they have fortified the road at Chena Redoubt as well as the bridge over the Yukon. Infantry, no matter how brave or skilled, cannot take positions like that without armor or air support." General Myslosovich pulled on his walrus mustache again. Squinting at Bear, he continued with an air of condescension.

"When you have fought as many battles for the Motherland as I have, understanding tactics will become as instinctual as mating with a woman." He broke into hoarse laughter. "And it can be a damn sight more fulfilling!"

Bear watched the old man crumple into a coughing fit. He felt doomed. This fool was like all the others.

Bear didn't think the Imperial Army had won a major engagement since the Great War. As far as he knew the troops had spent the past forty years balanced on the backs of the people of Russian Amerika.

Can it be I'm on the wrong side?

A vein of ice pulsed through his head as he considered his past decisions and present limited options.

I wish I had a bottle of vodka.

A dirt encrusted motorcycle, its engine sounding like an army of flatulent men, came up next to the car and the rider handed something to the guard in the front seat. After a quick glance at the paper, he passed it back to General Myslosovich.

"Excellent. The rabble are moving up behind their fortifications in front of Chena Redoubt. We finally have them in a position where we can smash them!"

"You will pardon me for saying so, General, but I've heard that before." Bear spat out the window again.

"If you continue to spout defeatist sentiments, I will have you shot in front of the troops as an object lesson."

Bear bit his tongue to keep silent. He had no doubt the old bastard would do it.

Time to cut my losses, disappear into British Canada for a few years.

Bear glanced at the General. "I feel boxed up in here. It's not to my liking. I'm a man of the forest."

"You're here to interpret anything I do not understand at first glance. If I allow you to leave you will instantly disappear like a jinni." He patted the holstered pistol on his hip. "I want you where I can get a good aim at you."

Bear estimated the time it would take to kill the guard in front of him. Could he get to the general before the fat bastard shot him? His fingertips caressed the haft of Claw in its oiled boot sheath; he thought about the razor-sharp edge.

Perhaps something would pull their attention outside the car. Bear knew patience—he was a hunter.

72

Flight Delta, 5 Kilometers Above British Canada

"Colonel Grigorievich." The headset provided incredibly clear communications. "Would you come up to the flight deck, please?"

"Certainly." Grisha pulled off the headset, unsnapped his harness, and picked his way between the rows of paratroopers who constantly examined and reexamined their equipment. The tension in the aircraft felt tangible. The sergeant major opened the hatch to the flight deck, waving him through, his black face impassive.

After days of total isolation Grisha was exultant to be heading north again. Colonel Buhrman flew in the lead plane, and Major Coffey flew in the second transport. Grisha had been more than happy to fly as senior officer in the third aircraft.

He wasn't sure where Benny Jackson and his Special Forces were, but it really didn't matter as long as they were in the fight.

"Over here, Colonel." The navigator, Major McDaniel, waved him to a seat in a bubble in the side of the aircraft. "Colonel Buhrman asked us to show you this. Here—" binoculars were pushed into his hands "—take a look down there and tell us what you think it is."

Grisha estimated their height at five kilometers. He saw two other transports, each with huge propellers on their four engines reflecting perfect circles, droning along in formation with them. A P-61 Eureka fighter passed in the distance. He peered down at the ground.

The RustyCan wound across the ground like an indolent reptile—whose scales glistened as he watched.

"What the hell?" Grisha sharpened the focus and tapped the enhancer control. The ground quickly swam up at him and he could clearly see an extensive armored column moving north up the highway.

"Those aren't Russian," he said. "Where are we?"

"Over northern British Canada." Major McDaniel lowered his binoculars and studied Grisha. "At first we thought they were Canadian, but look at the insignia."

Grisha strained his eyes to pierce the distance and dust. He anticipated the Union Jack and felt amazement when he saw the stylized Cheyenne war shield. "They're from the First People's Nation. What the hell are they doing this far north?"

The major grinned. "It looks like they're going to hit the Russkies in the ass. This war is beginning to get interesting."

"But their fight is with the British, not the Russians."

"Perhaps, Colonel, they're coming to help their fellow Indians," Major McDaniel said.

"But how did they get past the British?"

"The word we got says they went through the British. The Brits're fighting two battles as we speak. They sent too much of their army south and now they're paying for the blunder."

"If the F.P.N. hits the Russians at Tetlin, the only forces we'd have to worry about are the ones at St. Nicholas and St. Anthony." Grisha felt his excitement grow.

"If they hit the Russians soon enough." The major peered down through the fleecy cloud cover. "But I'd bet a month's pay the Russians know they're coming."

Grisha chuckled. "If we got paid I'd be willing to take that wager. The Russians are incredibly arrogant. If they weren't so mule-headed they would have defeated us by now."

"I've wondered about that," the major said. "We know you guys are hell on wheels, but you're outnumbered by at least five to one."

"More like seven or eight to one. But the Dená Republik isn't nice, flat farmland like Canada back there." He nodded his head. "Russia depends on her air force and her armor. Our antiaircraft have pulled her aviation teeth and her armor is confined to the RustyCan."

"You can hold the highway?"

"That remains to be seen, Major. Perhaps if we arrive in time."

73

Chena Redoubt

Wing inspected the fortifications carefully. This was where the Russians would hit first. Both banks of the Chena bristled with mines.

The Dená weapons could traverse the minefields with impunity by lining up on the bright swatches of cloth tacked to trees on the far side. Even if the Russians noticed them, they wouldn't know how to interpret the markers.

Behind the minefield stood a reinforced log-and-rock wall spanning the highway and stretching into the muskeg on both sides. The muskeg itself aided defense, consisting of meter-wide pods of lichen, called pingos, rearing up to a half meter in height, where a hastily placed foot sinking between the thousands of pingos could easily break a leg. Beneath the muskeg was a watery gruel of soil and gravel, below that lay the implacable permafrost, frozen to a depth of fifty meters or more.

After fording the river the first few tanks might make it through the muskeg but the rest would bog down. Six newly imported artillery pieces from the United States had the area zeroed in, complete with range markers.

"Placing those markers is something we learned in the Great War," Captain Lauesen told her. "The advancing troops rarely notice them and it tells us their exact distance."

The initial assault would be horrendously costly for the Russians. Wing almost felt sorry for them. A Russian-built command car roared up. The Imperial two-headed eagle had been painted out and what looked like an eight-pointed star replaced it.

Malagni jumped out of the car and slammed the door.

"What's that supposed to mean?" Wing pointed.

"The North Star, of course! Made from dentalium shells. It's the insignia of the Dená Republik." He glanced around. A huge axe hung from a loop on his belt. "Are we ready for them?"

"God willing and the creek don't rise," Captain Lauesen said.

"Which God, white or Indian?" Malagni asked. Sometimes, Wing thought, he sounded as balanced as anyone else. But it never lasted long. "It could make a difference, you know." Malagni darted off down the fortification, talking to the heavily armed Dená who watched the distant tree line with flinty eyes.

"Is he always that, ah, exuberant?" Captain Lauesen asked.

"Malagni is a madman. But a very crafty madman. He has absolutely no fear. I don't think he will live through this war—I don't think he wants to."

"What did he do before the war?"

"There's always been a war here. It just took some of us longer than others to realize it."

Captain Lauesen stared at her frankly. "How about you, are you going to survive the war?"

"Only if the man I love does." She turned and walked back toward the command car. Her feet hurt and she worried about Grisha.

74

Russia–Canada Highway, East of Chena

The lead column sat in the middle of the road. Engines idled as men relieved themselves and slapped at mosquitoes. Bear heard the motorcycle before he saw it.

Filth caked the rider and the lenses of the smeared goggles looked unnaturally clean on his dusty face. The motorcycle came to a stop next to the command car. "General Myslosovich, we are two kilometers from the front."

"Excellent." He smacked the back of the driver's seat with his jeweled baton. Bear had already heard the story how the Czar had presented it to the general for pacifying the Yakuts fifteen years before. "Vladimir, spread the word, I want an officers' meeting in ten minutes."

Bear absently rubbed his scar and noted the insignia on each officer as they arrived. Captain of Artillery. Major of Infantry. Lieutenant Colonel of Armor. An Okhana captain.

Bad sign. The cossacks had a way of fucking everything up. Back in his grandfather's day cossacks had a reputation for being noble, honorable warriors. That was before they sold their souls to the Czar and joined his secret police.

The other officers edged away from the Okhana captain. General Myslosovich cleared his throat and all eyes fastened on his fat, red face.

Bear smiled. Put tusks under that moustache and the first Eskimo he came across would have him for dinner.

"Radio the main column to make all speed and catch up with us. We may need them to consolidate our holdings. I want an immediate artillery barrage on the barricade and everything within five hundred meters of it. Then I want armor to advance all the way to Chena Redoubt."

When Myslosovich spoke his jowls quivered, enhancing the walrus illusion. Bear looked away so they couldn't see his grin.

"Infantry will follow armor. Mop up anything the tanks leave behind. Short and sweet. Any questions?"

"General, I understand they have antitank weapons." The tanker lieutenant. colonel let his voice drift away as Myslosovich glared at him.

"That's what your cannon are for, Colonel. Besides, the Siberian Tigers are up there clearing out that sort of thing right now."

Bear felt impressed despite himself. The Siberian Tigers were the best commandos the Czar had. They all had to serve four years in the regular army before they could volunteer for the elite force. Their training proved so grueling that, of every one hundred recruits who began the program, three finished.

Bear almost felt sorry for the Indians.

I hope they leave Grigorievich for me. Of all the people to make colonel! The Indians must be in dire straits.

The officers hurried off, shouting orders. General Myslosovich sat back with a grunt.

"I want to fight," Bear said. Grigorievich's visage hung in his mind like a cloud of mosquitoes. "There are Indians out there I have sworn to kill."

"You swear a great deal, woodsman. Why didn't you kill them when you had the chance?"

"I did kill one of them, a traitor to the Czar." Bear let his voice carry insult. "He was a Russian Army officer."

"Do you know his name?" Myslosovich seemed guarded.

"Captain Nikolai Rezanov, an Okhana cossack."

"General Alexandr Rezanov's son? You killed him?"

"Yes. He joined the Dená. Because of him I will wear this for the rest of my life." Bear pointed to his scarred face. "The man who did this is still alive, and I must change that."

"You may join the infantry elements going in behind the tanks." The walrus eyes squinted to slits. "If you try to desert I'll have you shot."

"If I chose to desert and couldn't evade this band of street urchins, I deserve to be shot." Bear stepped out and slammed the door behind him. He retrieved his gear from the boot and went looking for the infantry.

75

Four Miles from Chena Redoubt

Wing paused in her inspection tour of the front line, puzzling over the whooshing sound.

Major Heinrich Smolst bellowed, "INCOMING!"

Everybody hit the ground as the first salvo smashed into the log fortification and the minefield.

Wing tried to run but the concussion of the exploding shells and detonating mines knocked her off her feet, pummeling her with invisible clubs. Bits of wood and rock whirred past her. She realized those splinters and stones could kill as easily as a bullet.

The six pieces of U.S. artillery fired at the same time, adding to the maelstrom of sound. One of them took a direct hit, wiping out the crew and throwing pieces of cannon into two others.

Wing hugged the ground, trying to make herself small, as the barrage continued. A peek at the rapidly disintegrating barricade over the highway told her their three weeks of hard work was for nothing. The exploding shells didn't seem as loud and she felt thankful.

A body crashed into her and she turned to see Major Smolst. His mouth moved but she couldn't hear his words.

"What?" she yelled.

Smolst frowned at her. "You must get out of here!" he shouted.

His words sounded distant, muffled.

Wing realized her eardrums had been damaged by the barrage. She yelled, "I tried to run but I keep getting knocked down."

Abruptly the Russian shelling ceased. Although the world seemed packed with cotton, her ears hurt.

Smolst pulled her to her feet. "C'mon, if I don't get you back to safety, Grisha will have my ass."

Wing laughed. "Why, are you responsible for me?"

Smolst looked troubled. "Of course not."

"You really are responsible for me?" She felt dumbfounded. She had been in the Dená army for ten years. Who did Grisha think he was? She had rescued *him* from the cossacks!

Smolst grabbed her arm. "Tanks. We have to fall back."

She stared through the cordite-rich smoke. A line of Zukhov battle tanks roared toward them at speed. Wing couldn't hear them.

"Yeah, let's go." They ran toward the second line of defense, a kilometer away. Many others ran with them.

A few heavily armed squads had dug in and aimed shoulder launchers and heavy machine guns toward the advancing machines. One of the launchers spat fire and Wing glanced back in time to see the lead tank explode.

Three of the U.S. field pieces opened up on the Russians. dropping shells on the road and into the APCs supporting the tanks. A Russian tank exploded from a direct hit.

A bullet hit Smolst in his upper left arm, blowing blood, meat, and cloth away in a miniature cloud. Crying out, he spun and fell. Wing stopped and reached down to help him up. Something snapped past her ear.

"Major Smolst, come on!" She tugged his good arm and he bared his teeth in pain but staggered to his feet.

She looked up and saw men in camouflage attacking from the left flank. They had her people caught in a cross fire. She jerked Smolst down into a firing pit where one of three men still moved.

"Where'd they come from?" the trooper asked. She recognized Leroy, one of Blue's cousins from Nulato.

"Are you hit?"

"Not yet. Help me load this thing."

Smolst tore at his bloody sleeve. "Shit, shit, shit!" He pulled a belt off one of the dead troopers and cinched it around his bicep.

Leroy and Wing struggled with the heavy ammunition belt until it clicked into the feed slot. He snapped the bolt back once, took aim at the figures advancing from the tree line, and commenced firing short bursts.

Wing saw two attackers go down. She pulled a rocket launcher from beneath one of the dead men. The tanks were now five abreast and approaching the far side of the Chena. She waited, wondering if all the mines had been detonated by the barrage.

As if in answer, the right track blew off the middle tank. The other four continued down the bank. Another artillery round exploded between the tanks, throwing mud and moss over everything.

They don't have any idea how deep the Chena is along here, she decided.

Guess they're about to find out.

Two of the tanks stopped and the other two rumbled into the river and completely submerged. They didn't come out. Wing took careful aim and fired the antitank rocket. One of the remaining tanks gushed fire and the crew boiled out of the turret hatch as the machine began to burn.

Something knocked the rocket launcher out of her hands and she realized the enemy flankers hadn't gone to ground. Leroy fired again and two more men dropped.

"Are we the only people left alive out here?" she yelled. The ground heaved and pieces of tundra and permafrost rained down on them. The tanks made deadly forward fire bases despite their inability to cross the river.

The Russian ground troops enfiladed the U.S. artillery positions and killed two crews. The last 105mm swiveled and put three rounds into the woods where the Russians had taken cover. One of the remaining Russian tanks zeroed in on the cannon and hit it with its second shot.

Wing searched the firing pit and found two more rockets. She tried to load and discovered the launcher had been smashed by a bullet.

"Damn!" She grabbed one of the heavy automatic weapons, leaned it on the edge of the firing pit. Wing squeezed the trigger and the stock slammed against her shoulder like a string of hard punches. Her teeth clenched as she concentrated on putting the rounds where she wanted them.

She hit four of the camouflaged attackers and the rest took cover.

"How many are there, Leroy?" When he didn't answer, she glanced over to find him on his back with a surprised expression across his face, eyes turned up as if trying to see the bullet hole in his forehead.

Smolst pushed himself up and pulled Leroy's weapon from his dead hands. "Help me get this on the edge of the hole," he said, breathing heavily.

She grabbed the tripod and lifted it to the rim as Smolst crawled up behind the weapon. He fired a long burst.

The ground lurched again and debris bounced around the firing pit. Smolst and his weapon fell heavily on top of a dead trooper. The major lay there, panting, and Wing realized he was going into shock.

A lassitude washed over her like a warm tide as she realized they would die alone out here. Her determination to take as many as possible of the Czar's fools with her didn't diminish—she just stopped being careful.

Bullets spattered around their position and she knew one or more flankers were trying to pin her down while others advanced. She popped up and squeezed the trigger while moving the muzzle from side to side. Three more men went down before the others, so many others, dropped from sight.

Gunfire chattered from her right and left and she spared quick peeks to see that some of her people were still in the fight. She and Smolst wouldn't die alone. A round whined past her head and she involuntarily ducked as others followed.

Wing slammed in a fresh banana clip and popped up again, spraying the advancing enemy while cursing them in Athabascan.

76

Chena Redoubt

As he lay on his cot trying to rest, Malagni heard the thunder of artillery. He was halfway out his door when Sergeant Major Tobias trotted up.

"The Russians are blowing the fortifications to pieces, Colonel. Colonel Demoski's people will never hold them."

"So much for Plan A!" Malagni hurried down the hall, calculating madly. "Saddle up the reserve force. No sense in waiting for them to hit us here."

"Very good, Colonel." Tobias ran down the hall.

Malagni stopped in his office, grabbed a machine pistol, and put spare clips in his dungaree pockets. He looped a cord around his axe and tied it to his belt to keep it from flopping if he had to run.

Somewhere in this army his little brother, Nik, was preparing for this battle. Malagni had already lost one brother to the damned Russians and the spirits indicated the Russians would get him, too. He fervently hoped Nik would make it through.

Malagni felt the presence of Slayer-of-Men. "I'll avenge their treachery, brother!" he said to the room. "It's a good day to die."

He looked at his U.S.-supplied helmet and grinned. Let the rest of the Dená Army use them, he wasn't a soldier anyway—he was a warrior! He hurried out into the courtyard.

The artillery barrage overwhelmed all other sound. W*ing must be going through hell.* His reserve consisted of three tanks, five armored cars, and three hundred men.

We are outnumbered so bad I won't even try to figure it out.

A wave of elation swept over him. "Are you ready to fight?" he screamed at them.

"Yes!" they roared back.

"Then let's kill Russians!" Malagni jumped into the command car. Sergeant Major Tobias grinned from behind the wheel.

"I thought you were a pencil pusher, Tobias."

"I earned my stripes in the field, Colonel. I wouldn't miss this donnybrook for love nor money."

Malagni gave him a wide grin. "Then carry on, Sergeant Major, carry on." He threw back his head and screamed his war cry.

They tore through the gate with the entire garrison following.

77

The Russian Front Line, in the 2nd Battle of Chena

Bear Crepov cradled his Kalashnikov and trotted behind the ranger unit along the bank of the Chena. The Siberian Tigers had thrown a "hurry-up" bridge across the water a half kilometer upstream from the highway. These troopers seemed to know what they were doing. Not a cossack among them.

They arrived at the bridge and a guard waved them across the three-tree bridge. No chatter vied with the brutal cacophony of the artillery.

Across the river without incident and into the trees, the rangers kept up the pace and Bear began to feel his years and habits weighing on him. He gritted his teeth and maintained speed.

He wasn't going to let these kids show him up.

The barrage ceased. The silence felt unnatural. The ranger captain pumped his right arm twice and they increased speed.

Bear's breath came in hard gasps now. He couldn't do this much longer. Small-arms fire broke out ahead of them.

Bullets whined past, thwacked into trees. One punched into the man ahead of Bear. The ranger whuffed and fell to his knees.

Bear stopped beside him, not to help or out of concern, but because it gave him an excuse to rest for a moment.

The soldier turned his camouflage-painted face to Bear, tried to speak. His eyes rolled back in his head and he fell on his face. More bullets ricocheted through the forest and Bear sat down next to the soldier and leaned against a tree.

What I'd give for a shot of vodka, he thought.

The firefight heated up. Bear waited until his breathing returned to normal; then pushed himself to his feet.

Hope they saved some Indians for me.

He trotted toward the sound of battle.

78

117th Fighter Squadron Over Russian Amerika

Major Ben Hurley scanned the horizon, craning his neck up he searched the sky all around his P-61 Eureka fighter, *Jenny Love*. Nothing. Flying support for the paratroop transports had been a milk run.

He read his gauges and dials. According to his computations the Republic of California aircraft had just crossed the border between British Canada and Russian Amerika. He radioed the lead transport.

"Flight Delta, this is Foxtrot One. We have seen no enemy aircraft. Flight Foxtrot will now go to Plan B."

"Roger that, Foxtrot One. Thanks for the company and good hunting."

"Thanks, hope your delivery goes well."

The fifteen fighters peeled off and flew directly west.

"Okay, guys," Hurley said, "stay awake, the highway should be about a hundred and fifty miles ahead of us."

The flight dropped until they were a thousand feet above the terrain and bored onward, their propellers radiant in the Alaskan sunshine.

Tank Kommander Colonel Boris Lazarev breathed a sigh of relief when he received the radio communication from General Myslosovich. Immediately he told his driver to go to full speed. He

373

knew the other tanks and armored personnel carriers behind him would keep up. He once had broken a captain to the ranks for not maintaining pace, after that it had never again been a problem.

Being the lead tank gave him the advantage of not eating any of the dust they threw up in stultifying clouds. They traveled in battle formation, each tank staying within thirty meters of the machine in front of it. Colonel Lazarev glanced at the column behind him as it wound up the series of switchbacks to reach Baranov Pass, the only road pass in the Alaska Range.

Every tank commander stood in his hatch, goggles and helmets facing forward. His command had arrived in Russian Amerika less than forty-eight hours previously. This was quite different than patrolling the China/Russia border. For one thing, the scenery from absolutely striking.

On one side of the road the mountain rose at an angle nearly impossible for a man to traverse, on the other side of the road, below the switchbacks, lay a valley at least four hundred meters deep. Across the valley a long ridge, displaying a variety of hues as if painted by a gargantuan artist, ran for miles. The locals called it Rainbow Ridge.

Abruptly he thought of the transport plane from their small armada that had crashed on takeoff, killing twenty of his men and destroying one tank. He detested waste, and flying.

They sped along at thirty kilometers per hour, steadily climbing toward the summit. He hoped the Indians would hold long enough to insure his men would not be cheated out of combat; they had come a long way for this. He had it on good authority that the Czar used political maneuvering in order to gain time for this buildup. He also understood that the Indian rebels had gone along with it completely.

"Colonel Lazarev!" the voice in his headset all but shrieked. Before he could bark an admonition, the voice went on, "Aircraft!"

"Where?"

"East, northeast, coming straight at us."

"Man your machine guns!" He stared at the incoming planes; so far he counted seven, trying desperately to identify them. Could they be friendly? The Dená didn't have aircraft as far as he knew.

He finally recognized the slim profile with the underfuselage air scoop. "Oh, my God, they're R.O.C. P-61 Eureka fighters. And we're roosting chickens with a wolf in the henhouse."

Vainly he looked for options. "All personnel out of the troop carriers, fill the sky with fire!" He glanced back to see men scurrying like ants around the halted column.

No cover, we have no cover.

Major Hurley spread his flight out like a wide wave heading for a distant beach. Intelligence said there were a lot of Russian tanks and APCs headed north out here somewhere, and unless they were stopped the Dená were going to lose their asses. He spied a ribbon undulating across the landscape in the distance.

"Is that it, guys, dead ahead?"

"Negative that, skipper," Lieutenant Donaldson replied. "That's the Tanana River."

"You sure there's a road out here, Major?" First Lieutenant Christenson said with a laugh.

"Damn sure, we have pictures—"

"Tally ho! This is Foxtrot Nine, the road's over here to the southwest, just past another river."

"Good going, Captain Shipley. You heard the man, boys. I want two waves. We should find them under a big dust cloud."

"I see it, there they are!" Hurley wasn't sure who the voice belonged to, it didn't matter anyway.

"My gawd, they're sitting ducks," Christenson exclaimed.

"They're heavily armed ducks, don't forget that," Hurley snapped. "Get the troop carriers first, those tanks aren't going anywhere. Drop your gas."

A series of microphone clicks told him his people understood. Two all-but-empty long-range fuel tanks dropped from beneath the wings of each fighter, instantly giving the aircraft less weight and drag. The planes suddenly seemed agile as ballerinas.

"Okay, gentlemen, rank has its privileges. Follow me!"

He put his fighter into a long turn and came up the mountain behind the armored column. As if the stationary vehicles had lost a load of diamonds, the ground suddenly sparkled with muzzle flashes. Hurley grinned and pulled the trigger on the front of his stick, relishing the roar of his six .50 caliber machine guns.

Both of his wingmen opened up as they bored in, passing over the first bend of the long, snaking column. All of the Russian APCs carried twin .30 machine guns mounted over the driving compartment. Immediately the entire column fired at the aircraft.

"Shit, Skipper, I'm taking hits from above me!" Christenson said.

"Pull up," Hurley ordered. "We'll come at 'em from a better angle."

All three aircraft pulled up and twisted away in different directions. One of them trailed smoke.

"Major Hurley, this is Cooper. I'm hit."

"How bad, Coop?"

"My engine is smoking and my oil pressure is headed for the Spanish border. I think maybe I've got five minutes."

"Head straight north for Dená country, now. If you have to bail out, do it near a road, that's pretty wild country down there. Kirby, you escort him, try and make the field at Fort Yukon."

"Yes, sir. Sorry about this."

"For what, following orders? Good luck, Coop."

"Same to you, sir. Cooper out."

"I'll write often, Skipper, don't worry," Kirby said with a laugh.

"You guys be careful and that's an order."

Two comm clicks answered and Hurley grinned.

The two aircraft buzzed away.

"Okay, guys, this time let's hit them from the top of the mountain. There's thirteen of us now, let's make that an unlucky number for the Russians."

Roaring down out of a wide circle, the first three Eurekas screamed down at the leading elements of the column. The side of the mountain blurred a hundred feet below their polished aluminum bellies. Only the Russians on the highest switchback could fire at them without fear of hitting their comrades.

"Plug 'em up, use your rockets on these bastards," Hurley said with a growl.

The tanks quickly grew in size.

Colonel Boris Lazarev shrieked into his microphone, "What do you mean there are no aircraft in Alaska? I am being attacked by fifteen of them."

"My apologies, Colonel, I meant to say we have no aircraft in Alaska capable of assisting you at this time," the man seemed uninterested, lethargic.

"Pass my request on to High Command before resuming your nap!" He slammed the microphone down. "Where are they?"

Sergeant Cermanivich, his gunner, pointed up the mountain. "I predict they will come from there, Colonel."

"Another five minutes of attacking from below and we'd have killed them all."

"I don't know what kept that wounded plane in the air," Cermanivich spat over the side of the tank and flexed his hands before again grabbing his machine gun. "I think I hit the son of a bitch a hundred times myself."

"We're in a bad spot here, Rudi, shoot straight—"

"There!" Sergeant Cermanivich's twin thirties blasted up at the onrushing aircraft.

"Fire!" Lazarev bellowed. The 150mm cannon fired an antiaircraft shell, which passed the first planes completely before detonating. Bullets splanged off the side of the tank.

The three leading aircraft fired rockets.

"Take cover!" Lazarev shrieked, dropping into the hull.

The tank rocked with the multiple explosions but the terrified crew detected no breach in their armor. More explosions went off and a shower of debris from two directions rang against the tank.

"They keep missing us," Cermanivich observed.

Lazarev peered through the periscope but could see nothing but scenery. "To hell with this." He stood and opened the hatch, cautiously peered over the rim.

The tank behind them burned like a bonfire in autumn. He turned and looked up the mountain, and his heart lurched. A boulder twice the size of his tank had been blasted from the mountainside and tumbled down, coming to rest against the side of the road, less than a meter from the left track.

Who knew how long it would stay there? But for the moment it was a perfect wall against the R.O.C fighters. Abruptly he scrambled out.

"Come on, Rudi, we have work to do. Ivanivich, reload the gun with another antiaircraft shell."

"Yes, Colonel," the burly Georgian bellowed, grabbing a shell.

"Rudi, I'll tell you when they're almost on top of us. Blow them out of the air when they go over." Lazarev stood on the turret and peered over the top of the boulder. "Get ready, here they come."

Major Hurley whipped his P-61 down to hug the mountainside again. Only eleven of them were still in the fight. Barton, in the second wave of fighters down the mountain, had run right into an anti-aircraft shell. He crashed into the mountain and his plane exploded, blowing a huge boulder down the steep slope. At first Hurley thought the lieutenant was going to score a posthumous kill, the boulder tumbled straight at the leading tank—and stopped at the slightly elevated edge of the road, creating a perfect barrier for the Russian.

The fight was not one-sided. Four of the tanks behind the leader had become incinerators for crew members who hadn't moved quickly enough. Sixteen tanks still fought for their lives.

Seven of the fifteen armored personnel carriers would never operate again and all but one of the ten troop carriers burned brightly. The valley provided a natural draft, pulling the smoke away from the battle site, thereby awarding the fighters a clear view of their targets.

Two bullet holes in the plexiglas of Hurley's canopy and the absence of part of his left wing flap attested to the skill of the Russian gunners. He didn't want to know what the rest of his bird looked like. Not that it mattered, he was still in the air.

"We have to stop these guys," he grated over his radio, "or our Indian buddies are so much meat."

Christenson now flew on his left wing and had accelerated to pull twenty feet ahead of Hurley. They both fired their cannons at the huge rock but it absorbed their efforts. They zoomed over the protected tank and fire laced the entire length of Christenson's Eureka.

"Oh, shit, Ben! That son of a bitch got me!" Fire suddenly engulfed the aircraft and, as Hurley watched in horror, it exploded.

Tears abruptly pooled in his goggles and he tore them off to dry his eyes with his sleeve. They had flown together for seven years. Mike had been his best man when he married Jenny, and ended up bedding her best friend, the maid of honor, the same evening. You never knew what he was going to do next. He'd made captain twice and was busted back to lieutenant both times for crazy stunts, mostly involving women and alcohol.

He took a deep breath. No time for this now. They had a battle to win.

He went into a tight turn and came back at the road from the valley side. Two tank turrets turned and fired flak shells at him. Ten machine guns clawed after him and he thought this might be his last pass.

He wanted the leader, whose turret now swiveled to fire point blank. One of the flak rounds exploded directly under *Jenny Love*. The controls instantly went mushy and he knew there wasn't much time left.

Then he saw it; the mammoth boulder supporting the road with the lead tank right there on top of it. A scree field gave mute testimony that the roadbed wasn't solid here, but built up. The plane dropped slightly, not his doing.

The lead tank fired and the shell burst ahead and above him, shredding his cockpit, and him, with burning bits of razor-sharp metal. His last act aimed the plane at the base of the mammoth boulder.

"Jenny, I'm so sorry." She smiled at him and opened her arms.

"Beautiful shot, Ivanivich!" Lazarev screamed. "You got him, he's going down. Save your ammo, Rudi, he's going to hit the side of the mountain." Lazarev stood to peer over the rock again and heard the enemy plane explode downslope behind him.

The turret suddenly dipped beneath him and he fell onto the machine gun. "What the hell—"

"The road is collapsing," Rudi blurted.

Before they could react, the road dropped away under them. The tank fell, tumbling over, crushing Lazarev and throwing Rudi into the void before continuing its roll, crushing the three screaming crew members to death with their own ammunition. The huge protective boulder obligingly rolled after them.

Men and equipment filled two of the five switchbacks below them. The growing avalanche picked up speed and widened, taking out six operational tanks on the first switchback and everything on the second. Only on the tight curves were there still living Russians, and their machines would stay there until the road was rebuilt at some point in the future; the men would have to walk out—if they could.

Captain Shipley surveyed the devastation and took notes on his knee pad. Ben Hurley had been a personal friend and he wanted the recommendation for his Medal of Honor to be as complete as possible. Then he and the remaining seven fighters headed north.

79

Behind the Dená Front Line

Malagni viewed the battle through his binoculars as Tobias bounced them along in the command car. A young soldier hung onto the .30 caliber machine gun mounted in the back. They couldn't go into battle without a man on the gun.

Malagni spoke into his headset. "Tanks, spread out and commence firing at the Russian side of the Chena. No short rounds or I'll have your ass!"

He saw the Dená fire into the woods, peered through the binoculars at their targets. "Sweet baby Jesus, Tobias. They got Russian troops on their flank." He spoke into his microphone, "We need infantry on the left flank up there. Now!"

Malagni watched the Russian troops, noted their expert deployment and discipline, much better than their regular army.

These guys know their stuff. Not good.

As he watched, more Russians emerged from the woods. New guys, different uniforms, maybe they were not as experienced. Many of them fell to Dená fire before the rest stopped their rush and took cover.

"That way, Sergeant Major!" Malagni pointed at the Russian-filled woods. He twisted around and shouted at the young Athabascan on the machine gun. "When you think you can reach them, knock the shit out of them!"

The young man gave him a wicked grin and fired the machine gun. Behind them, armored troop carriers raced to keep up. Farther back, scores of infantry ran doggedly after them.

Maybe we waited too long? Malagni felt a flash of apprehension.

Shell fire crashed into the wide meadow between them and the woods. The Russians had spotted them and were trying to find the range with their artillery.

"Don't drive in a straight line!" Malagni shouted. "They'll shaft us for sure."

"Yes, sir!" Tobias shot back. He turned the car as sharply to the right as he could without rolling it. They headed directly toward the Russian line on the highway.

A shell whistled past and exploded behind them. Tobias veered left and another shell destroyed tundra where they would have been if they hadn't turned.

"Some son of a bitch has plans for us," Malagni bellowed.

The machine gunner kept up a steady fire that laced the tree line despite the violence of Tobias' driving.

The Russians don't have all the good gunners.

Malagni smiled, felt his heart hammering and his senses keen as razors.

He heard the one that got them. The shriek sounded far too loud to miss. Malagni didn't hear the explosion, but the front of the car flew apart as the shell detonated directly in its path.

The shattered car body flew back in a lazy spin, throwing the men out to be buffeted by the sledgehammer concussion of the round. Malagni landed on the stump of his right arm. Pain vomited through him and he screamed. He rolled over and came to his feet, involuntary tears streaming down his face.

Tobias, still clutching the steering wheel in his hands, hair scorched by the explosion, sat on the ground peering about owlishly. "Wot the hell was that?"

The decapitated body of the machine gunner lay kicking in the sphagnum moss and early forget-me-nots, blood jetting from the mangled neck. An armored troop carrier roared up and men leaped out, picked up Tobias, and tossed him in the back.

"Can we offer you a ride, Colonel?" the sergeant driver asked.

Malagni jumped on the running board. "Let's get them."

The troop carrier bounced toward the enemy. The Russians had dug in and fired at them with good effect. Bullets splanged off the roof and hood of the carrier.

"Okay, Sarge," Malagni said casually. "Let's let them off here."

Another enemy shell screamed over but landed in the tree line, taking out at least five Russians.

"Damned sporting of them," Malagni shouted, grinning.

The artillery fire ceased. Now it was an infantry fight. Dená troopers poured out of the carriers and spread out, returning fire and digging in.

Malagni started to speak into his microphone before he realized the headset wasn't hooked to a radio any longer, so he jerked it off his head and threw it over his shoulder. He turned toward the double-timing troops, who had closed to two hundred meters, waved his arm over his head and pointed to the trees where the Russian line thinned to nothing.

Maybe we can flank them.

A dozen rounds stitched across the ground toward him and he took cover behind a mossy rock. One round hit the rock, spraying tiny chips across the back of Malagni's neck. He thought it felt like mosquito bites. Big mosquito bites.

His troops slowed, spreading out in a wavery hundred meter line, with little or no cover, and taking too many casualties.

"Enough!" he bellowed, jumping to his feet. "Let's take them once and for all!" Malagni fired out the clip in the machine pistol at the Russians and threw the weapon over his shoulder.

He slipped the axe free, swung it over his head, and charged the enemy. Shouts echoed up and down the Dená line as his men rose and charged with him.

80

Rainbow Valley

First Lieutenant Gerald Yamato found himself in the twin-thirty cross-fire from three tanks. He felt *Satori* shudder with each hit, and there were a lot of hits. For a blissful moment he thought he could stay in the fight.

Then his controls went mushy and the solid stream of smoke from his engine compartment burst into bright flame washing back over his cockpit. Another minute in this situation would kill him. He immediately ejected the canopy and, after jerking his seat restraints free, threw himself into the smoky wake of his doomed P-61, which screamed out of control down into the awesome canyon a thousand feet below the battle.

Lieutenant Yamato wrenched his chute around so he could see as much of the battle as possible. While he watched, one of the Eureka fighters suddenly flamed, trailed smoke and exploded.

"Looked like Christenson's ship," he said to himself, feeling his heart lurch. Mike was the squadron mascot, a classic brilliant, self-doomed fuck-off.

A tree drifted past and he realized he had better pay mind to his own predicament; for him the fight with the Russians was over. An explosion from below pulled his attention to the bottom of the valley. His fighter had impacted at the edge of a river.

Someone had claimed it was the Delta River.

The wind pushed him farther down the huge canyon. The artist in him took a quick moment to appreciate the majestic beauty of the valley. The miles-long ridge on the far side rippled in shades of reds, pinks, greens, and even light purples, like a Technicolor layer cake cut and toppled on its side.

Then the pragmatic flier took over and he worked his chute in order to come down near the river, rather than hang up in the middle of the forest bordering both sides of the obviously swift-moving water. Even before the ground rushed up and grabbed him, he wondered what equipment he had and would it be enough?

His landing was textbook; take the shock with his feet together and collapse in a rolling tumble. Unlike the field back in the Napa Valley, this one was covered with boulders and rocks the size of his head.

He landed on a small boulder and his feet slid off to the right. He threw his arm out and instantly jerked it to his side again—he couldn't risk breaking it. His shoulder took the majority of the impact and immediately went numb. Jerry threw out his hands and stopped himself.

The parachute settled on the rocky floodplain, began to fill from the constant breeze moving alongside the water. He pushed himself up and jerked the shroud lines, collapsing the silk. His shoulder hurt like hell but he swiftly pulled the lines into a pile at his feet.

Just as his hands touched the silk canopy, he heard a massive explosion from above. He looked up the incredible slope. At first he saw nothing but smoke pouring down from the road on the canyon rim. Then he saw awful movement.

At least nine Russian tanks avalanched down the steep wall, rotating in deadly descent, thunderously smashing flat the rocks and trees before crashing into each other or bouncing farther out into the canyon. Huge boulders and entire swaths of trees boiled in a descending dust-shrouded dance of death.

Behind the maelstrom tumbled a boulder larger than any tank, gouging out sixty-meter-wide swaths of mountainside before spinning out into the air again, following the doomed Russian war machines into the abyss.

Lieutenant Jerry Yamato felt sorry for the poor bastards in the tanks, even though they were all probably dead at this point; that was a hell of a way to go.

Some of the tanks didn't explode when they finally hit bottom. Some did. And Jerry wasn't sure how many tanks the boulder hit when it landed. Everything ended about a quarter mile from him.

With the river twisting along the bottom of the valley, and the trees bordering the floodplain, the end result was completely obscured. A huge cloud of dust swirled into the breeze along the river and quickly dissipated.

A Eureka fighter suddenly roared down through the valley and screamed over him as he wildly waved his arms. Then it was gone. All of the beautiful, darting silver planes disappeared and the valley went silent, as if resting after the extensive disruption.

Jerry Yamato felt very alone. He looked around at the valley walls, the trees, the rocks, the now-audible river. For the very first time he realized he was completely on his own.

The Republic of California fighters were on their way north to Chena Redoubt where the Dená Republik Army, their new ally, was fighting for its life against the Imperial Russian Army. The transports held 960 R.O.C airborne troops who hoped to make a difference. The fighters would do everything they could to aid the Athabascan revolution.

But how long would it take Major Hurley to remember Lieutentant Yamato and where he was shot down? Did Hurley even know Jerry was still alive? The plane that flew over hadn't come back; had the pilot seen him at all?

They were on their way to next part of the battle; would any of them make it to Fort Yukon? It might be months before anyone came looking for him; or never.

"Okay, airman," he said aloud. "Time to take stock."

He stuffed his chute between two rocks and put his flight helmet on top of it to keep it from blowing away in the vigorous breeze. In moments he emptied his pockets and stared down at the result. Two protein-concentrate bars, a canteen of water, a survival knife, his service .45 automatic, and two full clips of rounds constituted his total belongings.

He felt grateful he wore good combat boots and a warm flight suit. Stuck down in the front of the flight suit was his garrison cap. Not three months ago he had gone through a survival course refresher.

With the abrupt start of the North American War he had been eligible for full flight status because he had remained current with training and preparedness protocol. Otherwise he wouldn't be here.

Jerry Yamato laughed out loud. He peered around at the stunted spruce, which grew at a forty-five degree angle, then up at the sky which still held a couple hours of daylight. The thinning smoke from the wreckage of his P-61 caught his attention.

He shrugged out of his parachute harness and carefully propped it up on the highest rock within ten feet. He didn't want to lose what little he had. Stuffing the PC bars in his pocket and putting the rest of his gear in place, he started toward *Satori*, his beautiful fighter.

She had nosed in at full speed and exploded on impact; what was left burned. The lump in his throat surprised him. The P-61 had just been a machine, a very beautiful one to be sure, but still . . .

Wiping away a tear, he looked around the crash site, maybe something usable had been thrown clear. He found nothing and searched the sky again. The smoke would draw any aircraft in the area.

Two billowing columns of smoke a half mile away caught his attention. The tanks, he thought.

Maybe there's something salvageable.

Keeping a moving eye on the terrain all about him, he moved carefully down the river.

As a boy he had been a member of the Bear Scouts of California, he had earned every woodcraft badge possible. In flight school he was first in the class in the survival portion of training. He'd just had that refresher a couple of months ago.

So why did he feel frightened? *Must keep one's morale up, that's what it says in the book*, he thought.

Turrets, ripped off the tank hulls in their descent, lay randomly amongst the bent and broken steel. Tracks and bogeys lay scattered, macabre prizes from the Devil's pinata. Only small flames remained in the two burning machines but he could feel their heat from fifty meters away.

Jerry thought the destroyed machines looked naked.

"You cry over your plane and now you're sad about enemy tanks?" he said out loud. "Did you hit your head when you ejected?"

He stared at the ripped hulls, knowing there might be items inside that could enhance his odds of survival. He also knew the remains of the crews rested in the heavy metal. This was part of why he had elected to join the air corps rather than the infantry—he didn't want to see stuff like this up close.

First Lieutenant Jerry Yamato, RCAF, took a deep breath and walked over to the first hemorrhaged hull and peered inside. Trying to ignore the heavy, rusty-colored slime coating the interior, he looked for equipment. When he saw the uniform pierced through with bone splinters, he turned and vomited.

He flipped off the canteen cover and rinsed his mouth. *What a wussy I am*, he thought. There hadn't been anything obviously useful in the tank.

For long moments Jerry eyed the closest turret, trying to justify skipping the whole thing.

"Gotta look, dammit," he said and spat off to the side.

He trudged over to the turret. The barrel stub of the .88 cannon bent to one side, looking for all the world like a comma with a ragged tail. The inside lay empty.

"Damn." Jerry leaned against the metal bulk and slid down to a sitting position, staring at the other wrecks. Was there nothing here he could use?

He stared up at the canyon wall. Should he try to climb out here, or follow the river until it either joined a larger body of water or went past a town? His destroyed charts mocked him; he should have looked at them more carefully.

"Who knew?" He shrugged and let his head fall forward.

Splaang! A bullet impacted on the turret where his head had just rested. The boom of the rifle pierced him through with terror and echoed off down the valley.

He jerked in fright and threw himself behind a large rock. Two more bullets smeared across the turret where his body had leaned. This time the rifle reports were just sounds.

Yamato made himself small and squirmed behind a boulder.

Adrenaline kicked in and his terror turned to anger. He pulled out his .45 and peered up the slope. Where was the son of a bitch?

He thought for a second. *Who* was the son of a bitch? Had one of the Russian troopers come all the way down here from the road to check for survivors?

It wouldn't take a genius to know there could have been no survivors. Sudden doubt washed through him. Could one of the crew have survived? Or had he run into an unfriendly local?

The odds against both were astronomical. Nobody human could survive that steel avalanche and it was scores of miles to the nearest village. But someone out there was trying to kill him. Yamato decided to go with the assumption he faced a surviving Russian.

Okay, that meant the man was close to the path the tank made on its way down. Jerry thumbed on the safety of the .45 as quietly as possible. He didn't want the damned thing going off accidentally while he was moving.

Fortune had given him something. Medium to large boulders lay scattered across the floodplain. Taking his time and moving as quietly as possible, he squirmed his way from boulder to boulder toward the canyon wall.

He had to outflank the bastard. His shoulder ached and he had to piss. He tried to ignore the distracting elements, knowing his life depended on it.

81

Russian Front Line, Second Battle of Chena

Bear Crepov carefully made his way to the front line of the Russian advance. The Siberian Tigers were excellent marksmen—many Dená lay splayed and torn in the meadow. The Russian artillery waited in silence, but shells from behind the Dená lines now fell on the Russian rear.

It's up to us to turn the tide, he realized.

A small armored column appeared from the direction of Chena Redoubt. Bear expected it to meet the Russian armor attempting to ford the Chena. A thrill of excitement ran through him when most of the column turned toward his position, spread out, and charged.

The Russian artillery resumed with a vengeance. A half-track took a direct hit. At this distance one couldn't differentiate between truck and human parts as they rained across the meadow.

The people around him stopped firing as they watched the gunners on the far bank try to hit the command car. Like a bumblebee, it dodged and darted across the meadow toward them. The machine gunner in the back of the car tried to bring his weapon to bear on the men in the tree line, but the bouncing vehicle allowed only a few rounds to sing harmlessly past them.

For the troops holding the tree line the war fell into a bubble caught in time as they watched the nimble car. Even Bear found himself holding his breath, as the uneven duel lengthened.

The front of the car abruptly disintegrated and the explosion blew its body backward in a slow flip.

The spell over the tree line shattered. For long moments they had all empathized with the enemy driver, man against death. A collective moan of disappointment rose and men hurriedly fired at the advancing Dená, now less than three hundred meters away.

Another Russian artillery round shrilled over the meadow. Bear realized the gunners had lost the range, and that the shell was going to land close to him. He threw himself behind a fallen tree trunk and hugged the ground.

The blast killed a score of troopers and blew down twice as many trees. Even though it was their own shell that hit them, the Russians cursed the Dená and intensified their fire.

The column abruptly halted at two hundred meters and troops spilled out, taking cover and returning fire. An armored personnel carrier stopped last and two of the Dená from the command car jumped down. One of them was huge, and Bear could see the man didn't have a right arm.

Bear rested his Kalashnikov across the tree trunk and blazed away. Two rangers and a Siberian Tiger shared the cover with him. The Siberian Tiger said, "Oh!" as a bullet pierced his head just under the lip of his helmet, snapping his head backward and knocking him flat.

"Fuckin' Dená are good shots," he muttered to himself. "Better go off automatic and see if I can pick them off one at a time." He wished he had his 'scoped hunting rifle; it was far more accurate than this crappy assault weapon.

Suddenly the huge Indian was on his feet. His voice carried clearly, "Enough! Let's take them once and for all!" And they charged the Russian line. The large man waved an axe over his head.

The Russians paused in their fire, laughing at the insane audacity of the Dená, especially the one-armed man with the axe. Wagers flashed back and forth as to who would hit him first.

Bear felt a rush of kinship with the madman. Finally, here was a foe worthy of him. "No!" he screamed at the men around him. "He's mine."

The line went silent as he threw down his Kalashnikov, pulled Claw from its oiled sheath, and charged the huge Indian.

The Dená charge wavered, stopped, and went to ground as the two massive men closed.

Bear bellowed at… the Dená, "You are mine!" and put his left hand behind his back, gripping his belt. This would be fair, by God!

"Then come and get me!"

When they engaged, Bear brought Claw down in a killing strike but the Indian parried it with his axe handle. Neither lost his balance as they danced away from the other. Bear realized they were a perfect match and a fierce elation gripped him.

The Dená swung his axe and Bear jerked back, heard the whisper as blade sliced air. He laughed. "I am Bear Crepov, a bold *promyshlennik* and killer of beasts and Dená! Who are you?"

The man's eyes blazed in hatred. "I am Malagni, warrior and Colonel in the Dená Republik Army. Killer of Russian scum, especially cossacks and *promyshlenniks!*"

Bear darted in and swiped at Malagni's arm. He might be fighting with only one hand, but he was using everything else he had. As Malagni fell back Bear leapt forward and kicked him in the chest.

Malagni rolled over backward and landed on his feet, pulled his arm back and sent his axe directly at Bear. Bear threw himself to the side, falling in the process. At least the man was empty-handed now.

The axe whistled a foot past where Bear's head had been. A thong hooked to the axe handle on one end and tied to Malagni's wrist on the other jerked the weapon back to Malagni's hand. The Indian never slackened his charge—he rushed toward Bear and savagely swung down at him.

Fear lent wings to Bear's feet as he rolled away and jumped up. He stifled the desire to throw Claw at Malagni, knowing a miss meant he was a dead man. Instead he threw himself at the Indian, slicing a shallow wound across the moose hide–covered chest.

As blood welled from the cut and soaked into the shirt, Bear suddenly became aware of the Dená surrounding them and the Russian weapons pointed at them—all in a frozen tableau. Neither of them could win this thing.

The certainty of death released him from his few inhibitions and he snapped—went berserk. Screaming in rage, he rushed Malagni and jammed Claw deep into the man's chest.

Malagni jerked away, knowledge of death in his eyes, and swung the axe in a vicious arc that ended at Bear Crepov's head.

Bear's last cognition was the stink of hot blood on sphagnum moss.

82

3rd PIR over Russian Amerika

A tap on his arm pulled Grisha away from the window. The burly, black sergeant major put his mouth to Grisha's ear to be heard over the stultifying roar of the engines. "They want you on the comm system, Colonel."

Grisha nodded. "Thank you, sergeant major." He went back to his seat and plugged his headset into the comm box. "Grigorievich here."

"Colonel, this is the pilot, Major Verley. We are within ten minutes of a major battle between your people and the Russians. We were going to have our people jump on Fort Yukon to act as ready reserve. But if you want, we can let you out behind your battle line."

"How large is the attacking force? What's the situation right now?"

"Our intelligence captain with your forces says the Russians have broken through your first line of defense and are advancing on Chena Redoubt itself. Your casualties are high and your people are heavily outnumbered."

Wing was at Chena—commanding his troops! "Can you drop us between the fight and the redoubt?"

"Jesus! That would be dicey, Colonel. The whole drop would be in range of the Russian advance."

"Then let me out there and you drop the rest behind our lines."

"Whatever you say, Colonel. Good luck."

"Thanks, Major Verley. And thanks for the ride." Grisha took off the headset and moved next to the sergeant major, who stood by the ramp controls.

The sergeant major listened intently to something on his headset. He replied and pulled the set off his head. He plucked a microphone off its wall mount and flipped a switch.

"Lissen up, people! We're on top of a firefight. The Dená are losin' their butts. The skipper said we was gonna jump at Fort Yukon, way behind the lines, and get fed in where needed."

Grisha turned to gauge the interest of the paratroopers. Every man stared at the sergeant major, hanging on his words.

"Now that's all changed. Colonel Grigorievich here, is gonna jump into the battle and the rest of us are 'sposed to jump behind the lines." His eyes moved across them, challenging them.

"The skipper says anyone wants to volunteer to jump with the Colonel has his okay. Who's goin' besides me and him?" He snapped his rip cord onto the cable running the length of the cabin.

All one hundred twenty men stood, hooked up, and began checking the gear of the men in front of them.

Grisha felt a lump swell in his throat. He turned back to the sergeant major. "You honor me and my people, Sergeant Major. Thank you."

"Ain't every day a troop runs acrost a straightleg colonel with balls, sir. We're the ones proud to be jumping with you."

The red light over the ramp winked on. The sergeant major worked the controls and the ramp in the back of the plane yawned open. Grisha stepped forward and snapped his cord onto the cable at the front of the growing line.

He grinned around at the serious young faces. "I got the most rank, so I get to go first."

They laughed and roared their approval.

The green light snapped on with a buzz.

"Go!" shouted the sergeant major.

Grisha ran the few meters to the end of the ramp and threw himself into space. The parachute snapped open with a loud crack and the harness jerked him upward, the straps cinched tighter on his thighs. Relief rushed through him.

The damn thing really opened.

He had never liked the idea of parachutes.

He looked around. Chutes blossomed above him in increasing numbers. Off to his right and left flew two of their companion aircraft. Men poured out the ends of both filling the air like giant dandelion seeds in a stiff breeze.

Something snitted past his face and he looked down on a scene of chaos. A firefight raged at close quarters at the front of the tree line. Russian tanks fired at pockets of soldiers who weakly returned fire.

Destroyed armor littered the meadow. From the woods around the battlefield small-arms fire winked up at the paratroopers.

Grisha unlimbered his AR-15 and returned fire. The ground rushed up at him.

83

Rainbow Valley

Sergeant Rudi Cermanivich rubbed blood out of his eyes and peered at the tank again. His body throbbed with pain and every time he swallowed he tasted blood.

Where was the damned flier?

If he hadn't had to blink the blood from his eyes he would have nailed the bastard with the second shot. He wondered how long he had to live, if the horrific fall down the valley would claim his life later or sooner.

Things had happened so quickly. As the road gave way under their tank it flipped, throwing him and Colonel Lazarev out of the hatch. Cermanivich had been tossed wide of the tank's path of death and fell into the scant tree line.

The first tree he hit slowed him but took off half his scalp in the process. The next time he hit the branches caught him and he fell grabbing, cursing, shrieking down through them, unable to defy gravity. The tree bordered a scree pile and he landed in it with crushing force that gave no mercy or pause.

Down he tumbled in the loose, jagged rock, tearing and cutting his hands, feet, legs, ass, face, knees. He bounced into one of the large boulders scattered throughout this barbarous valley and slammed shoulder-first into the loose rock. When he could move again he wiped away the blood streaming down his face.

He saw one of the Velikoff rifles they carried in the tanks, not three meters from him. It looked completely unharmed.

Moving created more anguish than he thought possible or reasonable. But he must see to his comrades, it was the tanker way. Using the rifle for a crutch, he slowly made his way over to the once proud command tank hull and peered inside.

Corporal Ivanivich's uniform held what was left, but most of him coated the steel walls. No sign of the colonel or Kalkoski, the gun server. Sergeant Cermanivich hobbled over to the turret and found no trace of his commander or subordinates.

He surveyed the devastation around him, realized that most of the column lay before him and he was the sole survivor. Without hesitating or caring for his injuries, he started up the grim path left by the tank avalanche. After a hundred meters the pain became unbearable and he sat on a rock, promising himself he would just take a short respite. While he sat there trying to ignore the pain, he saw movement down by the river.

Slowly he eased off the rock and positioned himself behind a slightly larger boulder. He wiped his sleeve across his eyes to clear the incessantly seeping blood from his vision. Focusing on the man, thank the saints it wasn't a bear, he realized it was an enemy aviator.

Who was the enemy? he wondered. The Dená didn't have an air force that he was aware of. And the air attack was nothing if not professional. U.S.A.? C.S.A.? Kalifornia?

"They were good enough to wipe us out," he muttered.

An intense hatred for the downed flyer suffused his being and he laid the rifle on the rock in front of him. As quietly as possible he chambered a round and took aim.

He decided to wait for the man to stop and rest, or else get much nearer. Between the seeping blood and the other injuries he had endured, he didn't trust his ability to take the target on the wing, as it were. He chuckled silently.

"As it were," he whispered. An old friend used to say that so often that when he said anything, at least half the people listening would intone together: "As it were." Harris had been an English deserter who wound up in the Czar's tank corps. Harris died in Afghanistan a year ago, instantly, when he stepped on an antipersonnel mine.

Sergeant Cermanivich shook his head angrily and immediately regretted the action. His head all but burst with the pain of a dozen hangovers smashed into one. He held himself very still as the wave of anguish washed over him and slowly receded.

I cannot afford the luxury of reminiscence, he told himself fiercely. *I would relinquish vigilance.*

The flyer, an officer, he suddenly realized with a smile, peered into the command tank hull before looking away and vomiting. Cermanivich grinned, happy to discover his enemy was weaker than himself.

The pilot-officer walked to the turret and stared inside again without hesitation. Well, he didn't lack guts, the sergeant decided. Then the flier leaned back against the turret and sank to his butt.

Sergeant Cermanivich quickly steadied the rifle across the rock, took careful aim between the man's eyes. He took a deep breath and held it, the muzzle didn't waver a millimeter, and squeezed the trigger—just as the flier dropped his head over and down between his knees.

Cermanivich, cursing the fates, the bolt action of the rifle, and goddamn pilots in general, chambered another round, took quick aim as fresh blood obscured his vision and fired. Hands remembering what brain had forgotten, he instantly chambered another round and fired. And missed again.

His quarry went to ground. But the man must be unarmed else he would have returned fire, no? So the obvious solution was to wait for him to break cover and then nail him once and for all.

Cermanivich eased his aching butt back up onto the larger rock, wiped blood from his eyes, and waited with his rifle across his lap.

84

Second Battle of Chena

Like everyone in sight of the contest, Wing watched Malagni battle the huge Russian. Even before the quicksilver blade of the *promyshlennik* darted into Malagni's chest, she knew she witnessed his last moments.

Soldiers from both sides watched the titanic struggle, ignoring their enemies and shouted orders from those not in line of sight, totally mesmerized by two men fighting it out hand to hand on the battlefield with naught but steel between them.

Then the first fatal blow, and Malagni jerked back and with all his remaining strength and might, swung his axe in a blurring arc and decapitated the Russian. Malagni toppled forward, dead.

Wing exhaled, not remembering when she had first held her breath. The Dená and Russians surrounding the meadow edge where the giants had fought stared at the the twitching, bleeding bodies for a long moment and as if on command, raised their heads and regarded the enemy.

A Russian sergeant cut down three Dená soldiers and the spell shattered.

Sergeant Major Tobias shrieked, "Charge!" and the Dená line hurtled into the Russians. Hand-to-hand combat raged. Wing considered picking off Russians, but none were far enough from her own people to shoot safely.

The Russians began to fall back under the intense attack. But the combat had exacted an insurmountable toll on the Dená army and they faltered. Russian fire from the woods increased and more and more Dená fell.

As Wing laced the woods with machine-gun fire she saw three Russians shooting into the air. She dropped behind the rim and gazed up at their targets—hundreds of parachutes filling the sky.

Men still spilled out of three aircraft overhead. In the distance she could see three more planes winging away. The Russians were shooting them in the air.

She jumped up and tried to make every shot count. She took out fifteen men before her clip ran dry. Frantically she searched for a full clip. There weren't any.

Smolst had passed out. Wing pulled his hand off the handle on the heavy machine gun, checked the belt feed, and started scything down Russians. A man shouted and they brought their firepower to bear on Wing. Bullets whined past her, made angry buzzes past her ears, smashed against the inadequate earthwork around the firing pit, dirt and small stones sprayed over her.

She dropped to the bottom of the pit. Knew they would be on top of her in moments. This was it.

"God, am I thirsty!" she screamed.

Even with her damaged ears, she detected the increase in weaponry. The bullets ceased seeking her out. Curious, she stuck her head up for a look.

The Russians retreated toward the river. Paratroopers hit and rolled, cut shroud lines, and fired at the Russians. The woods boiled with friendly soldiers.

One man limped among them using a rifle for a crutch, directing, shouting orders, and firing at the Russians with a pistol. The man stumbled and fell and two soldiers who had been waiting for his injury to take over produced a litter and rolled him onto it. They carried him back toward Chena Redoubt from where a number of auxiliary vehicles emerged and roared toward the battle zone.

The last unscathed Russian tank reversed up the far bank—onto an antitank mine. The explosion ripped open the bottom and set off ammunition inside. It went up like fireworks on the Czar's birthday.

Two soldiers in khaki jumped into her firing pit. The charging grizzly-insignia of the Republic of California Army adorned their left shoulders.

"You okay, buddy?" one asked. He stopped and took a harder look. "Sorry, ma'am, didn't expect to find a woman out here."

"Water," she pleaded.

He gave her a plastic canteen and she gulped down a third of it.

"I'm Major Wing Demoski, D.R.A., who is your leader?"

"Some Dená colonel, what's his name, Ernie?"

The other soldier thought for a moment. "Griz-something, I think. I don't know, they never introduce me to the senior officers any more."

"Hell of a guy, though," the first one said.

But Wing was already running toward the distant litter as tears threatened her vision.

85

Rainbow Valley

Yamato, drenched with sweat, stopped his drive for the canyon wall and carefully rolled over onto his back behind a large rock. Muffling the sound with his fingers and thumb, he unzipped his flight suit all the way to his navel. Never, he decided, had he been hotter than this, ever.

He briefly closed his eyes and willed his heartbeat to slow closer to normal. Being in superb physical condition, his heart rate dropped to normal after two and a half minutes. He edged up and peeked over the rock.

Not fifty feet away a man sat on a rock with a rifle across his lap, staring fixedly at the tank turret where he had almost nailed himself a lieutenant. Fifty feet was at the edge of accurate range for a .45. Jerry wondered if he could hit the man before he could return fire with the rifle.

At fifty feet the rifle wouldn't miss, not that one anyway. He eased back down and rested, weighing his options. The guy looked like crap, all beat up and bloody.

Hell, if I just take a nap, he thought, *when I wake up the guy would probably be dead.*

It was the "probably" that kicked doubt loose in his mind. He couldn't afford to take the chance, not if he wanted to try and win Andrea back. The vision of his ex-fiancée's naked body undulated through his mind for a moment before resentment kicked in and he refocused on his current situation.

His shoulder ached and he realized this was an excellent opportunity to void his bladder. Easing over onto his uninjured side, he unzipped and quietly pissed into a windblown depression under a rock. He groaned with pleasure, figuring the constant breeze would whip the sound away from the stonelike sentinel.

They hadn't covered this situation in flight school or survival school. If the guy was charging from a hundred meters away, or attacking him with a knife at close quarters, Jerry would know what action to take. But when your opponent is at the extreme range of your only weapon and possesses a weapon of superior range, what the hell do you do?

Woodcraft didn't work here, so he had to think with the military part of his brain. Was it possible to get another fifteen feet closer to him? He knew at thirty-five feet he could hit his target.

The soldier looked next to death. But was he? What had he ever heard about Russians?

Alcoholic peasants with a penchant for exhibitionist self-pity. But he realized he was basing his opinion on Elena, an old girlfriend from the Ukraine, and was probably mentally slandering a lot of fine Russians. His friend John had married her.

He couldn't worry about John, he had to look out for himself. What had they said in the briefing? He hadn't been paying attention to the usually boring preflight facts. Once they identified the mission and gave the pilots the weather forecast, Jerry usually allowed his attention to wander because most of the rest of it was for flight commanders and superior officers. First lieutenants performed as ordered.

He knew he had heard it, could he remember what he heard?

Oh, yeah. They said "seasoned combat troops."

So was this guy sufficiently handicapped that he wouldn't hear a clunky pilot squirming up behind him? Options being limited, he was going to find out the hard way. He felt rested and hungry, time for dinner.

He rolled onto his knees and elbows and began squirming toward the soldier.

86

Second Battle of Chena

Grisha's leg radiated agony throughout his body. When it snapped during landing, shock and adrenaline walled off the pain. But now that they insisted on bouncing him around on a litter his adrenaline had ebbed and the shock didn't dissipate anything.

"Ouch, dammit! Can you people slow down?"

"Sorry, Colonel," the one in back puffed. "But there's lots more people need picked up back there."

Immediately chagrined, Grisha said, "I'm sorry, soldier. Halt, both of you!"

They stopped and stared at him.

"There's an ambulance coming, or what serves for one. I'm away from the fighting. Leave me here. Go take care of someone who really needs help."

They sat the litter down and gently lifted him onto the moss and flowers. Both men stood and saluted. "We'll follow you anywhere, Colonel," the corporal said. They raced away toward the carnage where a few bursts still stuttered.

Grisha lifted his binoculars and viewed the Russian line on the far side of the Chena. Smoke poured from shattered tanks. Russian soldiers ran toward the rear, only a few pockets here and there retreated in an orderly fashion. For the moment, the Dená Republik Army held the field.

He wondered how much time the Russians would need to regroup before hitting them again, and how long they had before the full column arrived. Could they stop that much armor? Even the lowest private could see they had already given their all.

Four P-61s roared over the battlefield followed by three more, flying wingtip to wingtip. The Dená and R.O.C. soldiers cheered. The Russian retreat picked up speed. Grisha felt the tide of battle shift to their side despite the imminent threat of more Russian armor. Owning the sky made a hell of a difference.

He heard the ambulance close behind him. Somebody ran toward him from the battle zone. Grisha peered through the binoculars again.

At that point the figure threw off her helmet and the deep black hair fanned out in her wake.

"Wing!"

Something in his chest released and tears of joy ran down his cheeks. He had been so careful not to think about her, not to worry, not to dwell. And the whole time he'd kept her locked carefully in his heart, knowing he really didn't want to live without her.

The ambulance skidded to a stop next to him and two U.S. Army medics jumped out. "Where ya hit, Mac?"

Grisha spared them a glance. "Left leg broke when I hit the ground." He turned his attention back to Wing.

They slit his pants leg open. One made a small sound in his throat. "Simple fracture, but this is still gonna hurt a bit."

Wing waved urgently, wanting to be seen. He waved in response and she slowed to a trot. His eyes searched her as she approached, looking for harm, fearing damage.

Sweat ran through the streaked gunpowder on her face. One of the epaulets on her field jacket flapped, cut by a bullet. Dirt and moss matted her hair.

Grisha had never seen a more beautiful woman in his life.

She panted as she came up to him, stopped, and saluted.

"Good . . . to . . . see you, Colonel." She smiled, the scar on her cheek wishboned together. "Christ, I've missed you, Grisha."

The medics pulled back and watched in astonishment.

He spread his arms and she knelt and hugged him close.

"Hell, Sarge," one of the medics said. "Maybe we're in the wrong outfit."

"Officers!" Sarge snorted.

Grisha pulled her face to his and kissed her.

"You want us to come back later, Colonel?" Sarge said with heavy sarcasm.

Grisha and Wing pulled away from each other, laughing.

"No, Sergeant, I'll be right with you. I just have to ask the lieutenant colonel something." Grisha stared into Wing's face. "I know the war isn't over yet. But, will you marry me anyway?"

"Yes." She kissed him again and broke away. "Okay, guys, fix him up. I need him in good shape for the honeymoon."

"Not to mention the war," Grisha said.

The corporal grabbed him around the chest and the sergeant gripped his ankle and expertly pulled his leg straight.

Spots danced in his vision, thickened, grayed out everything around him.

"I'm so very tired," he said. Then he slipped away from them.

87

Rainbow Valley

Sergeant Cermanivich began to wonder if he had actually hit the pilot. Most people would have moved by now. He had seen nothing.

Anxiety abruptly surged through him. Could he see anyone moving if they stayed on the ground? How to know?

He stretched his leg out, setting off the waves of pain. *Some soldier you are*, he thought, *can't even get off your fat ass*. He stopped moving, waiting for the sharp pain to subside.

Metal scraped rock behind him and he twisted, bringing the rifle up to his shoulder. Trying unsuccessfully to ignore his sudden, debilitating agony and to see through fresh blood, he hesitated. A weapon fired and his rifle burst out of his hands, nearly taking his trigger finger with it.

The impact slammed him sideways and he felt his butt slide off the edge of the rock. He fell onto the rock-riddled ground. Magnified pain shot through him and he screamed his way into darkness.

"C'mon, wake up."

Something stung his cheek.

"C'mon, Ivan, wake up."

Again the stinging. Rudi Cermanivich tried to open his eyes, but they would not obey him.

"C'mon—"

"Do not strike me again," Cermanivich said in English, the language in which he was being addressed. "I am injured all over, my body does not respond as it should."

"I have a pistol. If you make any sudden moves I will hurt you."

Cermanivich barked a laugh that turned into a painful cough. "If I make sudden move *I* will hurt me." He slowly raised his hand to his face and rubbed at the bloody crust around his eyes.

"Do you have water? I need some on my face."

A moment later a dollop splashed in his eyes. He rubbed briskly and felt his eyelids tug open. The light blinded him and he squinted. The throbbing in his head intensified.

"What's your name, Sergeant?"

Rudi blinked up at the man, realizing for the first time his opponent was an Asian. "Sergeant Rudi Cermanivich, Imperial Tank Korps, Flash Division. Do you wish my service number also?"

The pilot smiled for a moment. "No, that's enough. This battle is over for us, why are you still trying to kill me?"

"For you, perhaps the battle is over. For me, never. Who are you and why are you on Russian soil?"

"First Lieutenant Gerald Yamato, 117th Fighter Squadron, Republic of California Air Force. I'm not on Russian soil, I'm in the Dená Republic, I think."

"Kalifornia? For what reason do you make war on us?"

"Ask the politicians, I'm just following orders."

"Who do you fight for, and against?" Rudi demanded.

"We're aiding the Dená Republic and fighting against you, the Russian Empire."

"There is no Dená Republik, how can you aid what does not exist?"

"The Dená Republik has been a recognized country for a week, at least. Are you guys supposed to be pretty hot in combat, or what?"

"We are—were crack tank group. Four days ago we disembark from ship which picked us up near Chinese border week before. We did not anticipate aircraft nor any other opposition."

"You're in a war zone, it isn't like 'San Diego—Day of Infamy' or anything like that."

"We were surprised, but nothing on the scale of your 1931 defeat, no." Rudi grinned, which hurt. "But I was not aware of your country's role in this insurrection."

"This is our third day at war, so don't feel bad about not getting the word. Where are you hurt?"

"Shorter list if you ask where I am not hurt."

"Can you stand?"

"I don't know. Will try."

He pushed himself up and the pain level rose with him. Rudi leaned against the rock he had fallen from and tried to breathe without hurting. Never before in his life had he endured this much pain.

Am I going to die here? he wondered. His heart slowed from a stampede to mere gallop and the pain receded. Slowly he turned and faced the rock, put his hands at shoulder level, and tried to stand.

Stars danced through his head and blurred his vision. Sensation deserted him as darkness charged.

"Just what I need, an injured prisoner." Jerry Yamato spat on a rock and finished adjusting the sergeant's comatose form on the litter he had fashioned from the plentiful willows along the river.

His stomach growled and, as if in response, so did the sergeant's. Food needed to be found, and soon. Jerry worked his eyes slowly over the terrain, hoping to see movement.

They had been relatively quiet for some time now. Perhaps game might be available.

And I will get it how?

The sergeant's rifle was junk. The .45 slug had smashed the receiver and trigger mechanism. At the time, he had been aiming for the Russian's head.

The man was probably going to die long before he could get him any medical help. The temptation to just shoot him and put him out of his misery passed through Jerry's mind. He shuddered in revulsion, disgusted with himself.

"I've got to at least try and help him."

He figured he was about a half mile from his parachute and harness. Dragging the sergeant that far shouldn't be too much of a problem. Then the harness and chute would be of immeasurable help.

Bouncing the litter over the rocks, Jerry was glad the Russian had passed out. He was also making far too much noise if he wished to find game within a mile. Doggedly, he continued dragging the litter.

After twenty minutes by his own watch, he stopped and sagged onto the nearest boulder. He felt completely done in, and had yet to spy his cache. With extreme care he lowered the litter to the ground.

Yamato pulled himself onto the largest rock within three yards and looked for his harness marker. A glance over his shoulder gave him the wisping smoke from the wrecked Eureka and farther away the tendrils from the tanks as a gauge. Unless his memory was playing games with him, he should be on top of the cache.

He faced forward again and caught motion out of the corner of his eye. A quick step and he was sliding off the rock, turning to face the unknown and unholstering his .45 all at the same time. He landed beside the boulder with both feet spread wide, his elbows resting on the rock and his weapon pointed at . . . a frightened young woman?

Dressed entirely in soft leather molding to her voluptous curves, abundant dark hair framing her porcelain-fine features, she held his parachute bunched in her arms and stared at him like a frightened fawn.

"Who are you?" he asked, not lowering the pistol.

"Sm-small English," she said. "Ruski?"

Jerry shook his head. He found her beauty disturbing. What was she doing out here all al—

A stunning blow knocked him against the boulder, turning his legs to jelly and his mind to star-speckled mush.

"Good work, Magda," God said just before Jerry's wits slipped into the void.

88

Tanana, Dená Republik

"I think he's coming around, now, Colonel."

Wing grinned despite herself. Her unexpected promotion to colonel was still new enough to feel disproportionately grandiose. She watched Grisha's face as his eyes fluttered and finally opened.

He frowned at the ceiling.

"You're in the hospital, Grisha," she said in a low voice. "Don't try to move, they have your leg in traction. The longer you stay quiet, the quicker they'll let you out of here."

He looked down at the sling and pulley arrangement in which the doctor had trapped him. "Pretty fancy. Where are we?"

"Tanana. The U.S. fixed up the old Russian military hospital." Wing glanced around and sniffed appreciatively. "It actually looks, and smells, like a hospital now."

She smiled down at him, wondering if he remembered asking her to marry him. "How do you feel?"

"Weak, and I don't like it." He frowned, looked up at her, and the frown slid away into a smile. "And in love. Pretty strange situation all the way around."

She bent over and kissed him.

Grisha took a deep breath. "What's the military situation?"

"We have both the Diomedes. The bridge still stands but we can vaporize it if the Russians try to use it for military purposes. All

Russian units between the town of Bridge and Chena Redoubt have been neutralized or eliminated."

"We've won the war?"

"Not quite. From what we can gather, there's a massive Russian retreat toward St. Anthony Redoubt. Those are the guys we fought outside Chena."

She gave him a moment to appreciate the victory. "There was a second column advancing over the Alaska Range from St. Nicholas, but the RCAF hit them with a fighter squadron—"

"The 117th?"

"Yes. And they not only destroyed the majority of the tanks and other armor, but they cut the road. The only threat we have to worry about from St. Nicholas is aircraft."

"How many birds did the 117th lose?"

"Almost half their strength. Their commanding officer has been recommended for a posthumous Medal of Honor."

"How can we ever repay them?" Grisha whispered.

"We will, don't worry. There is also a column moving north from Tetlin, no idea as to strength."

"What about the F.P.N column?" Grisha's eyes seemed normal again.

"What F.P.N. column?" Wing wondered how he could have military intelligence that she didn't.

"How long have I been in here?" He waved at the room.

"Since late last night. The Battle of Chena happened yesterday."

He told her what he had seen from the transport. "From the air their column looked to be about five miles long."

"I wonder if they're going to claim all territory they take?" Wing said. "This could be a whole new problem."

"Is the U.S. or the R.O.C. claiming anything they've fought for up here?"

Grisha's mind was clear as ever, she thought. "No. But the U.S. and the Californians established a liaison with us before committing troops. The F.P.N. is just attacking."

Grisha surveyed his left leg and the cat's cradle of wires hooked to it. "How long do I have to be in here?"

"Two weeks, minimum, if you ever want to walk normally again. It was a worse break that they thought, Grisha."

"In more ways than one! Okay, I want a radio operator, a desk that I can actually use from this position, a telephone, and some routing boxes for papers, whatever. If I can't be in the field I'll do what I can from here."

"You were wounded in the line of duty, Colonel Grigorievich," she said with feeling. "Nobody will think you are shirking if you're flat on your back in a hospital bed."

"I know Malagni can handle—" he was looking at her face while speaking and what he saw there stopped him. "What?"

"Oh, Grisha, I thought you knew." She told him about the epic man-to-man contest, how both sides had stopped fighting to bear witness, and how it ended.

"Things were moving so fast," he said. "When we dropped on Chena we just watched for muzzle flashes and didn't pay attention to anything else." Grisha stared through the wall; Wing wondered what he was seeing. "Malagni is really dead, that is so hard to believe. Do we know the name of the man who killed him, who he killed?"

"Bennie Amos from Venetie said the *promyshlennik*'s name was Boris Crepov—what?"

The blood seemed to drain from Grisha's face in seconds. "Did he have a scar on his right cheek, a big one?"

"Yeah, made him look even more fierce, they say. I was too far away for detail like that, and, afterward, I had other things to do."

Grisha relaxed and his color returned to normal. "He's the bastard that almost killed me on the trek from the slave camp. I'm the one that gave him the scar, that day on the trail when Nik and I ran into Valari's ambush. Crepov was the man I cut."

"Small world, isn't it?"

"I was afraid of that man, knew he would hurt me some day. I just didn't know how badly." He sniffed and rubbed his left eye. "How soon can you get me a desk?"

"Today. How soon can you marry me?"

When he grinned like that she knew how he looked as a boy. "Don't you want a husband who can carry you over a threshold or jump over a broom at your side?"

"I want to marry you before you can get away from me."

"Well, for the next two weeks you know exactly where I'm going to be. It won't be much of a wedding feast, and our first night together will probably lack a lot of the things I had in mind, but you get a holy man in here and I'll marry you this afternoon."

"You have a deal, General Grigorievich."

"Colonel," he said, still smiling. "I'm just a colonel, remember?"

Wing snapped her fingers. "I knew there was something else I had to tell you. The War Council of the Dená Republik promoted you to general as soon as they heard about your actions yesterday. And I think they're working on a suitable medal to go along with the two stars."

"I'm a brigadier general? Does that mean I'll be stuck behind a desk for the rest of my career?"

"It means you're in charge of the Dená Army, Grisha."

89

USS Enterprise, CV5 in the North Atlantic

Captain David Thiessen hoped their intelligence was correct, he was taking a big chance pulling Task Force 1 this far north. The weather in the Newfoundland Basin seemed to work hard to earn its reputation.

"Pure crap," he growled as the bow of the aircraft carrier nosed into another mountain of green water. But they had managed to launch a recon bird three hours earlier before the weather changed yet again. Now he was worried they wouldn't be able to get Lieutenant Todd back onboard in one piece.

The quartermaster striker on headphones piped up, "Captain, the radio room reports sightings from Prowler 1."

Prowler 1 was Lieutenant Todd in his Hellcat.

"Tell them to put it on the bridge speaker."

"Aye, aye."

A burst of static issued from the speakers on either side of the bridge and then the lieutenant's voice said, "—six ships with her."

Captain Thiessen picked up his microphone and clicked for attention. "Sam, this is the captain. Please repeat your report, we didn't get the first part on the squawk box."

"Yes, Captain. I have sighted *HMS Endeavour* accompanied by two Simcoe Class cruisers and four destroyers."

"Well done, Sam. You sure it's the *Endeavour*?"

"Positive, Captain. I went aboard her in '82 when I was an ensign."

"Just the battleship group with no birdfarm?"

"I have seen no aircraft carriers other than the Big E, Captain."

"Good work, Sam. The weather out here is getting worse by the minute, so I want you to fly into Reykjavik and land there."

"Captain, I'll be interned, the Danes aren't in the war."

"I know, Sam, but you'll still be alive. And don't forget, the place is crawling with good-looking, buxom blondes who appreciate sailors."

Lieutenant Todd laughed. "Aye, aye, Captain. I'm just sorry I'll miss the fight."

"So noted, Lieutnant, *Enterprise* out."

The officer of the deck, Lieutenant Commander Stephens, watched his skipper with a gleam in his eyes. "We going to engage the limeys, Captain?"

Captain Thiessen grinned. "Bet your ass, Louie. But we're going to wait and nail them when they come out of the storm, all beaten to shit and their brightwork dulled. Quartermaster, steer west, southwest, half speed, notify the task force."

90

Rainbow Valley

"What have you done to us, Lieutenant?" Rudi Cermanivich's voice possessed sharp claws that ripped into Jerry's aching semi-consciousness.

"Don't shout," he mumbled. "M'head hurts." He tried to raise his hand to his throbbing neck but couldn't move his arm; either arm. He cracked his eyes open and nearly wept at the intense pain riding the light waves into his nervous system. Tightly wrapped bonds proved to be his own parachute shroud lines.

Without looking he knew his pistol was gone. So the Russians had come looking for Rudi after all. He swung his painful gaze around and found Rudi still in his willow litter, firmly tied with more shroud line.

"What's happened?" Jerry whispered.

"I thought you would know. When I wake up I am in this, this cradle—"

"Litter, I made it for you. So I could move you."

"As you will, litter. Did you also truss me into it like a Christmas goose?"

"No. I suspect—"

"Ah, both of our guests are awake."

Jerry looked up, borderline fearful to see who owned that massive, booming voice.

A bald, muscular giant looked back at him. Wearing soft leather clothing like the woman Jerry had seen somewhere in his past, the giant seemed sprung from the earth. The worked hide covering his chest boasted resplendent beadwork depicting a creature eating the tail of an identical, but darker, creature which in turn was eating the first creature's tail.

The thought *dog eat dog* crossed Jerry's mind but he didn't share, deciding this wasn't a good time.

Suddenly Jerry noticed the giant possessed blue eyes, and what little hair cowered about his ears definitely was not as dark as his skin. Coffee with lots of cream, he decided.

"You're not from around here, are you?" Jerry asked, smiling through his pain.

"You're very perceptive, Lieutenant. No, I'm not. But I have been here for a very long time. My question to both of you is: why did you bring war to our valley?"

"Accident, pure accident," Jerry said. "This is where my shot-up plane crashed and my parachute brought me. Rudi, here"—he nodded his head—"fell down along with his tank, which had also been shot up. Nothing personal, but this is just where we landed. That okay with you?"

The giant considered the question. "No, it isn't. But what can one do?"

"Are you both madmen?" Rudi asked in a low voice.

"Probably," Jerry and the giant said in unison.

Jerry laughed. He hadn't laughed for real since his orders had come through three weeks before. But this got to him; his laughter came from some place deep within him that had been pent up far too long. His headache eased.

The giant laughed with him, but a different cast had taken over his eyes and Jerry realized he was being measured for something and he hoped it wouldn't hurt.

"I like the way you think," the giant said. "What's your name?"

"First Lieutenant Gerald S. Yamato, Republic of California Air Force. My comrade here is Sergeant Rudi Cermanivich, Imperial Russian Tank Corps. Who are you?"

The giant frowned. "Then I was correct when looking at your uniforms; you are enemies."

"We were. I think Rudi may have shot me down. But we both seem to be out of the war and we might need each other."

"But I heard shots, which is what attracted my attention."

"There was much gunfire up on the road," Rudi said, tossing his head back and then shuddering in pain.

"I heard that." The giant's frown deepened. "But I also heard rifle shots down here by the river."

"We had yet to come to an understanding," Jerry said. "But we did. So, who are you?"

"I am Pelagian, I rule this valley and all in it."

"Where were you born?"

"In the Swedish Triumvate, Denmark, to be exact."

"Your accent doesn't sound European and you don't look Swedish."

"My father was Danish and my mother was French and Algerian. I spent nine years in the British merchant marine and decided to change careers."

Jerry laughed again. "From sailor to king, right?"

Pelagian didn't laugh. "Well, not quite that abrupt a change. I trapped for a decade before realizing my gift for uniting like-minded people."

Jerry didn't smile, even though he wanted to. A different cast clouded Pelagian's eyes and his countenance precluded levity of a sudden.

"Like-minded people?"

"The people of this valley and the flats beyond were getting pushed about by the cossacks as well as the *promyshlenniks* for *yasak*. The first time the cossacks came to my humble cabin and demanded 'tribute' I told them to go to hell. They did their utmost to persuade me to comply with their demands."

"You told cossacks to go to hell?" Rudi said in a wondering tone. "Did they not try to kill you?"

"They did. I killed them instead. It seemed the only thing to do at the time."

"What did the authorities do?" Jerry asked.

"They were the authorities. I was left alone for over a year."

"So what happens now?" Jerry said, trying not to fidget. "Can we use your, uh, facilities?"

"First you must pledge your fealty to me."

"Pledge my what?"

"You must accept me as your king."

"Before I can take a piss?"

"If you try to run away I will kill you."

"I believe you. I will not try to escape, I promise."

"Magda, release him."

The raven-haired beauty materialized beside him and deftly untied the knots.

Jerry tried not to stare, but he knew it would be easier for a moth to resist the flame than to not look at her. Her fingers flew over the shroud lines and suddenly he was free. She looked up at him and smiled.

"Thank you," he said. "Now please turn away."

Magda gave him a puzzled look and Pelagian said something to her in Russian. She snickered and turned away.

Jerry moved two boulders away before voiding. Now he felt he could deal with anything, including the baron. He walked back to Rudi's side.

"How are you feeling, sergeant?"

"I couldn't hold my bladder in both hands at this point. I feel someone has dropped large bolts into my transmission while operating at high speed."

"Bad, right?"

"Very bad."

"What are you saying to your enemy?" Pelagian asked.

"He is severely injured. Is there a doctor in your valley?"

Pelagian moved over to them and looked at Rudi. He untied the shroud line so quickly that at first Jerry thought he cut it. Grabbing the sergeant's blouse with both hands he calmly pulled it open, raining what few buttons remained among the rocks.

Rudi's body featured heavy bruises, lumps where none should exist, dried blood from an unseen wound, and he smelled bad. Pelagian ran his hands over the wounded chest. Rudi sucked in his breath in pain and fear but said nothing.

Pelagian turned and shouted, "Bodecia, bring your bag."

"Is he badly hurt, Father?" Magda asked at his side.

Father? Jerry thought. He studied Pelagian's face and discerned the faint network of lines around his eyes. To be her father he would have to be nearing forty or forty-five. From six feet away the man could pass for thirty-five or even younger.

"He is in grave danger of leaving us for another realm, whether he wishes to or not."

"Would like to stay a while," Rudi said through a grisly smile. "If not too much bother."

"You have been a soldier for a long time," Pelagian said.

"Thirty-one years and never demoted. Have been sergeant for twenty-two years. Is as bad as I think?"

"My wife is the healer here, she will tell us." He moved to the side and an older version of Magda stood there examining Rudi's torso.

Jerry hadn't seen her walk up. He felt positive she had just materialized on the spot. He looked at Magda, who had moved next to him.

"How did she do that?"

"Do what?" Magda's words no longer carried the heavy Russian accent.

"Get in front of us without me seeing her."

"You were looking at me, we could parade a wolf pack past and you wouldn't notice."

"I thought you said 'small English'?"

"Do you give a potential enemy leverage?"

"Yes, my unmilitary lack of attention when you're around."

She laughed and her perfect teeth flashed in the sun.

"Is Bodecia your mother?"

"Of course she is. Do not worry, your friend is in no danger while she is present."

Jerry mulled over the thought of calling Rudi his "friend." After all, not more than a couple of hours ago, the man had tried his best to kill him, twice. But he did feel something for the proud old soldier and let the comment pass.

"Where do you people live?"

"Within twenty miles of here. Where do you live?"

"In the city of Castroville, Republic of California. Ever hear of it? My dad grows garlic, lots of garlic."

"I know of garlic, and have heard of your republic. It is far from here."

"Yes," he said. "In a great many ways."

Bodecia squatted next to Rudi, whose litter now lay in a convenient swath of rock-free gravel.

"Why do you fight Russians?" Magda asked, her eyes following his gaze.

"We are allied to the Dená Republic and they are fighting for their lives."

"Dená?" She turned and spoke in Russian to her father.

In a heartbeat Pelagian stood in front of Jerry. "The Dená are openly fighting the Russians? When did this happen?"

"Why did you think we were here? The first concentrated Dená attacks happened earlier this year. They simultaneously struck at all the major redoubts in what they claimed as their traditional territory."

"How do you know so much about it?"

"Our government always explains why they want us to declare war. When we got the first stories about the heroic Athabascan Indians fighting the evil Czar, we all voted to kick Russian butt."

"Why do you sound bitter?"

"Just being sarcastic. I voted against the war, but then I've had more education than the majority of the electorate."

"Does that make you right and them wrong?"

"No." The word sighed out of him. "Nothing that yin and yang. I wish it were. I wish life was all dark or light, but the sky is always changing."

"So, what happened?"

"To what?"

"The 'heroic' Indians who attacked the bad Russians, Lieutenant."

"Oh, sorry. Well, they pretty much won the day. They even took Chena Redoubt, which I gather was a very big thing, but the Russians bombed it flat after the Dená occupied it. They lost a lot of their cadre."

"Cadre? I was in the merchant marine, not the bloody navy."

"The ones running things. In charge."

"Lieutenant, are you feeling well? Your mind seems to be wandering overmuch."

Yamato focused. "Well, I'm almost to the point of starvation. Breakfast was at oh-four-hundred California time on Tuesday and it's been a long day." He squinted upward.

"For about a fortnight this time of year it really doesn't get dark. 'Land of the Midnight Sun' and all that."

"I thought it was six months."

"They didn't tell you everything about Russian Amerika, did they? Here, chew on this." Pelagian tossed him a strand of flesh.

Jerry sniffed it and his mouth watered. He chewed off a bite.

"That's a strip of smoked salmon. We call it 'squaw candy.' I quite like it."

Jerry nodded agreement and kept chewing. He wondered if Pelagian was going to tie him up again.

Sergeant Cermanivich gasped loudly. Jerry stopped chewing and watched Bodecia shift her stance and grab Rudi again.

"This one will also hurt, but you will feel better after." She abruptly twisted his torso.

Rudi shrieked and went limp.

Bodecia's hands continued to move over the sergeant's torso and arms, pulling tugging, pushing, twisting before suddenly stopping and dropping her head to his chest.

"He is a strong man." She straightened to her feet. "He will live, I think." She stared at Jerry. "Now tell me about the Dená Republik."

Jerry told them everything he could remember hearing about the Dená revolt that had touched off a continentwide war. He felt exhausted and wrung out.

"Oh, the French and the Spanish also sent their fleets out—"

"Who cares, the Dená Nation is mostly landlocked," Bodecia said. "Do you remember any of the names of those killed at Chena, the cadre?"

"Only one name sticks in my mind. Slayer-of-Men, how could I forget that one?" Jerry's near-chuckle died before it reached his lips.

Bodecia's face froze and Magda emitted a small gasp. Pelagian stepped between them and Jerry.

"You just named one of my wife's cousins. He was one of my best friends."

"I'm sorry to bring you sad news. I wish I could remember more."

Bodecia spoke to Pelagian in a different language, not Russian or French. He answered and both women turned and walked away toward the dense willow thickets bordering the rocky river shore. In moments they had vanished from sight.

"What is your plan, Lieutenant Yamato?"

"Plan, what plan?"

"How were you going to get out of here and back to California?"

"I was sort of making it up as I went along, didn't really have a plan."

"You are twenty miles from the nearest *odinochka*, which is a fortified trading post. They will give you all the compassion you can pay for, maybe less. You are thirty miles from the nearest Russian redoubt, but I think perhaps you might not care for that, either."

"Is that thirty miles following the river or going cross country?" Jerry nodded at the huge colorful ridge.

"Both."

"What do you think we should do?"

"We?"

"The sergeant and me."

"I believe you have only one option, to come with us."

"Aren't we your prisoners?"

"I am not at war with either of you. The ropes were used to meet you both without use of firearms."

"Makes sense. Where are you going, back to your, uh, fort?"

"No, we are going to the village of Delta, near St. Anthony Redoubt."

"Why?"

"My wife has family there. She is angry with me for still being out here where no one can find us."

"What are you doing out here?"

"I am visiting the length and breadth of my land, where I am honored as a leader, while returning from my trapping camp."

"Are you a leader in Delta?"

Pelagian gave him a grim look. "I am not ignored."

"I think you're right. May the sergeant and I accompany you?"

"Of course you may. I think you both would die if we left you here."

"I won't argue that one, either. Are there telephones in Delta?"

"Yes, they all go through the Russian Amerika Company switchboard."

"Oh. Well something will turn up, I'm sure." Jerry surveyed Sergeant Cermanivich, who had yet to regain consciousness.

"He will not wake for some time. He has a lot of healing to do. We will need to carry him."

"I'll take the first turn."

Pelagian laughed. "Do you know how long it took you to go a half mile?" He pointed back toward the destroyed tank. "Almost an hour."

"Well, I didn't want to hurt him any more than he already was."

"You misunderstand, we have a better way."

Magda reappeared from the windblown willows, leading four large dogs wearing harnesses. Under her arm were four long poles and some of the parachute shroud lines. She spoke and all four dogs stopped.

In minutes she had Rudi's litter slung between the dogs, an animal at each corner. The sticks worked as spacers to keep the dogs in the same configuration. Jerry's parachute harness was hooked to the front of the litter and a makeshift sling tied to the back.

"One person in front, one in back," Pelagian said. "That way we all share the load and can go long distances."

"I'll bet I'm in back."

"You can't be in front, you don't know the way."

Jerry couldn't argue with that. He looked around, wondered how far they had to travel and what they would meet along the way. He glanced at Magda and she smiled at him.

Something told him this adventure was just beginning. He smiled back.

91

Republic of California Ship *Eureka*, BB7 off Vancouver Island

"The Russians refuse to heave to, Captain," the signalman second class said.

"Just what I thought they'd do. Mr. Gorin, put a shot across their bow."

"Of which ship, Captain Llerena? There's ten of them out there."

"The one in front."

Commander Gorin spoke into the microphone on his headset and one of the five-inch 38s immediately fired. The shell splash in front of the leading Russian destroyer was easily seen by all on the bridge of the *Eureka*.

Three Russian destroyers immediately opened up on the *Eureka's* task force. One shell whistled past the *Eureka's* bridge and landed in the water.

"All ships," Captain Llerena barked, "fire at will!"

The *Eureka* rocked to starboard as all twelve sixteen-inch guns on the four mounts fired simultaneously. The heavy cruisers *Sacrameto* and *Los Angeles* and destroyers *Hemme, Hepner, Bear,* and *Mitchell* all fired their main batteries within seconds of the task force commander's order.

Battleship *Gorki* and destroyer *Severin* of the Imperial fleet both disappeared in a stunning blast of explosives and flying metal as the salvos hit them with more shells than the rest of the Russian fleet combined, setting off their magazines. *Gorki* had flown the flag of Admiral Buldakov, commander of the Russian Pacific Fleet and chief tactician.

The surviving Russian ships, nearly in a straight line, steamed at flank speed toward the California fleet, which had formed a great C shape and was able to bring nearly every gun to bear on the hapless, enraged Russians.

The entire Battle of the North Pacific took less than an hour before the Russian destroyer *Tolstoi*, crippled and taking on water, lowered the remains of her flag.

"My God," Commander Gorin said. "It was like 'The Charge of the Light Brigade' in reverse!"

"And just as stupid," Captain Llerena said in a tone of disgust. "I almost wanted to give them another chance after the fifth ship went down. Did we lose anyone?"

"The *Hemme* took three hits but is still moving under her own power, and the *Mitchell* is dead in the water. The *Los Angeles* is preparing a tow for her. Between the two ships we lost about ninety men, including the skipper of the *Hemme*."

"Gary Cole was a good sailor and a fine skipper," Captain Llerena said. "Those ninety men gave their lives for a great victory. The Russians can't even protect their own coast now."

"Captain, do you think we just won the war?"

"Perhaps, Mr. Gorin, perhaps."

92

Fort Chena, Dená Republik

Grisha carefully formed each letter as he wrote out his report. The War Council had asked he record everything about the Chena campaign while it was still fresh in his mind. He had been at it for the past two days.

Wing sat at a small desk near the door, working on troop allocations and placement. After only three days in hospital, Grisha already yearned to be in open air and talking to his troops.

"Colonel?" a soldier said from the doorway.

Wing and Grisha both said, "Yes?" They also laughed at the same time.

"Sorry," Grisha said, "this 'general' stuff will take some getting used to."

"What is it, Sergeant?" Wing asked.

"Sorry to bother you, ma'am, but Captain Lauesen is here to see you, says it's urgent."

"Who?" Grisha asked with a frown.

"U.S. Army, good man, real smart," Wing said. "Please show him in, Sergeant."

"Yes, ma'am."

"He's an intelligence officer, has more facts in his head than most schoolbooks," Wing explained in a soft voice that made Grisha think about actions other than military. "We're lucky to have him on our side."

Captain Lauesen walked in accompanied by a second man. He stopped and came to attention, saluted.

"General Grigorievich, it is an honor to meet you, sir. Colonel, I am very happy to see you again, too. You both are truly awesome."

"It was urgent that you tell us this?" Grisha asked, feeling uncomfortable.

"No, General." He turned to the man with with him. "It seems we have a new ally."

The man looked familiar to Grisha. As tall as the captain, the man possessed broad shoulders, an athletic body, and dark, penetrating eyes. He wore military dungarees and a clean bandage on the left side of his forehead.

"You are Grigoriy Grigorievich, son of Anna from Akku, of the Killer Whale kwan, Raven phraety."

Grisha stared at the man as his mind rushed back through the years to childhood. He grinned.

"You finally cut your hair, Pietr, or is it Paul? It's been so many years." Grisha extended his right arm. Pietr stepped forward and they grasped forearms.

"You have brought great honor to our kwan."

"Thank you, my cousin. Allow me to introduce you to my wife, Wing."

"My cousin has an excellent eye." He glanced at her collar tabs. "And a woman of rank, in addition," he said approvingly.

"Pleased to meet you, Pietr," Wing said. "I'm Athabascan, so please forgive me if I don't know what 'kwan' means."

"Clan," Pietr and Grisha said at the same time.

"Grisha and I used to play together at our grandfather's house in the old village when we were boys. The last time I saw him he was a lieutenant in the Troika Guard. We thought we had lost him forever."

"I didn't know it mattered," Grisha said as old memories swept over him.

"It did, and does. But I have not come to refresh old pain."

"I don't recognize your uniform," Grisha said, happy to change the subject.

"The uniform was a gift from an ally."

"'Ally' of what, or who?"

"This thing seems to run in the family." Pietr smiled; Grisha thought it genuine. "I am a captain in the Tlingit Nation Army. We have received a good deal of material aid from the Empire of Japan."

"Japan!" Grisha and Captain Lauesen said simultaneously.

"According to the Honolulu Treaty of 1950 the Empire of Japan is barred from becoming politically involved in any North American nation," Lauesen said.

"Unless invited," Pietr said.

"What is happening at home?" Grisha asked softly. "Why, exactly, are you here?"

"The Council of Toions realizes there is little time before what the Dená have done here will be finished. The Czar's government will relinquish this land and hold tighter to what remains. What remains are the Eskimos and us.

"We know we can ask the Japanese for military aid, even intervention. But if we do that we are forever part of their empire. That's a future war we know we cannot win."

Grisha glanced at Captain Lauesen and back to his cousin. "You want to join us?"

Pietr smiled again, somewhat sheepishly, Grisha thought.

"The Dená War took us unawares. We had no idea such unrest existed in these cold lands, nor were we aware of your alliances with other North American countries. It has occurred to us that were we to join forces we all might eventually create a united republic in Alaska."

The room stilled and Grisha let his mind run with the thought. It seemed perfect, both geographically and politically. He wondered if his wish to see Akku once again shaded his perspective.

"Captain Chernikoff," Captain Lauesen said, "what do you need immediately?"

"Wait!" Grisha snapped. "Wing, please ask Colonel Jackson to attend us immediately. Captain Lauesen, I think both of my allies should have a representative present from the very beginning of anything larger than the Dená Republik."

"Point taken, General," Lauesen said with a wry grin.

"Has a treaty been signed between you and the Czar?" Pietr asked.

"Far from it. We are still at war. The Russians have at least one major ground force somewhere between here and Tetlin as well as a large force in retreat from the Battle of Chena."

Grisha realized he was trying to get out of bed again and forced himself to relax. "Forgive me, cousin, I keep forgetting I have temporary physical limitations."

Pietr laughed. "You were always on the move, and usually getting into mischief if memory serves."

"And I remember that you were always right there with me."

"May I apologize for the pain I and my brothers caused you?" Pietr asked.

"Children are cruel, youth are callow, that's part of nature. Thank you for the thought, but there is nothing to forgive."

"A party!" Benny Jackson said, walking into the room. "What's the occasion, Grisha? Did they make you president now?"

"Benny, it's good to see you!" Wing said, hugging him.

"Good to see you, too, Wing. I'm still willing to try women if you'll be the test case."

"Sorry, Colonel," Grisha said. "She's snagged herself a general."

"May I offer my heartfelt congratulations?" He shook Grisha's hand. "I am continually amazed at how perceptive the Dená are when it comes to choosing their leaders."

"Okay, Benny, put on your Special Forces Liaison hat, firmly."

"Sure, Grisha, uh, General Grigorievich. What's up?" He looked the two captains over with a professional eye.

"This is Captain Lauesen, U.S. Army, who is our intelligence laison. And this is my cousin, Captain Pietr Chernikoff, of the Tlingit Nation Army. Pietr, tell him what you told us."

"We need help, too. Without a navy we will never get the Russians out of our land and the rest of Alaska."

"How far south does the Tlingit Nation extend?" Benny asked.

"To what you call Dixon Entrance, that's where our Kaigani Clans live."

"All the way to British Canada." Benny grinned and with a glance at Captain Lauesen said, "Well, we just happen to have a fleet in that ocean."

A corporal edged up next to Captain Lauesen and pressed a sheet of paper into his hand before nodding and backing away.

"Bigger than the Russian Navy?" Pietr said with a scowl.

"I don't know how big a fleet they have—"

"Don't worry," said Captain Lauesen. "You do now."

"I do now what?" Benny snapped.

"Have a bigger fleet." He waved at Pietr. "This all may be solved as we speak."

"What's your message say, Captain?" Grisha asked.

"British Canada has sued for peace and all their forces are standing down. It seems they lost over half their Atlantic Fleet to the U.S.A. in a battle off Newfoundland." Lauesen grinned at them. "That's water as cold as you have up here and the weather's just as mean."

"But we were talking about the Russian fleet, not the British," Pietr said.

"I wasn't finished, Captain. Just hours ago the entire Russian Pacific Fleet was defeated off Vancouver Island. The Republic of California lost one ship, a destroyer. Twenty minutes ago, the Russian Empire asked for peace terms."

The room went dead still again. Grisha stared dumbly at the others who stared just as dumbly back.

Wing started sobbing. "Oh, I wish Slayer-of-Men could be here now."

Grisha opened his arms and she bent into his embrace. He kissed her on the side of her head, and whispered in her ear, "He is, where else would he be?"

"If you'll excuse me, General Grigoriy Pietrovich Grigorievich," Benny said with a smile and a salute, "I think my job just got a lot more complicated."

He left the room at a brisk walk.

"Captain Chernikoff," Captain Lauesen said. "My country will give you all the aid you need, I guarantee it, just wanted you to know. General, Colonel, I think I need to be somewhere else just now." He tossed them a salute and hurried through the door.

"So what does this mean, Grisha?" Pietr asked.

"I don't know, cousin, but it has to be better than what we had before. Doesn't it?"